Child of Loki

by

Richard Denning

Child of Loki
Written by Richard Denning
Copyright 2012 Richard Denning.
First Published 2012.
ISBN: 978-0-9568103-2-8
Published by Mercia Books

A catalogue record for this book is available from the British Library

Book Jacket design and layout by Cathy Helms
www.avalongraphics.org
Copy-editing and proof reading by Jo Field.
jo.field3@btinternet.com

Author website:
www.richarddenning.co.uk
Publisher website:
www.merciabooks.co.uk

In memory of my uncle Jeremy, whose spare room became to me a library that kindled a young boy's love of books and reading.

The Author

Richard Denning was born in Ilkeston in Derbyshire and lives in Sutton Coldfield in the West Midlands, where he works as a General Practitioner.

He is married and has two children. He has always been fascinated by historical settings as well as horror and fantasy. Other than writing, his main interests are games of all types. He is the designer of a board game based on the Great Fire of London.

Author website:
http://www.richarddenning.co.uk

Also by the author

Northern Crown Series
(Historical fiction)
1.The Amber Treasure
2.Child of Loki

Hourglass Institute Series
(Young Adult Science Fiction)
1.Tomorrow's Guardian
2. Yesterday's Treasures
3. Today's Sacrifice (Coming 2013)

The Praesidium Series
(Historical Fantasy)
The Last Seal

The Nine Worlds Series
(Children's Historical Fantasy)
Shield Maiden

Northern Britain 598 to 604 A.D.

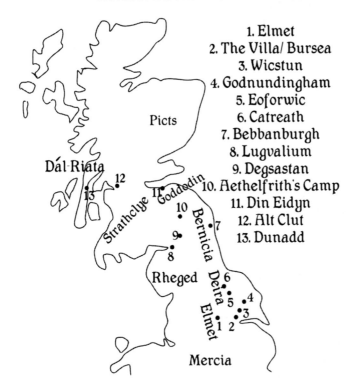

1. Elmet
2. The Villa/ Bursea
3. Wicstun
4. Godnundingham
5. Eoforwic
6. Catreath
7. Bebbanburgh
8. Lugvalium
9. Degsastan
10. Aethelfrith's Camp
11. Din Eidyn
12. Alt Clut
13. Dunadd

Names of nations, cities and towns

Here is a glossary of the main locations referred to in Child of Loki and what they are called today.

Alt Clut – Ancient capital of Strathclyde, modern Dumbarton.
Bebbanburgh – Capital of Bernicia. Modern Bamburgh.
Bernicia – Anglo-Saxon kingdom in Northumbria.
Bursea – Settlement and landing place on the River Fulganaess (Foulness), a tributary of the Humber.
'The Villa'/'The Village' – Cerdic's home at Cerdham - modern Holme-on-Spalding-Moor.
Catraeth – Catterick.
Dál-Riata – Kingdom of the Irish Scots from Ulster in what is now Kintyre, Argyle and Butte.

Degsastan – Battlefield in 603. Uncertain location. Possibly Dawstone in Liddesdale.

Deira – Anglo-Saxon kingdom north of the Humber.

Din Eidyn – Ancient capital of Manau Goddodin - modern Edinburgh.

Dunadd – Ancient capital of Dál-Riata. A hill fort near Kilmartin, Argyll and Butte.

Elmet – Welsh/British kingdom around the modern day city of Leeds.

Eoforwic – York.

Godnundingham – Site of Deiran Royal Palace. Possibly modern day Pocklington.

Loidis – Leeds.

Lugvalium – Carlisle.

Manau Goddodin – Welsh/British kingdom around what is now Edinburgh.

Rheged – Welsh/British kingdom in what is now Cumbria.

Strathclyde – British kingdom around Clyde valley, Dumfries and Galloway.

Wicstun – Market Weighton.

A note about the various races and terms.

Historians call the people that had once been under Roman rule and who remained in Britain after the Romans departed, 'Romano-British' or 'Britons'. These people became eventually absorbed by the invading Anglo-Saxons or displaced, moving west to occupy Wales and Cornwall. However at the time of this novel they also inhabited Cumbria and the Scottish borders as far north as Dumbarton. In this book they are the peoples that lived in Rheged, Mannau Goddodin, Strathclyde and also Elmet.

Further north, in the east of what is now Scotland, between Inverness and the Perth/Dundee area, were the Picts – a race that even the Romans never suppressed, or at least not for long.

To their west, an Irish clan called the 'Scots' had crossed over from Ulster around the time the Romans left and settled all down the west coast of Scotland as well as many of the islands. This is why, perhaps a little confusingly, Scots and Irish in this book refer to the same people and are interchangeable.

In time the land we now call Scotland will come into being as an amalgamation of these three main races and lands. Through alliance, conquest, battle and marriage a nation is forged.

Further south the invading Anglo-Saxons became the English. The 'English' of this book would probably not have called themselves that. The Anglo Saxon invaders of Northumbria were the Angles. In time the word Angles mutated via such words as Anglii and Englisc to English and the country became England. Although this process took some time I have used the terms English, Angles or Saxons interchangeably in this novel.

List of named characters
Denotes historical figure

Acha* – Sister of Edwin and princess of Deira.

Aedann – Once Cerdic's family slave but now his companion.

Áedán mac Gabráin* – King of the Dál-Riata Scots.

Aelle* – King of Deira.

Aethelfrith* – King of Bernicia.

Aethelric* – Prince and later King of Deira.

Aidith – Cerdic's woman.

Bebba* – Queen of Bernicia and first wife of Aethelfrith.

Bran* – Prince of Dál-Riata.

Cenred – Father to Cerdic. Lord of Wicstun and Earl of the Southern Marches.

Cerdic – Main character, Lord of the Villa and son of Cenred.

Ceredig* – King of Elmet.

Cuthbert – childhood friend of Cerdic.

Cuthwine – Cerdic's older brother, died in 597, also the name Cerdic gives his own son.

Cynric – Cerdic's uncle who died in 580.

Domanghast* – Prince of Dál-Riata.

Durwyn – Aidith's father

Eanfrith* – Son of Aethelfrith by Bebba.

Edwin*– Younger son of Aelle.

Eduard– Childhood friend of Cerdic.

Felnius – Captain of the Scots.

Frithwulf – Son of Guthred.

Grettir – Cerdic's family retainer.

Guthred – Lord of Bursea to the south of The Villa.

Gwen – Aedann's mother.

Harald – Earl of Eoforwic.

Hereric* – Son of Aethelric, Grandson of Aelle.

Hussa – Cerdic's half brother.

Herring* – Exiled Bernician nobleman.

Lilla – Bard and friend of Cerdic's family.

Mildrith – Cerdic's younger sister.

Osric* - Son of Aelle's younger brother.

Rydderch Hen* – King of Strathclyde.

Sabert – Earl of the Eastern Marches.

Samlen – Prince of Elmet.

Sunniva – Cerdic's older sister.

Theobald* – Aethelfrith's younger brother.

Wallace – Lord of Wicstun, died at the Battle of Catraeth, 597 A.D.

Chapter One
Loidis

Loidis was in flames. It was the price Elmet had to pay for choosing the losing side. I, Cerdic, once heard Abbess Hild talk of forgiving one's enemies: she said that a man should pray for those who curse you and bless those who mistreat you. These were Christ's words and we should heed them, she implored us, for they were words of love and words of peace.

But this day was not a day for peace or love. This was a day for vengeance and blood. Elmet chose to back Owain and his great alliance of the Northern British tribes. Together they attacked my land and my people - the Angles. They raided Deira, killed my brother and kidnapped my sister. Then they took their army and joined Owain at a place called Catraeth. There they hoped to destroy my land and my race forever.

But it was we who prevailed. We Deiran farmers and townsfolk from the wolds and moors and the lands along the River Humber, held on against the odds until our brothers - the Angles of Bernicia - had marched from the North and fallen upon the enemy.

There, at the great Battle of Catraeth, we destroyed them. The tribes from Rheged, Strathclyde and Manau Goddodin had been crushed. So now we returned to our neighbour - to Elmet - to make them pay for the hurt they had done us.

That at least was what Aelle - our king - had ordered. He wanted recompense from Ceredig, King of Elmet, and punitive steps taken to ensure he could not easily attack us again. For my

1

part, I had seen enough blood and death at Catraeth to last a lifetime. I would have been content to stay at home with my family and Aidith, my woman. But Aelle was our king and my father, Cenred, was Earl of the Southern Marches. Our family's lands around the village of Cerdham lay in his domain so when he called out the Wicstun Company that spring, a few months after Catraeth, he expected me, the Lord of the Villa, to obey the summons.

So we went - ten men and boys from the village - led by myself. Amongst them were my three friends: Eduard, - tall and broad-shouldered, a fierce warrior, utterly loyal and a true friend; Cuthbert, my other boyhood companion, short and delicate, yet agile and as much a master with the bow as was Eduard with his axe. Finally, Aedann, the dark-haired, green-eyed Welshman, who had once been my slave and was now a freedman sworn to my service. With us went the rugged old veteran Grettir, who had been our teacher once upon a time and was still full of the wisdom of a man who has seen many battles.

We left the village of Cerdham with its hovels and huts, and left too the Villa, the decaying old Roman house that my grandfather had captured and made into our family's home. Off we went with the rest of Aelle's army - six companies from the south of Deira - and invaded Elmet. We marched hard and fast, striking deep into the Welsh land and before he knew we were coming, King Ceredig was staring down at us in horror from the wooden palisade around his city of Loidis.

Aelle's orders had been strict and Earl Harald commanding us followed them to the letter. There was no offer of peace from Harald, no olive branch held out and no chance of reprieve. Not yet. Not until we had smashed our way through the city gates and burnt the houses that lined the main street.

2

I am an old man now and I have been in many battles, but despite all the sights I have seen I will never get used to the screams and cries for mercy from the innocent. The gods blow their trumpets and the Valkyries ride forth to choose who is to be slain and lead them to Valhalla, and men cheer and do battle for the sake of glory or wealth or honour. Yet it is the children and the women who suffer whilst we men wallow in blood.

So it was on that day. Demanding vengeance might sound a fine thing when you stand over the grave of your brother and smell the smoke of your own home burning, but see how you feel when it is someone else's brother, son or daughter who lies at your feet and their home burning whilst you stand nearby holding the torches that kindled the flames.

Yet it had to be done, did it not? They must be made to regret their attack and be prevented from doing it again. It was us or them; and frankly, when you have seen hundreds die you can harden your heart to the cries of the innocent. Or at least you can try ...

A little later, Eduard, Cuthbert, Aedann and I stood with our men amongst the Wicstun Company in a square at the heart of the city. Smoke from the smouldering hovels and the stench of burning flesh wafted across to us, but I tried to ignore it. In front of us was a long hall: Ceredig's royal palace. Lined up before us were two hundred Elmetae warriors, shields held high and spear points sharp and glowing red in the firelight. They were the king's last defence and we and two other companies were forming up in a shield wall to attack them. The rest of the army was elsewhere, ransacking the city and putting it to the torch.

"This is it, lads. One last attack and the campaign is over," Harald shouted. "One last attack and then we can all return home and forget about war."

3

"If you believe that you'll believe anything," I heard Eduard mutter, but loud enough that many of us heard it. We chortled wryly, yet we all hoped it was true. It was what gave us the strength to carry on. Maybe Harald was right. After all, the armies of Owain and his allies were scattered or dead. With Elmet suppressed too, who else was there to threaten us? I gripped my shield tighter, checked the balance of the spear in my right hand and waited for the order to advance.

Harald blew one sonorous blast on his horn and we were off. Behind us my father and his huscarls followed, and over our heads, flapping in the gentle spring breeze, our company's standard the running wolf visible through the drifting smoke.

Overhead a few arrows flew back and forth, but not many, for apart from Cuthbert we had brought few archers along with us and the Welsh had only a handful themselves. Nevertheless, one arrow found its mark somewhere amongst the company for I heard a curse over to my right. Glancing that way I saw a man from Wicstun tumble out of the shield wall, blood streaming down his chest and an arrow shaft protruding from just above his collar bone. He slumped to the ground and sat there, face screwed up in agony, each breath laboured and painful. Then he was forgotten as the army moved forward.

We were thirty paces from the enemy, who now locked their shields together, each one overlapping the next. Then they brought their spears down so they pointed towards us and with a clattering of ash staves on oak boards, we copied their move.

Twenty paces away now and my gaze fell upon one Elmetae spearman directly in front of me. In truth he was barely a man and from the faintest wisp of a beard on his chin and the gangly thin arms and legs I surmised that he could not have been above fourteen years old. His dark green eyes looked haunted and his

4

gaze darted this way and that. I had seen that look before, at Catraeth, on a hundred faces and knew without a doubt that today he was in his first battle. Next to him and older was a gruff veteran, a huge man with scars down his cheeks and bulging upper arms. His eyes showed none of the fear in the young man's eyes. Instead hatred and bloodlust lingered there.

Ten paces away and the spears of both armies interlaced like the fingers of a man bringing his hands together. Then the shields crashed into each other. The shock of the collision sent a judder up my left arm and it was all I could do to keep hold of my shield. Unbalanced, I stepped back just as a spear point lunged at me, missing my throat by only an inch. Recovering my feet I thrust back, realising as I did so that my spear was aimed at the young boy's neck. Maybe I hesitated for just a second, for it never reached him: the grizzled old veteran at his side hacked down at my ash stave with his sword, snapping it in two and leaving me with a useless stump. He then brought the sword round aiming to take out my throat with the fearsome edge. I was saved by Aedann who, standing on my left, took a step forward and drove his spear into the veteran's left shoulder. The man gave a roar of pain and recoiled. The youth, meantime, drew back his own spear preparing to thrust it forward again. In his eagerness and panic he fumbled, dropped it and then bent to recover it.

Panting hard, I took advantage of the reprieve and reached down to my scabbard grasping the hilt of my short stabbing sword. I had taken this blade from my first foe, whom I had slain during the raid on the Villa. It had served me well: it was with this sword that I had killed Owain, the golden King of Rheged, and it was in honour of that battle that it had earned its name: 'Catraeth'.

5

I dragged it up above my shield just as the youth advanced again, screaming as he thrust the point at me. I leant to one side, let the spear point go past and then following up, hacked over the top of the shield and felt Catraeth's edge cut through tendon and bone deep into the boy's arm. He let out a howl of agony and fell to the ground, shield and spear abandoned as his hands reached up to stem the flow of blood from the wound.

To his right the veteran roared in anger and then hurtled forward, his own wound forgotten, slamming his shield against Aedann's own, knocking my Welsh companion back through the rear ranks. Without pausing, the enemy stepped over to me and kicked hard against my shins. With a shout of pain I too tumbled to the ground.

Above me the light was blocked by the huge figure of the grizzled veteran standing astride me, his face a mask of rage, his shoulder pouring blood that dripped down onto my upturned face. Yet there was something in his features that reminded me of the young man I had just cut down. It was then I realised that the youth must be his son. Thirsty for revenge and consumed by anger, the old man swung back his sword and prepared to finish me.

'One last attack and then we can all return home,' those had been the words of Earl Harald just minutes before. They resounded in my head; hollow now. Then again, maybe he was right, but if so I would not be returning home to live in peace.

I would be going home to be buried.

Chapter Two
Home

In desperation I struggled to haul myself off the ground and put something in the way of the blow: my sword, my shield - anything. Down came the blade, cutting the air like a farmer scything through corn at harvest time. I just managed to raise my weapon enough to intercept the strike. The crash of steel on steel set my teeth on edge and I felt my arm go numb. I lost my grip on Catraeth and saw it spin away into the mass of men - Welsh and Angle - who pushed and heaved against each other. The bearded, scarred enemy warrior wore a humourless grin as he swung back his arm to finish me. His sword seemed to hang in the air for an age before he brought it down again, looking to cleave my head from my shoulders.

"Get off him you bastard!" bellowed Eduard. My huge friend appeared out of the swirling melee and without thought or care for himself barged straight into the veteran. His force and power were as irresistible as a charging beast and the older man cried in alarm as he was knocked sideways. Eduard's attack deflected the man's blow so that rather than landing on my neck, it skidded across my shield and then slashed down my flank, cutting through my tunic and cloak and carving an ugly trail from shoulder to hip. I screamed in agony, let my shield slide off me and then clamped both hands to my bleeding torso. Through my pain I saw my friend leap over me in pursuit of his prey.

Eduard followed up his attack hacking and slashing with his axe at the veteran who, having regained his feet, staggered backwards deflecting the blade with his shield. The axe bit deep into the board, which shattered, scattering fragments here and there. The veteran roared and thrust his spear back at my friend, aiming to skewer him like the boars we had once hunted in the woods near the Villa. Edward let him come on and then, at the last moment, he stepped to one side and swung his axe in a great arc parallel to the ground. The blade caught the old man in his belly. He gave a cry of agony and fell to the ground, guts spilling out onto the bloodstained earth. He twitched for a moment and then lay still. Eduard glanced over at me and, untouched as he always was by the carnage around him, he winked. I nodded back and then a wave of pain ripped down my side and the world went dark.

"Cerdic!" I heard someone shout then felt a hand grasp me by the neck of my tunic and tug me backwards out of the battle. "Cerdic," the man repeated, now leaning over me, "are you all right?" Through a haze of pain I tried to focus on the face that was now staring at me, anxiety etched on the features.

"Aedann?" I answered vaguely, "Am I dying?"

The only reply was to feel the Welshman lifting my tunic to examine the injury. His lips pursed as he contemplated the damage. He tore some strips off my torn undershirt and used them to bind the wound.

"Well," I said weakly, "will I die?"

Aedann shook his head. "Shouldn't think so. Mind you, another inch lower and Aidith would be very disappointed!"

I opened my mouth to say something rude, but my retort was drowned as our army gave a great cheer. I raised my head in an effort to see what was happening. Our numerical advantage was too much for the Elmetae, no matter how determined they were and how bravely they fought. Under the pressure of our battle-hardened companies the centre of their shield wall had given way. So now Earl Harald was leading a charge through the gaping hole. The enemy warriors on the wings of their army panicked as they realised they would soon be out-flanked and attacked from the rear. When a man is frightened it only takes the sight of his neighbour throwing down his spear and shield then turning and running, for resolve and fighting spirit to flee, terrified, like a lamb before a wolf. Crying out to their Christian God to save them, the surviving warriors fled down the alleyways and roads of Loidis.

Ahead of us lay the Royal Palace: undefended, full of treasure and the wealth of kings. I was suddenly anxious that I would be left out here whilst everyone else went through and saw the wonders inside. Grasping Aedann's outstretched hand, I pulled myself back on my feet and then using his spear as a crutch, I staggered up to where Earl Harald, my father and the other captains were approaching the doors. My father spotted that I had been injured and the old man's gruff face creased with concern. In two huge strides he stood in front of me.

"Woden's balls, son, are you hurt?" he asked, placing a hand gently on my shoulder.

"I'll live, Father. I would have been done for, but Eduard saved me."

"Thank the gods. Come then, let us see what this king has to say for himself."

We entered the hall of Ceredig, King of Elmet - the last Welsh Kingdom east of the Pennines. I will say this much for the man. Now that he had seen that defiance was futile, he had clearly decided to salvage such pride as he had left, regardless of the danger to himself. His armies had been defeated or had fled, he was defenceless and at our questionable mercy, yet, as we entered

9

the hall and walked past the long fire pit that ran down the centre of the room, he sat on his throne protected by just two loyal guards and regarded us with cool disdain, as if it were he who was the judge and we mere prisoners being brought out to hear his verdict.

Without getting up from his seat he called out to us, "Who are you pirates and barbarians that dare attack my palace, murder my people and burn their houses?"

Harald stepped out from amongst us and went to stand just feet from Ceredig. The king's guards tensed as he approached so the earl spread his arms wide to show that he bore no weapons.

"I am Harald, Earl of Eoforwic and trusted lieutenant of Aelle, King of Deira."

Ceredig snorted. "King of a land that was once ours! King of a people who plunder and murder at will."

"Aelle took your lands from you by right of conquest. If a people are weak is it a surprise when the stronger replace them?"

Sitting in sullen silence, Ceredig glared at Harald who continued to speak.

"As for murder and plunder, is that not just what your brother Samlen did when he raided Cerdham and Wicstun. Is it not what you had in mind had you triumphed at Catraeth?"

"Huh!" Ceredig grunted. "It is good for you that we did not. So then, Earl Harald, what now? What will you do to me and my people?"

"In return for leaving you in peace to rule yourselves you will pay a tribute to King Aelle and recognise him as your overlord. The tribute will be fifty ingots of gold and as many of silver. You will deliver to me all the weapons and shields your armies possess. You will also deliver a score of hostages to guarantee your goodwill. You will undertake to decline any approaches

10

from Rheged, Strathclyde and Manau Goddodin towards any alliance."

Ceredig listened to the list of demands without comment.

"Well, what do you say?" Harald demanded, having given the king some time to think it over.

"You ask a lot, Lord of Eorforwic. What if I decline?"

Harald's face was now grave with foreboding. "My king gave me one instruction, should that be the case. I was to destroy Loidis and carry its people and its king in chains into slavery."

"You have the advantage and you leave me no choice, Earl Harald. I will agree to your demands, but pray to your gods, for your sake and those of your countrymen, that I never get the opportunity to regain an advantage over you."

Harald stared at Ceredig for a moment, perhaps deciding whether it would be best to deal with the man here and now. Then he nodded his head.

"Very well. You have two days to deliver the tribute and the weapons. Good day to you."

Turning on his heel, Harald walked back to us. "Come, we will leave him to his solitude."

I glanced back at Ceredig and noticed that he was studying us, his face a mask of malevolence. "Is it such a good idea to leave him on the throne?" I asked in a whisper that only Harald, my father and my friends could hear.

As we moved towards the door, I leaning on my father, Harald shrugged. "We have no choice. We might have won here by virtue of a quick strike, but Aelle has not the strength of men to occupy Elmet. Best that we force tribute on Ceredig as well as disarming him; it will weaken him."

As we left the palace I wondered for how long. Ceredig did not look like a man who would happily pay tribute and sit around in

11

impotent rage. Then again, maybe I was wrong. Maybe he would bide his time even if he had to wait decades for the right moment to get his revenge. I shivered, then realised that I felt chilled to the bone. Weak also; the blood loss had taken a lot out of me and the pain was befuddling my mind.

"Let's get you home, son," my father said, eyeing me with a worried expression.

Home ...

Through my childhood years I had yearned to leave it, to travel to the wild lands of the far North, to battle sea serpents, ogres, trolls and dragons, to win lands and gifts of rings and swords from kings and nobles. Then I would take my place as a warrior amongst the sagas and never be forgotten. Yet Catraeth changed all that. The Villa and the woman that waited for me there was all the world I now needed.

The Villa - that was the name our family used for our home. My grandfather had liked the look of the old Roman house when he and a few followers had arrived there decades before. He had taken it as his own and my family had grown up there. Now it was mine. My father had been Lord of the Villa but after Catraeth he was given Lord Wallace's lands at Wicstun and had moved there to take on his responsibilities and in turn he had given the Villa to me.

After leaving the king's hall at Elmet, father had Grettir commandeer a cart drawn by two oxen. He then insisted that I make the journey back to Deira in that rather than on foot. My brief protest was cut short when a bolt of pain shot down my flank and fresh blood oozed through the dressing Aedann had fixed earlier and began to drip down my leg. Grettir redressed the wound, using a salve made from moss and some herbs he obtained from the fields outside the city such as mugwort, nettle and fennel mixed with egg yolk. So then, accepting the inevitable, I allowed myself to be hoisted into the cart. Grettir and my father mounted the front and then, with Harald's permission, the Village men, my friends and I departed.

We approached my home from the west, passing through the woods where my friends and I had once hunted boar on the day before the raid that had started the war with Elmet the year before. We crossed the open fields where Eduard, Cuthbert and I had once ambushed and killed three of the Elmetae who were taking our people away to slavery, and where I had taken my sword from the body of the man I had slain. Then we came to Cerdham which we all knew at the 'Village': the little collection of a dozen or so huts where the villagers who farmed our land lived. The women and children came out and greeted us. Thanks to the gods none from the Village had died and as it happened I was the only man wounded, so there was much joy at our return as well as a great deal of fuss made of me. In fact I was treated as some kind of champion even though I told everyone that I had done very little except fall over and Eduard was the real hero. The villagers still showered me with spring blossom, although I noticed a couple of the girls had taken a shine to Eduard. He winked at me as he disappeared behind one of the huts, one huge arm wrapped about each of them.

Finally we left the Village behind us and moved towards the Villa down the little track where once Sunniva, my sister, had met me and told me that my other sister, Mildrith, had been kidnapped, my father wounded and Cuthwine my brother slain. As the cart rocked from side to side I glanced up towards the low hills to the north where Cuthwine was buried and I sighed. Father heard me and saw where I was gazing.

13

"Yes, lad, I miss him too. Praise the gods that you live, though. There is much to look forward to now that Elmet is beaten. Peace at last, son. Think on that."

I nodded, although a feeling that it would not be as easy as all that crept into my mind and the gloom returned. Then I saw something that scattered all the storm clouds and it was as if the summer sun had broken through them.

The cart had rumbled its way up the track, round a little bend, past a beech tree and at last I could see the Villa. The west side, from which we approached, held the main entrance that led into the atrium, an entrance chamber where I had once seen my brother's corpse laid out. That day had been grim for I entered a house that was scorched by flame and cursed by the death of its oldest son. This day, however, I returned from Loidis - a place of death - to a house whose doorway contained a vision of life.

She wore a woollen dress, dyed deep green and over her shoulders she had cast a lighter green cloak, clasped at the shoulder by a golden brooch. Apart from the brooch she wore no other adornment save a small seax and a set of keys hanging from her belt. Her red hair cascaded like a waterfall down her back. In the spring sunlight she was stunning. She would have been just as stunning had it been pouring with rain. When she saw me lying on the cart, her hand went to her mouth and a moment later she was running towards us. My father sighed as she approached and before she was in hearing of us he whispered a few words.

"She is a fair beauty, that Aidith, there is no mistaking that. But what will you do, Cerdic, if a marriage to an ally could be arranged for you? One of Earl Sabert's nieces or Harald's daughter maybe, or else that of a local thegn. You could gain much influence and wealth."

14

I glanced across at my father and frowned at the question. Then, seeing that Aidith had almost arrived I smiled at him. "I have all the influence I desire and all the treasure I need right here."

My father gave me a sharp glance and I thought for a moment he would argue the point. Then he shrugged. "So be it, son. You are Lord of the Villa now."

Aidith rushed up to the side of the cart, her face pale and anxious. She leant over the side and stared at me. "Oh Cerdic, what happened? Are you badly hurt?"

Frowning, my father grunted. "He will live, Aidith. He took a nasty wound to the side but it is not mortal. A few weeks rest and he will be well again."

"Are you certain, Lord Cenred?" Aidith glanced up at him, "He looks so pale."

I grinned at her, "I lost some blood, lass. That is all. Come, let's get inside," I pushed myself up from the straw and shuffled to the end of the cart. I tried to slide off the tailboard meaning to launch myself onto my feet to show her I was fine. Yet when I got upright, I felt suddenly dizzy and staggered a few steps. Aedann caught me and Cuthbert rushed up to take the other arm.

"Steady there, Cerdic," Aedann muttered. "Let us help you inside." Without waiting for a reply he turned me towards the Villa and we made our way to the Atrium. Once inside I was helped into my room and laid down on my bed.

A moment later Father came in to say goodbye. "I wish to reach Wicstun tonight, lad. So I will leave you in Aidith's hands. Be sure to rest, Cerdic. I will ride over in a few days to see how you are. Oh, by the way, the east field is bare I notice. Have you not sown the barley yet?"

15

"I plan to rest the east field this year, Father. I am growing barley in the south fields beyond the orchard."

He opened his mouth, apparently ready to argue and then closed it again. "Well it's your land now, lad. So that is up to you." His gaze passed over Aidith before he added, "Along with a few other decisions it seems." He smiled and left without further comment.

"I wonder what he meant by that," I muttered and looked up at Aidith. Her face wore an expression of surprise as she looked towards the door through which my father had left. Then she came over to me and sat down on the bed.

"You father does not miss much, Cerdic, does he? I wonder if he is a little bit fey."

"Whatever do you mean?"

Aidith laughed. "Yet, it seems that you have not inherited his powers of perception."

"I don't understand ..." I stared at her dumbfounded.

Her smile did not drop. "We had best hope they pass to your son or daughter," she said softly.

I would not think of myself as stupid, but she was certainly right that it had taken a while for what was being said to dawn upon me. Yet suddenly I knew what she meant and a smile broke out on my stunned face. "You're pregnant! With my child?"

Her eyebrow rose archly. "Well, it is certainly no one else's, my love."

"When? When will it come?" I asked, my hand moving to her belly. It was as flat as usual and showed no sign of life growing within.

"I am only a few weeks along. Goodwife Algifa thinks the baby will come at Yuletide or perhaps a little before."

16

I pondered this for a moment. Before the turning of the year I would have a son ... or daughter and an heir to my lands. But that raised another question, one that had clearly been on my father's mind today and again I wondered how much he knew. Suddenly and unheeded, the thought of Hussa, my half-brother, came to mind. Born of adultery between Father and a woman from Wicstun, his illegitimacy had festered inside him like a sore and had finally erupted in treachery. For the betrayal of his country he was condemned to death, but spared when Father, out of a feeling of guilt or perhaps a desire to acknowledge the boy as his son, had paid a blood debt for him. And so he lived and was in exile somewhere; I neither knew nor cared where.

All that had stemmed from his bitterness at being denied his inheritance and place in our family. I did not want that to happen to my child.

"Shall we marry. Aidith? I mean, shall we ... er, would you like to ... that is, would you agree to be my wife?" I floundered on, but Aidith was smiling again.

I pulled her towards me. "Can I take that as a yes?" I asked, my hands moving to her breasts. "I think we should celebrate, don't you?"

"But Cerdic, your father said you should rest."

"I am in bed aren't I?" I winked and wrapped my arms around her, wincing slightly as the movement pulled the gash in my side.

"But what about your side, Cerdic?" Aidith's brow creased with anxiety.

I grinned at her, "It was not my side I was planning to use! And anyway, you will just have to be gentle with me, won't you?"

The following morning, I woke Eduard, Cuthbert and Aedann, who, after my father had given me the Villa, had moved in as my first huscarls – my house guards – sworn to serve and defend me, and now my companions. Together we strolled to the Village. My wound had stiffened in the night and was sore, but as I walked so it began to ease.

"Pregnant?" Cuthbert said, "You sure?"

I glared at him. "Aidith was pretty certain. Women do tend to notice these things you know," I replied as we ambled down the track. I had risen early, dunked my head in a bucket of water from the well and then changed into my best tunic, strapped Catraeth to my side and wrapped a cloak around me. I had tried to adopt the look of the young warrior lord.

"But marriage, Cerdic ... are you sure?" Aedann asked.

"What do you mean?"

"He means you are not the first lad to get a lass pregnant and won't be the last, but marriage is pretty final, " Eduard broke in. "You're a thegn, mate: a lord - even if Cerdham is an anthill on Woden's backside - and lords have to think of the future. Alliances and so forth. You sure you want to marry a ..."

I halted and spun round to glare at them. "A what?" I demanded, suddenly angry.

The air seemed to grow icy as the three of them exchanged glances. None of them spoke; it was I who broke the awkward silence. "I'm sorry, it's just that I think I should marry her ..."

We were fifty paces from the Village. Below us in the muddy track that wound between the huts, chickens picked at the soil and a child sat in the mud outside one of the doorways. I turned back to my friends.

"Do you think I am doing the right thing?" It was a silly question since they blatantly did not, but I pressed on. "Is it foolish to do this? Maybe I should think of the future and not just act on impulse ..." I trailed off and looked at each of them in turn, hoping for guidance.

It was Cuthbert who answered with a question. "Do you love her?"

I blinked and it was a few moments before I answered. "Yes ... yes, I love her."

They stared at me then Eduard smiled. "Oh, that's all right then. Marry the girl and bugger the politics!"

Aedann and Cuthbert just nodded and since Eduard had pretty well expressed my view there seemed no more to say. We carried on down to the village. Aidith's family lived in a large hut at the far end. I strode up to the door and rapped on it with my knuckles. In a moment it was opened and Goodman Durwyn stood in the frame. He was taller than my father and I suddenly felt naked in front of him. It occurred to me to wonder how much he knew about Aidith. He would know she had spent most of the winter in my company, but he had not seemed bothered. I imagined he would be soon enough once he knew she was pregnant. Indeed, at first he glared at me then cast his gaze across my companions and finally back to me. Then he seemed to recognize me for the first time.

"Master Cerdic ... how can I help you?" He seemed puzzled, but neither tense nor touched with anger.

"Who is it, Durwyn?" a woman's voice demanded from within the hut and a moment later Mayda, Aidith's mother, appeared at his side. She halted when she saw me and her eyes narrowed. Oh dear, I thought, did she know? I cleared my throat and at least as much to distract me from Mayda's glare as anything, launched into a speech I had prepared.

"I have come here today, along with my companions and sworn huscarls, to ask for your permission to marry your

19

daughter, Aidith. I seek alliance with your family and promise you and yours my protection. I offer you a *handgeld* in token of this agreement and promise to deliver it to you and to give Aidith her *brýdcéap* on the morning after we are married. If we can reach agreement today these men will witness the handshake by which we seal it."

I paused and took a deep breath while I waited for an answer.

Durwyn blinked. "What?" he asked, obviously utterly taken aback.

Mayda, however, was in complete control. "You old fool, husband. Master Cerdic wants to marry our girl. Invite him in," she insisted. Her icy expression of moments before had vanished. Was it the prospect of wealth and status or just happiness that I was looking after Aidith? I wasn't sure and didn't really care. I smiled at her as she elbowed her slow-witted husband to one side and dragged me inside, sat me on a bench and fetched mead and cups. In moments we were drinking a toast to the betrothal and Durwyn and I were shaking hands.

"That went easier than I expected," I smiled at Eduard.

"Don't know what you are so happy about, Cerdic. You just got engaged to be married!" He chortled as he sipped his mead, "And between *handgeld* payment to Durwyn and what you will give Aidith in her *brýdcéap* gift, you've promised to hand over about half your gold to do it!"

My people have never much cared about bathing. A dunk in a cold stream or having someone throw a bucket of water over you was about as far as it went when the grime and stench got too much. Yet the one day when a man and woman should bathe is on their wedding day. So it was that a month later, when May had given way to June, my wound had healed completely and all

20

preparations were made, I, accompanied once more by my friends, strolled down to the bath house. Most Angles would frown in puzzlement at the word, for my people certainly never built such extravagances. Yet we owned one, although of course we had never built it. The Villa was Roman and one forgotten owner of the estate had discovered a spring that emerged from the rocks a little way south of the orchard. Here they had constructed a pool and surrounded it with rooms.

It was many lifetimes since the Romans had lived here, but the building still stood - more or less. Some of the external wall had collapsed revealing the furnace, which Lilla had once said they had used to heat the water and the rooms. The spring water was clean and actually naturally warm, heated - Lilla again had said - by fires in the ground deep beneath the Villa. The pool was still intact as were two nearby rooms. In one we got undressed. In the other hot stones heated on a fire outside had been placed and water poured upon them. We closed the door, sat in the steam and sweated the dirt out of our skin. Then we jumped into the pool next door and washed it all off. At this point, I remember Lilla once telling me, the Romans would oil and scrape their skin, perish the thought!

As we reclined in the pool and relaxed for a few moments, the warmth of the spring water lulled me into a doze. I was woken by Aedann nudging my elbow.

"What is it?" I asked him.

"There is something on my mind, Cerdic."

"What? " I mumbled.

"This place - this estate - it was my family's once you know."

I opened my eyes and looked at him. "Yes, I know. Caerfydd told me once," I said, curious as to what was on his mind. "Do you resent it that my family own it now?"

"No - that's not it. Not any longer, I mean. I used to, it's true."

I nodded, thinking back to the sullen lad who had once hated me. "Then, what?"

"My people must have had status, land too - this land. We were nobles ourselves, once."

I nodded again, not sure where he was heading.

"I want land again."

I sat up and stared at him. "I don't have much land myself, Aedann. I can't give it away."

"I know. But your father is Earl of the Southern Marches. All of the south of Deira is in his authority. There must be land he can find for me somewhere."

I shrugged. "I don't know."

"I will ask him," Aedann said, a determined expression on his face.

"What, today?"

"No, not today. In a few days. He is staying on for a while isn't he?"

I nodded and then putting it out of my mind dragged myself out of the pool. "Come on everyone, let's get ready.

I dried myself and then dressed in my best tunic and britches, wrapped bright red and yellow strips of linen around my shins and buckled Catraeth to my side. When I was ready I turned to my friends.

"Well?" I asked.

"You'll do," Eduard said, "Come on, or we'll be late."

Just over the other side of the road to Wicstun was a sacred grove. My grandfather had planted it when he first came here and had a priest of Woden bless it. The elm and oak trees, which had grown and matured over my father's lifetime, now provided an

22

enclosure that was sheltered from the sun's heat. In the very centre of the grove was a single-storey wooden structure consisting of one room with a sloping roof. Not much, but it too had been built by the old man and to me and the villagers it was a sacred place, an *ealh* or temple. On holy days and festivals a priest would visit to say the words that the gods wished to hear.

When Eduard, Aedann, Cuthbert and I approached, the villagers had already arrived and were clustered around the small door leading into the sanctuary. I saw Grettir amongst them, resplendent in his finest warrior's garb. He nodded at me as I passed and the faintest hint of a smile reached his lips, which was an impressive show of emotion for the man. The other villagers were less stiff and grinned and cheered as I walked by.

Once inside I saw that my family had already arrived. Sunniva, my older sister, was beautiful but stern. We had never been that close and she always seemed aloof and cold. Married to a rich thegn from a village near Wicstun, she enjoyed her rank and wealth and took every opportunity to show it off. Today she wore a fine gown with golden thread woven into the garment. I nodded at her and she at least tilted her head in return.

"Cerdic!" my other sister. Mildrith, shouted and almost knocked me over as she bounced across the temple to give me a hug, attracting a disapproving glare from Sunniva and the priest alike. Millie's hair was braided with flowers and though her dress was much less fine than Sunniva's the effect on Eduard, Cuthbert and Aedann was dramatic. They all stared at her, mouths open in speechless amazement.

"Hello lads. You look smart today: must be all that bathing. Hope nothing got shrivelled up in the water," she teased mischievously as she returned to stand by my mother.

23

Eduard guffawed, Aedann's expression was lecherous whilst Cuthbert blushed and looked away. I grinned at their reactions then walked across to greet my parents.

"You look beautiful, Mother," I said as I kissed her on the cheek.

"Cerdic, I'm proud of you. I wish you happiness, my son."

Now I turned to look at my father. Cenred, the Lord of Wicstun and the Southern Marches wore a shirt of mail, an elaborate helmet with cheek guards and a mask that came over his eyes. I saw that he carried the sword that had once belonged to my uncle, which Samlen One Eye had stolen from my brother during the raid on the Villa and which we had taken from him when he lay dead near Catraeth field. That had been a day of three swords. I could have chosen to posses any of them: one was the family heirloom - my Uncle Cynric's sword which had such a history behind it; the other, a glorious weapon that Hussa had won in a tournament at the Villa. We had taken it from him when we seized him after Catraeth. I had counselled father to give it to Aedann, but he had not and I had not seen it since. Father never told me, but I believed he had returned it to Hussa, his illegitimate son, when they had parted. The last sword of the three was the one I had chosen - the short Roman gladius that I had named Catraeth in memory of that terrible day.

"Cerdic, you should wear this blade today," Father said, patting my uncle's longsword. "Then it will pass to your son."

I nodded and unbuckled Catraeth and handed it to him, receiving Cynric's in its place. We had already agreed we would do this as I had no desire to give up Catraeth just yet, but what was about to happen would involve yielding a blade to my bride as part of the ceremony. We had agreed I would give him back my uncle's sword after the wedding until such a time as the son I

24

hoped Aidith carried was of age to wield it. But today the great weapon would be an important part of the ritual. We now turned and waited for my bride.

We did not have to wait long: a disturbance in the crowd outside the temple heralded the entry of Peada, Aidith's cousin. He carried a cushion upon which there lay another sword. It was rather plain - just a simple iron blade with a wooden guard. Yet I knew this would have cost Aidith's family a good few coins so I smiled as Peada approached us.

"Lord Cerdic," he greeted me and came to stand near to the priest and myself. We then looked back towards the doorway. It seemed that an eternity went by as we waited. Then she was there. Aidith, my red-haired beauty, her dress a forest green the same colour as her eyes, patterned in yellow and held up by plain bronze clasps at the shoulders. She had chosen simple garb to emphasize her natural beauty. That day she looked like a woodland spirit, full of life and joy as she came up to me and smiled.

There was utter silence in the temple for a long moment and then the priest raised his hands high to the heavens and spoke.

"Hengest and Horsa, our fathers of old look down upon us mortals with benevolence. Woden, father of the gods grant us your blessing. Thunor, god of storm and thunder spare us your wrath, Tiw, god of battle and war release us from strife this day, Wayland, smith of the gods help us forge something strong. Freya, lady of love, bless this man and this woman and bring joy and offspring to their union."

Then he lowered his hands and held out his arms, describing a circle around the temple.

"Gods of Æsir and Vanir, I implore you to bless this place this day at this moment for one purpose, one task. Today we join these two as one."

Now he turned to me and his gaze was full of the gravity of the moment, yet kindly also. "Do you have the *handgeld* as you gave your oath you would bring?"

I nodded. "Yes, I have it here." I lifted a pouch. Then I turned to Durwyn and held it out. "I give you this, the *handgeld* as I promised to do. It is gold and silver taken from the foes I have vanquished, won in honour on Catraeth field."

Durwyn nodded and took the pouch from me.

The priest now turned to him. "Do you have the *brýdgifu* as you gave your oath you would bring?"

Solemnly, Aidith's father inclined his head, "Yes." He reached into his tunic and produced a pouch of his own, which he handed to Aidith. "I give you this, the *brýdgifu*. It is yours to have and hold all of your days."

Aidith took the offering. I knew it was the lion's share of Durwyn's wealth. It was his gift to her. A wealth independent of my own that would guarantee her and our children security from poverty should I ever abandon her.

The priest raised his voice and addressed the guests. "The *brýdgifu* and *handgeld* have been gifted and given. The holy oaths given have been held. Now let the bridegroom and bride exchange their oaths."

I turned to Aidith and tried to smile at her but suddenly I felt nervous and my throat dry. To mask my anxiety I reached down and brought out my uncle's sword.

"I give you this sword to save for our sons to hold and to use against our foes and in protection of our home."

Aidith took the sword, struggled with its weight and finally turned and handed it to Durwyn, who took it from her and held it with reverence. His father has been one of the men who had fought and perished with my uncle on that day outside Eoforwic.

Aidith now turned to Peada and he came forward, lifting the cushion up. She reached out and took the new blade from it. "Cerdic, to keep us safe you must bear a blade. With this sword keep safe our home."

I lifted the sword. It was long, more like my uncle's than Catraeth, and actually well balanced even if crude. It occurred to me that such a blade could be useful in fighting a man hand to hand, just as Catraeth was ideal for the crush of a shield wall. It would need a name, of course. Then I cast aside such concerns. This was a day for love, not thoughts of war. I dropped the sword into the leather strap buckled around my hips where my uncle's sword had hung.

Now the priest had us hold hands and exchange oaths. We swore to love and honour and be true to each other, and then he cried out, "I call upon the Goddess *Wær* to hear me and grant that these two are one."

It was done; we were man and wife.

"Well, I am glad I did not miss this moment," a new voice interrupted from the back of the sanctuary.

As one the entire company turned to stare, blink and then, jaw-dropped, stare again.

For standing in the doorway was Aelle, King of Deira.

28

Chapter Three
Aelle

The feast after my wedding would be remembered for the lifetime of all who attended. Not for anything that I did, but for the splendour of the occasion. My parents poured much of their wealth into it and, if that was not enough, Aelle had brought a company of his household warriors to wait upon us, two score barrels of the best wine and ale in the kingdom and the finest food in his cellars.

That night I did not give any thought to the extraordinary fact that the king had appeared and lavished his attention upon my house. Like many men who had seen battle, I had learned to live for the moment, not knowing how many more I might enjoy. That night Aelle could have drawn attention to himself, as would have been more than right, but he did not. He deflected any questions, refused any attempts to honour him and remained apparently content to sit to one side, sip at his ale and smile benevolently at me.

Yet the morning soon came and with it thoughts of what exactly Aelle was doing at the Villa. I had woken before dawn, despite the heavy load of wine I had consumed and the blissful attention of Aidith after the feast. Aelle was here for a reason, I was sure of it and after my new wife and I had finished our lovemaking and she had drifted to sleep, I lay awake pondering his visit. As the first glimmer of light filtered into the windows of the Villa, I disentangled myself from her arms, dragged on a cloak and britches and drifted towards the kitchen. When I opened the door, I found I was not alone.

I stalled on the threshold and blinked twice. The king wore no tunic and was standing in his britches and shirt, sleeves rolled up, his arms covered in flour to the elbows. His hands were plunged into a bowl where he was kneading dough. Gwen, Aedann's mother, whose domain was the kitchen, looked up at me as I entered, her face wearing an expression that seemed to be a mixture of irritation and awe. *Master*, her frown said, *there is a man in my kitchen and he is the king!*

"Ah, Cerdic, I hope you and your servant can forgive my intrusion, but there is something delightfully simple about making bread that I am finding soothing. Flour and fat, yeast and water: mix them together and in just a little while we have bread."

Aelle frowned as he lifted the unappetizing, congealed and rather grey looking mixture out of the bowl and attempted to shape it. Then he shrugged and let it drop again, moving away to the wash bucket to clean the sticky mess from his hands. He patted them dry on his britches, leaving smears of dough on his backside, then glanced at Gwen and seeing that she had retrieved the mixture and was already rescuing it from the atrocious state in which he had left it, he nodded at her with respect. "I can see you have a talent I never learnt. Come, Cerdic, and walk with me. I would like to stretch my ancient legs."

He led me out of the kitchen towards the orchard that lay to the south of the Villa. We walked in silence, but I could tell that something was on his mind. I said nothing. Aelle was the king and would speak when he wanted to.

We reached the orchard and he sat down on the stump of an old pear tree we had cut down the previous winter. I stood in silence, waiting. Finally he looked up at me. "I wish that being a king was as simple as baking bread appeared to be - before I made such a mess of it, of course," he added with a smile.

"My lord?"

"I am old, Cerdic. I will die soon. It cannot be long."

I said nothing. What was there to say? The man was old indeed and yet it seemed impossible to believe the day could come when he was no longer our king. Aelle was studying me.

"How old are you, Cerdic? Eighteen? Nineteen?"

"Not far off nineteen, my lord."

"Nineteen? I was not much older than you when I united the Deiran settlements along the Humber and made a people, where before there were scattered, leaderless villages and hovels under the domination of the Eboraccii. Since then it has been simple really. Get larger, add lands and villages; defeat the Eboraccii, keep Elmet under control and finally see off Urien and Owain. Through my life the enemy has always been the Welsh - Rheged, Elmet, Eboraccii, Pennines or whoever."

"My lord, you have protected us well. We are safe now. The danger is over."

Aelle shook his head. "Over? I thought you wiser than that. But I will forgive you. You are just married and must have a young man's dreams and hopes. But no, Cerdic, it is not over. The enemy may change. Friends may become enemies and enemies friends, but it is never over."

He fell silent again. In the trees above us the silence was broken by the shrill call of a bird heralding the new dawn. Soon it was joined by dozens of other voices. Aelle looked up.

"A new day has started. Soon my day will end and Deira will have a new king. That king will need guidance and courage. If he does not have it naturally, I will need you and others to give it to him. When a king dies, other kings will gather like ravens or

31

wolves looking for a weakness and waiting to pounce upon it. You stood in the hall at Stanwick Camp upon Catraeth field and persuaded Aethelric to keep the army there. You must speak out if you feel that decisions are wrongly made. Can I trust you to do that?"

"Decisions? Like decisions a king will make?"

Aelle nodded. "Aye. And decisions about who should be king, too."

I gaped, "About who should be king?"

Aelle nodded.

"I am confused, Sire. Surely Aethelric should be king?"

"You and the Witan will decide that, Cerdic. Not I. Just choose well and whatever the choice, guide him well. You, your father, Harald and Sabert, the four of you are the best to give guidance, so give it well. That is my last command to you. Other than this, I am leaving within the hour, so ... can we have breakfast now?"

I smiled. "Of course, my King."

The king left that morning as he had said. My family, however, stayed at the Villa for a full week after the wedding, feasting and relaxing. Indeed, they might have stayed longer had it not been for Cuthbert. My shy friend had taken a fancy to my sister and she, though having at first flirted with Aedann, had eventually returned the attraction. Mildrith lived at Wicstun now, of course, in my father's house - Lord Wallace's old hall in the town. As a result Cuthbert and Mildrith had seen little of each other in the year since Catraeth, though my friend would happily volunteer to take the *feorm* to Wicstun - the contribution from my lands destined for the king's tables at Godnundingham. Such trips were not that common, so he had welcomed the wedding and my family's visit to Cerdham as a chance to see my sister.

My friend might be shy, but he was a man after all and my sister a young woman and put the two together for any period of time and certain things tend to happen. So it was that a week after the wedding I was dozing on the verandah after the evening meal, my belly full of pork and mead, when I heard a terrible racket from the barn.

The voice that was shouting in rage I recognised at once as my father's. "I will skin you and hang you on a hook!" were the first bellowed words I heard.

In a flash I was off the verandah and galloping across the open ground to the barn. Eduard and half a dozen other villagers who had been around the Villa had heard it too and joined me as we burst in through the doors.

"Father, please don't hurt him!" Mildrith shouted.

She was lying in the corner of the barn on a heap of hay that was piled there, one hand was reaching up towards my father who had both hands around Cuthbert's neck and had lifted him bodily off the ground. Cuthbert's face was now bright red and he was choking. A brief memory came to me that it was pretty much the same spot that Aidith and I had made love only months before. Mildrith's clothes were rather rumpled and it did not take a genius to realise that my sister and friend were perhaps interrupted in a similar activity.

"Hurt him? I'll kill the little bastard!"

"Father, put him down!" I shouted, running up to them now and struggling to wrench his hand from my friend's throat.

"Leave off, Cerdic. I won't have this trash touching my daughter."

"Father, LET HIM GO!" I bellowed and to my surprise the old man released his grip. Cuthbert fell to the ground, both hands going to his throat. He coughed and then gasped.

33

"Sorry, my lord," he finally managed in a hoarse voice, "but I love her."

My father's eyes bulged. "Don't make me laugh; you are just after what is under her skirt!"

"Father, please! I love him too," my sister protested.

Father glared at her. "Keep quiet. You are in enough trouble as it is."

There is a wild streak in my younger sister and a liking for courting danger. I saw it the year before when she ignored the risk in order to sneak out of hiding and gaze at the raiders from Elmet - an action that cost Mildrith her liberty for a while and almost a lot more, had Samlen forced himself on her as he had threatened. Today it was father's wrath that she risked when she got to her feet and faced him.

"I do love him and I want to marry him. I am old enough to marry and I choose him."

Father's face was red again and I, like a man putting a pot on a fire, was waiting for the steam to rise.

"You have chosen HIM? What makes you think you have any choice in this matter? I will choose who you marry."

"But Father ..."

"Silence! I should have married you off last year. Had it not been for the raid and Cuthwine's ..." he gulped and for a moment the rage abated, but was quickly rekindled. "Had it not been for the fact that your brother died and we went to war I would have made arrangements. I see now that the time has arrived that I should."

"No, Father!"

"Get ready to leave. We return to Wictsun today. As for you, little runt," he added aiming a vicious kick towards my friend, "Mildrith will marry who ever the Lord of the Southern Marches says she will. Understood? Some thegn and certainly not some peasant! Come, Mildrith!"

With that he reached out, seized my sister by the wrist and stomped towards the Villa. It was at that moment that, with the height of mistiming, Aedann walked up to him. I could see from the look of determination on his face that my Welsh friend was going to broach the subject dear to his heart, which he had mentioned in the bath house just days before. Frantically I waved my hands to try to draw his attention, whilst shaking my head vigorously. It had no effect at all.

"My Lord Cenred," he began in a loud, confident voice.

Father stopped in his tracks and stared at the Welshman for a moment. "What in the name of Woden's balls do you want, Aedann?" he asked.

Aedann was clearly taken aback by the ferocity of the response but rallied and continued. "My lord, I wish to ask for a favour. I would have a name - I would have land. Please consider me when allocating the estates at your command."

"*What?*"

"I fought for you, your king and your son. I think I deserve something."

"*Deserve?*" he spun round to fix me with a baleful stare. "Your friends seem to be making free with my family and our lands, Cerdic." Then he turned back to Aedann, " So, you think you deserve reward? You Welsh bastard! You will get nothing from me - nothing. Now get out of my way."

He stomped off with Mildrith trailing along behind, casting a mournful glance back at Cuthbert, who had staggered out of the barn and joined Eduard, Aedann and me.

"That is one pissed-off man," Eduard grunted.

35

Aedann was still staring after my father and then finally he turned to face me. "Not a good time I take it?" he said with a wry smile.

True to his word, Father left with Mildrith and Mother later that afternoon. I tried to see him before he left, meaning to put in a word for both Aedann and Cuthbert, but he was in no mood for conversation and I, having learnt from painful experience that I would get no sense from him for some days, bade him farewell and watched him set off on the road to Wicstun.

Cuthbert and Aedann were rather tense the following day and Cuthbert in particular seemed hurt and upset. I decided we needed activity to keep them occupied and to fill our days over the summer months. The crops were planted and there was little to do but watch them grow till autumn, so I turned my mind to the task of building the new hall that I had often discussed with my father. It had long been on his mind to put up a new structure to be the centre of the Village - a mead hall for the people to gather in and hear tales, riddles and gossip. Better than making do with the barn as we had until then. The Villa itself was deteriorating. Grandfather might have taken a liking to it fifty summers before, but like the rest of our race he knew nothing of stonework. Tiles were missing in patches on the roof, the walls and plaster crumbling. The fire that had been started by the Elmetae during their raid the summer before had only made the problem worse. One day we would have to abandon it and live alongside in halls of wood and thatch just as the rest of our people did. So building a hall would be in preparation for that day. But for now it would serve as a gathering hall for feasts. It would also be used to store mead, ale and smoked food.

A week after my father had left, Aidith and I spent sometime deciding on the spot for the hall. We settled on a location between the Villa and the Village and soon I had the villagers busy marking out the perimeter. Then we set to the task of building the foundations. First we dug a large rectangular hole in the ground. This was some six feet deep. Six inches above the base of this hole the sides were taken back to create a ledge running around the outside. Two small square pits were dug in the midline of the hole. These would later serve as the supports for the sturdy posts that would take the weight of the roof.

These had first to be made. Eduard led a party of strong men into the woods where a sturdy oak tree of at least three hundred summers was felled and the branches trimmed away to leave the trunk. A series of wooden wedges were now hammered in a line along the tree. As the wedges bit deeper the trunk began to split until, with a crack, it was sundered from end to end. Using more wedges the halves were split again to create the planks. These were planed and smoothed until ready. The work was hard and the days still warm so for the most part we laboured without shirts. The village girls gathered about and giggled or whistled, but went screaming away when Eduard chased after them offering to strip off completely.

That was as far as we had got before we had to leave the job to go and gather in the crops and preserve the food for the winter months ahead. Aidith took to this task with zeal, eagerly overseeing the preservation of the food and its storage and then locking it away with the keys that had once been Mother's but now fell to her. Through the summer and autumn her belly had been growing and just after dawn one day I had to stop her from lifting a barrel to carry it down the stairs to the cellar storeroom.

37

"Oh, don't fuss, Cerdic. I will be fine," she said as she reluctantly surrendered the barrel to me. Besides which, that is pretty much the end of the work."

"A good thing too," I muttered as I reached over to pick up an apple and bite into it with a crunch. "Winter is close and you are getting fat!"

My reward was a punch to my belly.

"None of that, you need to be careful of yourself," I retorted.

Aidith rolled her eyes, "I am getting fed up of hearing that from my mother and yours too when she visits. I can't drink mead - not that I feel like it, it makes me sick at present. I'm not permitted to leave the Villa and travel far. I'm not supposed to eat anything too salty, nor too sweet. I can't have my meat too fatty. Does it not occur to you that this describes all the good stuff?"

I laughed, then frowned. Aidith's face had scowled into a pained grimace, her hands clutching at her belly.

"What is it?" I asked, dropping the apple.

"I think the discussion about what is good for me is now pointless, Cerdic," she replied between gritted teeth. "I think the baby is coming. Help me inside the Villa and send for my mother."

An hour later Aidith was settled in the bedroom, her mother and several women from the Village in attendance and a message sent to Wictsun to summon my mother. Ejected from the Villa, I strolled down the path to the foundations of the hall and pondered the situation. I glanced back up at the Villa and bit my lip as I thought of Aidith and my unborn child.

"Worried about the lass?" Eduard's voice disturbed my thoughts. He and my friends were standing by the building site with half a dozen men from the Village, including Durwyn. I shrugged, trying to appear nonchalant and then nodded.

"Well then, best to keep busy. How about we see about giving the baby a new home?" Durwyn said.

I nodded again and looked back at the foundations. We were clearly ready to lay the wooden planks we had laboured on some weeks before. And so we got on with it. The planks were laid across the base of the hole from ledge to ledge to create a floor to our cellar. Then more planks were added vertically, lining the cavity to keep the damp out and stop the sides collapsing into the hole. Another floor of wood planking was placed across the top of the hole to be the base of our hall, these reinforced by joists. In this floor we had already cut square holes for our posts and a trap door was created to allow access down into the cellar.

With eager hearts and strong arms we had set to our task and in a day the cellar and the floor of the hall above were finished. Eduard was right that the work had proved a distraction and yet every half hour or so I could not prevent myself from glancing up at the Villa and wondering how Aidith was. It would do no good to go and find out. The Villa was the domain of the midwives and the women of the Village until the baby was born. My sisters and mother arrived later in the day and went at once into the Villa. A little later I saw Mildrith go to the store room and rushed over to her.

"How ... how is she?" I asked her.

Mildrith was just emerging from the storeroom when I intercepted her and she jumped on seeing me. She was holding a parsnip as well as a bundle of dried herbs.

"Cerdic, you surprised me. I thought you might be ..."

I nodded. Clearly she thought maybe I was Cuthbert coming to see her. "Cuth is out hunting with his father," I explained. "Perhaps you can see him later."

"Father forbade me to."

"Oh, and you always do what Father says don't you? So you certainly won't be trying to sneak off and see him, will you," I grinned.

She made a face at me but we both knew that given half a chance she would do exactly that and I did not blame her.

"What of Aidith?"

"Oh, she is fine, but the labour is taking a while."

"Why? What's wrong," I asked, fear gripping me by the throat.

"Cerdic, relax. It's her first baby. They sometimes take a long time. Old mother Algifa is going to give her parsnip water to ease the labour."

From the Villa I heard a scream then a pause and a moment later a sound that still echoes to me down through all the long years, as does the clamour of battle. This was a different sound though, not the echo of death but the call of new life: the sound of my son crying, though I didn't know it then.

Mildrith laughed, "Looks like she does not need the parsnip after all. I will take it anyway and the holly oak in case the afterbirth will not come."

She rushed back, leaving me alone, keen to see my wife and my child. I did not have to wait long. My mother emerged from the Villa a short while later and waved at me to join her. I handed Eduard the hammer I was holding and ran over. Mother took me inside to where Aidith was sitting up in bed looking exhausted and pale. At her breast was a tiny figure wrapped in strips of cloth. Only the top of the head was visible and there I could see the smallest wisp of reddish hair.

Aidith looked up as I entered and smiled at me. "Here is your son, Cerdic. What shall we name him?"

A son! I came closer and as I did the baby stirred and for a moment his unfocussed gaze flicked over to me, before again returning to the important matter of feeding. It was not much of a glance, but in it I saw something I had not done for a year and more. I saw my brother. I looked over at my mother and replied.

"Cuthwine, Aidith, we will call him Cuthwine."

Later that week I took Cuthwine with me to show him the work being done on the hall. Wrapped in my cloak to ward off the winter cold, I carried him to the site and stood watching the activity.

Whilst I had been away, two thick posts had been lowered through the holes in the floor and then located in the pits we had dug for them. More post holes were dug around the corners of the hall and the posts added to create the skeleton around which was placed the timber and planks of the walls. At one end a doorway was fashioned and the frame carved with symbols of Woden and Thor and my name rune. The thatched roof had openings in each end to allow the smoke out and some air in.

I looked down at the small form in my arms and found that he was awake and two dark eyes were staring at me. I smiled at him.

"This will be your hall one day, son, when you are full grown and then four generations of our family will have ruled the valley from this spot."

Aedann and Eduard looked up from where they were helping bundle thatch for the roof.

"I don't think he is listening to you, Cerdic," Aedann teased and nodded towards my son who, warm and snug in my arms, had drifted off to sleep. I sighed in contentment and watched a while longer.

Whilst the men laboured to complete the hall, the women of the Village had set to work weaving tapestries, moving into the new building once it had a roof. Some would take weeks to finish, but I was determined that my hall would be the envy of the whole South Marches. One of these tapestries showed our ancestors in longboats passing over the great sea to land in Britannia. Others showed scenes of battles, including Catraeth. Cuthbert swore that one of the archers depicted in one scene was himself. He may have been right; his mother did help with that frieze. Even more villagers, meanwhile, were fashioning benches and tables, moving them inside as they were complete. I heard a footstep behind me and saw Aidith there.

I smiled, "Here it is, my love. Our new hall. It will be finished before Yuletide," I said. "And I have an idea for the best way to celebrate our first feast in it ... if I can find him, that is."

That winter we feasted on great oak benches and tables in the hall beside a roaring fire and as always tales were told of battle and valour. I still enjoyed them but realised they failed to fire my soul as they once had. They were stories that no longer applied to me. Entertaining and amusing but not relevant. Or so I thought. Nevertheless, there was one man who did stir my spirit just as he had when I was a child. This man wove magic in with his words and blended awe into every breath. This was the man I had sent out to find: Lilla the Bard.

Lilla was now in his mid thirties, but still looked as young as ever. His hair was golden like the sun, not silver like the moon, and his body both strong and agile. Far more important than mere appearance and stature was the man's charisma and that enchanting voice. Even though I had seen the horror of Catraeth field and felt the terror of the flight from Elmet, I experienced that familiar glow in my chest and my heart pounding with passion and yearning as he spoke of war.

"The British have a name for Aethelfrith," he said. "They call him 'Twister'. They seek through it to insult his honour and suggest he is not to be trusted. I say to you, though, that the King of Bernicia has taken that name and changed it. So, like a wolf chasing a deer through the forest, he twists and turns. Try as they might to evade him, in the end his jaws lock upon his prey, biting into his foes, bringing death and destruction upon them."

The villagers cheered. I looked across to Cuthbert and saw in his eyes the same memory of those times, just bare months before, when we had cheered at news of Aethelfrith's victories and those of his father in Rheged and the North. For us, though, this had all changed at Catraeth. Then I heard Eduard cheering harder and louder than the rest and smiled. Eduard was not troubled by thinking too much. He did not find these tales hollow at all. To him we were ALL living through the sagas and truly becoming one with them.

"In the year since the great victory at Catraeth, the warlord has not ceased his warfare nor stayed his hand. He has marched north and extends English rule and English power in the land between the walls ..."

Now, despite myself, I felt my pulse quicken as Lilla drew us away from our valley and our humdrum life and told us tales of lands that were almost a legend to us.

"Aye: the land between the walls; that is where the Bernician armies are fighting even now. In that realm between the great stone wall to the north of Catraeth, which runs through Bernicia, and the earth ditch and embankment even further away. Few men

43

have seen it but ... so the stories say, it was built to keep out the wild people: the Picts."

There was a low rumble of voices as men and women muttered curses. We had heard of the Picts but not many of us had seen them, though some were at Catraeth I heard tell.

"Picts, which means the painted people. Theirs is a cold land north of the earth wall and full of mountains and moors. Their men are tough, brave warriors and their women fearsome and strong. Yet those are not the only enemies he faces."

The bard now held up one finger. "Firstly, the Picts in their mountain stronghold. Secondly, the British that survived Catraeth. Aye there are still many left in the kingdoms of Rheged in the West, Manau Goddodin in the North, and Strathclyde. They lick their wounds and mourn their dead and look upon us with eyes full of vengeance and hate. Catraeth was a fearsome blow but it was not mortal, not yet."

Now he was holding up three fingers and he circled the hall, dragging out the tension like the master storyteller he was.

"Three, the Scots of Dál-Riata. They are kin to the Irish and have crossed the sea from Ulster to settle along the far west coast. They are led by a man hungry for conquest. He is Áedán mac Gabráin and I met him last winter."

Lilla's voice dropped almost to a whisper as he recalled his visit. "The Picts and the British have always been here - leastways as long as any can recall. The Scots, though, are like us: a people from a far land making this land their own. Only the gods know if there is space enough for us all. If there is not, if some are pushed into the sea, then mac Gabráin will make sure that he is the one with his feet on dry land. If he comes south, driving Picts and Britons out of his path, then we may have cause again to go to war."

44

Now his gaze fixed on me and I knew what he was thinking: that in such a war there would be a need for warriors and leaders, and I, the man who had killed Owain at the gates of Stanwick Camp, would be in demand.

But no. That was not my fate. My fate was to be here with my wife and my child and to rule this little valley. This was all the life I needed. The sagas would have to find other heroes and Lilla a new warrior to sing about.

Chapter Four
A New King

It was a good Yuletide and I let myself believe that my wishes would come true. Life would go on like it had these last few months and I would raise my son and other children and live out my years in this idyllic place. It was a small valley after all. Maybe the gods would ignore us and we could get on with life. I have an abiding memory of sitting with Aidith in our kitchen beside the glowing embers of the bread oven. It is almost time for bed, but I am too comfortable to move. Cuthwine is snuggled warm against my shoulder, gently snoring and my beloved wife is smiling at me. It is an image I will carry with me until the day I die.

In this contentment another two harvests slipped by. My baby son, the light of my life, was rising two and into everything. To give Aidith a moment's peace, I often took him with me as I went about my valley overseeing the men who tended my fields and livestock. He would toddle after me or ride chortling on my shoulders: a farmer in the making. It was the life I had dreamed of since Catraeth and for a long while it seemed I would get my wish. However, one god chose not to ignore us: Loki, it seemed, was bored with it all and did not appreciate stability and security. That winter he decided to change the rules of his game.

Aelle had been our king for as long as most men could remember. For almost fifty years he had led and protected our people: a strong, seemingly indestructible figure. Yet even compared to when I had first seen him not that many years before, he had become an old man. All men die eventually and in the heart of winter, when gales swept bitter cold across the frozen fields, the Valkyries decided it was time to call this old warrior to his rest.

It did not surprise me that it was Lilla who had somehow caught wind of this before anyone else. He woke me far too early one morning after we had all drunk too much ale the night before, by hammering on my door.

"What in the name of Woden's buttocks …?" I roared as I opened the door and saw him on the threshold. I trailed off when I saw a serious expression on his usually jovial face.

"I just got a message that Aelle is dying, Cerdic. You have been summoned to Godnundingham straight away. Get dressed and I will ride with you."

The king's hall at Godnundingham - a day's journey north and east of the Villa - was enclosed by high, palisaded, earth embankments and a reinforced gate, and was a vast wooden structure two stories high. At its heart lay the massive mead hall where Aelle had once entertained the nobles and warriors on the eve of the council that sent us to battle at Catraeth. That day it had been full of noise and song, ale and laughter. Today, even the fire pit that ran along the floor in the centre of the room seemed subdued, its dying embers echoing the fate of the hall's master.

At the far end of the hall was the high table where Aelle, with Aethelric and his other son, Edwin, his grandson, Hereric, and daughter, Acha, had sat that other time. As we approached I saw that three youths lounged at it now, drinking small beer and studying us as we went by. Edwin was thirteen, a lanky youth with dark brown hair and intelligent but dark, brooding eyes. His expression was hostile as we passed, as if asking who came to see his dying father this day. Sat next to him was Hereric. A year or two younger, Aethelric's son was an overweight youth whose

48

spotted face showed little interest in us as we walked by: a boy whose intelligence was as limited as that of his father, or so it seemed to me.

The third lad I did not recognize. He was younger, perhaps about seven, and sat a little apart from the other two as if afraid to be in their company. I inclined my head into a slight bow, which none of them acknowledged, and then turned to Lilla.

"Who is the younger one?" I whispered.

Lilla glanced at the boy before answering. "Osric. He is Aelle's nephew; the son of his brother, Aelfric, who died a few years ago."

We reached the far end of the hall and climbed some stairs that led to the king's private chambers. Two guards armed with spears and carrying shields marked with the king's own symbol barred our way, but stepped back when they saw Lilla and me. One man I recognised as having been with us at Catraeth and exchanged a nod with him.

The door led to a solar: a room occupied by chairs and tables where the king's family could relax away from the public eye. It was lit by the light of winter sun, which was now dying in the south-western sky, though still filtering in through a high window. I saw that a servant was lighting candles dotted around the room. Two guards directed us to an interior door.

Lilla paused at it and cast an appraising eye over my travel-crumpled attire, tutting as he straightened my cloak and tidied me up. "The king's chamber is through here. Much of the court will be present. Let's make you presentable." Lilla, as ever, was immaculate, despite the fact that we had just ridden over twenty miles. Satisfied that he had made the best of a bad job, he nodded at me and tapped gently on the door. It openly slowly and I saw my father standing on the threshold.

49

Entering the room I saw that Lilla was correct and a large number of the nobles of Deira were assembled: Earl Harald and Earl Sabert, my father and around twenty others of all ranks. Sitting near the bed was Prince Aethelric, the king's son and heir. Everyone else was gathered in the shape of a horseshoe around the bed.

I allowed my gaze to pass beyond them all to the man who lay there and saw at once that we had arrived only just in time. Aelle, King of Deira was panting hard, beads of sweat were hanging on his forehead and his lips were a blue-grey colour. The man was certainly dying. His expression was vacant and I thought him oblivious to all of us, but after a moment he seemed to focus upon me and just for a heartbeat I saw in that gaze the same spirit and drive that had pushed him to conquer a nation. Then the flame dimmed and when he spoke his voice was thin and rasping.

"Ah ... Cerdic. Join us," he said, breaking into a fit of coughing. After a moment, with obvious effort he continued, "I am glad to see you once again. As you see, I am dying and go, I hope, to feast with the gods."

"The gods should be glad to have such a great warrior and king join them, my lord."

"Maybe ... I shall soon see. Thank you for reminding me I was a great warrior. I was just remembering my first victory as king, so it is fitting that the hero of Deira's last victory is here with me. You were there when we needed you, Cerdic."

Now he looked around the room, "Indeed, I need you again ... every one of you. When I am dead my successor - whoever he is - will need all your support and all your counsel. Choose him wisely." Then he slipped into sleep again, his breath coming in short rasping gasps, which filled the shocked silence that followed his words.

Close by the bed, Aethelric wore a puzzled expression. He was not the only one. All around the room the earls and lords were glancing at each other. Aelle had not declared who his successor should be. In so doing he had raised a doubt that the crown should and would pass to his son - to Aethelric. He had pretty much said what many of us were privately thinking - that Aethelric was no king and that Deira under his rule would be at risk from its neighbours.

The man on the bed slumped back onto his pillow. His eyes were glazed, unseeing. He was a man who cared no longer for the concerns of this world. If he saw anything it was his journey to the next: a world that we could not see, not yet anyway. His breathing slowed, he gave a rattling cough and then he was still. I had seen it before on a thousand faces at Catraeth. King Aelle was dead.

"Father?" Aethelric said and then, realising what had happened he bowed his head and covered his face with his hands.

We buried Aelle near to Godnundingham. He had directed that a mound be raised a mile to the north, on high ground so that he could look down upon his kingdom. Three days after his death a procession left the palace. Aethelric led the funeral party and every noble that had been present went along. The king's huscarls - those who had taken oaths to serve him and in turn had received rings and other gifts as symbols of that service - formed the honour guard and carried his body the whole way.

At his tomb we laid the old king with great honour into his final chamber and around him were placed spears, swords, shields, axes and bows: weapons he had used to forge a kingdom and trophies taken from the vanquished. To these were added a wealth of precious stones and gold jewellery and a fine pair of

51

drinking horns. Finally, Acha and the women of the court came forth and deposited offerings of food: apples; boiled eggs; a side of beef; shellfish and a flagon of mead. Aelle was going on a journey to the gods and it was fitting that he had food and drink to nourish him and perhaps gifts to present to Woden and his kin to show how great he had been in life. Then the priest came forward and appealed to the gods to receive this great warrior into their halls.

When all was done, we withdrew and sealed the tomb. Then, as dusk came on, a fire was started and we stared into the flames as the oldest nobles - those who remembered much of the king's life - came forward and spoke of his deeds. We heard of his valour and courage, his bravery in battle and wisdom in judgment. When the battle in which my uncle had died was mentioned, I glanced at my father. His eyes were distant and I saw that his hand was resting on the pommel of Cynric's sword, which he had retrieved from Durwyn after my wedding. Then, as if feeling my gaze upon him, he looked over at me and smiled a sad smile. My mother once said to me that every wedding she went to reminded her of every other one, including her own. I guess that is also true of funerals. We remember not just the person who has died, but all those who have gone before them along the same route and waited for them in the company of the gods ... waiting for us too, when the time comes.

Finally, Acha came out into the firelight and sang a song of mourning for her father. The princess was beautiful, but I don't think she ever looked more like a goddess than on that night at Aelle's funeral. The song tore at the soul and left a deep aching and yearning inside us. Each of us felt something: a feeling that even if it had been for just a few months that King Aelle had touched us and inspired us, we were nevertheless the better for it.

Then the song ended and the fire died and we were left with darkness and silence to ponder our loss.

"Gods, Cerdic, but I need a beer," Eduard muttered, as ever not quite quietly enough, for half the company must have heard it.

"Indeed, goodman, I think we all do," Aethelric said at last and led us back to the palace for a funeral wake.

"We are here to decide who will be king," Lord Sabert announced, looking around the hall. It was the day after the funeral and the Witan had gathered. Every bench was filled with nobles, great and small from all over Deira: from the smallest estate such as the Villa, through the thegns who held the villages and towns, to the earls, Sabert, Harald and my father. Sabert was standing at the end of the hall near Aelle's vacant throne. Near it, on another chair, sat Aethelric and beside him were Edwin and Hereric.

"The most worthy should be king; that is the tradition. That is the law. If a dying king indicates his wishes on the succession we would take that as a strong guide as to who should inherit," Earl Sabert continued.

"But Aelle did not indicate who should come next," Harald said, "so this council must decide out of the candidates."

"What is there to decide?" Prince Edwin interrupted. "Aethelric is the only choice."

"I am his oldest son, Earl Harald," Aethelric agreed, his voice as vague as ever and devoid of any enthusiasm. "That probably means it should be me."

Harald glanced at Sabert. I could see the hesitation on both their faces.

"What are you waiting for?" asked Edwin. "Perhaps you have another candidate in mind? Osric, Hereric and I are too young and would not in any event put ourselves in front of my brother, but we are Aelle's only close kin."

Edwin was right. There were no others of the blood line old enough or able enough to become king. The problem was that we all knew Aethelric was not the man for the job. Yet no one said anything. I recalled the conversation with Aelle in the orchard on the morning after my wedding. I knew I had to say something, but what? There was really only one man here whom I would choose.

Throwing caution to the winds, I opened my mouth to speak. "What about Earl Harald?" I suggested.

There was silence after I said those four words and every man turned to look at me. Some faces were lit up with hope that perhaps what they had been secretly thinking was at last spoken aloud. Others shocked that someone as junior as myself should speak out in front of the whole Witan. My father's face was full of admiration. Aethelric looked confused, but not upset, almost as though he was hoping for a way out. Sabert, thoughtful, seemed content, as if all along he had been waiting for this. Harald, flushing and embarrassed by the suggestion, which to my mind reinforced my judgement that he was the right man: one who would never put himself forward. Yes, lots of expressions and lots of reactions, but it was one face that I recall all these decades later. A scowling youth of thirteen summers, who jumped to his feet and shouted one word: "No!"

"I was taken aback by the ferocity of Edwin's outburst.

"My Prince, I mean no offence ..." I started to explain myself.

"Silence! Tell me who you are."

"I am Cerdic, Lord of the Villa of Cerdham and son of Earl Cenred."

"The Villa? You mean that crumbling Roman ruin in a tiny valley?"

I nodded, despite the insult.

"Hah! You own a few pigs and cows and you presume to speak at the King's Council?"

There was a polite cough and Sabert spoke. "My Prince, Cerdic was well thought of by your father. He was the hero of Catraeth."

"Hero indeed. I see no hero. I see a farmer ... nothing more."

Sabert coughed again. "Even so, as thegn he is entitled to speak here. Maybe we should discuss his suggestion of Earl Harald. That is, if Prince Aethelric does not object?"

Aethelric shook his head, looking vaguely from Sabert to me, "N-no ... n-not at all."

Edwin scowled again. "Brother, you should object. This is nonsense. Father was king and it should pass to one of us here," Edwin waved at Aethelric and Hereric, both of whom gazed back with the same belligerent expression. Edwin sighed and I have to say that at that moment I felt my first feeling of sympathy for the lad. It was clear that nothing of Aelle had passed to his older son, whilst the younger had all the fire of his father. Yet even if that were so, Edwin was too young to be king.

"You are too young, my Prince and so is Hereric," I said. "As for Aethelric, I am sorry to say this, lord, but I don't believe King Aelle thought you the right man to succeed him."

There were gasps around the hall as I said this, but I had gone too far to stop now. "It is true. I am sorry, but he was anxious about the future. He worried about the North, the Picts and Scots and others. The land needs a strong man to command it."

"Silence, farmer!" Edwin screamed.

55

"I will be silent, Prince Edwin, but I had to say this. Your father asked it of me."

"My father is dead!" Edwin glared at me, "How is it that he said none of this to me, to my brother ... why to a farmboy?"

Sabert again came to my defence. "Because he knew you would not listen, my Prince. And he knew that two years ago this man," he pointed at me, "argued against us all and kept the army at Catraeth. He put his trust in the man who saved the nation then to help us make the right choice now."

"What choice is that?" Edwin snapped. "I am too young and so is Hereric. It must be Aethelric!"

"Does he want to be king?" I asked. "Your brother? Does he want to be king?"

"Of course he wants to be king. It is his birthright."

I raised my eyebrow at Aethelric, surprised that he should allow his young brother to speak for him. He made no comment and I was again struck by how out of place he was.

"What of Harald?" Sabert asked. "Would he want to be a candidate?"

We all turned to look at the Earl of Eoforwic. Harald had not said a word while this conversation was going ahead. His head was bowed and he was staring at the embers in the firepit in the centre of the room.

"Well, Earl Harald, what say you about all this?" Edwin said.

Harald looked up. For a moment I thought he would confirm that he would stand as candidate and let the Witan decide. Around me all were silent as every noble studied him, half hoping and half fearing he would accept. Then something changed in his expression. His eyes widened and it was if he was seeing Edwin for the first time.

56

"I pledged allegiance to the house of Aelle before you were born, my Prince, or you Cerdic of the Villa. Kingship rests in Aelle's house, one way or another, and I will not be the one to break that dynasty. I will not stand against Aethelric as king. I will serve him as I did his father."

I could not believe this. I had been certain Harald would agree to stand. Deira needed a strong leader like him. Why now had that strength wavered? Why support a weak king when there was danger of the wolves gathering against us?

Sabert glanced across at me and shook his head, waving at me to sit down again. "So then," he said, "Harald will not stand, nor Edwin or Hereric. Is there another here who the Witan deem kingworthy?"

No one answered.

"Then shall the Witan elect Aethelric, son of Aelle as King of Deira unless any would now speak against that?"

I stayed silent, my gaze fixed on the same coals Harald had been staring at. Then I felt that I was being watched and looking up saw Edwin glaring at me as though daring me to speak.

"So be it," Earl Sabert said after a moment. "Aethelric is king. May Woden and Thunor and all the gods bless him with long life, wisdom and might. Let us all come forth to swear allegiance to him," he commanded.

We lined up and one by one knelt and swore to obey and follow Aethelric or die trying.

When we had returned to our seats we waited for Aethelric to make a speech, which he did in a few halting words. When it was finished, Edwin leant over and spoke to his brother and Aethelric nodded. Edwin stood up.

"Cerdic, son of Cenred, Lord of the ... er, *Villa*," he added the last bit with a sneer, "it is fitting that a messenger be sent to convey news to Bernicia of my brother's succession. You, Cerdic, shall carry that message north.

Chapter Five
Messenger

"You're g-g-going where?" Cuthbert asked the following night after I had returned home. The household and many of the villagers were drinking in the mead hall and it was there where my friends and I were sharing a meal. Aidith had retired to nurse Cuthwine, who seemed to be getting colic a lot these days.

"Bebbanburgh in Bernicia, like I have already told you five times," I answered, skewering a roast chicken with my seax and dropping it on my trencher.

Watching me tear off a leg he nibbled at a crust of bread before stammering another question. "Th-that's a l-l-long way isn't it?"

I shrugged and looked around the tables and then spotted Grettir sitting alone nearby, sipping at his ale, his eyes distant. I called over to him.

"Lord Cerdic," he answered coming to his feet.

I waved him back down. "Cuthbert asks how far Bebbanburgh is."

He scratched his grey beard as he pondered the answer. "Four days for a horse and rider, twice that and more on foot."

I nodded my thanks and looked back at Cuthbert. "And you are coming too?"

"M-me? W-w-why?"

"Two reasons. Firstly because all you do around here is mope and sulk over my sister." He opened his mouth to speak but I raised a hand to stop him. "Yes you do, there is no point trying to

59

deny it. Anyway you need a change of scene and this will give you that."

"And the other reason?"

I hesitated before answering, "Because my father insists I take you. With him at court a lot at present and me away he seemed to think you would try to see Mildrith."

Cuthbert scowled at me.

"Don't look at me like that. You know it's true."

His face was still dark.

"Look, be patient," I said, "he is not rushing to marry off his last remaining child and he might come round to you if you keep out of his way for a bit. Mildrith is not going anywhere."

"Aye, but w-w-we are. Those northlands are full of d-d-demons and giants."

"That's balls," Eduard put in with a belch as he poured himself another tankard of ale.

"Who b-b-built the Wall then?" Cuthbert challenged, talking about the great stone wall that was supposed to stretch clear across the country not far south of Bebbanburgh.

Eduard took a pull at his ale and shrugged with disinterest.

"My father always said it was the Romans," Aedann chipped in, and I recalled that Caerfydd had once told us about the Wall and how he had seen it as a youth.

"I should like to see it, if I can come too," Aedann said. "Besides which, those lands are wild and I may get a chance to make a name for myself," he added, persisting with the thought that he wanted rank and land.

I nodded noncommittally for I did not see that a simple journey to carry a message was likely to give us much by way of adventure. "I don't think we will have much trouble. Indeed, I hope not. I will take my sword, but don't plan to draw it," ... *ever again,* I added silently as I thought about Aidith and our infant son, and getting to my feet made ready to join her.

"Oh, I hope there is *some* trouble," Eduard grinned. "I assumed I was coming too, but just carrying a message seems a bit boring. Hey - maybe we will meet some Picts to fight," he added brightly before returning to his ale.

"Must you go?" Aidith asked me later as she lay in my arms." Cuthwine is barely two. You only seem to go away to fight and I don't want him growing up with no father."

"I am not going to fight anyone, my love. Just to carry Aethelric's message and come home. Two or three weeks at the most and I will be back."

"You promise?"

"I promise I will be there to watch Cuthwine grow tall and strong."

She looked across the room to the cot where our son lay. His breathing as he slept was all we could hear for a full five minutes. We lay in silence and listened. Then she turned to me and pulled me towards her and we kissed. In that moment I felt blissfully happy. I had all I wanted in that place: a wife, a family, and a house to grow old in and one day leave to my son. It was all that I had asked the gods to bless me with. Yet not all the gods were benevolent and one in particular was mischievous and vindictive and liked his tricks and his games. For this brief time my piece on the gameboard had lain dormant at its edge, not part of the chaotic swirl of kings and warriors at its heart. Now an ancient hand reached over and took my piece and that of my friends and pushed them into the maelstrom along with another piece, that of my half brother.

That of Hussa.

61

Grettir was right about the distance to Bebbanburgh. It was over one hundred and fifty miles. A long way for a man on foot I decided. So we would take horses. That was when the fun began. I had my own horse: a chesnut mare my father had given me, which he had named 'Autumn', for her coat was the colour of leaves at harvest time. She was fast enough when called upon, but more than that she was reliable and would keep a steady trot for mile after mile. Eduard, Cuthbert and Aedann would have to content themselves with the smaller horses that we kept on the estate. I had ridden Autumn many times, but the boys had done little more than haul themselves onto the backs of their beasts when trotting around the fields surrounding the Villa. Aedann took to his mount with ease and showed no difficulty controlling the animal.

"Bollocks to that idea," Eduard complained when I told him how we were to reach Bernicia. "I'll bloody walk."

"You bloody won't. It will take three times as long and I don't want to be away that long, so get on the damned horse!"

It did not end like that. Eduard went on about it for a full hour before finally I threatened to take Aidith with me instead and leave him to play nursemaid to my son. Grumbling, he heaved himself onto the animal then sulked at me for another five minutes until I turned away and went off to sort out Cuthbert.

"I ... I ... c-c-can't." Cuthbert stammered, shaking with fear at the thought of getting on his fat little horse.

"Cuth, just try."

He tried. He climbed up. He fell off.

He tried again and smiled at me as he perched astride the animal. His smile turned to a terrified grimace as he slowly tilted sideways ... and fell off again. In the end Grettir appeared with a length of rope and we tied the man to the back of his patient mount.

When I turned back to see how Eduard was getting on, he was prancing around as if he was one of the Gododdin cavalry and not someone who minutes before had sworn at me at the very idea of getting on a horse.

"Come on, Cerdic. Last one in Bebbanburgh buys all the beer," he said and galloped off down the lane toward Wicstun leaving the rest of us gawping after him.

The road north took us through the city of Eorforwic. Seeing it again brought mixed feelings. The huge Roman fortress to the east of the river and the decaying civilian city on the other side were still impressive, but I was reminded that it was here, two years before, that we had passed through on the way to Catraeth. I had seen it again after the battle, for here was the place that my half brother Hussa had been tried for treason. He had betrayed Deira and his people and he should have died but father, feeling guilty over having abandoned him, had pleaded for his life. He had bought Hussa's freedom with blood money by handing over my mother's priceless amber necklace. My mother had been furious when she found out. After all, the boy was the result of my father's infidelity. But that day, with Aelle's permission, Hussa's sentence of death had been commuted to banishment and father took Hussa away to the bridge at Catraeth and there they had parted.

We passed over the bridge the day after leaving Eorforwic. The old Roman bridge had been made of stone, but neglected after the legions left, it had begun to decay. It seemed the stomp of armies back and forth in the last year or two had caused even more damage. I saw that attempts to repair the structure were

63

underway, but not in stone - such skills were beyond us. Instead, although the existing stone piles were being re-used, wooden planking had been laid between them. The hooves of our horses clattered hollowly as we trotted across.

Coming this way again I found myself thinking about my half brother, whose resentful betrayal had almost led to my death. I knew he had gone north into lands controlled by Bernicia. Was he still there? What was he doing? I had the strangest feeling of foreboding as if fate was bringing us together again.

One morning, when we had not been travelling that long, we came over a small rise and there was the Wall. Without a word we each reined in and stared at the spectacle. The road we were on was Roman, of course, heading north from Eoforwic into the wild northern lands. We could see it ahead of us heading straight as an arrow's flight to the Wall, passing through a fort and presumably continuing on the far side.

The Wall stretched across our path as far as we could see and disappeared to the east and west, rolling up and down the dips and rises in the ground. Dotted along it were small towers each one in sight of the next. As we approached we could see that the Wall was maybe twice the height of a man. From a distance it had seemed white, but now I saw this was because the Romans had plastered the surface and painted it white - maybe so it could better weather the winter storms. The Romans were long gone, of course, and the paintwork was cracked and in many places had come away entirely. In other places the Wall itself was missing huge chunks of stone work. I frowned in puzzlement at that and Aedann, seeing my expression, pulled his horse over to me.

"My father said that after the Roman soldiers had gone, some of the local British tribes came to steal parts of the Wall and take the stone to build their own houses with."

"Ah yes, so he did, I remember," I nodded, recalling a long ago conversation in the kitchen of the Villa with Aedann's father. Those days had been good ones for me. Everyone I loved was in that valley. Now Caerfydd was dead, killed ironically by a warlord of his own people, who had also killed my older brother. The years had rolled on and now I was Lord of the Villa, yet it was still the case that most of those I loved were there - save that my parents and my sisters had moved to Wicstun. Aedann was looking sadly at the wall.

"What is it?" I asked.

"I am thinking of my father. He came here once. Did he stand here and see this sight I wonder? He was free in those days - before your people came to the Villa. Forty years ago, perhaps more. He had land and lost it. I was born with nothing but the stories he told me of the world that was ours before your race invaded."

"We have been in Britain more than forty years, Aedann," I pointed out.

"Yes, but not in the valley, not until just after Da came here and at that moment he was free and had hope. "

"You are free," I said, gesturing to the sword at his side, "a proud huscarl and a fierce warrior."

"But what *hope* do I have? I want more. I want land again, Cerdic."

I was not sure I liked the way this was going. "I will help if I can, Aedann. But I hope you don't mean the Villa," I said with sudden need to be clear on that matter.

65

He turned and stared at me and opened his mouth to reply, but at that moment Eduard, who had ridden ahead with Cuthbert, galloped back to us.

"Come on, you two, I have good news. Some locals have set up a tavern in that abandoned fort down there next to the road and I have had them open a barrel of ale and told them you are paying, Cerdic!"

The ale was good; very good in fact. Yet I could not fully appreciate it. Eduard was his usual boisterous self, laughing and joking his way through the evening and then managing to incite one of the local girls into a room. Love-struck, Cuthbert sat in sullen contemplation, his gaze like his thoughts far away. I was pretty certain I knew where. Aedann kept looking over the table at me, seemingly about to speak and then falling into silence again and gulping his ale.

When Eduard left us I retired for the night. But then I found that I could not sleep. I kept thinking of the Villa and how it was my home and how I wanted to be there and not here on this errand. When I did drift off, thoughts of the Villa were replaced by images of Aedann's face. This was not the first time he had mentioned his dreams of land and title and of belonging. But it was the first time he had seemed so blatant about *what* land and *what* title he wanted. Did he really want the Villa, and if so, would I be forced to fight him for it?

The next two days we continued northwards along the great road that ran on, so the stories went, to the lands of the Goddodin. Uncertain of the way, we asked locals in villages we passed. Some were clearly British tribesmen, now ruled by the Angle kings from Bebbanburgh. Most British men and women avoided us as we passed, mounted and armed as for war. Was their treatment under Aethelric rough I wondered? Others regarded us with hostility. These ones reminded me of those Eboracci we had seen in Eoforwic before the battle of Catraeth. Like the British in Deira, all these people had once ruled the lands around us in their own right and just as Aelle had taken it from Aedann's ancestors and people like them, so had Aethelfrith's forefathers come to dominate these lands.

There were also many villages of Angles who were more responsive to us and who, in their gruffly accented English – or so it seemed to us - directed us on, away from the great road and towards the coast.

Aethelfrith's ancestors had chosen a magnificent spot for their stronghold. There upon the coast of the German sea, where the waves crashed with fury on the rocks at its feet, stood a hill. Its seaward side ended abruptly at cliffs that fell sheer to the sea below. The approach to the landward side was a path that swung back and forth up the hillside. Upon the hilltop surrounded by a palisade was Aethelfrith's hall. An army wishing to attack him there must either climb the cliffs or this path, in which case they would be forever under attack from those walls.

As we climbed we were watched closely from the battlements by the warriors on guard, who did not let us in the gates at the top until I had presented them with the credentials Aethelric had provided. Inside, the gates opened onto a wide space atop the hill. This place was not unlike the palace at Godnundingham. In the centre was a huge wooden hall with a vast door leading into a gloomy interior. This was surrounded by dozens of smaller huts and workshops for making weapons and armour, curing animal hides or butchering cows. There was also a forge on the far side of a large corall. Yet the forge, just like all but one of the workshops, was unoccupied and the corall contained a half dozen cattle at

67

most. Indeed, now we were inside, it was obvious that only two or three score warriors were here and very few craftsmen. That being so, I doubted Aethelfrith himself was present. Yet if he was not here, where would he be?

I got my answer when we were presented in the great hall. Here the fires were subdued and most of the torches extinguished. At the far end, gathered at the high table and with Aethelfrith's throne empty behind them, sat a dozen women busy embroidering tapestries, such as those that decorated the walls around us. Each was an elaborate tableau of Bernician victories and the deeds of their warriors. There were only two men on guard. When we were announced one of the women looked up sharply from her work, put down her needle, turned to climb the stepped dais behind her and then sat at a chair beside the throne. I noticed that a young lad of about ten years joined her and sat on the steps beneath her. The lady was about thirty-five years and pleasing to look at whilst not of stunning beauty. She certainly exuded a strong personality. Her hair, which was blonde, was plaited and drawn into a long tail at her back. She wore a red-coloured robe cinched at the waist with a belt from which hung keys, a seax, a strike-a-light and other small tools that chimed together as she moved.

"You are Cerdic, son of Cenred of the Villa? she asked, perusing my credentials.

"I am," I nodded.

"I am Bebba, Queen of Bernicia and its ruler in the absence of the king. This is Prince Eanfrith," she added with a wave in the direction of the lad.

"King Aethelfrith is not here then. May I ask, Your Majesty, where he is? I have a message for him."

"At war. He is on campaign fighting the Gododdin, up north. You can leave your message with me or ..."

"I was instructed to give him my message in person, Highness," I interrupted "Can you tell me where he is?" I added, with a sinking feeling. I turned to the others and muttered, "Looks like we won't be going home straightaway."

"Did she say war?" asked Eduard, his face lighting up with anticipation.

The following day, after a comfortless night in Aethelfrith's stronghold – Queen Bebba's hospitality having been somewhat meagre in the absence of her lord - we continued on our way. The road we had been following from Bebbanburgh curved westwards to avoid some low hills and then continued on north and west, edged by a tumbledown stone wall. Yet another Roman road with its cobbles and reliable surface, though here, as elsewhere, two hundred years of decay had begun to show. The grass was poking up through cracks and in some places whole sections were missing. It seemed that just like with the Wall, the locals were mining it to provide materials for their own building work. Even so, it struck me as impressive that so much of what the Romans had built remained for us to see and I wondered what would be left of my people when a similar time had passed.

"How much further is it do you think?" Eduard asked grumpily, disturbing my thoughts.

I squinted up the road. Aethelfrith's camp could not be far now - we were practically in Manau Goddodin. I could not, however, see any sign of it yet. There was movement further up the road, though. I blinked and looked again. Yes, definitely movement. It looked like a dozen horsemen coming quickly towards us. Behind us the late afternoon sun broke through the clouds and shone upon the riders and I caught the reflection of something blue.

Something blue! I had seen that colour on men on horseback before.

"Get off the road!" I bellowed.

For a moment everyone stared at me and then sharp-eyed Cuthbert joined in. "M-m-move it everyone," he shouted, "Goddodin cavalry!"

Now every face reacted with shock and anxiety. Every one of us had seen the Goddodin charge at Catraeth. We might be mounted on this occasion, but even so we would be no match for these trained horse warriors.

To the eastern side of the road - in the direction of distant hills - the ground was broken with undulations as well as scattered with boulders and rocks. We turned our horses that way and I spotted, a short distance from the road, a small hillock with fairly steep sides. Steep enough - I hoped - to slow down even this enemy. When we reached the hillock we dismounted and led the horses behind it, hobbled them then climbed the rise. Examining it at close quarters, it seemed too circular to be natural. Most likely a barrow or tomb: a resting place of some long forgotten king or warrior. Fitting, I thought, for the scene of what might turn out to be our last battle. I had promised myself after Catraeth that I would not fight again - then done so after Loidis and here I was, at it again. Damn the gods!

"I don't want this," I muttered.

"What?" Eduard grunted.

I glanced at him and then back at the oncoming horses, now but a hundred paces away. I counted a dozen of them and sighed, "Very well. Eduard, Aedann, ready shields and spears," I ordered, adding, "Cuthbert - your bow."

We readied ourselves on the mound, three of us overlapping our shields, I in the centre flanked to my left by Aedann and to the right by Eduard. We stood a few steps below the crest of the barrow whilst behind us on the very top waited Cuthbert, his bow at the ready and half a dozen arrows thrust into the ground at his feet.

The horsemen had reached the point where we had left the road. They paused at the gap in the wall to study us. We stared back. They were, without a doubt, Goddodin cavalry in their familiar blueish armour and helmets: more of the heavy cavalry that had charged us at Catraeth. Just seeing them there took me back two years to that battle. I heard again the thundering of hooves on the turf, the crash as they reached our lines and the screaming of the men cut down and I shivered. Yet, I reminded myself, we had won at Catraeth. Most of the Goddodin had been destroyed that day. So they were not invincible and whether these men had been at Catraeth or not, after that battle Aelle had strived to come to some agreement with the enemies we had defeated. A truce had been reached and although Bernicia was up here north of the Roman Wall fighting the Goddodin, officially Deira was not at war with them at all. Not yet anyway. So maybe it was worth talking to them.

I raised a hand and waved at them.

"What ...what are you d-doing," Cuthbert stammered.

"I am going to try diplomacy."

"Eh?" Eduard asked.

"Diplomacy - talking to them."

"You think they want to talk?" he asked, doubtfully eyeing the lances several carried and the sharp swords of the others.

71

At that moment one of the Goddodin rode out of the gap. Behind me Cuthbert tensed and raised his bow, but the man held his hands in plain sight to show us that all he held were the reins.

"You Bernician?" he shouted, his voice thickly accented and clumsy.

"No, we are Deiran. We are not at war with you. Will you let us pass?"

The man looked puzzled and glanced back at his companions. "I … not … understand."

Eduard grunted. "I don't think his English is very good."

"No. I agree - Aedann you try."

Aedann lowered his shield and shouted some words in Welsh. The man stared at him for a moment and then he replied.

"What did he say?" I asked.

"He wants to know what I'm doing with a party of Angles. Seems to think I'm betraying my people."

"B-but w-what about the l-letting us p-pass part?" Cuthbert looked doubtfully at Aedann.

"Wait a moment, I'll try again," Aedann said.

There was another exchange of words. Aedann was frowning when he turned back to me. "Their orders are to let no English pass this way. It seems that Aethelfrith's camp is not far away and these Goddodin are trying to prevent any reinforcement reaching him."

"Did you tell them we were Deiran?"

"I did, but that did not seem to help. Seems he was at Catraeth and some of his family died that day. He insists that we surrender and be taken to the Goddodin king. What shall I tell them?"

"Tell them to bugger off," I replied.

"You sure?"

I looked at Eduard and Cuthbert. Eduard just nodded. Cuthbert looked his usual anxious self. "If we are c-captured we will be k-killed or made slaves, m-might as well fight."

"Very well. Aedann, what about you? No need for you to die here. You are Welsh. They will let you go."

"No they won't."

"Why?"

"Well firstly, they think I am a traitor and secondly, I told him he was a fat horse's turd."

"Why on earth did you do that?" I asked aghast, resolving that if we survived this day to learn some Welsh.

"I didn't like him," was all that Aedann would say.

"So much for diplomacy," Eduard snorted as Aedann shouted our refusal.

The envoy spat once in our direction, yanked at his reins and galloped back towards his companions. They now all emerged onto the grass on our side of the wall and spread out into a line, tidied themselves up and started moving towards us at a walk, their horses' hooves slipping and sliding on the steep sides of the mound.

"Get ready," I ordered. There was a clatter as we once again overlapped our shields and raised our spears. I frantically twisted my head around looking for an escape route: a wood, buildings, anything that we could dash to for cover and escape these horsemen. But there was none. The gently undulating ground rose slowly towards the hills, but they were a mile away at least and we would never reach them. The only hope we had was that the steep slope of the barrow would slow the Goddodin down and from our height we could keep them at bay until ...

Until what? Nightfall was still hours away and even if it did get dark what good would that do us?

73

The hungry look in the eyes of the Goddodin captain and the smug expression on his face told me he knew we were doomed. "Rhuthro!" the cavalry officer shouted. "Attack!"

And on they came.

The one advantage we did have - and it was not much of one - was that they could not all reach us at once. So whilst the captain hung back, five of his men made the first attack. As they moved to charge us, Cuthbert let fly with his first arrow. The missile buzzed past my ear and plunged into the chest of the leading horse. It reared up, veered to the side and then collapsed, throwing its rider to the ground. Another horse collided with the first and the two were soon an entangled heap on the ground. The other three veered round the debris and plunged on up the little slope.

Though the Gododdin carried lances, our spears were longer and as they approached we thrust them forward and braced for the blow. Carried onto our points by their momentum, two of the three horses were impaled on our spears and tumbled away. That, however, meant that with a jerk the spears that Aedann and I were wielding were yanked out of our hands. Eduard had angled his over the horse's head and lunged it into the chest of the third rider, who roared, veered away and circled back to his captain.

In front of us one of the stunned horsemen got to his feet, but another of Cuthbert's arrows took him in the throat. Both hands around his bleeding neck, the man collapsed gurgling to the ground.

In the pause that followed I took stock. Two of the enemy were dead and three wounded or unconscious and out of the fight for the moment. Yet Aedann and I had lost our spears and Cuthbert was down to only two arrows - the rest being on his horse away behind the hill. If they charged again it would surely be impossible to stop them. Watching from near the road the

Goddodin captain must have had the same thought because he moved towards us, gesturing to his men to follow. Next to me there was a rasp as Aedann drew his sword and I, doing likewise, waited amongst my friends for our doom to arrive.

This time they did not all come straight at us. Three did, but two veered to our left and two to our right and circled around so as to fall upon our flank or rear. With shouts and whoops all seven horsemen charged at once. Cuthbert turned to the right and loosed his last two arrows. One caught a horse in the leg and the beast stumbled, the rider struggling to keep his seat. The second clattered off the helmet of his companion. The man's head flung back with the stunning blow and his eyes glazed for a moment. Then he shook his head to clear it and reined in his mount.

In front of us the three riders led by the captain reached us and thrust their lances at us. One point slammed into my shield and flung me over onto my back. Aedann gave a scream of agony as his opponent's lance slid off his shield and sliced across his thigh. He fell writhing to the ground. With the two of us down, the enemy horses pushed on up the slope and it was only its steepness that slowed their progress and Eduard's intervention that saved us.

As the third man closed upon him, Eduard leapt to one side letting the point pass him and then stabbed back with his spear catching his man in the throat. The horse's momentum carried the man onto the spear point, which punched straight through him and out the back of his neck. Letting go of the spear, Eduard pulled his axe out of his belt and as the two other riders urged their mounts up the steep slope he hacked at the closest. He missed, but the rider was forced to parry the blow with his lance and then he turned to attack Eduard. The third rider, bellowing something incoherent, tugged on his reins so that his horse reared

75

up as he tried to bring the hooves down on Aedann. I scrambled to my feet and raised my shield in an effort to get in the way, but the blow as the hooves landed was devastating. My entire arm went numb and my hand lost all its strength. Having lost my grip on the shield I felt it slide away from me and roll down the hill.

Behind me I heard Cuthbert gasp and risked a glance that way. He had dropped his bow and drawn his seax and was pointing it towards the two other horsemen, who were coming from our left. They had reached the barrow and having found a shallow section to the slope, now thundered towards him. Meanwhile, the first two riders Cuthbert's arrows had brought down had recovered and were closing in on him from behind.

"Woden help us ..." I muttered.

Chapter Six
Rescue

As the horsemen closed in upon us, their hooves carving great gouges in the turf, the air was filled with a sudden high pitched whirling sound. A moment later there was a dull thud and one of the riders, who had almost reached Cuthbert, tumbled soundlessly out of his saddle and landed face down on the grass. The back of his head was covered in blood. Another thud and the man fighting Eduard let out a cry of pain and dropped his lance, his left hand moving to grasp a smashed right elbow. Eduard saw his chance, stepped up to the man and hacked at his shoulder, the blade cutting deeply through sinew and bone. The man screamed and steered his horse away.

Two more missiles found their marks on the men riding up from our right. One man was knocked clean from his mount, the other taking a glancing blow to the cheek, steered his away. For a moment I gawped around, searching for the cause of the chaos. Finally I spotted them. Slingers! Over near the road a score of foot soldiers had arrived. Some were using slings to pelt the enemy with a hail of stones whilst the rest formed up into a shield wall and advanced toward the barrow. Fortunes had changed and it was now the cavalry that were outnumbered.

After a moment's hesitation and with a final venomous glance at my friends and me, the Goddodin captain spat out an order and led the survivors of his battered patrol at a gallop away to the north.

The Bernicians - for I could see now that it was clearly a party of Saxon warriors - pursued them on foot a short way, sending yet more slingstones after them. Then, when the horsemen had ridden out of sight, a single voice called the Bernicians back to rally next to him.

A cold chill shot down my spine as I recognised that voice. My head snapped round and I saw the man I had half hoped and half dreaded to see again.

Hussa!

Mounted on a horse standing on the road, my brother wore a shirt of fine mail visible beneath a richly embroidered, green cloak. He shouted another order to the men who had rescued us and then turned to look towards us. Those dark eyes that had watched me so often from out of the shadows beside his house at Wicstun were now turned upon me once more. He studied us for a full minute and then clicked his tongue and tugged on the reins. His horse turned and walked through the gap in the wall and over towards us. When he reached the bottom of the barrow he halted.

"Hello, brother. I thought it was you. It was lucky we came this way, my men and I, or our father would be mourning another son."

"Your men?" I replied, looking around at the well-armed party of huscarls that now gathered about him.

"Indeed, I have come a long way since we parted two years ago. Such are the rewards of loyal service."

Eduard spat. "Loyalty? You? Who to ...." He faltered, clearly changing his mind about whatever insult he had been about to utter and instead said, "Whom do you serve?"

"I serve the king."

I gaped, "But King Aelle banished you."

"That old fool is not my king, Cerdic. Aethelfrith is my lord now."

"Does he know about you, Hussa? Does he know how you betrayed your country?"

"I have told you before, *brother*, that Deira was never my country. I never had much feeling for it and I have no ties there anymore. Not since I crossed the bridge at Catraeth. I came north and swore allegiance to Aethelfrith and soon proved myself useful. I am a captain of his huscarls now, Cerdic, with lands of my own and women too. How is the Villa anyway? What of the lovely Aidith?"

"Leave her out of it," I growled.

"I am just being civil."

"I don't want to have a chat, Hussa. I came with a message for your lord. Take me to Aethelfrith so I can deliver it and go home."

He smiled a slow, mocking smile and said no more.

After we had retrieved our horses and remounted - this took some time as we had first to patch up Aedann's thigh, which was bleeding profusely, but was not as deep as I had feared - we fell in with my brother's patrol. Hussa led us northwards up the road we had been travelling along earlier. As we rode I asked him a question.

"Those Goddodin came down the road. Where did they come from?"

"We are within the old borders of Manau Goddodin here," Hussa replied. "Last year Aethelfrith took from them those hills over there," he pointed, "and the valleys in between. This year we are driving towards Din Eidyn, their capital. Aethelfrith's camp is an old village we captured a week or two back. The Goddodin took such a pounding at Catraeth that they seem reluctant to meet

79

us in battle, but are content to raid, try to cut our lines of supply and prevent us getting reinforcements. I imagine that is why you got attacked. How fortunate that I happened along at that time," he added, his voice dripping with insincerity.

"Quite," I commented and we fell back into an icy silence.

Aethelfrith's camp was indeed as Hussa had described: a small gaggle of hovels not unlike our own Village. Around the buildings makeshift shelters had been thrown up to provide space for the Bernician army. As we rode in we passed no fewer than three blacksmiths, each with a forge surrounded by furious activity: spear points being hammered in one, red-hot sword blades being thrust into cold water to temper the metal in the second, and in the third, panels were being curved around an anvil ready for welding together into helmets. Further along, ash staves were being fashioned into spear shafts and bronze bosses attached to wooden shields. Everywhere there was the industry of an army in preparation for the coming campaign season.

There was a time when such a scene would have thrilled me and I would have been eager to have been away with them on their conquests of these lands. But I was different now. Catraeth had changed all that. I just wanted to get home to my valley and leave the fighting to warlords like Aethelfrith.

I saw Eduard stop by a man with a crooked nose. The man looked up and I recognised him, remembering that he and Eduard had argued the last time we met the Bernicians. Eduard had broken the man's nose back then, but you would not have thought so now to see Eduard hold out his hand and the man smile and take it. A moment later Eduard had dismounted and the two appeared to be deep in conversation about an axe the man was sharpening. Maybe Catraeth had changed me, but not my friend. He still truly belonged in such places.

Leaving Eduard to his reunion, we spurred our mounts on until Hussa reined in outside what once must have been the headman's hall. It was not much of a place but was bigger by far than the others. We dismounted and entered.

The interior was more roomy than I had at first expected. Nothing to compare to Godnundingham, of course, or Bebbanburgh, but comparable with the new mead hall I had built at the Villa. It was gloomy though, despite the fire flickering in the central hearth. A score of Bernician warriors were gathered in small huddles here and there around the room, sitting at the half dozen long tables or standing around the fire. One pair sat playing Taefel whilst nearby another two were arm wrestling. As we entered several men looked up and stared at us, hands reaching for their swords. Then they saw Hussa was leading us and relaxed, returning to their entertainment. All, that was, except a large man with bulging upper arms and a full beard of air hair. He was sharpening his sword on a stone at the far end of the room near the high table, upon which he rested his booted feet. Beyond the table was a screen, which was decorated by tapestries embroidered with scenes of battle and the deeds of warriors. As we approached the table he examined first Hussa, then the rest of us, before his gaze returned to my brother.

"Who are these people you bring uninvited into my brother's court, Hussa?" he said in a low voice.

"Envoys from my former country, Prince Theobald. Sent by their king to carry a message to Aethelfrith. May I present Lord Cerdic of the Villa and his huscarls?" Hussa answered, politely enough, although I felt I could detect tension in his voice.

81

Theobald looked back at us, each in turn – myself, Cuthbert and Aedann – his gaze lingering on the latter for a moment before returning to Hussa.

"What does the King of Deira wish to pass on to the King of Bernicia?" Theobald asked.

"That message is for the King of Bernicia himself, Highness," I said.

"I act for the king, what is so important that Aelle sends a special envoy to find Aethelfrith?"

"The message comes not from Aelle, but from King Aethelric. That indeed is the message. Aelle is dead and his son is king in his stead."

There was a sound of a chair scraping on the floor beyond the screen and a moment later a man emerged from behind it. I recognised him immediately. This was only the fourth time I had seen Aethelfrith of Bernicia. The first time he had been leading his armies at Catraeth, dressed in full armour and looking like a warrior god of old. Then I had seen him at the feast to celebrate the victory of Bernicia and Deira, and finally, on the day we left Deira he had come to see us off and - or so it seemed to me - to see what manner of men we were. Aethelfrith had got the better of the negotiations after that battle and though our men's blood had run into the soil of Catraeth field, it was Bernicia that had ended up owning it. Today, however, was the first time I had seen the man up close. He was an impressive sight: taller by an inch than his brother, Theobald, and even broader in the shoulders. There was a sense of force of will there that I had seen only in one other man: Aelle. Or perhaps Edwin. Yes, Edwin had it. But Edwin was young and Aelle dead, which left this man Aethelfrith as the force in the North; the leader of the pack. To me, he and his wolves seemed powerful, almost invincible.

"It is true, then," Aethelfrith said, throwing himself down in the headman's high-backed chair. "It is true that Aelle is dead?"

"Indeed, Your Majesty," I replied.

"He was a strong man. My father and I respected that strength as we do all men who wield it well." He stared at me and not knowing if he expected a reply I just nodded.

"Yet you say that Aethelric is king now?"

"Indeed, lord."

There was something about the way he said 'yet' that suggested he was drawing a distinction. Aelle he had respected; Aethelric maybe not.

I spoke to fill the silence. "Aethelric sends his regards, expresses his friendship and says he wishes to continue the alliance that has hitherto existed between Bernicia and Deira. One people should stay together to help each other out, he said. That is the message."

Aethelfrith nodded. "Stay with us and accept our hospitality tonight, Lord Cerdic. I will send your new king a message in the morning if you are willing to carry it."

"Of course, lord."

Aethelfrith turned away, but Theobald was not ready to let us leave.

"Your companions - your thegns - the pasty-faced thin one is an Angle is he not, though a feeble looking one …"

I cut across the insult, "Cuthbert is the best shot with that bow of his in Deira, and I would wager he would give your best archers a decent match."

"That's as maybe, but he don't look like a man who would be any good in a shield wall. But still, he is an Angle, yes?"

"Indeed he is, from my village."

"What of the other man, the dark-haired youth. What did you call him?"

I felt Aedann tensing beside me. "I did not, but his name is Aedann, son of Caerfydd."

Theobald jumped to his feet, sword point flying up, blade held out straight at Aedann. Aethelfrith looked up, eyes narrowing.

"A Welshman?" Theobald spat. You bring a Welshman into the king's presence? An enemy spy mayhap?" He moved towards Aedann.

My friend's hand drifted towards his own sword, but I shook my head at him and he froze. I stepped between them. "He is no enemy. He is a brave warrior who fought for Aelle at Catraeth."

"Huh! To gain your trust no doubt. Given half the chance he will be off to his friends with news of our strength."

"He had that chance before in Elmet, and he stayed with us. "

"Why? Out of loyalty to you?"

Before I could respond, Aedann drew himself up to his full height and answered, "In part, but also to gain revenge on Samlen One-Eye, the man who killed my father. I took his life at Catraeth."

"That is true, My Prince," Hussa confirmed. "I was with Samlen at Catraeth and was captured after he was killed. Aedann is no friend of mine, but he is a friend of Cerdic here – I know this because Cerdic is my half-brother."

Theobald remained unimpressed by this new information. "Hah. Your recommendation means little to me, Hussa. I did not approve of my brother making you a captain in his army. You, a man who sided with the enemy and who now, it seems, has a half-brother who has a Welshman as a huscarl! If I were king I would not permit your presence ..."

"But you are not king, brother," Aethelfrith interrupted, "I am. Hussa is one of *my* captains. That choice was mine, so obey it. Cerdic is an envoy from Deira. You will treat him and those under his protection with respect. Do you understand me?" He spoke mildly enough, but there was an edge to his tone. This was a man who was used to being obeyed.

Theobald stared at Aedann, Hussa and me without answering.

"Well?" Aethelfrith asked again, his voice suddenly dangerous.

Theobald nodded at last. "Yes, Sire, of course I will obey you."

Aethelfrith nodded, satisfied, but like a cat watching a mouse, his brother's gaze did not leave us for a moment.

Chapter Seven
A Diplomatic Mission

The following morning, in the hut where Hussa had arranged for us to sleep, I was abruptly woken from slumber by an outburst of shouting just outside the door. When I opened my eyes I found that it was full light and perhaps as late as mid-morning. Tired from our journey and still aching from the fight of the previous day, I had fallen into a deep sleep from which no one had disturbed me. I looked around the room for my companions. I heard rather than saw Eduard, for he was snoring heavily, buried in furs on the far side of the hut. Cuthbert was sitting up on the makeshift bedding laid out on the floor not far from me. Rubbing the sleep from his eyes, he yawned and then glanced over at me.

"What was that?" he asked sleepily.

I opened my mouth to reply but never got the words out.

"Come here you Welsh turd!" A voice bellowed again from just outside.

Cuthbert and I exchanged glances and then looked over at Aedann's cot. We were not surprised to see that it was empty. Groaning, I rolled out of bed, dragged on my tunic, shoved Catraeth into my belt and picking up the longsword I had received at my wedding, stumbled to the door. Cuthbert followed suit, grabbing up his bow and quiver.

In the space between our hut and its neighbour we discovered Aedann, fists raised, fending off three huge brutes with scarred faces and arms that seemed like the width of tree trunks. At

Aedann's feet lay a fourth thug, out cold and with blood tricking from his nose.

"Come on then you Bernician bastards," Aedann roared. "Let's have you all at once or one at a time, I don't care!"

His three opponents grinned at each other and started towards him, one of them pulling a seax from his belt and twisting it as he approached.

"Stop right there!" I shouted, raising my sword and stepping into the gap between Aedann and his assailants.

The man with the blade turned to me with a scowl. "Keep out of this, it don't concern you. It's a matter between us and this spy."

"This man is my huscarl. Back off!" I replied and held up my left hand, palm facing out to him.

"What is going on here!" A new voice cut across us. I looked up to see Hussa over near the track that ran through the village. "Is this how we treat guests of the king? I think not. You will show Lord Cerdic the respect due to a man of his *rank*," Hussa said, his lips curling slightly as the word 'rank' rolled across them.

The three men hesitated for a moment and then one of them snorted in derision. "We don't take orders from you."

"I know who you take orders from. Now go and tell him that the king will hear of this. Go!" Hussa commanded.

With some reluctance the three men walked over and helped their friend, who was now stirring and moaning, to his feet before moving off down the track.

Hussa turned to me, "Are you hurt?"

"Would you care if I was?" I snapped at him.

Hussa shrugged, "Probably not, but the king made you his guest and it would not please him if I stood back and let you be injured."

"I imagine not."

"I did not come to rescue you, however," he said, apparently having lost interest in the matter.

"Why then?" I asked.

Hussa gestured to the headman's hall. "Aethelfrith asks that you attend him today. There is a delegation from Dál-Riata arrived nearby early this morning. He assumed that your king would prefer it if Deira were represented when he goes to meet them today."

I nodded and returning to the hut, woke Eduard, who had the amazing ability to sleep through anything. Once dressed, we walked the short distance to the king's hall. I drew up sharply as I entered for I had just spotted that Lilla was present and talking to Aethelfrith. I should not have been surprised. The bard seemed to get everywhere and had after all often spoken of visiting the Bernician court. He glanced up at me, a twinkle in his eyes before turning back to the king.

Aethelfrith looked away from the conversation as we carried on into the hall. "Ah, Cerdic, your party has mounts yes?"

"Yes, Your Majesty. We rode here from Deira."

"Then fetch them and join us on the journey today," he commanded, dismissing us with a wave of his hand and turning back to Lilla.

We went to do his bidding and once mounted, gathered outside the hut. Soon we were joined by a party of twelve huscarls commanded by Hussa. A moment later another dozen arrived with Theobald. Lilla accompanied them. He came over to me and clasped my hand in welcome.

"What are you doing here, Lilla?"

"Carrying a message. When I left you at Godnundingham after Aelle's burial I travelled north. Dropped in to see Aethelfrith and then went west to Dunadd on an errand. I accompanied the Dál-Riatan party here and arranged a meeting."

I nodded. Aelle's death had not come as a surprise to Aethelfrith when I broke it the day before. I had wondered how he knew, but news was Lilla's stock in trade, of course.

Aethelfrith was with us shortly. He glanced over at me, nodded then tugged on his reins and we were away, galloping west over the fields, churning the mud under our hooves. We rode for maybe five miles or so before Aethelfrith reined in his sweating horse and we all came to a stop. Just ahead of us was a grassy mound on which were a dozen weatherbeaten standing stones. Ancient people had once toiled to place them there in a circle, for whatever reason such folk built such places. We dismounted and several huscarls took the horses into woods nearby and secured them. Then we strode up the hillock and waited. Aethelfrith sat on a stone and one of his huscarls brought him a cup of mead.

The Dál-Riatan party arrived soon afterwards, about thirty of them. They too dismounted and approached the mound. I was impressed by my first sight of them and could see from the start that these men were tough bastards. Many wore short tunics, a few wore britches, but most were coated in furs and animal skins, though the leaders had fine woollen cloaks with a kind of crisscross pattern of hatched lines in blue and green. A couple of the warriors had no clothing save britches. They walked behind the leaders, bare-chested and with spears at the rest across their muscular shoulders. Others were armed with fearsome blades, a little shorter than Catraeth but somewhat broader.

90

These were the same race that had crossed the seas from Hibernia - from a country even the Romans had not been able to conquer - and carved out a land north of the Wall. They drove off all those who lived there: Picts or British - it did not matter, for they had slaughtered them like sheep. Now, because Aethelfrith was pushing west, they had sent an envoy to meet us, the Angles.

Two figures strode forward from the Dál-Riatan party and stood in front of Aethelfrith. Both wore full beards, rich clothing and had fine swords.

"I am Domanghast, a prince of Dál-Riata and this is Bran, my brother. We are sons of mac Gabráin and come bearing gifts and offers of friendship to Aethelfrith of Bernicia."

"I am listening," Aethelfrith replied, not rising on their approach but sipping at his mead.

"Your enemies are our enemies," Domanghast continued. "Does that not make us friends? We are both new to these lands - your people and ours - you from the East and we from the West. Together we can defeat the British rabble here in the land between the walls. Strathclyde, the Gododdin and the Picts further north still."

Aethelfrith nodded slowly and seemed to be considering the wisdom of the alliance. Then his sharp eyes focused on another figure standing further back amongst the huddle of Dál-Riatan warriors. He stood suddenly and handed his goblet to the huscarl with such force that the contents splashed over the side and drenched the man's tunic. Domanghast gawped at him, apparently taken aback by the Bernician king's action.

"Your Majesty?" he asked and then glanced behind at the man Aethelfrith was staring at.

"Ah, you recognize your kinsman perhaps. Come forward, Herring."

The man concerned was not a tall man, though broad in the shoulders and muscular in the upper body. He was almost bald, but wore a short, neatly trimmed beard. The cloak that was thrown around his shoulders was of Angle fashion, not Irish to my eyes. He moved forward with obvious reluctance, one hand not straying far from the pommel of his sword.

"Cousin, how are you?" he asked Aethelfrith tentatively.

Aethelfrith's eyes were bulging with obvious anger. "You ask me that, you dare to ask me that? You were banished, Herring, when I became king. Why do you think I would forget that? Why would I?"

"That was six years ago, cousin. My father was wrong to challenge you. I will accept that. But I was young then and did not go with him to fight you. You sent me into exile nonetheless. So I found a home in Dál-Riata. I am no threat to you."

"No threat! You were not then, for you were but twelve, but now you are a man full grown: a man who might want my throne, to inherit what he thinks he should have had before, maybe."

"That is not my wish," Herring replied, but Aethelfrith had turned his attention back to Domanghast.

"So this is what mac Gabráin wants is it? These offerings of peace are falsehoods. You would draw me in and then strike me down and place your puppet here in my place to rule through him."

Domanghast shook his head. Herring said nothing and the moment might have passed had Bran, the other Dál-Riatan prince, not spoken. "Mayhap that would be best," he snapped.

Bran, a year or so my junior, was a young man speaking his mind without the wisdom to know when to keep quiet. "Herring is my friend and has learnt much by my side from our scholars. More than a petty bandit knows anyway," he sneered.

At that Aethelfrith leapt to his feet and took two huge strides to bring him face to face with Bran, his hand raised as if ready to strike the prince across the cheeks.

This could get nasty very quickly, I thought and was about to say something, but Lilla beat me to it.

"Friends ... let this meeting be one of peace not bloodshed," he purred in his soft voice. "Both parties can gain much from an alliance surely?"

Aethelfrith hesitated and glared at him then stepped away, returned to his stone and took back the mead. I breathed out a long breath, thinking that perhaps Lilla might have succeeded in bringing calm and order again. This might have been the case had the hot-headed Theobald not intervened.

"What did you just say?" he demanded of Bran, who looked back at him blankly.

"Just now," Theobald said, "after my brother stepped back and could not hear you."

I craned to look. Theobald was off to my left on the other side of Hussa. Bran looked up at him, obvious confusion now plain on his face. Hussa said something to Theobald, but I could not hear what and then Theobald stepped towards Bran just as his brother had done moments before. "What did you call my brother, Irishman?" Theobald snarled.

"I said nothing more, I swear it!"

"*Liar!* You called him a coward," Theobald roared, dragging his sword from its scabbard.

The act sent a shock through both parties and in the blink of an eye swords had been drawn on both sides of the stone circle.

Eduard, Cuthbert and Aedann glanced at me, unsure what to do. Then the nearest Irish warrior to me took a few steps towards us.

"Oh bollocks," I cursed, "here we go again!" In a moment Catraeth was in my hand and an instant later Aedann also was armed with a sword, Eduard with his axe and Cuthbert, stepping back to the edge of the circle, notched an arrow on his bow string.

Even now Lilla tried to find a peaceful solution. He looked appealingly at Theobald in particular, crying out in the stentorian voice of the trained bard, "Please put down your weapons!"

Hussa, standing next to Theobald, was talking animatedly, apparently trying to persuade him to back off, but no effort to quench Theobald's anger seemed to work. I reflected that if Aethelfrith had set up this meeting in an attempt to gain allies it seemed foolish in the extreme to have brought his brother along.

"Irish bog filth!" Theobald roared and charged towards Bran, who pulled his sword up to face his enemy.

"Treachery!" Bran yelled. "Kill them!"

Chapter Eight
Stone Circle

That was the signal that set everything off. The sides in this fight were fairly even. Around thirty Irish faced a similar number of Angles. No one seemed to have an advantage and as such the two parties just hurtled towards each other.

A half dozen of the Irish warriors, led by one of the bare-chested brutes, charged at us Deirans. Eduard roared at them and slashed his huge axe in a circle that caught one youth in the throat, ripping out his wind pipe and sending him hurtling into another man and knocking him over. The bare-chested man reached me and swung his sword. I stepped away and parried, wishing I had my shield which, with my longsword, was back with the horses. As my opponent recoiled I stepped forward again and lunged at his belly, but like a man swatting a fly he irritably slapped Catraeth aside and thrust out a fist aimed straight at my jaw. The blow only just connected, but still sent me spinning back to the edge of the stone circle. He came at me again and I barely had time to block once more with Catraeth and then I tripped over one of the stones. My sword went spinning away from me and landed down the slope. I thought I was done for, indeed, I should have been, but at that moment an arrow took him deep in the right shoulder. He screamed in agony, dropped his sword and pulled back, one hand grasping the arrow shaft.

I got up, flashed Cuthbert a grateful smile and looked about for Catraeth. Lilla had retrieved it and tossed it to me. I nodded my thanks, saw that Hussa had finished off my foe and had a brief moment to take stock of the little battle, my legs still trembling from my close brush with death.

It was not over yet. Aethelfrith and his huscarls, over beyond Theobald, were hard at it engaged with Domanghast and his men. In the centre Theobald and two of his huscarls were exchanging blow and counter blow with Bran's party. Yet it seemed that the Irish were more numerous and I could see that Theobald had now realised the danger, for he and the two huscarls were facing six Irish. I staggered forward. Hussa was next to me in line, weaving and bobbing around, cutting at a man and then swaying to avoid another warrior's axe. Finally, my friends and I were on the end of the line. We were getting the edge over our opponents, thanks mainly to Eduard. In a shield wall his axe could be effective enough, but here, with no shields to protect them, the huge blade swinging wildly left and right and already having cut down two of their companions, he brought fear to the enemy. I took a chance and left him to it, covered by the ever vigilant Cuthbert, and grasping Aedann by the tunic pulled him to the centre of the fight.

"What're you doing?" he gasped.

"Allowing you to make that name for yourself," I muttered.

"Huh?" was the incoherent reply.

"Come on!" I yelled as I led the way back around Hussa and past Lilla, who was standing unarmed at the rear watching proceedings as usual.

"Will this be in one of your tales?" I puffed as we ran past him.

"Rather depends if we all die doesn't it?" he answered.

We arrived near Theobald just as an Irish warrior wielding a huge, two-handed blade cut down one of the Bernician huscarls and advanced on Aethelfrith's brother. A moment later

96

Theobald's other bodyguard was slain and now two killers in mail shirts closed in on the Bernician prince.

Aedann did not hesitate. He launched himself at one of the huge brutes, sword flickering like a flame back and forth. I intercepted the other fellow and drove him back. I seemed to have the edge on him until he fooled me by dropping his sword point. Foolishly I lunged forward. The brute let me come and then twisted out of my way. As I tumbled he followed up with a resounding strike to the back of my helmet. The blow was sickening and had I not been wearing the helm it would have caved in the back of my head and I would have joined Aelle in Asgard. As it was I crumpled to the ground as a wave of blackness threatened to engulf me. The man could have finished me there and then, but through the haze I saw him leave me to advance on Theobald, who turned to the new threat and brought his sword up to challenge him. The brute smashed his own blade down with such fury that the prince's weapon shattered.

Theobald staggered backwards, tottered and landed on his behind, looking in astonishment at his sword hilt - pretty much all that was left of his blade. Then a shadow fell over him as his enemy stood astride him.

With a tremendous roar, Aedann stabbed his own foe through the belly and then, not sparing him a glance as he fell twitching onto the bloodstained grass, the Welshman brought the blade back and round in an arc and slashed it across the other warrior's face. The man, who was about to kill the prince, screamed, dropped his sword and holding his lacerated face in both hands backed off. Aedann then stepped over to stand in front of Theobald, daring any other Irish to attack. By this time I was on my feet again, more ornament than use, but I moved to Aedann's side and waved Catraeth in what I hoped was a threatening manner. Bran glared at us, but both he and his men hung back, wary of the ferocity of the Welshman's counter attack.

Over to our right there was a sudden shout. Aethelfrith had joined the fray and had reached Domanghast. The roar was the triumphant exultation as the Bernician king brought his sword down like a scythe, cutting Domanghast in two.

There was a moment's stunned silence and then Bran, shouting his grief and rage, charged towards Aethelfrith. But Herring was at Bran's side and now, one arm wrapped around the other's chest, was dragging him away.

I looked around and saw that we had won. Only a half dozen enemy remained on their feet and we had lost but five men. The remaining enemy bodyguards now formed a wall as best as they could, whilst Herring continued to drag Bran towards their horses. Suddenly, the prince wriggled free, dodged the remaining Irish and Herring's arms as they reached out for him and charged once more at Aethelfrith. He never got to his target, however, because Hussa moved across and with the pommel of his sword smacked Bran hard on the back of his head. The prince dropped like a stone, unconscious.

Herring and his huscarls started towards him, but Cuthbert fired two shots, one of which buried itself in the throat of one huscarl. Herring hesitated, gave one despairing look back towards us and then he and his companions mounted and spurred their horses west into the trees and out of sight.

At last silence fell upon the stone circle, interrupted only by the groans of the injured and a question posed by Cuthbert. "W-w-what just happened?"

It was a bloody good question, I thought. This had started as a peaceful meeting, a coming together of tribes who, whilst having no basis for trust, were fighting the same enemies - the British. An alliance was sensible. Yet a few misplaced words and the lost temper of two hot-headed princes, Theobald and Bran, and a dozen men were dead and as many wounded. What chance an alliance now?

Theobald and Bran may have started it - or leastways it seemed so to me at the time - yet Aethelfrith, in slaying the son of mac Gabráin, had done the one thing certain to cause endless animosity between Scots and Angles. Not only had he killed Prince Domanghast, he had captured Prince Bran. Even now, Herring would be riding like the Valkyries westwards towards their lands to carry the dread news: news that could only end in war.

So whilst I shook my head at the impetuosity of Theobald and Bran, I now stared at Aethelfrith. What kind of man was he, I wondered? There had been no need to slay the prince as he had done. He saw me watching him and came over, sword still slick with Domanghast's blood. Lilla drifted along behind.

"This worries you, what we have done here this day?" he asked in a low tone that only I and Lilla would hear.

"I would not question the actions of kings, my lord."

"But you do question it, don't you? I can see it in your eyes."

"I was just thinking that we could have used allies like these, my lord. But that is out of the question now."

Aethelfrith shrugged then bent to clean his sword on the cloak of a fallen Irishman. "There never was much chance of that. Not for long anyway. Conflict with these Irish Scots, as with the British, is inevitable if we are to expand and grow. Besides which," he added, fixing me with a steely gaze, "with allies like you - our fellow Northumbrians - we need no other help. I can trust on Aethelric to support me when the time comes, can't I Cerdic?"

99

"I cannot answer for my king, lord, but I will convey your message, of course."

I would convey his message and I would do my best to persuade Aethelric to be cautious of alliance with this wily man. At Catraeth it was a question of survival, but now what madness was this Bernician pulling us towards?

I did not, of course, voice these feelings to Aethelfrith, who just nodded at me and then turned away to look at his brother. Theobald was talking to Aedann. Last night the prince had almost killed my Welsh friend and this morning he had set his bullies upon him, and yet now he was embracing him.

"I was wrong about you, brave warrior," Theobald said. "You saved my life, Welshman. I will find a way to reward you."

Aedann smiled at him and then wryly at me. I grinned back thinking that maybe he had earned his name after all. Then another face caught my eye: Hussa's dark gaze was fixed on Aedann and his eyes smouldered with anger.

Chapter Nine
Back in Deira

'He's mad! He will get us all killed. Keep well away from him!' That, at least, is what I *wanted* to say to Aethelric about Aethelfrith, but what I actually said was, "I am anxious that King Aethelfrith and his brother might let their temper and aggression affect the wisdom of their judgment at times, Sire."

It was ten days after the skirmish within that stone circle. Theobald had insisted on holding a feast in honour of Aedann, we had all drunk too much ale and Lilla had sung a song about the Welshman who saved an English prince. The prince had given Aedann a gift of a new sword and the two of them had spoken long in the corner of the headman's hut.

In the opposite corner Hussa had sat watching them, his expression unreadable. The effects of the ale meant that we slept long the following day and as a result it was the day after that when we had finally taken leave of the Bernician king and ridden south as quickly as we might. Aedann kept himself to himself on that journey and seemed preoccupied by whatever Theobald had said to him. He avoided my gaze and did not respond beyond a shrug when I asked him about it.

Since childhood, ours had been a complex and strained relationship. When we were young he had clearly resented my position of seniority and I in turn had felt a certain amount of guilt, for it was my forebears after all who had enslaved his family. Yet a friendship had emerged nonetheless and when he could have walked out on me at Calcaria, he rescued me. Circumstances meant that we had a common foe, of course, but I think our friendship was more than just an alliance. For my part I had lifted him from slavery and he in turn had sworn loyalty to me as his overlord.

Whilst on the surface we were friends – indeed, we had saved each other's lives on more than one occasion - bubbling underneath were tensions we had not yet resolved. It was becoming increasingly clear that Aedann had expectations of land and status that I was simply unable to satisfy. I had barely enough land for myself without giving any away. I pondered this as we rode, but as usual, unable to think what to do about it, I shovelled the problem to the back of my mind.

The skies were heavy with rain clouds and the ensuing downpour, which went on for days, coupled with the need to avoid raiding parties of Goddodin and the villages still held by them, meant that it had taken longer than I had hoped to get back to Deira. We were all eager to get home now, but I needed to report in at Godnundingham before I could go on to the Villa.

We arrived at the king's hall as the dark skies broke and the first sunshine in a week appeared. The bright weather was not matched by our reception inside. Storm clouds would have been better.

"What do you mean by that?" Edwin asked in response to my carefully worded advice concerning Aethelfrith and his brother, his adolescent voice shifting from a deep growl to a high pitched whine.

He was standing next to Aethelric's throne. The king himself was staring at me with his customary expression of confusion, his face glowing red from too much wine. His eyes were dull and when I looked at him I found it hard to believe that Aelle had been his father.

102

"Well?" Edwin snapped, fixing me with an intense glare, which in complete contrast was every bit that of his father's, if tinged by the arrogance of youth.

So I told him. I told him how a simple diplomatic meeting with a potential new ally turned into a bloodbath. How Aethelfrith and his brother were hotheads who allowed arrogance and anger to cloud their minds. How it was now the case that we had a new enemy to deal with. A potent one - the Scots of Dál-Riata: a race that would now be spurred on by a thirst for revenge. I might as well have been trying to talk to the moon for all the good it did. Edwin just sneered at me throughout my explanation.

"Have you finished?" he asked when I had stopped talking.

"Yes, Highness."

Edwin shook his head and turned to his brother. "You see, Sire. I told you that he was just a farm boy with a farm boy's understanding of the ways of kings."

Aethelric nodded although I doubted he had been listening to much of what Edwin or I had been saying. Then he surprised me with a comment that suggested I might have been wrong in my assumption.

"Maybe Cerdic has a point, Edwin."

"We sent him to pass on a simple message. Not to make judgments on fellow rulers!"

"But, my lord, we can't fight everyone!" I retorted. "If mac Gabráin sends an army against the Angles all we gained at Catraeth could be undone."

Edwin snorted at that and then pointed a finger at me. "You think so do you, farm boy? Tell me how you know such things - did your corn tell you that – or was it your pigs?" He sniggered.

"Fighting a battle taught me that, Prince. A battle that happened when you were just eleven!" I snapped at him and

103

realised I had gone too far. Edwin's face turned red with fury. Aethelric's was even more confused and uncomfortable. He just wanted to be somewhere else as always. Not here, bothering with politics. He looked at Edwin and then at me and chose the easier option.

"Maybe you should go back to the Villa, Cerdic. Thankyou for your help."

Edwin glared at him and then at me. "Yes, go on back and count your cows. You will be sure to let me know if you think the bullock's judgment is at fault, won't you. I might take notice of that."

I was aware that my face too was now bright red, though whether from embarrassment or fury I was not so certain. I bowed at Aethelric, shot Edwin a cold glance and turned and stomped out of the hall, followed by Aedann, Cuthbert and Eduard."

"What a brat!" Eduard said when we got outside. "One of these days I would love to slap him."

I looked at him and grinned. "You and me both, mate. Come on, let's go home!"

We mounted and left as quickly as we could. It was not yet noon and I wanted to sleep the night in my own bed. As we rode I let Eduard and Cuthbert drift ahead and hung back with Aedann. He saw me studying him and after a moment scowled at me.

"What?" he asked.

"Are y ou going to tell me then?"

"Tell you what?"

"Tell me what you and Theobald had to say to each other. What you have been mulling over all the way home but refusing to comment on."

"Oh that," he replied and then his head drooped, his gaze fixed on his mount's neck and we fell into a silence punctuated only by the clip clop of our now weary horses.

"Aedann!"

He finally looked up. "Theobald offered me land, Cerdic."

"What?"

"Because I saved his life. He offered me my choice of a village and estates up between the walls. A title too, as one of his thegns."

Now it was my turn to fall into silence, but only for a moment. "I must say he changes his mind easily enough," I retorted, stung. "Just the night before he was all set to kill you and he had his huscarls attack you next morning .... " I trailed off when I saw Aedann was shaking his head.

"Theobald denied sending his huscarls. He insisted none of them came anywhere near me."

"Do you believe him? Don't you think he was just trying to look good? After all, you had saved his life."

Aedann shrugged. We rode on without a word for several minutes and then, as we were fording a small stream not far from Wicstun, I asked the question.

"So, what will you do? Will you join him?"

"I swore to your father, Cerdic, and to you. I would not break my vow. You must know that."

I did, of course, and as always my guilt rose in my throat. "But what if we released you? If you were free to choose ... what then?"

Again silence. If ever there was a race for brooding it was the Welsh. I've known a few in my time – later, in the court of Gwynedd, in Powys and elsewhere - but none could perfect the state of silence like Aedann could. Finally, after what seemed like an hour he deigned to speak.

105

"I would not be honest if I said that Theobald's offer is not tempting, Cerdic. I want land and I want a title. But two years ago I was a slave. At least now I am a free man and I have you to thank for that. As a free man I chose to stay with you for friendship's sake and I think I would do so again now, were I given the choice."

I nodded at him then smiled, not sure what to say.

"Besides," he muttered, "it is not *that* land that I want is it?"

"Aedann!" I yelped.

He grinned, "I am joking, Cerdic. I know that my family's land is lost to me." He paused then added, "Nothing else would do for me, though. Better a huscarl on my family's land under another lord than having land elsewhere."

I studied him for a moment, uncertain if he was telling me the whole truth. It was always hard to judge with Aedann. He seemed sincere, and yet …

After a moment he asked me a question, which effectively changed the subject. "Er … where are Cuthbert and Eduard?"

I looked along the path and realised that our two friends were not in sight. Had they picked up the pace? If so, why? Spotting Wicstun through the trees up ahead I answered my own question. Wicstun: my father's home … and the home of Mildrith. It was not hard to guess where the two clods had gone!

I swore. "Cuthbert you fool and Eduard you're double the fool for going along with him!" I muttered under my breath. "Come on, Aedann. Let's catch up with them before Cuth has time to do something stupid."

"He usually doesn't need much time," he laughed.

I glared at him and dug in my heels.

Chapter 10
Cuthbert

Aedann and I galloped into the centre of Wicstun and reigned in outside the headman's house. Once Lord Wallace's abode, it was now the residence of the new Earl of the Southern Marches - my father. I slid off my horse and then scanned the town for a sign of Eduard and Cuthbert. After a moment Aedann shouted and pointed down the Eoforwic road. There, just along the rear of the house where a hedgerow grew, we could see their horses tied to a tree. We tethered our blowing mounts beside them then scampered along, pushing through the adjacent bushes into the small field beyond.

Eduard was sitting alone on a tree stump, dozing in the late afternoon sunshine. Meanwhile, Cuthbert was not alone. He and Mildrith were sitting side by side on a bench against the rear wall of the house. In alarm I scanned the main entrance, expecting to see Father burst forth in fury and probably lynch my friend then and there. I made a step towards them when I noticed that Mildrith was crying and shaking her head.

"Cuthbert!" I hissed at him, thinking he had said or done something to upset her, but when he looked up at me I could see his eyes were red too. He took another longing look at her and said something that I could not hear and she again shook her head. At that he stood up, walked past me with an oddly vacant expression on his tearstained face and vanished through the bushes. I took another step towards my sister, but she now stood, held out her hand palm outwards to keep me away and sobbing, ran into the house.

"What in the name of Woden's buttocks just happened?" I demanded as I followed Cuthbert out onto the road. He was standing by his horse fiddling with the saddle.

"Do you think it hurts to hang?" he asked me, ignoring my question.

"*What*?"

"Hanging; I f-f-figured ... " he turned towards me and showed me the coil of rope he held in his hands, "... I f-f-figured that if I c-c-climbed this tree and jumped with this round my throat, it would break my n-n-neck and not hurt too much. Of course, I don't really give a d-d-d-damn if it does, it could be no worse ...."

I sighed, exasperated. "What are you saying? Does Mildrith not want to see you anymore. Don't she love you?"

"Yes, she loves me and I love her."

"Well then, what's the problem?"

"The problem is I c-c-can't see her ever again."

"Why in the name of the gods?" The man was mad, had to be.

"Because she is betrothed."

"*What*!"

He nodded. "Yes, your damn f-f-father's arranged for her to m-m-marry the youngest son of Guthred."

"What, the Lord of Bursea?" I asked, naming the lands between the Villa and the Humber.

"Yes." Cuthbert proceeded to uncoil the rope, running it through his hands and looking up into the tree.

Eduard had now joined us. "Well, that's a bugger," he said, "but put down the bloody rope, Cuth. We aren't about you let you kill yourself are we!" He patted Cuthbert's shoulder and with one big hand reached for the rope.

Cuthbert flung it to the ground his face crumpling, eyes wet with tears held barely in check.

"Wait, Cuth," I sighed. "Look, I will talk to my father."

"Huh. D-d-do you think it would do any g-g-good ... I m-m-mean really?"

I shrugged. He was right. But I was going to try anyway.

"Cerdic!" My father roared as I entered the house. He was sitting at the same bench in the ale hall where once he and I had drunk beer with Lord Wallace as we discussed the goings on in Bernicia and Rheged. It was not distant politics that was on my mind this day, though, but the future of two people that I cared about. As he leapt to his feet and, despite his fifty and more years, came bouncing over to me, something about my expression must have suggested I was not happy, because when he reached me, instead of enfolding me in a hug he put his hands on my shoulders and studied me intently.

"You'll have a scar there," he observed as he pointed at a wound I had picked up from a glancing blow when the Gododdin had attacked us.

"It's nothing, we were ambushed, but we survived." I cleared my throat, "Father ..."

"So how was Aethelfrith? Where did you find him? Looks likes you had to go further than Bebbanburgh."

I nodded, "Aethelfrith was at a camp up near the lands of the Gododdin." I reluctantly went on to give a quick summary of our journey to the North. I kept trying to change the subject to talk about Cuthbert and Mildrith, but he was pushing me for more details of the encounter with Dál-Riata. I was in two minds as to whether to tell him about Hussa, but decided for the minute not to.

"You are right about Aethelfrith, son. He is a firebrand and has a short temper as does his brother. He does what he feels,

109

confident in his own strength and his will to make things happen. He does not care who gets hurt in the process."

"So an alliance with him is risky. I have said as much to the king, but Edwin said I was ... well, never mind what Edwin said," I grimaced.

My father considered this. "We needed Aethelfrith at Catraeth, but I think that battle showed us which of Deira and Bernicia are stronger. Bernicia's star is rising and Deira's is weak, fading and perhaps failing."

"Are you talking about the countries or the kings, Father?"

"Both of course. A king *is* the country, Cerdic. When you have a weak one the country too is weak."

I nodded. "What should we do?"

He blinked. "Do? Nothing. Aethelric is king and that is all there is. But we can watch and wait for the moment he needs our help."

I nodded again. My father took a long swig of his ale and I took the chance.

"Father, Mildrith is upset ..."

"What?" he asked vaguely.

"She's unhappy because you want her to marry."

"Yes, well, she is getting on a bit, what is she now, eighteen? Should have got her married a year or two back, but it all got a bit busy if you recall."

"Yes, it did, but she does not want to marry Guthred's son."

"Well ... I am sure she will accept it in time. She is my daughter - daughter of an earl. Who she marries is all about what is best for Deira and for our family. Union with Bursea strengthens our position in control of this region. She will do what is best for us."

"But she is in love with ..."

110

My father's eyes bulged and he cut me off. "I don't care if she does love that peasant you used to run about with when you were a brat, Cerdic. She is not going to marry him. She will marry whom I choose. If she is that bothered about this Cuthbert she can one day take him as a lover no doubt." He grinned, "Only, NOT before she is married off and safely away from here!"

"Father, please!"

"No, Cerdic, don't ask me again. I will NOT change my mind! It is my intention that Mildrith will marry during the harvest festivals. That's my last word on the subject."

He turned away and that was that. I stumbled outside and went to tell Cuthbert the bad news.

My friend sighed, turned and dragged himself onto his horse.

"Come on," I said, "let's go home. I need some mead."

Going home. There is something wonderful about those words and as we turned down the lane to the Villa and Aidith came out to meet me, little Cuthwine toddling along behind, I let out a sign of contentment. Then I looked at my companions and knew that two of them were not feeling what I felt. Eduard adapts pretty well to any situation and indeed, was already no doubt deciding which of two girls in the Village to call on and see if he could entice her into his bed. Maybe even both of them, knowing him. But my other friends were not happy. Aedann was gloomy and wanting something I could not give him. Likewise, Cuthbert looked forlorn and lost and I could not help him either. I thought back on the trip north when we were twice in peril of our lives, my thoughts moving on to Aethelfrith and his ambitions. Not for the first time I resolved to turn my back on the world. It seemed to me that it could not be long before the Scots came against the Angles, desperate for revenge and for the return of their captive prince. As I folded my wife and son into my embrace, I hoped fervently that I would not be involved.

Over the next few weeks, I listened with trepidation to all the tales and rumours from the North. Yet as the year went on and we heard no news of armies on the march - precious little news at all in fact - I dared to hope that my prayers were answered. How futile, though, are the hopes of men when pitted against the will of the gods. How fragile are our bodies and how vulnerable our souls.

There are moments in life that change everything. It is something upon which I ponder in quiet moments. Many years later, Paulinius - when he was a bishop in Northumbria - told me that there was once a great flood that drowned all the people apart from six. These six built a huge arc and saved themselves and all the animals of the world. It seemed unlikely to me that all the men and women in the whole world came from just those six, but he showed me the passage in the Bible where it is written, so it must be true. Not that I could read back then ... or at least, not that well, but I took his word for it. That flood swept away whole cities and nations in a night. God's judgement, so Paulinius said, for the sins of the world. I remembered Aedann and his mother, who followed the Christian God, telling me He was a god of love. It seemed an odd god to me that professed to love yet punished people so. My own gods, on the other hand, played their games and rewarded those who played them well. But was it that judgemental Christian God or the meddlesome gods of my youth who brought upon us the plague that in a moment changed my world?

112

That spring, Lilla brought us word of a pestilence. Arriving for the festival of the goddess Eostre which celebrated the fertility and new life of the lengthening days, he spoke of his fear and foreboding of coming deaths.

"Plague and famine are ever a fear among men," Lilla said, prowling around the fire pit that burned in the centre of the room. "When we were young our fathers told us of the great yellow plague that ravaged the land sixty years ago. It came, so the tales tell, from the fabled land of the pyramids: from distant Egypt to southern Gaul and then carried by traders to the south of Albion, along with wines and glassware. They sold these to merchants, drank the local mead and dallied with the daughters of the merchants. The traders would take tin and silver away with them. Some, though, did not return to Gaul. They died in Dumnonia and Kernow and were buried there, but not before passing on their pestilence to the merchants they dealt with or perhaps to their pretty daughters.

"In the five years following this, the plague raged across the land. Thousands perished without regard for class or status. Infants were particularly vulnerable. My father recalled those times to me. His childhood companion, Aelwulf, had died, as had his beloved sister. But it was the British lands that were hardest hit. This in part was British folly as they had avoided trading with us English, choosing instead to trade with foreigners and indeed, even avoided sending their priests to the so-called lands of the heathen. The plague came to Deira, certainly, but it devastated the Welsh. Was this a curse from their god as their priests believe? Perhaps, for the children that did survive were in much reduced numbers. When Ida of Bernicia, and later Aelle, rose up against them it was the plague as much as our force of arms that reduced their numbers and won our freedom!"

113

Lilla paused as the villagers cheered, hammered mugs on the tables and guzzled their ale. He tilted his head and stared at them without humour. One by one the cheers stopped as we realised that he had something more to say - something we might not care to learn.

"Indeed, that plague served to help us. But I am sorry to say that this is not just a tale of long ago. No, indeed, it is now a tale of our own time. I have heard that the plague is back in the lands of the Britons and the Scots. In Dál-Riata, in Rheged, in Powys and Gwynedd and now, even now, there are victims as close as Loidis and Lincolne. So heed my warning: keep safe, my most favourite people; keep away from others and keep safe."

But how safe can a man be? We must trade with others and visit market to sell and buy goods. As summer came in that year, which Aedann told me was six hundred and one years after the birth of Christ, a trader visited the Villa, his cart piled high with woollen tunics and fur cloaks, warm and thick and just right for the cold months ahead. Perhaps the disease was brought to the Villa and nearby farms by him or was somehow carried in his furs. However it happened, when he arrived he did not look an ill man. That night though, as we spoke in the ale house, I noticed that he was sweating, did not touch his food and seemed to have a fever. He excused himself and retired early to bed. He died overnight right where he had been sleeping in the great barn. As one of the estate workers rolled his body into a hastily dug grave, I noticed that the dead man's skin was covered in weeping boils and blotches. A few days later the same estate worker developed a fever and a sweat then a cough. He deteriorated rapidly and perished a few days later.

In the month or so, half a dozen more villagers, including Cuthbert, developed the symptoms. Two died, but Cuthbert,

114

although fearfully weak, survived. We locked ourselves away from the world, avoided travel and all trade ceased. Through that terrible summer we hid and prayed that we would be spared this terror.

That autumn, with the plague still abroad, a messenger rode into the Villa from the North. I recognised him as one of my father's huscarls, but nevertheless, wary of what contagion he might carry we kept inside the building and away from the rider, calling down to him from the windows. Yet, though the man was fit, he brought terrible news.

"Lord Cenred is ill, my lord," the rider shouted up to us. "Your mother bids me bring you as quickly as you can come."

I hugged my wife and son, expressedly forbidding them to leave the house in my absence, then dashed to Wicstun, galloping along in the wake of the huscarl and then, in increasing anxiety, passing him and leading him into town. Sliding off my horse, I did not wait to tie it up or take notice of where it went. Leaping across to my father's door I yanked it open to be greeted by an ashen-faced Mildrith.

"Millie," I croaked my throat dry and sore, "how is he?"

"He is getting worse," she said. I followed her inside feeling that a certainty in my life was falling apart. What more did the gods want from me? Had I not seen misery enough with my brother's death, with the horrors at Catraeth?

In the bedchamber my older sister, Sunniva, and our mother rushed to embrace me. We turned back to look at the man in the bed and I felt the breath catch in my throat when I saw that Father was indeed very ill. This was the man who had always been so strong, the centre of my world and of all our lives. Now he looked so weak and I, just past twenty-one years old, felt far from ready for this.

115

It was less than a year since we had all stood by the deathbed of Aelle and watched him wither before our eyes, and now here was my father, who last time I had seen him had been fit and strong and powerful, reduced to a husk of the man I had known: an old, old man, dying. He waved me towards him and then held out his hand to stop me. "Not too close, Cerdic. You must not catch the plague."

"Father ... I am sorry if my words were harsh when we last spoke," I gabbled.

"You spoke from the heart about a matter of the heart. That does not matter now. Millie remains unmarried because of the plague. Who she marries will soon be your decision."

Of course, I thought, Mildrith should have married Frithwulf in the autumn but the plague had prevented all that. My sister flashed me the briefest of hopeful smiles and I expected she was thinking there was a chance for her and Cuthbert after all, then her face grew grim again as she looked back at Father. I said nothing to her because I was thinking about what my father said about it being my decision. It would only be my choice, of course, if my father died. I looked at him and he seemed to know what I was thinking because he nodded.

"Now, though, you must put your heart to the side. When I die ..."

"Father ... no!"

"Hush, son. I am dying. I know that. It does not matter. I have lived a good life. "

"You have, Father, you have," I said, careless of the unmanly tears flooding down my cheeks.

"But I will go to our ancestors soon. I will go to be with Cuthwine. I am content. But it is not me that I worry about. It is you, you and the family and the country."

116

"Deira?"

"You worry too, son. You worry about the king and how weak he is. You worry about Aethelfrith and how controlling he is."

I nodded.

"Try to steer Aethelric away from too close alliance with Bernicia. But if all else fails, if we are drawn into a pact with Aethelfrith, you need to be careful. Aethelric's rule may fail us. If that happens you must make sure his heir is safe."

"Who? Hereric. He is a fool like his father."

"Not Hereric. Aelle's spirit was passed on to another, Cerdic. To his younger son."

"Edwin?"

He nodded.

"But Edwin is stubborn and just a youth," I sobbed.

My father coughed, his voice growing weak. "He is fifteen now, Cerdic. He needs protection and he needs guidance. He needs a friend."

The old man was mad. A friend? Edwin despised me. "Edwin and I are hardly friends, Father."

My father pulled himself up onto his elbow and bent forward, summoning all his strength. "Make him one!" he insisted and then, strength failing him, he lay back down, panting heavily.

"Make him one, Cerdic," he mumbled. "Promise me you will try."

It seemed an odd promise for a dying man, yet how could I deny him? I nodded. "I promise, Father."

That night he died, the last in Wicstun to do so. This was not a great plague like the one of which Lilla had spoken that half a century before had changed the face of Britannia, yet it was devastating enough. In Wicstun thirty died as did dozens more in the surrounding estates and villages. Nobles and commoners

117

alike were struck down. Even royalty was not immune. We heard a rumour that Aethelfrith had died. Then another saying it was not him but his wife - Queen Bebba - whom I had once met. She perished around the time my father did. The North in general was hit pretty hard and not just we Angles, but the British and Scots too. We had our answer: this then was why the Scots had not yet attacked us. An army would not march through plague lands. Travellers avoided the area.

Though it was devastating for us, it barely merited a mention in the chronicles the monks wrote in later years. A single line, perhaps, in a local record. Yet what the chronicles do not mention is that one more member of my family would contract the plague before it burnt itself out.

We took father home - to the Villa - and buried him on the north ridge beside my brother and our grandfather. I buried him with his seax, shield and spear to recall the warrior he could be if the need arose, along with a single sack of seeds in remembrance of the farmer that he truly was. Cynric's great sword I did not bury with him. That now belonged to Cuthwine and I put it in our basement store room, wrapped in oiled rags to await the day my son would wield it.

Mildrith, Sunniva and my mother cried themselves hoarse, but I was silent in my horror and grief and I stood unmoving. Beside me, though, Aidith was not still. She was shivering. Then she coughed. As I turned to stare at her, she gave a little groan and fainted into my arms.

We sent for help from Wicstun, but the apothecary could do little for her. I watched her weaken, fever raging, her coughing and shivering getting worse. When the fever was at its height I walked through to the common room where I kept Catraeth as well as my wedding sword which Aidith had given me. I took down the latter from its stand and sat cradling it.

How I wished then that I had a human enemy to fight: to strike with sword and spear. But this enemy, this fever, I could not hurt. How impotent and useless I felt. I prayed to all our gods: to Woden, to Thunor and to any who might intervene. I walked to the grove and fell on my knees and there I first worshipped them and then cursed them. I threatened and cajoled the gods. But it was clearly in vain. They did not hear or if they did, if my cries of anguish reached Valhalla, it seemed the gods did not bother to turn away from their games. Maybe they just laughed at this mortal and his pathetic pleas.

In the end I gave up trying for it was clear that the gods did not care.

Chapter Eleven
Pact with Loki

The next days were the most terrible of my life. Aidith's fever grew worse with each passing day and she became gradually weaker. Cuthwine, my son, was not yet three and wanted his mother, but I had to keep him away from her. Sunniva, my older sister, stayed on after our father's funeral, along with Mildrith and our mother, and between the three of them the lad was well cared for. Despite that, I watched him like a hawk, conscious of every sniffle and breath that sounded out of place and filled with dread every time Sunniva remarked that he seemed tired or was not eating as much as did her own children at his age.

About three days after Aidith fell ill, Lilla came to the Villa. "I am sorry about Cenred," he said, as soon as he had dismounted. "He was a brave man and a strong one too - a hero like his sons. How is Aidith?"

I shrugged, "Not well, Lilla." I led him through into the mead hall and indicated a stool by the high table.

"Sorry to hear that," he said, with true concern in his voice, "and doubly so, because you won't like what I have been sent to tell you." He paused, sinking to the stool. I, my heart lurching, waved at him to carry on.

"Aethelric has sent me to summon you to Godnundingham."

"What? I can't go now. I can't leave Aidith like this!"

"He was most insistent, Cerdic."

121

"Aethelric was?" I said and the surprise and doubt must have been obvious in my voice because Lilla raised both his hands in apparent surrender.

"Oh, all right then, Prince Edwin was."

"You can tell the little brat he can bugger off!"

"He won't be happy about that."

"He can go to meet Hel if he thinks I care."

"I figured you might take this attitude, but I have not told you the whole news."

"What is the rest then?" I asked in a tired voice.

"I have not told you WHY you have been called for, have I?" Lilla helped himself to a jug of mead on the table and poured some into a mug. He lifted the jug to offer some to me, but I shook my head.

"Well, go on then," I said, "why have I been called?"

"Bernicia has sent a diplomatic mission. They arrived at Eorforwic last night, will spend Yuletide with Earl Harald and are expected at the palace in a week."

"Oh?" I said, not sure why I needed to be involved.

"I have not told you who is leading the expedition yet."

"Theobald?" I guessed. Lilla waved his hand in a so-so gesture.

"*Hussa* and Theobald," he corrected.

"Hussa in Deira? But he was banned and sent into exile."

"So you see Edwin's and Aethelric's dilemma. Aelle threatened Hussa with death were he to return and yet return he has. But he is part of a diplomatic mission from Bernicia. What is Aethelric to do?"

"Indeed," I said drily. "There are many who would happily see Hussa swing for his betrayal of Deira."

Lilla looked up from his mug, "You perhaps?"

I frowned. "I am not sure what I feel about him."

122

"So you see why they want you there. You met Theobald."

"So did you," I pointed out.

"Ah, but I am just a storyteller. High policy and affairs of state I merely report on. I observe but I do not direct. This is a moment for the likes of you, Cerdic."

"I can't leave Aidith," I repeated stubbornly.

"Let me look at her. When I was away from here I happened upon a wiseman who was treating the plague in Elmet. He taught me some healing. Maybe I can help a little."

"Could you?" I asked, suddenly hopeful.

"Don't hold your hopes up, but maybe I can. Go pray for her."

"The gods are not listening to me."

Lilla leant across the table and as he did so a pendant swung forward from the open neck of his tunic. It was hung on a silver thread and plainly I saw the symbol of two snakes coiled around each other. The bard glanced down, saw where I was looking and shrugged. He stood, pulled the slender thread over his head and after staring at the pendant for a moment, pressed it into my hand.

"Take this and try again," he said flatly as he sat back down.

I was going to argue, but then I thought, why not try again? What after all had I to lose? I left Lilla to go into the Villa and then I turned and walked across the fields to the road, crossed it and entered the little grove and the small shrine.

I was not sure which god to pray to. Freya and Frigga were the women's goddesses, but Woden was the warrior's god as well as being the chief of them all. Then there was Thunor, god of thunder and storms. I had prayed to them and to Eostre, Tiw and all the others. I had prayed to them all, save one. I had not prayed to the one god who, it seemed, guided my destiny. Lilla's pendant - the pair of snakes twisted around each other - was the symbol of

123

that one particular god. Throughout all the chaos, along the twists and turns of my life I had not prayed to this one. It was Loki. I had cursed him for his interference, but never had I prayed to him.

So now I did. But I was not exactly reverent in my approach to worship. "Loki! Do you hear me, Loki? I am Cerdic. When I look at the world and how chaotic and random it appears to be, it is right there that I see your handiwork, for you are the trickster god. You like your jokes, don't you Loki? You like your pawns in this world. I turned away from you, from the world, but that was not enough for you was it? You drag me back to the world. It seems that every time I think I have escaped it you conspire to involve me once more. Well then," I fell to my knees, "I accept. I will play whatever role you have in mind. Just one thing: heal Aidith. If Aidith lives I will go with Lilla to the palace and I will let you take me where you will. Do you hear me Loki? Heal her and I am yours to do with as you please!"

I returned to the Villa and went into our chamber. Lilla was giving Aidith a drink of some potion he had made, urging her to sip at it, whilst her mother and mine looked on anxiously. Lilla turned to look at me, tilted his head in unspoken question and I replied with a brief nod. A pact had been made, a promise given. Now to see if the god had heard.

I sent everyone away and slumping down exhausted beside the bed, settled to watch my wife through the night. I looked at her feverish face, longing for her to come back to me. Then I drank some ale and a crust of bread and let myself doze.

That night was the longest of the year: the Winter Solstice. Just after it, every year, my people would celebrate Yuletide. There in the midst of the darkest month we made our own brightness. In all the previous years the Villa would have been full of noise and music and laughter. I had hardly been aware it was coming that year for the plague had taken away from all of us any yearning for the joy and the festival. Sorrow and fear had taken their place. Yet in the deepest part of this, the longest night, I felt something touch my arm. I stirred from my slumber and looked up, expecting to see Mildrith, perhaps coming to take over the watch. But there was no one in the room. No one save one other.

"Cerdic?" a weak voice whispered.

I turned towards the bed and gazed at Aidith slumped in the furs. She still looked exhausted, but of the beads of sweat, ever present on her brow since her fever began, there was no sign. Her face was no longer flushed, her skin pale as death, but her eyes were clear and focused. She smiled a weak smile at me and tried to grasp my hand, but clearly had no strength in her limbs.

"Cerdic," she breathed, "I feel like I have been a long way away from you."

"You have, my love, far away; almost beyond my reach. But you have come back to me. It was Lilla that brought you back ... Lilla and Loki."

"Loki? What do you mean?"

"Nothing, my love, you are back. Let us be glad of that."

"Cuthwine ...? She gazed up at me with anxious eyes.

"Is fine."

Reassured, she sighed, "What day is it?"

"It's the start of Yuletide. When the morning comes I will have the men bring out the best ale and mead, the finest food and we will celebrate your return to us."

She smiled at me and laughed. It was weak, faint, but a laugh nonetheless and I had not heard it from her for days. "Yes, we will celebrate," I said.

125

And then I would have to leave to go to the palace, and find out what Loki had in store for me. But I did not tell her that. Not yet.

Lilla and I set out for Godnundingham three days later. He was not happy at the delay but I insisted on waiting until I was certain of Aidith's recovery. I also wanted to be sure that Cuthwine was unaffected and that no more cases of the plague had happened in the Villa and Village. Finally, I was determined to enjoy Yuletide at home. When I left I took Aedann along on the journey instead of Eduard, who was in no fit state having got himself outrageously drunk the night before and ended up face down in a plate of boiled chicken. Grettir came too and I also took Cuthbert. As far as I was aware Mildrith was, despite my father's death, still betrothed to this Frithwulf and I had no idea what I was supposed to do about that, but I wanted to keep them apart whilst I sorted it all out. Because - and this was only just dawning on me - I was the son of the late Earl of the Southern Marches and until the king decided otherwise, I had inherited that role. Earldoms, of course, did not pass on in the same way as did the titles of estates and lands. I owned the Villa because my grandfather had, and my father after him, and he had granted it to me. But Earl of the Southern Marches was an appointed role and could be taken away by the king. Did that matter to me, I wondered? I wanted only to be left in peace in my valley, yet I would not happily allow the standing my family had gained to be eroded easily.

This created a problem: with my sister married to the son of another thegn, my own position, despite my youth, would be strong. The man who killed Owain, who kept the army at Catraeth, linked by marriage to another noble family - such a man would not be easy to set aside. Father had believed I needed to be

126

close to the king. He had feared the times ahead. Yet, to follow through with that marriage would destroy the friendship I had with Cuthbert and my relationship with Millie, who I knew was hoping I would make things right for her. It was a problem I would have to deal with. My pact with Loki was only days old and I was already regretting it!

The Bernician deputation had not yet arrived at the palace when we turned up. Sabert, Acha, Aethelric and Hereric were there, however. So too was Prince Edwin.

"Nice of you to spare us time from your pigs, Cerdic," he muttered at me from where he was playing stones with Hereric on one of the long tables in the main hall.

"My fault entirely, Highness," explained Lilla with an elaborate bow. "The Villa is really a very exceptional place to spend Yuletide as I have done several times and I insisted on staying for it this year. The ale is very good."

Edwin glared at him for a moment and then smiled. "You old rogue. You like your ale, Lilla," he said and ignoring me went back to his game.

I shook my head in amazement at Lilla. His silver tongue could enchant anyone, even a spoilt prince - or so it seemed. I wandered further down the hall to where Sabert was waiting for me.

"I was sorry to hear of your father, Cerdic," he said softly. "He was a great man."

I nodded my thanks and then tilted my head towards Edwin. "He wanted me to ... felt I needed to somehow gain the trust of Edwin. Said he was the main hope for the Deiran line," I glanced at the prince, "he just seems like a sarcastic young puppy to me."

Sabert considered the youth across the hall. "Your father was a wise man. He looked beyond Edwin's immaturity and saw two

127

things, Cerdic. He saw that maybe the boy is just insecure and feels he has to prove he is as good as you, or better perhaps."

I gaped at him, "Me? Why me?"

Sabert shrugged. "You were only two years older than he is when you rescued the company from Calcaria and when you held the gate at Stanwick Camp. Many would have thought you incapable. Me for a start," he admitted. "He is a prince and seems to have a need to prove himself. You, because of your relative youth, even now, remind him of that."

I turned back to the prince and saw him glance briefly in my direction before a look of irritation flashed across his face and he focused back on the game.

"Hereric seems easier going," I commented, finding Sabert's assessment hard to believe.

"Hereric is like his father and as suited to being a prince as Aethelric a king. You were right to raise doubts that day."

I grunted. "Much good it did me, but you said just now that my father saw two things in Edwin?"

Sabert pointed at the game going on between the two princes. It was clear that Edwin had trapped Hereric's king and that Hereric was losing badly yet had not seemed to notice the fact. His eyes remained dull, yet jovial as ever as he made another bad move. Quick as a flash, Edwin spotted the error and with a holler of triumph finished the game.

"I have seen only one other man as good at Tafael as that boy," Sabert murmured. "Edwin needs to learn to apply his skills to life away from the table, but your father spotted that he is clever. The boy has fire in his belly; he's determined, focused and ruthless. Like his father - like Aelle. He just needs a guiding hand."

I was considering my reply when I felt a tap on my shoulder. Turning I saw an overweight, dark-haired man in his fifties with hints of silver in his beard. Behind him there stood another much younger man, handsome and very tall. I had seen them both occasionally at Wicstun and once or twice over the years visiting father at the Villa. These were two men I had hoped to avoid for a while: Guthred and his son.

"Might I have a word, Lord Cerdic?" the older man asked. He nodded at Sabert, who returned the greeting then left us alone.

"Yes, Lord Guthred."

"I think you know my son, Frithwulf and I expect you know what this is about."

I had intended avoiding this conversation until I was ready for it, but here they were. "Of course, Lord Guthred, you wish to speak of the ... betrothal?"

"Indeed. Your father and I shook hands on it before the plague came. The marriage should have occurred by now had it not been for that and for the untimely death of the good Earl Cenred. When shall we arrange for the ceremony?"

I stared at him, rather taken aback by the abruptness of the question, but before I could reply the young man spoke.

"Father, perhaps we should first extend our sympathy on the loss of such a great man, " he said, then turning to me, added, "I was truly sorry to have heard the news. Please accept my condolences."

Well the son was polite even if the father was not, I thought. "Thank you," I muttered.

"Yes, yes indeed," Guthred blustered. "But returning to my question - shall we discuss the location and date? Mildrith is getting on in years. She is what, nineteen and unwed? Frithwulf's mother was pregnant with him when she was but sixteen. Time is pressing."

129

This was true maybe, but damn it all, I could not betray Millie and Cuth. Despite my earlier misgivings, I came to a decision then and there. "I regret that we will have to cancel the arrangement. My sister is not available for this marriage," I announced.

Father and son exchanged a confused glance.

"We do not understand. Your father and I shook hands on it. We had an agreement. You cannot now back out," Guthred said, his voice becoming threatening.

"I know it is unfortunate, but I am not my father. He shook on it, but I did not. I would ask you to release us from the agreement."

"I am sorry, but I have to insist. If you break this agreement, made in good faith and in front of witnesses, I will seek recompense from your estates. The law is clear on it. Half of what you own is forfeit. Think on *that!*"

Without another word, the pair stomped off down the hall and stood on the far side, talking to each other and occasionally casting dark looks at me.

"What will you do about that?" Lilla asked, coming up beside me. "I couldn't help hearing … Your family can't afford for you to keep giving away treasure to buy your way out of trouble, you know."

I glared at the bard and returned to silent thought on the problem. While I was still pondering this, a guard entered the hall and walked up to Sabert. "Prince Theobald, the Bernicians and the traitor are here," he announced.

"So how was Yuletide with Hussa as a house guest?" I asked Harald sometime later. He was on one side of me and Sabert the other. We were standing amongst the nobles gathered on either side of Aethelric's throne, where the king was sitting nodding

130

congenially at the various thegns and earls. Edwin, perched at his side, was studying us all with less joviality, more as the leader of a wolf pack inspects the secondary males, testing their loyalty and trying to be sure whom he trusted and whom he was not so certain about.

"I did not see much of him, truth be told, Cerdic," Harald replied. "Theobald was the life and soul of the party - quite a good fellow actually. Hussa generally kept out of sight."

"I wonder what he was up to then," I muttered.

"What makes you think he was up to anything? Last time he was in my hall he was almost executed for treason. You can forgive a man for not feeling comfortable. What I will never forgive him for is siding with that bastard Samlen. I would have strung him up myself had he not been with Theobald. Reckon he could feel that. Reckon he just knew better than to get in my way."

I shrugged. "I guess you are right. The question is what now? What does Aethelric do? How does he handle Hussa?"

We had our answer soon enough. The great doors at the far end of the hall opened and the Bernicians entered, led by Theobald with Hussa at his side. They strode up to the throne and Theobald gave the slightest bow of respect. Hussa hung back behind him at this point and glanced over at me and then, defiantly at the nobles in the hall. Thirty and more pairs of eyes were fixed in his direction, thirty men who would happily see him dead.

Aethelric, however, did not seem to have noticed Hussa.

"Welcome, Prince Theobald, to my palace. We rejoice at your visit. Let it serve to further strengthen the bonds between kindred lands ..."

131

Always good at speechmaking was Aethelric. I think he would have gone on, but at that point Grettir, standing a little to my rear, pushed between Harald and me and pointed at Hussa.

"Grettir? What are you doing?" I hissed.

"Traitor!" he shouted, pointing at my half-brother, not hearing me or at least not listening. "That man, Sire, is a traitor," he bowed towards Aethelric, "whom your father condemned. Will you have him stand here in your hall - your father's hall - as if none of that happened?"

"What is that you say?" Aethelric asked cupping his ear, confusion echoing in his voice.

"Hussa trained with us, under me, he was one of us, even if a surly companion. He was part of the Wicstun Company till he betrayed us and went to serve Samlen. He should have been hanged after Catraeth, but escaped his just punishment," Grettir said loudly.

"Is that so?" Edwin stepped forward to look into Hussa's eyes. "What are you doing back here, traitor? Your life is forfeit."

"This man is under my protection," Theobald interceded, "and that of my brother, King Aethelfrith. Believe me, I would happily hand over the fellow as we don't get on, do we Hussa? But my brother has made it plain that he is not to be harmed. So now he is Bernician and under the Bernician king's protection."

"This is Deiran soil," Grettir insisted. "That man committed treason against Deira and it is not in the power of the Bernician king to forgive that or to make other arrangements."

I looked around the room. Of those present only Aethelric, Sabert and Harald were fully aware of the circumstances of the outcome of Hussa's trial. Those three had been there that day. A few of the other thegns and the odd huscarl had also been present, but were not here today. All had agreed afterwards that

132

Hussa's guilt lay with Hussa alone and that the taint of his crime should not be laid on the rest of my family. Father had paid for his part, such that as it was, with the Amber Treasure. He had bought Hussa's life dearly with the blood money he had paid that day, for the treasure, my mother's necklace, was without equal and I am not sure she had ever forgiven him. Not all of the thegns would have kept silent, of course. After all, many like a good scandal, but we had heard no more about it. The praise and honour poured upon my father and me for our part in the victory had been enough to keep it quiet. Grettir, though, had not been with us when we captured Hussa, nor at his trial, and afterwards, wishing to put the past behind us, neither my father nor I had felt like telling him the full story. I should have done so, I realised that now. I glanced at Aedann and Cuthbert. Aedann shrugged at me whilst Cuthbert bit his lip nervously.

What should I now do? I looked at Aethelric, hoping he would intervene, but he watched the confrontation with the awkward air of a man hoping it will sort itself out. Harald and Sabert were both studying me waiting to see what I said, maybe feeling some obligation to keep quiet, perhaps not wishing to reveal the full truth until I had spoken.

I cleared my throat and all eyes turned to gaze at me. "It was not the Bernician king who let Hussa live, it was the Deiran one. Aelle agreed that he should live." I said at last.

"Why?" Grettir and Edwin chimed in unison.

"Apologies, Highness," Grettir said, "but, my lord, why would the old king let the traitor go?"

"Indeed, Lord Cerdic, why?" Edwin asked.

I hesitated for a moment then spoke, "Because he was paid *wehrgeld*."

"Blood money? What wealth could pay for such treachery?"

"The Amber Treasure that was my mother's."

There was collective gasp and a low murmur buzzed around the hall.

"Your father paid *that*?" Grettir asked. Then he glanced at Hussa. "So it is true, this man is his son. Your father kept it quiet or thought he did, but there was a rumour. It explains a few things."

"I don't want to talk of it here, Grettir. But Aelle agreed that Hussa would live - agreed it with my father."

"He also said that the man's life was forfeit if he ever returned to Deira," Harald pointed out.

"Admittedly, but he also accepted that his heir should decide the boy's fate should he come back," Sabert put in.

"You are Cerdic's brother?" Edwin asked Hussa, his tone still hostile.

Hussa inclined his head, "Unfortunately it is true that we shared the same father. I hear he is dead now."

I looked at Hussa in surprise. Had he heard of our father's death whilst in Eoforwic? How had it affected him, I wondered. It was impossible to tell for his voice was devoid of emotion.

"But yes," he went on, "we are half-brothers. Much to my shame I am closely related to the great hero of Deira!" Hussa sneered.

Edwin blinked, glanced at me and then seemed to reappraise my brother. "Maybe we should spare his life. I would like to hear his version of the story of the great Lord Cerdic," he said, more than a touch of irony in his voice.

"Sire, I would happily hand the man over, but not to be hanged," Theobald said. "If Hussa were to die, King Aethelfrith would not like it."

134

"What is your decision, Sire?" Harald asked Aethelric, who blinked at him as if he had not understood the question.

"Let him live, Sire," I pleaded, "for my father's memory; it is what he wanted. Hussa has found service and honour in Bernicia. Do not risk the peace with our friends for the sake of old revenge." As I spoke, I was aware that Hussa was staring at me, his mouth open.

I am still not sure now, all these years later, why I spoke up for him. He was my half-brother, but I disliked him intensely and there was no doubt the feeling was mutual. Damn it, why did father have to save his neck? After the death of Cuthwine, the kidnapping of Mildrith and the losses at Catraeth, I probably had wanted Hussa punished as much as anyone else, and yet I also understood, at least a little, the pain my father had suffered. I knew of his guilt in fathering the boy then neglecting him; his further guilt because of what that boy had gone on to do, most likely as a result of that neglect. I had inherited Father's estates and rank and I suppose I knew there and then that I had also inherited his obligations – and his guilt - for I could understand why he had acted as he had. And so, as my father had done, I pleaded for Hussa's life.

Aethelric stared at me for a long time, so long that the hushed mutterings in the hall at my plea died away and everyone fell silent, waiting.

Slowly nodding his head, the king said, "I agree. Let the boy live, providing he leaves with the Bernicians."

Glancing around, I saw more than one face scowling at this decision, particularly Grettir's.

Hussa stepped forward to stand beside Prince Theobald. I could see now why he had come on this journey. Theobald was hardly a man blessed with the gift of diplomatic speech or with a silver tongue. It seemed, however, that Hussa was. He glared once more around the room and then bowed to Aethelric.

"I am glad the matter is resolved, Your Majesty. You spoke a few moments ago about the bond between Deira and Bernicia. Prince Theobald has asked me to reply by saying that we are indeed happy to be here, for it is of that link between us that I am instructed to speak. The prince's brother, King Aethelfrith, wishes to make the bond even stronger. Indeed, there is no stronger alliance, no stronger bond than that made by marriage."

Aethelric's mouth dropped open, "Marriage?"

"Indeed, Sire. We are here to propose a marriage between the House of Ida and the House of Aelle. Between Bernicia and Deira."

"Who is to marry whom?" asked a female voice from behind Aethelric. All heads turned as Acha emerged from around the throne. She fixed Hussa with a cold, imperious stare.

Hussa seemed taken aback by the intensity of the challenge, but then recovered and the slightest hint of a smirk now curled across his lips.

"You should rejoice, Highness, for King Aethelfrith would be delighted to marry *you*, Princess Acha!"

Chapter Twelve
Alliance

Later, of course, it would be bloody obvious what was going on and I suppose we should have been wise to the sudden romantic approach of Aethelfrith to Acha. Royal marriages are always arranged for a purpose and fool that I was I should have thought it all through. Yet then again, I probably imagined that marriage might mean peace. As ever, this was my problem. I just wanted to be left alone. Why could I not just go back to the Villa, to Aidith and Cuthwine and live out the rest of my life? I thought that maybe, if Aethelfrith wanted marriage to a wife of Deiran blood, this might be his motive too. This was my greatest mistake - thinking that somehow the marriage would bring us peace and security. Damn fool for wanting that in the first place. Double the fool for imagining this was what Aethelfrith had in mind!

Still, then and there few objected, even Acha, interestingly enough, did not look as upset as I would have thought. I mean, does any woman want to be wed to a foreigner or a man she has never met? Yet Aethelfrith was not only a king but the greatest king in the North at that time and as a princess of a royal house I think Acha knew what was coming. Her role was to marry a prince of another country to ally Deira to that land. She probably thought she was lucky. She might have been sent to the land of the Picts or to an obscure Welsh kingdom where no one spoke the same language as she did, and here she was marrying Aethelfrith, an Angle from a neighbouring land and a man of power. No, she did not look unhappy that day in the palace. In fact, as I remember, I rather feel I saw a smile on her lips.

Not so Guthred! Betrothal was still on his mind. Not, of course, that of the princess and Aethelfrith, but of Frithwulf and Mildrith. Two days later I was summoned to the king's presence for a hearing on the charge of breaking off a betrothal agreement. Guthred was correct in that the law specified that half my wealth might pass to him and Frithwulf were I found to be in breach of a firm and binding agreement.

"I am in a mess, Lilla," I commented to the bard on the morning of the hearing. "There *was* an agreement, Father said so and Guthred confirms it."

"Was it formalised? Had there been an agreement on the specifics of gifts?" he asked.

"Not that Father told me," I answered with a shrug.

"Leave it to me, then."

A moment later Guthred entered the hall in company with his son. They threw me a dirty look and stomped to the other side of the room.

Aethelfrith now came in and we stood whilst he took his seat, then the proceedings began. The claim against me was first in the order of business.

"This man," Guthred gestured dismissively at me, "broke a betrothal agreement between his sister and my son here. It was an agreement that his father and I reached."

"Was there *handsellan*?" Aethelric asked, looking vaguely from Guthred to me.

"There was, Sire," Guthred answered, confirming that my father and he had shaken hands to seal the agreement.

"Do you deny this, Earl Cerdic?"

It was the first time I had been publicly addressed as 'Earl' and slightly confused, I stood and prepared to answer, but Lilla pushed me back in my seat and stood forward.

"Sire, I will respond for Lord Cerdic. His father and I were friends and I would not have either name besmirched."

"What do you know of this matter?" Guthred asked.

"I know tradition; our traditions and our laws. Can any man say they know them better than I?"

No one spoke. They all knew Lilla was speaking the truth. As bard, he maintained the old knowledge and stories. They were his stock in trade. I felt a spark of hope.

"Cerdic was not present at the *handsellan* IF it happened," Lilla said.

"What do you mean IF? Guthred snapped."

"Can you provide witnesses to the event?"

Guthred looked uneasy. He finally shook his head. "No, I cannot. It was an arrangement between Lord Cenred and me."

"Can you describe the agreement on the *Brydgifu* and the *Handgeld*?"

"We had not reached an agreement. The plague came before we could finalise it," Guthred admitted.

"Then, Sire," Lilla turned to the king, "with no witness of the *Handsellan* and no specific details of *Brydgifu* and *Handgeld*, I submit that this agreement was nothing formal and merely an expression of intent. Earl Cerdic cannot be bound to such an informal understanding."

Aethelric looked around the room, seeking the feeling of the other nobles. Most were nodding their heads.

"Very well, so be it. I rule that no formal agreement was made and that there is no binding undertaking here. Cerdic is free to arrange a betrothal for his sister to whomsoever he chooses."

"Thank you, Lilla," I muttered.

"No problem, Cerdic," he whispered, "but I would watch out for Guthred. I hear he would like to be Earl of the Southern

Marches in your place and this defeat might give him another reason for enmity."

Guthred glowered at me, but said nothing. I made a note to be wary of him. I still found it hard to believe that I was indeed Earl of the Southern Marches, yet it seemed that Aethelric, who had himself addressed me as 'Earl Cerdic', was content to have it so. As such I would have cause to have dealings with Guthred in the future. I was aware that they might now be difficult.

Since that row with my father about Mildrith, out of respect for the old man's memory, I had kept my sister and Cuthbert apart by finding work for my friend and dragging him along on every trip to court, Eorforwic, or anywhere else I went. I knew I was in one sense being mean, but Father had made a ruling and I had promised to obey him. That promise had bound me until just now when I was released from it by the king. In walking away from an alliance with Guthred I was perhaps not acting in the best interests of my family's prosperity, but I was young and inexperienced and my sister and Cuthbert were close to my heart. I could not wait to see their faces when I told them the news.

When I got home I called the pair in to me. Masking my features into an expression of gravity befitting an earl, I looked from one to the other. "I have spoken with Earl Guthred concerning your betrothal and imminent nuptials, Mildrith ...."

I could see she was holding her breath; Cuthbert transferred his gaze from me to the floor. Both looked agonised and neither spoke. I waited a moment drawing out the tense silence, but could tease them no longer.

"The arrangement was not binding and I have cancelled it. You may now see each other freely, but I will make no decision on betrothal until after the royal wedding in the summer. I think you two need time to be sure of each other and besides, I am sick of betrothals for the moment," I finished grumpily.

My words were all but drowned out by Mildrith's shriek as she flung herself at me. Even the usually shy Cuthbert hugged me and I, enjoying their gratitude, found I had no reason to be moody. "Go on; bugger off the pair of you," I grinned at their happy faces. "Just behave yourselves. I don't want to be an uncle again anytime soon. The brats Sunniva is raising are enough for the moment."

Unlike me, Aelle's daughter had not had enough of betrothals. Now she was about to be Queen Acha of Bernicia she took every opportunity to hold feasts and entertain the Deiran court and the Bernician guests. She looked happier still, if a touch apprehensive when seven months later we travelled north. The princess was accompanied by a grand procession of all the thegns and earls in the kingdom. We were also instructed to call out one man in two of the fyrd to act as escort. It took us a full ten days to reach Bebbanburgh. Each city and town we stopped at would play host to us and outdo each other to provide the most elaborate feast or entertainment. We had horse races at one stop, boar hunting and wrestling at another, riddles and music at still more.

At last we reached Bebbanburgh. As we approached, a fanfare of trumpets and horns played to greet us. From the battlements a hundred flags flew - those of Aethelfrith and of Aethelric and of all the noble houses of both countries.

The wedding ceremony was not unlike my own, except it was conducted in the open air at the top of the cliffs, which fell sheer to the crashing waves far below us. It seemed to me that Aethelfrith was calling upon the very forces of nature to witness the deed.

141

The celebrations went on for a full week after the actual ceremony. Aethelfrith had spared no expense in bringing in the greatest of entertainment, which overshadowed the best we had enjoyed on the journey north and I did wonder at the extravagance of the festivities. Aethelfrith seemed happily relaxed about it all, ordering new barrels of drink opened, emptying his cellars onto the tables with apparent glee. His new wife, Princess Acha - or Queen Acha as I had to get used to calling her - seemed to have put behind her any apprehension she might have had in the days before the wedding, taking on the role of hostess and cup bearer to the king with obvious enthusiasm, her enjoyment at being the centre of the festivities plain to see.

"Well," Eduard quipped with a grin, "Aethelfrith must have given her something to smile about, if you take my meaning." We were eating breakfast the morning after the royal couple's first night together and Edwin, sitting a few yards away, scowled at him, but several of Aethelfrith's huscarls roared with laughter.

Whatever the truth of the matter, Acha was everywhere, smiling at any greetings, filling the cups of even the minor thegns and radiant in her beauty. At the time I thought little of it. Later I realised that like her brother, Edwin and their father, Aelle, the Deiran princess - now Queen of Bernicia - was politically shrewd. She knew how to play a role and had clearly realised her best chance for power and influence was through this match. To what extent she was willing to manipulate those around her to gain that power we would have to wait and see. I noticed that the old Queen Bebba's son, Eanfrith, though present for the wedding was not often visible for the celebrations and I did wonder what he thought of all of this. His mother was dead less than a year and Aethelfrith had already taken a new wife. Eanfrith was his heir, but she was Queen and nothing in our customs said that the oldest had to inherit. If Acha provided Aethelfrith with a string of sons, how safe would he be? That set me thinking about how much of all of this was the celebration of a romantic union and how much politics in disguise.

There was little disguised about the conversations Theobald had with Aedann. The Bernician prince approached my Welsh friend and again offered him a position as one of his huscarls and a parcel of conquered land north of the Wall. Aedann saw that I was watching the exchange, but he made no effort to avoid my seeing it. When I asked him later if he had changed his mind and if Theobald's offer was tempting him, he shrugged.

"Yes it is. But I don't know if I want to leave the Villa," he answered, sounding more doubtful than before and wandering off without saying any more.

Aethelfrith left it until the very last night of the week, the eve of our departure for home, to make a request of Aethelric. It appeared to be casual enough, but now I am not so sure. At the point the question was asked, Aethelfrith had been topping up Aethelric's cup with the finest red wine in his cellars, brought from distant Burgundy. Aethelric was in a jolly mood by this point and was clapping along to the music, or tapping the table to keep pace with the dancers. One of the jugglers, acting the fool, pretended to slip and fall, to gasps around the hall. Then he landed agilely, rolled and managed to catch the plates and goblets he had been playing with. Aethelric roared his approval.

It was at this moment that Aethelfrith leant across to the Deiran king sitting at his right hand and spoke. It appeared to be idle conversation, yet loud enough that a score of men and women heard it: Hussa, Theobald, Edwin, Acha, Sabert, Harald and I, with a dozen others.

143

"Your Majesty, it saddens me that you will depart on the morrow."

Aethelric nodded and smiled back at him.

"Yet I am delighted that your sister is my queen," the Bernician continued, "daughter of a noble house - a house of warriors."

"Yes, warriors," Aethelric agreed.

"Your father before you and you yourself, who fought so bravely at Catraeth," Aethelfrith's words dripped like honey from his lips.

By way of reply Aethelric belched happily.

"I look forward to the time when Deiran warriors march beside Bernician ones once again," said Aethelfrith.

"As do I," Aethelric nodded vaguely.

He had missed it, but both Sabert and I had realised where this was leading.

"My King," Sabert put in, "you look tired. Perhaps we should retire."

"Indeed, Sire, we have an early start and a long journey tomorrow," I urged him.

Aethelfrith looked over at us and a flash of anger passed across his face, but before he could speak, Edwin entered the fray. "I am sure my brother can decide when he is ready for bed without advice from you, Cerdic." The prince slurred his words, having had a good amount of wine himself.

"So," continued Aethelfrith, choosing to press on. "Shall we be brothers in arms, fellow warrior kings driving back the hordes of barbarians?"

Again Aethelric nodded then looked up in surprise as the Bernician King jumped to his feet.

"My friends, thegns and huscarls; warriors all. My queen," he added, with a tilt of the head towards Acha. "I rejoice in my new

144

bride and my land's new queen. Doubly do I rejoice, for this day the King of Deira has agreed to join with me in sending a force of mighty warriors north. Together will we destroy the Goddodin, sweep aside Strathclyde and crush the Picts. And if mac Gabráin should dare to come against us he will find twice the strength to oppose him."

The Bernician warriors roared in approval whilst the Deirans stared at Aethelric in dumbfounded shock. Aethelric looked confused and turned to Acha, who sat on the other side of Aethelfrith, "Did I just agree to that?" he asked.

Acha did not hesitate and at that moment I knew she had chosen to throw her lot in with Aethelfrith. She was no longer Acha, daughter to Aelle and princess of Deira. She was Acha, Queen of Bernicia.

"Yes, brother," she answered firmly, "you did."

I noticed Lilla looking at Aethelfrith with admiration. He caught my eye and shrugged and then fingered the icon of Loki at his throat. I knew what he was saying. The god was up to his tricks, had rolled his dice and laughed in delight as once again we were drawn into his game. Whatever was his goal I did not know, but I knew that we were off again, to war!

Chapter Thirteen
North Again

I was not surprised when Cuthbert asked me after the royal wedding if he could marry Mildrith. I could not think of any reason to say no and I was happy for them, but I was just too busy that winter raising the fyrd to organise anything before the campaign.

"Soon as we get home, Cuth. Then you can marry the girl."

"If we get home, Cerdic, if we get home," he replied gloomily. He seemed to have lost his stammer in recent weeks and I wondered if that was the effect my sister was having on him; restoring his confidence perhaps, or maybe he was just more relaxed now she was to be his wife.

"Oh, cheer up," I teased, "I just agreed to let you marry Mildrith. You should be happy."

He flashed me a shy smile, which dropped away quickly as he returned visibly to his worrying – not so relaxed then!

Aidith was not happy with us going away either, of course. At the best of times no wife wants her husband to be away for long, even less so when the man is going to war and might not come back. Added to that, by the time the men and I prepared to leave the Villa the following spring, she was still far from strong. The plague had left her weak and she was often fatigued. There were new lines around her mouth and eyes, and the colour of her skin was pale yellow, reminding me of beeswax. To me, Cuthwine seemed frail as well. It wrenched at my heart to think of leaving the little fellow. How many days would I be away? Weeks

147

certainly. When I looked at him I knew that I did not want to miss even a single day of him growing up. But I had no choice.

"It won't be for long," I told Aidith, "Sabert is in command and he and Harald have Aethelric's blessing to bring the army home by harvest time. The fighting will be over by then."

Aidith nodded, but I could see the anxiety deep in those green eyes. So I reached over and took her hands in mine. "Don't worry my love. We beat these Gododdin before. There will not be much fight left in them. Just some marching about, lining up in front of the city of Din Eidyn and they will surrender. That should satisfy Aethelfrith and then we can come home. I'm leaving Grettir here to look after you. He is getting a bit old to be in a shield wall in any event, but he will make sure no harm comes to you and Cuthwine."

I could see she was trying to smile and as we parted she gave me one last kiss. I had made it sound reasonable enough, but something in Aidith's expression suggested she did not believe it would be that easy.

Aethelfrith had managed to persuade Aethelric to send five hundred spears from Deira, maybe one half of those we would be likely to muster for home defence. That part was not so easy - not many Deirans saw the need to send an army to the far borders of Bernicia.

"What are we doing up there, Cerdic?" Cuthbert asked on the day we left. "Didn't we beat this lot at Catraeth?"

"I have told you before about second guessing the wisdom of kings, young lad," grumbled Grettir as he helped me organize the men of the Villa for departure. His scowl shut up any dissent, yet Cuthbert was not alone in asking such questions. Many outlying villages, particularly up on the moors, sent far fewer men than they should have done. Guthred in particular was stubborn in his refusal to cooperate with me, even setting his dogs on Aedann whom I had sent to deliver the summons. That was hardly surprising but his influence amongst the farmsteads and villages along the Humber was considerable and deprived me of a number of good men. That meant the burden lay on places like the Villa and Wicstun - places under the direct control of an earl. We could not so easily shirk our duty whatever our private feelings.

In fact, the reluctance of the fyrd to answer the summons and the need to gallop around visiting the villages ourselves meant that any attempt to march north in the spring was abandoned and summer was upon us before it was clear we had as many men as we would manage.

Edwin, speaking for Aethelric, had insisted that the earls ensure they each brought their allocated numbers. I did not want to give the young prince any excuse to criticise me. Despite my best efforts, however, the Southern Marches fell short by about ten men of the eighty we should have provided. Edwin was quick to point this out loudly: this despite the fact that I had brought nearer my quota than either Harald or Sabert had managed.

"Don't forget, Cerdic, that it will be me and not a jumped-up farmer who will need to explain to Aethelfrith that we have fewer men than my brother promised," Edwin scoffed.

"You?" I asked. "Forgive me, Highness, but I thought Earl Sabert was in command."

"I am," Sabert said, "but the prince has persuaded the king that he should come along and learn about war first hand."

"But you are only fifteen, Highness," I protested. "Is it wise to risk your life?" I did not really want him along because he was a pain in the arse, but I could hardly say that could I!

149

"There were boys my age in our army at Catraeth and the …
er, *hero* of Catraeth was not much older," he added, thrusting his
finger towards me, a sneer on his lips.

I was not in good spirits when I joined my friends that night at
table.

"Why the scowl, Cerdic?" Eduard mumbled, his face around a
leg of mutton.

"Edwin is coming with us."

Eduard dropped the haunch onto the table with a loud clatter
that turned heads nearby. "Great! From what you tell me, the
little runt is not going to be much company."

I glanced towards the top table, "No, he isn't."

Soon, though, we were off, north along the great Roman road,
past the Wall and eventually into the wild lands beyond. Our
arrival at Aethelfrith's forward camp swelled his army to
something like sixteen hundred men. It was as well that in the
two years since our last visit there, when we carried news of
Aelle's death, the village had grown. More houses had sprung up
and the headman's hall had been enlarged, but even so, the place
was bursting at the seams.

With his army thus reinforced, I expected that the Bernician
king would not delay long before launching his campaign. Sure
enough, after just two days he called the senior leaders from both
armies to a council of war. Edwin, Sabert, Harald and I
represented Deira, with Aethelfrith, Theobald and Hussa amongst
other nobles present for Bernicia. The Bernician leaders seemed
distracted as if anxious about some news they had not yet passed
on to us.

Aethelfrith unrolled a sheet of vellum on which a crude map
had been drawn. It was nothing like the beautiful map that Earl
Wallace had once owned and which had come into my

150

possession. That map was of Roman make and showed the lands in exquisite detail, the roads, forts and towns clearly laid out with the precision that Rome had brought to Britannia. A precision now long lost. Wallace's map had passed to my father when he became earl and in turn to me. I did not mention it; I was not certain what I thought about Aethelfrith yet, and anyway, I had not wanted my half-brother getting his hands on it, so had left it at home, but I wished now I'd brought it with me.

Prodding with a dagger point at our location Aethelfrith pointed to a cross he had marked along the coast line north of our camp. "That is Din Eidyn, a fortress on a rock and the capital of Manau Goddodin. Little more than seven hundred Goddodin warriors remain at arms; precious few of those are cavalry, thanks to Woden. Most of the Gododdin are scattered in their villages and not many in the city. If we marched soon, with the spears we command it would not be too difficult to take it. But that we cannot do."

"Why not?" Edwin asked.

Aethelfrith nodded to Hussa, who moved over to the door and gestured that someone outside should join us. A warrior entered, his cloak splattered with mud and his face etched with fatigue.

"Tell us again what you reported just now," my brother demanded.

The warrior glanced around at us, nodded and responded. "I was on patrol with a dozen men, out west a day's march. All was quiet for several days as we circled from southwest to northeast. Suddenly, the day before last, we came across a camp. A dozen or so Strathclyde warriors were there."

"Strathclyde? Why were you so far west?" Sabert asked.

"We were not that far over, my lord. I swear it. We were not in Strathclyde lands – of that I am certain. This was Gododdin territory."

I frowned, "What were they doing there then?"

The man shrugged. "I do not know. They hadn't bothered to post a watch and there was good cover nearby, so I told the men to hide and then I snuck down to the camp, away from their fire, but near enough to hear them talking."

"Well?"

"I was not there long when a couple of Goddodin horsemen rode into the camp, jumped down and greeted the Strathclyde as if in the manner of old friends."

"Friends?" Harald asked.

"More than that, I'd wager. I listened as they talked about their plans - I speak a little Welsh, you understand, enough to catch most of what they were saying."

"Plans? What plans?" Edwin asked.

"Alliance, Highness. Strathclyde has six hundred spears not two days journey away. They have agreed to march to Gododdin's aid and attack us. They believe they will outnumber us and given the element of surprise will slaughter us."

"Did they see you? Do they know that we know this?" Sabert asked.

"No, my lord. I was careful. I am certain we got away unseen."

"Then..." Harald started, but it was Hussa who reached the conclusion first that the advantage had switched to us.

"But they don't know about the Deiran army. We outnumber them. Only a little, perhaps, but if it is we who launch that surprise attack then we can finish this war quickly in one blow."

Aethelfrith's camp was to the west of the main Roman road that headed up towards Din Eidyn. From the road a hundred yards to the south a lesser track branched off westwards towards the lands of Strathclyde. From that road the Strathclyde army would come, whilst the Goddodin approached via the Roman road. Our plan was simple enough. The Deiran army relocated that morning half a mile south and west where a shallow wooded valley would provide a hiding place. The Bernicians remained in camp.

The following morning we kept the army in the low ground whilst the lords went up to the shallow ridge line and peering from around the trunks of tall ash trees, we waited. I had taken Cuthbert along with us. His eyes were sharp and after about half an hour he suddenly gestured towards the track. I squinted and after a moment I could make out what he had seen. Westwards about a couple of miles away there was movement along the track – a cloud of dust above the marching feet of hundreds of men. Shortly, the vague outline of figures became visible in the haze; then we could see spears, shields and pennants flapping over their heads.

"It's Strathclyde all right," Sabert muttered, "I recognise one of the flags. Saw that one at Catraeth."

"And there are the Gododdin, now," Cuthbert said, pointing to the north of the Bernician camp.

From the camp we could now hear the Bernician horns braying, calling our brother Saxons to arms. Soon we could see companies of Aethelfrith's men forming up. The king was taking command of the companies facing the Goddodin, whilst Theobald was closer to us and facing the Strathclyde. Hussa was not in sight, so maybe he was in reserve.

"When do we attack?" Cuthbert asked.

"Now," Edwin replied, drawing his sword.

153

I glanced at Sabert and Harald; they appeared to be waiting for me to comment. "Not yet. Not until Strathclyde is committed to the attack on the village. That is my advice."

Sabert nodded. "Just so, don't you agree Harald?"

"Indeed it is the best advice," he started to answer, but Edwin interrupted him.

"What? Why this cowardice? Are you scared, farmboy," he said scathingly to me.

"Only a fool is not scared of battle, Prince, unless, like my huscarl, Eduard, they live for the joy of battlelust. Believe me, everyone else is terrified, but fights anyway because he must. It's not cowardice," I spat, "it's bloody strategy!" I caught Sabert's faint shake of the head and added, "... er, Highness."

"Strategy? The enemy is right there marching toward the camp. Why not just attack them?"

"If we attack now, Strathclyde would maybe just run away, or move north and link up with the Gododdin. You want to win this battle don't you, my lord?"

"Of course!"

"Then we wait. We wait until they are engaged with Theobald. Then we swing out fast and hit them from behind. We trap them like a stone on a Tafael board, do you see?"

Edwin's eyes twinkled at that analogy and for once I really felt I might have got through to him.

As we organised the army in companies just below the crest of that valley, Harald wandered over and murmured in my ear, "Smart talking, Cerdic. I think he understood what you were saying to him."

"Maybe," I shrugged, for I had this little niggle of doubt.

The Wicstun Company fell into place around me, under the charging wolf banner we had carried at Catraeth. We were on the righthand side of the line, with Sabert's companies and those of Harald further to the left. Edwin and a half-company of the king's huscarls waited in reserve behind our centre. Cuthbert was the best archer in any company and we had given him three dozen skirmishers. They would run ahead of us and then veer towards the nearby village. Just outside the settlement was a small orchard. It would give them cover to fire upon the flank of the enemy.

We waited another few minutes, perhaps a quarter hour, and then moved the army up to the crest line, though still shrouded by the ash and beech trees. Cuthbert's men started filtering down the slope, taking care to stay behind the trees or in cover in the undulating ground to our right. Straight ahead of us was a ploughed field, bare and exposed ready for sowing winter wheat. Dug ground, which might be easy to bury the dead in later, I thought morbidly. I was still thinking this when Strathclyde's companies passed by on the far side of the field and formed up just fifty yards from the village. Beyond them, another five hundred yards away, I could see the Goddodin foot soldiers had also arrived. Around fifty of them were mounted. This was a worrying sight, yet not as intimidating as the three hundred horsemen that had been present at Catraeth.

"We move out when they charge the village," I announced.

"My lord!" Aedann shouted to me. He was over on the extreme right of the company with Eduard: two strong warriors to protect our flank. I glanced over at him and lifted a hand questioningly. Then I lowered it as I saw him gesturing wildly beyond the end of the line. There was a gap between the end of the army and the orchard that even now Cuthbert's men were stealthily approaching. It was not Cuthbert's nigh invisible light troops that Aedann was pointing out, however. Swinging into

155

that gap, marching quickly, were the fifty huscarls under the Wyvern Banner, the royal banner: Edwin's flag! Striding ahead of them, sword already out was the prince himself.

"Damn him!" I swore.

"Well at least the lad has balls," Eduard muttered as he stomped towards me to find out my orders.

"Not for much longer," I replied between gritted teeth. "Company advance," I bellowed. Sabert and Harald came scampering over to me.

"What in Woden's name ...?" Harald demanded and then caught sight of the prince.

"Advance *now* - everyone advance!" he yelled. "Bloody fool's going to get himself killed."

Five steps took us hurtling down the front slope of the crest, swords and armour, shield and strapping clanging and cracking. As we moved I prayed that the Strathclyde would hurry up and charge the village. Once pinned by Theobald they would not be able to turn on Edwin. Ahead of us the Strathclyde warriors were banging spears on shields, hurling abuse at Theobald and challenging him to come out and face them. Theobald stayed put and the enemy started to move forward towards him.

"Yes!" I let out an explosive breath as it seemed the gods were listening.

Then an enemy spearman saw Edwin's company approaching them and shouted in alarm. In a flash the enemy commanders were barking out orders and half of their shield wall sheared off, turned and headed straight for Edwin.

Three hundred men against fifty! The boy was surely dead.

Chapter Fourteen
Hussa the Hero

Impetuous youth that he was, Edwin kept marching towards the enemy. Then I think some common sense must have filtered between his ears, for he halted abruptly, stared for a moment and then started yelling orders. The huscarls formed up around him, locked shields and waited. The enemy bore down upon them. They were fifty yards from Edwin, whilst we were still more than three hundred paces away. Too far - much too far.

"Run, you bastards, run!" I shouted and Sabert and Harald, even Eduard and Aedann took up the call.

We were still tired from the long march north, weighed down by heavy weapons and shields and the ground was churned and muddy under foot. We weren't going to make it!

Ahead of us the British charged forward. Their centre crashed into Edwin's men, the blow sending men on both sides flying onto their backs. Spears splintered and shields shattered and then the killing began. Meanwhile, the Strathclyde warriors, outnumbering their foe six to one, started outflanking them, both wings wrapping around their enemy. Soon they would be surrounded. Then it would all be over.

Dropping out of the sky like a score of hawks swooping down upon their prey, arrows fell upon the wing nearest us. Most fell short or wide, but five struck home: five men lay dead or groaning in the mud as the warriors swept on. Cuthbert had reached his orchard and was directing his archers to target the enemy. Even as I staggered on I saw another storm of shafts fall, this time more accurately and more men went down. The enemy slowed, shields were raised to block the arrows. A smile came briefly to my face. "Good man, Cuth!" I muttered. "Keep going, you are buying us time."

Then my smile dropped. On the far side of Edwin's beleaguered band the other wing of the enemy was wrapping around between the village and his right flank. Too far away for us to reach and mostly blocked from Cuthbert's archers by Edwin's company. The first Deiran men fell, others turned as they realised the threat and started to step backwards. In moments panic would set in and then they would be finished.

I could do nothing to help for we had arrived in front of the Strathclyde right wing. Our company did not falter but charged in at them. Soon we were heavily engaged, shields crashing at they met, swords hacking down and coming back bloody. Men screaming. I let the company pass me and pulled back a step. To my left Sabert and Harald were swinging past us to charge the rest of Strathclyde's force, who now had ceased any attack on the village and had turned to face us. I left them to it and turned the other way, running to my right. I dragged Eduard and Aedann out of the fight and pulled them over towards Edwin. Beyond him the Strathclyde army had truly enveloped them and despite our aid to his left, Edwin's company was doomed.

A British warrior with a huge, two-handed sword was hacking his way into the prince's bodyguard. He cut down two huscarls in one swing and suddenly was in front of Edwin. Now we were fifty paces away, moving fast but still too far away to help him. The mighty sword went up and then swung down. Somehow Edwin managed to get his blade in the way, though the blow threw him onto his backside and he lost a grip on his shield. The huge sword went back again for the killing strike.

It never came. The British warrior let out a cry of agony and dropped the weapon and then looked down at his belly, staring in disbelief at where the end of a long sword was projecting through it. He collapsed. Behind him, a grim expression on his face, bloody sword dripping in his hand, was Hussa.

All around him, Hussa's own huscarls were cutting and slashing into the Strathclyde force. My brother's force, kept in reserve, had been thrown into the battle and arrived at the critical moment to save the Prince of Deira. Behind the enemy more horns sounded. A moment later, Theobald leapt over the barricades and led his companies out of the village in a charge that crashed into the enemy, now already heavily committed to the fight against Sabert and Harald.

After that, against all the odds, it was just a few moments before the enemy started to drop weapons, hold up hands and surrender. I could hardly believe it. Over on the other side of the battlefield I could see the Goddodin foot soldiers falling back, pursued initially by Aethelfrith's warriors until the small number of cavalry charged forward, cut some Angles down and then shielded their infantry during their retreat. Strathclyde was destroyed, the Gododdin falling back in disarray. We had won!

That night both armies celebrated the victory in Aethelfrith's camp. The battle had been light in terms of losses. The worst casualties had been, of course, amongst Edwin's company - caught in the open and outnumbered. Almost half had been killed or wounded. The other companies had fared much better. In the Wicstun Company only one lad was dead - some fellow called Alf, from Wicstun itself. Even one death causes sorrow and his family would suffer when they learned of it, but outside the boy's immediate circle there was relief that the battle had been so easy

159

for us. Caught by surprise, the army sent from Strathclyde had been almost destroyed and although the Gododdin had withdrawn blooded but mostly intact, it was clear that we Angles were on the rise and those old British kingdoms in decline. It was a plenty good enough reason for ale and song that night, but I was not so cheerful as the others. I had not forgotten Bran and Domanghast and that incident in the stone circle a couple of years before and nor, I was certain, had their father mac Gabráin. There was trouble ahead, of that I was sure.

If anyone else shared these thoughts I was not aware of it. As darkness came, the ale and mead flowed and the men sang and cheered as Lilla improvised a tale of their valour. I listened along with everyone else and then I was distracted by a huddle of figures outside the firelight. Over towards the end of the hall, to the side of his throne, Aethelfrith, Hussa and Edwin were talking. Edwin, excited and eager-faced was recounting a tale and slapping Hussa on the shoulders as he did so. Aethelfrith was smiling and nodding his head. When Edwin had finished he shook Hussa's hand once more and then returned to the high table. No one else was looking, but after Edwin had left them, Hussa turned to Aethelfrith and gave a short bow. Aethelfrith nodded at him and winked before walking across to join Edwin and picking up a goblet, drank deeply from it. As he moved away Hussa saw me watching. His dark, brooding eyes studied me for a moment before he strolled across to join his men. What was going on there, I wondered.

I went back to my friends and found that Aedann was missing. Glancing around the room I spotted him at the far end talking to Theobald. I was fairly sure they were not discussing the weather. When Theobald left a few moments later I wandered over.

"Still tempting you, is he?"

160

"Yes, Cerdic, it is tempting. Land and title; a chance of glory and more land. What can you offer me? You just want to go home and enjoy the Villa, tucked up cosy with your lovely wife and son. I don't blame you, but there's not much chance of glory there for me is there."

"I don't need glory, I have Aidith," I commented, stung by the challenge in his tone.

"Well, I don't! I hardly see you sharing *her* around - even less chance of that than sharing land," he grinned, but there was an edge to it.

"Aedann, I told you, I don't have land to spare. You expect that I can just hand it out to anyone who asks?"

"Not anyone, but to a friend: a friend whose family owned that land. It belonged to my family, Cerdic.

Fuelled by guilt, my temper flared. "It DID belong to your family. It does not now. Were it not for me you might still be a slave instead of a huscarl. Why can't you just accept your lot in life like the Welsh do who live in Eorforwic?"

"Because it is MY land; my people's land!" Aedann yelled, glaring at me.

"Not any longer!" I yelled back.

In the past we had skirted round the issue, kept our tempers in check for the sake of our friendship, but this was open confrontation and a part of me was saddened by it.

"In that case go back to your Aidith and enjoy your land," he spat. "When the army goes home I am staying here. I will take my own land and serve a lord who understands glory, not one who only understands pigs."

I recoiled at that insult for he sounded just like Edwin. "So be it. I release you from my service and the bonds to my house. I

161

hope you find your glory," I muttered and sick at heart I left him to return to Eduard and Cuthbert.

We started to think we would be going home soon. We had come north, won the battle and defeated the threat on the border of Bernicia. Now almost all the British lands that neighboured Northumbria were subdued - Elmet, Strathclyde and the Gododdin. A couple of weeks after the battle, emissaries from the latter two arrived to ask for peace. Aethelfrith negotiated even more land from them, together with an agreement to pay a tribute and not to aid any enemies of the Angles.

There were now only three powers in the North that were a threat: Rheged, the Picts and the Scots. The former we had beaten at Catraeth, but no lasting settlement had been reached. The others were separated from us by the defeated lands of the Gododdin and Strathclyde.

"We can end this campaign if we can agree a deal or pact with them, we will be secure and then we can all go home," Aethelfrith said. "So I plan to keep the army here in defence against a counter attack from Rheged."

"*What!*" I gasped.

I was not the only one. Harald and Sabert both looked up sharply.

"Your Majesty," I said, "I understood that our army was here for one campaign, one season. Now that summer is well advanced our men would expect to go home ere much longer, they will be getting anxious about the harvest ...."

Sabert and Harold nodded, but Aethelfrith ignored them.

"I am sure Prince Edwin here would not want Deira to miss out on the final campaign against Rheged that we started together at Catraeth. A chance of glory for us all, eh?"

162

I groaned. Edwin was not stupid, but he was full of dreams of glory. I had also felt that call once so I recognised the shine in his eyes.

"Surely we should consult with our king, your brother?" Harald said to Edwin.

"Yes, we can do that. You can go, Earl Harald. But the army stays here, ready for the next campaign," Edwin ordered.

Aethelfrith smiled. "Meanwhile I will send envoys to the Scots and the Picts. We will secure peace with them and then fall on Rheged."

"I find it hard to believe that the Scots will talk to us. Last time we tried it ended in bloodshed and the death of a prince," I retorted. "Why would they talk to us?"

"To get back their other prince, that is why," Hussa said. "Bran is still our captive."

"Exactly so," Aethelfrith agreed. "So then, in a week or two we will send a diplomatic mission. We will offer peace and promise to hand back their prince if they will give it to us. They can dominate all lands north of the earth wall and we all the lands between the walls."

"Who will go?" Harald asked.

"I will go!" Edwin said at once.

"That is impossible. If we send you they will just capture or kill you, My Prince," Sabert said.

"Hussa will go on behalf of Bernicia," Aethelfrith said.

"Then let his brother go too for Deira. Let Cerdic go," Edwin said, looking down his nose at me.

And because I could not think of any excuse, that was that and off I went.

Chapter Fifteen
Brothers

"You and Edwin seem very friendly all of a sudden," I said to Hussa after we had been riding in silence for most of the day. The two of us were accompanied by a couple of Hussa's own huscarls for protection, but no one else. Eduard and the others had objected to me going off alone, but I saw no reason to drag them even further north and I hoped that in my absence Harald would manage to persuade Aethelric to recall our army and then my friends at least could go home.

Hussa was scanning the horizon to the west. The early evening sun was moving around to our front and beginning to cast long shadows as it sank towards the skyline. Coupled with the low, rolling landscape and woodlands it would be almost impossible to spot anyone waiting in ambush. I shifted in the saddle, my hand straying to Catraeth's hilt. These lands belonged to Strathclyde. With the defeat of his army, their king, Rhydderch Hen, had sent his peace envoy to Aethelfrith and so in theory we were passing through lands that, if not exactly friendly, were not now hostile. Yet four men alone in the wilds would be easy prey for bandits or even a group of survivors from the recent battle who, bent on revenge, would have their share of fun out of our corpses. None of Rhydderch, Aethelfrith or Edwin would ever know if we were attacked here.

"He seems to have got the idea that I saved his life," Hussa finally replied with a brief glance my way before returning his gaze to the distance.

165

"Well you did rather, didn't you?"

"Believe me, Cerdic, the last thing I want is to go about rescuing princes of Deira. You know how I feel about the country. You do recall that most of the king's court would have happily seen me strung up after Catraeth and then again before the wedding!"

"Can you blame them? You betrayed us, Hussa. Your country, your people ..."

He glared at me, "We have been down this road and had this conversation before, brother. I felt no connection to Deira when I lived there. Even less so now."

I laughed at the irony of it.

"What do you find so amusing?"

"Saving the life of one of the heirs to the throne I think pretty much guaranteed you that connection."

He seemed to ponder this for a while. Then he shrugged. "Come on, let's pick up the pace. We have a long way to go to get to Dál-Riata. Let's see if we can reach Alt Clut tonight."

I snorted, "Hardly a place to welcome us."

"Maybe, but Rhydderch has made peace and will offer us hospitality. That is unless you would prefer to sleep out in these hills?"

I looked about me at the inhospitable countryside, made somewhat more foreboding by the gathering dusk. I shivered, "Very well," I replied, digging in my heels.

Later, when the light had almost gone, we passed a junction between a north-south road and the road we had been following from the east. Slowing the pace to spare our mounts, we turned north up the road towards Alt Clut. I was suddenly tired and felt my head nodding and my eyes heavy.

166

"Cerdic!" Hussa's sudden call brought me fully awake with a jolt.

"What is it?"

"Look down at the road."

I did. Like many roads it was a muddy, rut-filled scar across the land. Here and there stones and cobbles showed through, suggesting that it may once have been a Roman road abandoned long ago.

"Well, lots of mud! What of it?"

"Tracks!"

I peered more closely. He was right. There were hoof prints and the impressions of boots and shoes mixed in with horse turds. Tracks made by men and horses: a great many of them - all travelling south.

"It will be the army that we attacked," I suggested.

Hussa shook his head. "Why are the prints so clear just here then? We did not see many further east. And why are these so fresh? To me they look like they were made only a day or so ago. That other army had foot soldiers. They could not have been here two days ago and then attacking our camp on the same day."

I yawned, "Maybe it rained here just before they passed so that the tracks went deeper in the mud. They'd show up easier than in the dust to the east." I shrugged, wanting nothing more than to rest my weary bones. "What else could it be? Come on, let's get moving."

We pressed on, though Hussa looked unhappy and I caught him glancing down at the tracks as we rode along.

Alt Clut, ancestral home of the kings of Strathclyde, was located on the north bank of the River Clyde on and between two rocky outcrops that thrust skyward on a small peninsula projecting out into the river. The lands in the immediate vicinity were still fairly low-lying with only occasional hills. Yet, as we approached along the river, the outlines of mountains were visible to the north and to the west. It was into those highlands that we were heading come the morrow.

The path took us towards the city built near the fortress and then, just before it entered the city walls, it branched and we followed the southerly route, which led us through a high wooden palisade built across the neck of land leading into the small peninsula. Once through the wall we found ourselves amongst a collection of shacks and huts housing blacksmiths, tanners, farriers and store houses. Beyond these, overshadowed by two watch towers high up on the rocky outcrops, was a king's hall. We dismounted, left the horses with our escorts and walked towards it.

As we passed across the open space, which was lit by flaring torches, I was aware of the hostile stares directed at us by the Strathclyde warriors scattered about on the wall and up on the towers. But I noticed something else: there were very few of them; remarkably few men at arms considering this was the palace of their king.

"There are only - what - fifty men? Not many," Hussa observed echoing my thoughts. "Maybe we did kill or capture most of their army at Catraeth, or else earlier this summer."

"We? It was not *we* at Catraeth, Hussa! You were on their side then and don't you forget it. But that is the point. You will know better than I. They had what - two hundred men there?"

Hussa shrugged, "Yes, about that."

"Few got home. If we accounted for another three hundred this year then maybe there really are only a handful left. It makes sense that they agreed to peace then - doesn't it?"

168

Hussa said nothing, but he still did not look happy. Was he thinking about those tracks again?

"So these are the envoys of the great Kings of Northumbria?" King Rhydderch asked us on being presented to his court. The king was an old man, perhaps the same age as Aelle was when he died - or not much younger. Lilla told tales of his wars when he was a youth, but that was long ago and Rhydderch seldom left his fortress these days. His armies, such as those he had sent to Catraeth five years before and to attack us this time, were commanded by his sons and lords.

"Yes, Your Majesty. We bring messages of peace to you and seek permission to travel on through your lands to Dál-Riata."

"Peace that you have forced upon us, bought by the blood of our men when you ambushed and attacked us."

"With respect, my lord, it was *your* army on its way to attack *us*, which we ambushed." I shook my head, adding, "The chances of fate and fortune in the game of war."

"A game Aethelfrith has won *this* time."

I glanced at him sharply. What did he mean 'this time'? Hussa picked up on it too, "Surely there need be no next time, now we are at peace?" he asked.

Rhydderch smiled a thin smile. "I am hardly in a position to argue. You slaughtered my army and as you see around you, I have few other fighting men left. But you will forgive me if I am reluctant to spend time with the enemy of my people. I will have you shown to your room and food and drink brought to you - fear not, it will not be poisoned! - then you may sleep here tonight and be about your business in the morning."

169

The following morning we were up very early. Feeling the hostility of our hosts we were eager to depart and were underway before dawn. The roads became even worse the further north and west we travelled. Soon the land began to rise around us. Hills became mountains separated by deep lakes and dense forests, which channelled blasts of icy wind along the roads. My spirits sank as I rode on. The mountains and lakes were magnificent, but I felt so very far from home. I had begun to believe my chances of once again seeing Aidith and little Cuthwine were diminishing by the day.

Finally we forded yet another river and emerged onto a low-lying plain. The mountains were away to the north and ahead of us a river twinkled in the sunlight as it meandered across a boggy, marshy land. In the centre of the plain was a single, steep-sided hill and perched on the top an imposing fort. We had come at last to Dunadd, the capital and chief fortress of the kings of Dál-Riata.

As we approached the fortress we were under constant observation from the high stone walls that loomed above us. The path slanted uphill and entered the fortress through a rocky defile. This natural, narrow passageway had been turned into a superbly defensible portal. We passed a pair of huge wooden gates, which would have provided a challenge to any attacker, pelted and fired upon as they would be from those walls as they assaulted up though the narrow channel.

We emerged into an outer courtyard and were challenged by an imposing warlord, who peered at us with dark green eyes beneath a pair of bushy, black eyebrows. He spoke to us in Gaelic at first, but neither I nor Hussa spoke the tongue. He did not understand our English, so we communicated who we were in Welsh, which Hussa spoke well and myself hesitatingly. He

170

introduced himself as Felnius, Captain of the King's Guard. I mentioned that we had news of Bran for the king.

"Which way did you come here?" he asked.

"By way of Alt Clut and the lands of Strathclyde," I answered, thinking he was curiously interested in our travel arrangements, but I let it pass.

He glanced at our horses and nodded. "Come with me," he ordered and led us across the space full of workshops between the outer and inner walls. There was the usual array of blacksmiths and so forth, but we passed more than one hut in which men were smelting gold and silver. I paused at one to take a closer look and saw a smith pouring molten metal into moulds. Another was breaking open the moulds to reveal exquisitely detailed necklaces, almost as beautiful as my mother's had been. These lands might be wild, but their craftsmen were skilled, their kings and lords were wealthy and their coffers full of the spoils of victory.

I watched a moment until Felnius turned and beckoned me to catch up. We passed through a further archway into yet another courtyard. I expected to see the great hall here, but instead was greeted by further workshops and the dwelling places of the king's warriors, men who eyed us warily as we passed, then returned to sharpening their axes and huge, two-handed swords. Another doorway led to a third open space, this time with finer and better appointed structures, presumably populated by the lords and ladies of the court. I was aware that I was gawping like a country boy, but I had never seen such grandeur before. Finally, a fourth gateway led up even higher, to the very summit. Here at last was the king's hall.

Like many of the buildings around us, the hall was made from slate and granite slabs, insulation against the harsh winters, I

171

thought, but cool perhaps in the summers. It was a huge, round building with a steeply-sloped roof. We passed more of the king's guards and walked through a narrow doorway into the interior, which was lit by torches and a roaring fire in a central pit.

Sitting in a throne carved from a block of granite was a middle-aged man of perhaps five and forty years, or maybe a little older. Across his knees lay a sword. His chin was bare but he wore hair on his upper lip, drooping to either side of his mouth and dark brown, like the long, straight hair on his head, though with hints of grey about it. He was garbed in a kilt and sandals and a green shirt that left his arms bare. I could see these were muscular but scarred: here was a man who has seen more than one battle and lived to tell the tale, I thought. A man accustomed perhaps to victory. He wore gold rings on his arms, finely wrought, as was the torque around his neck. This then was Áedán mac Gabráin, King of the Scots of Dál-Riata. He studied us carefully as we entered.

"Did you kill my son?" he demanded, brushing aside our greeting. "Are you one of those who killed Domanghast?"

I glanced at Hussa briefly, but answered at once. We had expected this question, albeit not in such an abrupt way.

"No, my lord, Prince Domanghast died in battle."

"That is a lie!" mac Gabráin spat, leaping to his feet, one hand wielding the sword.

"You speak the truth, Sire," another man put in. I recognised him. It was Aethelfrith's cousin, Herring. "He was cut down in cold blood, he was murdered."

"That is not quite what happened," I protested. "It is unfortunate, but tempers ran high and voices were raised on both sides. Yet it was Domanghast and Bran who started the fight," I tried to explain.

172

"You would say that, Angle," Herring replied.

"You are an Angle too, Herring," Hussa put in. "A man in exile and in whose interest it is to paint Aethelfrith as the culprit here."

"Who are you two anyway? I don't remember you from before I left, yet I recall your faces. You were there at the stone circle; you were with Aethelfrith and yet you are not Bernicians, are you?"

I shook my head. "We are Deirans, at least, we were both born there. I still live there. I am Cerdic, son of Cenred and Earl of the Southern Marches. Hussa here is ... from Deira, but now serves the King of Bernicia."

"How so? I wager there is a tale there?" Herring asked.

"I am not interested in the tales of you two runts," mac Gabráin said, coming closer. "I want to know what happened two years ago and I want to know where my other son is. The captain of my guard says you bring news of him. Speak quickly. If you were there when my son died I could order you killed here and now."

"If you do that, Sire," I replied, "then there is no chance of your seeing Prince Bran again. Aethelfrith wants peace and sent us to carry that message."

The king stared me down. "I am told that Manau Goddodin and Strathclyde have made peace and that only Rheged remains at war. Aethelfrith just wants peace so he can finish off what he started at Catraeth. Then with the Britons defeated it will be we Scots who are next on his list."

I thought of Aethelfrith and his plan to rest out the winter. Then what? He had spoken vaguely of falling on Rheged, but no other indication of when or how. He had told us that our mission here would be the end of the matter and yet I recalled his words when I spoke before of the hopes for peace with Dál-Riata: *"There never was much chance of that. Not for long anyway. Conflict with these, like with the British, is inevitable if we are to expand and grow."*

173

Mac Gabráin was not stupid. I think he saw something of this in my eyes.

"You know it is true, Angle. Aethelfrith is a wolf who would devour us all. Nothing will sate his hunger till we all lie bloody at his feet."

"That is not true," I replied weakly.

The king snorted and stalked towards the door. "Follow me, Deirans," he ordered and did not wait for a reply. Felnius indicated that we should do as we were bid.

Mac Gabráin led us out of the building into the brightly lit courtyard. Then he turned and climbed up the hill, which rose still a little higher. We followed. The path took us to a flat area on the very top of the fortress where a single beacon flared into the sky. Here the stone had been cleared, flattened and then carved. There were strange markings in runes that I could not read and the carving of a wild boar. This was reproduced in black on a white background on the flags that flapped about us and I knew it to be the symbol of the mac Gabráins. The king walked towards another symbol: a man's footprint incised into the bare rock.

"You see that? My ancestor Fergus had that made more than a hundred years past when he conquered this land. He made it to show that he was both part of the land and master over it. My grandfather, my uncle, my father and I each in turn stepped into it when we became kings. We claim the land as we do so. Now look out there."

He pointed west and a little south to where the river that passed the base of Dunadd flowed into the sea. There was a wide bay there - a perfect anchorage. It was some miles away, but lit by the rising moon I could make out the shapes of boats: quite a lot of them.

174

"That and a hundred other bays and coves are where my people came ashore from Ireland. We are not natives. Like you we came from over the sea - you from the East and we from the West. We came to carve out a new land for ourselves. My domains stretch right up the coast for a hundred and fifty miles. I have thousands of my people here now. We are expanding, pushing Strathclyde and the Picts back, forcing them to make peace with us on *our* terms. So you see, I know Aethelfrith, though we have never met. I know him because I am him and he is me. We are conquerors and victors. We are wolves."

Hussa, I noted, did not deny any of this. Instead he asked a question.

"If that is so, what then of Bran? Even a wolf cares for his pack. If there were a chance to save your son would you not take it?"

The king's face grew pale and I put myself in his place. I thought of Cuthwine, and how I would feel if my own son was lost, how indeed I had felt when Millie was taken from us. For the first time I saw him not as a powerful king but as a grieving father.

Mac Gabráin was silent for a moment. He looked down at the sword in his hand. "This was Domanghast's, you know," he said suddenly. "One of his men brought it back from where he died. It is all I have left of him." He stared out from the fortress eastwards towards that distant stone circle.

Then he sighed and turned to me, "The answer is yes, yes I would take that chance. You can stay here tonight and then go back. Go back to Aethelfrith and tell him I will come in the spring. I will come and meet him and we will talk. Now leave me!"

Felnius led us to a small hut near the king's hall. "Your men can sleep in the stables. You two can use this tonight. It belonged

175

to a man who died at the stone circle. No one uses it now," he said simply and pulled the door to.

The hut was basic: a bed to one side, a single chair and a table. A fire burned low in a central firepit and did little to dispel the chill in the room.

"So much for Irish hospitality, eh," Hussa muttered as he threw himself on the bed.

I grunted, tossed my pack onto the floor near the fire where I guessed I would sleep and poked at the embers to try to stir them into life. There was a knock at the door and a guard opened it. A maid entered and placed a tray on the table with a jug of ale, two goblets and bowls, a hunk of bread and a steaming pot of stew. Without saying a word, they left.

"Well, we might as well enjoy the food," Hussa said, as he ladled chunks of lamb into his bowl and tore off some bread. "You noticed the bay?" he asked between mouthfuls.

"It seemed full of ships, you mean?" I said, gulping down the stew. It was not bad.

"Yes, lots of them. Now why so many do you suppose?"

"Dál-Riata is a seagoing power. It needs ships," I suggested.

Hussa grimaced, "Yes it does, but you would expect them scattered up and down the coast. Why so many here?"

"Maybe we should go look?"

Hussa nodded. "Tomorrow then," he said.

The following morning we were up early saddling our horses and making ready to depart. Felnius joined us in the lower courtyard and escorted us to the entrance. There we found a patrol of half a dozen warriors mounted just outside.

"My men will set you on your way," he explained in a voice that allowed for no discussion.

We set out at once, eastward through the bog towards the road that would take us to Alt Clut. Hussa coughed and I looked across at him. He scowled at me and I knew what he was thinking: how could we investigate the bay on the west coast with this escort taking us east?

We rode on for an hour, ambling along before Hussa spoke to the sergeant in charge of the riders. The man's Welsh, like our own, was patchy but we got through.

"How far along this way are you going?"

"As far as the road beyond Loch Gachan there," the man pointed to the small lake we were skirting. On the far side was the track that wound its way around this convoluted coastline to distant Alt Clut.

It took about another hour to circle the lake to the road. Once there, the patrol sat on their mounts and watched us ride away northeastwards. This we obediently did, staying in plain view until at last we passed out of sight into low hills. There we sent our two escorts on ahead to carry a message to Aethelfrith that mac Gabráin was coming in the spring for talks, but that we had something to investigate before we returned. When they had ridden away, we allowed our horses to graze. Taking it in turns to keep watch while the other dozed, we waited out the day.

Finally, under cover of darkness, Hussa and I rode back the way we had come. Keeping Dunadd on our right, silhouetted against the starry sky, we circled the fortress. At last we came round a hill and rode down into a bay: more of a lake, which emptied at one end into the sea just visible far to our left. Projecting out into the still water were the wooden quays of a harbour crammed with fifty or more longships, with tall masts projecting like a bare forest into the sky. Facing the lake and

177

surrounded on three sides by a wooden fence, was a large settlement: the shipbuilders' dwellings no doubt.

"Is it an invasion fleet? What do you think?" I asked Hussa.

As he opened his mouth to reply we heard the sudden clatter of horses' hooves on the road behind us.

"I'll tell you what I think," a voice growled, "I think you should have gone home when you had the chance."

Spinning round, we saw Felnius and Herring riding out of the gloom where they must have been hiding, listening to our every word. They were accompanied by twenty warriors.

"Alas, I don't think you will be going home now, or ever!" Herring said.

Chapter Sixteen
Winter

"You should have gone home as I suggested, Angles. You would have been safely on the way to Alt Clut and far from here," mac Gabráin said.

We had been marched back to his fortress and then our weapons taken from us before we were thrust into a cell dug deep into the rock of Dunadd beneath the main hall. There we were chained to the walls. There was no window and when the door was shut we were plunged into darkness with only the dripping of water down the cold walls and the sound of rats scuttling around to keep us company. We were left for what felt like days, each one interrupted only by a guard bringing us skins of water and crusts of rock-hard, often mould-encrusted bread, or coming in to take away and empty the one bucket that Hussa and I shared, stinking, between us.

We were half-brothers and yet we hardly knew each other. Nor did we like each other much. But you cannot be chained up with a man in conditions of such deprivation - a man you cannot even see - without getting to know him better. Before his betrayal we had shared very few conversations and on the occasions we had spoken since it had always been about the army or the plans of kings, and not much else. But bit by bit and day by day we started to talk of little things: of people we knew in Wicstun; a particular brew of ale we discovered we both enjoyed; about old Grettir and a certain day we remembered when as youths we'd trained with him in the woods, or any of a hundred and one other topics.

179

Sometimes we spoke of our fears for the future and of lost hopes and dreams, for it seemed unlikely that mac Gabráin would let us out of there alive.

We might almost have become friends, save for two obstacles: the ghost of our father, his guilt and his sorrow, seemed always to stand between us, and so while we talked of many things, by unspoken agreement we both skirted around the issues of our different childhoods, which had always festered between us and would lead only to anger. Secondly, though I started to feel that I might even be ready to understand and forgive his betrayal, there was a barrier there: a point beyond which it seemed Hussa would not go, for whenever I hinted that this might be the start of a new fraternal relationship, he fell silent and I learnt to avoid that line of conversation. Yet there in the dark, no longer sure if it was night or day, wondering if we were fated to be buried forgotten in this hellhole until we died, I think that were it not for my brother's company, I would certainly have descended into raving madness.

Maybe a week after being incarcerated - though I had lost track of the days - the door was flung open and in the flickering torchlight that hurt our eyes, mac Gabráin, Herring and Felnius loomed over us. Half a dozen of the king's largest huscarls waited in the outer chamber, presumably in case we tried anything. Not that we could. We were still chained to the wall and even had we not been, we were stiff, weak from lack of food, filthy and exhausted, both of us with running sores where the manacles had rubbed our ankles and the lice and fleas had made a meal of us.

"You were meant to be carrying a message of peace back to your kings. But no, you had to sneak back and spy on us. You had to go to the harbour and see our fleet," mac Gabráin said, wrinkling his nose in disgust as he gazed down at us.

180

"Why are you so worried about that if you have nothing to hide?" I mumbled. "It's an invasion fleet isn't it? Where are you going with it?"

Herring stepped forward and struck me a violent blow across the face and when he stepped back I could see my blood on his arm and feel it tricking down my chin.

"We will ask the questions and you will answer," Herring spat, his fists bunched.

"So then," mac Gabráin grinned, "now you will tell me what I want to know. How large are the Northumbrian armies and what is Aethelfrith's plan? Where will he attack next spring?"

"Sire, you are wrong. Aethelfrith and Edwin want only peace," I mumbled, knowing I was lying. Edwin might want peace - I was not even sure of that - but Aethelfrith certainly did not, and this Irish Scot knew it as well as I.

Mac Gabráin shook his head. "I told you last week, Aethelfrith is a wolf. He will always be wanting to attack and expand. It is his way. So let's try again. *Where* is he heading? Where is he going next?"

"I have no idea. I told you already we came here to arrange peace. Prince Edwin wants to take the army home as soon as we are sure there'll be no more war."

The king snorted. "Edwin of Deira might want that, but what does Aethelfrith want?" he asked, echoing my own thoughts.

"He wants peace," said Hussa. "We would not have come here if he did not. Why else would he have sent us as his envoys?"

Mac Gabráin plainly did not believe this and I could not blame him because, to be honest, I did not believe Hussa myself. Aethelfrith was not the type to want peace unless it was on terms that suited his purposes. I was fairly sure he had only been stalling for time when he sent us here.

181

The king was thinking this too for he again shook his head. "No! That does not follow. Aethelfrith is up to something and I want to know what it is."

Now it was I shaking my head. "Even if he is up to something, we don't know what it is, Sire. We are just simple envoys. King Aethelfrith does not divulge his plans to the likes of us."

The king regarded me thoughtfully, but Herring stepped forward and thrust a finger towards Hussa. "What about you? If you serve Aethelfrith as you say you do you must know what he is plotting. Tell us now."

Hussa shrugged. "I don't know anything either. I am not a king or a prince, nor even a noble - just a captain of the king's guard. Why would he entrust me with his plans?"

The king's face grew grim and threatening. "If in truth the pair of you know nothing then I am afraid you are in for a very long, cold and painful winter. We will leave you to think about that." Turning on his heel mac Gabráin stomped out of the cell.

Herring took a step closer to me and then leant forward, jabbing my chest with his index finger. "I don't believe you. You will tell us what we want to know. You will tell us what my cousin is up to."

Hussa gave a derisive snort. "What has mac Gabráin promised you if you help him to defeat Aethelfrith? You will be King of Bernicia in your cousin's place, perhaps? You surely cannot believe the Bernicians will accept you back? If you help Dál-Riata defeat us, *everyone* will see you as a traitor."

Herring's eyes widened in anger, "What do you know of it, a man without a nation?"

"Oh, I know a great deal about how a man like you would be received at home," Hussa shrugged. "I would suggest you give up any hope of a glorious homecoming and make what life you

182

can as a minion in your new adopted country, at mac Gabráin s beck and call," he sneered.

Herring's arm went back to strike him a massive blow and he lunged towards my brother, but Felnius called sharply from the doorway, "Come along, Herring, time for that later. Let them think on it for a while."

His arm arrested at the top of its swing, Herring glared at us then swung away and strode out of the cell. The door slammed shut behind him, plunging us into darkness once more.

"Idiots," muttered Hussa.

"Idiots or not, they are out there and we are in here."

That was the problem. Outside summer was fading to autumn. I imagined myself at home. Grettir would ensure that the harvest was gathered. The barn and the food stores would soon be bulging with smoked meats, salted pork, the best cheese, ale, dried fruits and grains in Deira. The thought of it drew saliva into my mouth and I spat, trying to ignore the hunger pains in my gut. With the nights closing in, my people would come to the great hall for food, drink and company. I missed them. I missed the work on the estate. I missed the laughter and the teasing and I missed even grumpy old Grettir.

But more than all of this I missed my family. I missed Mother, Mildrith, Aidith and little Cuthwine. As the leaves fell from the trees and the days grew short and cold, was he asking his mother where I was? Was he asking for his father? What could Aidith tell him? That I would come home? Each day that I did not return she would look northwards along the Roman road that led to these wild lands and ask herself the same question. And each night as she closed up the Villa she would wonder whether I ever would return.

Each day that we were left to rot in this awful cell with no hint of light and just mouldy food to sustain us, I had the same thoughts. There was, however, another thought ever present on my mind. Or rather, a fear that gnawed at me and twisted my empty guts into knots. I have felt the fear of battle more than once. A man is a fool if he is not afraid when the enemy bears down upon him. Yet he can do something about that fear. He can roar and shout and hammer sword on shield. He has men by his side, can feel that company around him and knows they will stand with him. In that dark cell with just my treacherous half-brother for dubious company, I felt no such comfort. For here it was the fear of being tortured that weighed upon me like a stone tied round my neck. I tried to keep count of the days, but each day I felt myself growing weaker and I knew Hussa felt the same. We had stopped talking long since, neither having the energy even had there been anything left to say.

They left the two of us alone for what by my reckoning was another week before they returned. First they took Hussa away. They did not take him far, however, for I could hear him screaming. I heard thumping and banging and the scraping of metal on stone. Finally, I could hear him whimpering. They dragged him back into the cell and from the brief flash of light as the door opened I could see that his face was swollen and bloody.

When they had fastened his chain and shut the door I reached out towards him, but as my hand touched him I felt him recoil.

"Hussa, it's me, Cerdic, how are you?"

"You damn fool! How do you think I am?" he asked between gasps.

"Sorry, stupid question. I meant are you all right? What did they ask you?"

There was a groan as Hussa dragged himself closer to the wall and slumped against it. "The same as before: what Aethelfrith is up to, what his plans are, where he is taking his armies come the spring."

I sighed. "But we don't know that do we?"

Hussa did not answer.

"So this is it then. They will torture us until they finally realise that fact, and then they'll kill us," I sighed.

Hussa barked out a dry, cough-like laugh. "Yes, it's going to be a fun winter isn't it?"

I expected that our captors would come for me at once. But they did not. They let the days drag on by and each day the anticipation grew worse until one day I yelled out, "Come on you bastards, come and take me if you want me!" But all I heard in response was silence.

I calculated from the daily ration of bread and water that it was sixteen days after Hussa's ordeal that they finally came for me. I think I was dozing, but in total darkness day after day, the mind starts to play tricks, so when the door scraped open and two guards stepped into the cell, I was not sure at first if they were real. In the flash of light from the doorway I caught sight of my brother and I would not have recognised him. Beneath a new straggly beard his bruised face was gaunt and pale and his eyes had a haunted look as he cowered against the wall. I supposed I must look much the same. The guards unfastened my manacle, lifted me under my shoulders and dragged me out. I was halfway along the corridor outside before I realised my time had come; my turn to be beaten to a pulp.

"I don't know anything," I muttered, as they propped me on my feet.

185

There was laughter from the corner of the room they brought me to. Squinting against the light I saw Herring standing there with Felnius.

"Oh, don't spoil our fun; it's our job to find that out," Herring said drawing a long blade that looked a little like a seax and then dragging the blade along a stone so that it made a terrifying scraping sound that set my teeth on edge.

"Shall we begin?" He said with a deep growl as he stepped closer to me and waved the knife back and forth.

My eyes were drawn to the point of his weapon as it circled inches from my face and I, like a young hare pinned by the malevolent stare of a stoat, could not look away from it, so did not notice Felnius moving round to my left until his fist smashed in to my belly, blasting the air out of my lungs. I collapsed to the ground gasping for breath, wheezing, "I told you, I don't know anything!"

"And we told you we wanted to ask the questions," Felnius hissed as he loomed above me.

I tried to climb to my feet, but before I could do so a boot kicked me in the ribs and I went down again. "Tell us where your army is going to attack in the spring!"

As I floundered on the ground I craned my neck upwards and fixed Felnius with what I hoped was a defiant glare. "I don't know!" There was the crack of a whip and searing pain tore across my shoulders.

"Tell us!" Herring demanded.

And so it continued.

Eventually they tired of their sport and I was tossed back into the cell. From then on our captors took it in turns to torture me and Hussa. It went on day after day until just the sound of the cell door opening had me shaking and gibbering, shamed by my relief

186

when they took my brother instead of me. I don't think either Felnius or Herring actually believed we knew anything. It did not matter whether we did or not. Like all bullies, they simply enjoyed tormenting helpless victims. Always they stopped short of life-threatening injuries, yet seemed able, by various means, to inflict excruciating pain. After a while and to my eternal shame, in desperation I told them some facts about the Angles' army, but whether I told the truth or lied, the torture and the beatings continued.

As the weeks went by time blurred and I lost all track of the passing days. After that I think I just accepted that I would die there. Indeed, I had begun to long for the release of death and thinking to hasten it stopped eating. We were both emaciated and riddled with pus-erupting sores by this time and our captors, perhaps fearing they would soon lose their sport, sent in a horse surgeon to clean and salve our wounds. On his instructions, bowls of greasy mutton stew now accompanied the daily ration of stale bread; we were given ale instead of water and a torch was left burning in the cell for a while each day – to stop us losing our wits, he said. It was enough to start me eating again, my will to survive flickering back into life along with thoughts of Aidith and my son.

One day I found myself thinking back to the deal I had struck with the trickster god. Was this part of his plan for me? Was Loki laughing at my expense - I who had dared to bargain with him?

"Hussa, do you believe the gods have plans for us?" I said into the darkness, for the torch had burned out and would not be replaced until the morrow.

I heard my brother groaning as he stirred from the half asleep, half awake state we both seemed to drift into. Hussa had been back in the cell for maybe an hour after his latest ordeal, which seemed to have gone on even longer than usual. It may not have been the best time to ask such a question and his voice was sour as he spoke.

"I think they laugh at us a lot. I don't think they care much what happens to a man, though. If they have plans for us they haven't shared them with me."

"My friend Aedann is a Christian ..."

Hussa snorted, "He is Welsh and most of them are. So what?"

"He says that God has laid plans for everyone and if we put our faith in him as the one god we will be saved."

"One god? The Christians believe there is only *one* god? Does that make sense to you? Do you see one all-powerful guiding mind behind our lives? Doesn't the world seem chaotic, brutal and dark to you? No, brother, our gods are real enough. Their arguing and plotting is what causes the chaos of our lives. That is what makes sense to me and that is why I worship Loki, brother."

I considered this for a moment. Odd that he and I should both worship Loki, I thought. "Hussa - do you have his symbol, Loki's I mean?"

"Yes," he answered, "Lilla gave me one."

"You too?" What was the storyteller up to? What game was he playing with my brother and me? Sometimes I wondered if there was not a little of the trickster god in him as he did so like to be part of all the big events - almost as if he himself was controlling them. My fingers strayed to the pendant at my neck and not for the first time I wondered why Herring and Felnius had allowed me to keep it. Did they fear its power or was it just unimportant? After all they could take it from me whenever they cared to.

We fell into silence again as I pondered our predicament. Mac Gabráin had gathered a fleet. Through the winter he could add to it and come the spring he could take an army anywhere he wished. There was no way he would let Hussa and me go free with that information. We did not know where he was heading, of course. However, it seemed likely, given the fact that Aethelfrith had slain his one son and captured the other, that he was going east. The Scots of Dál-Riata were powerful and their army numerous. If it fell upon the Angles, it would go very bad for us.

"Hussa?"

"What now?"

"We need to find out where mac Gabráin's army is going and then escape with that knowledge, brother."

Hussa didn't answer at first. We had, of course, discussed this at length before we became so weak. Escape had seemed hopeless enough back then; even more so now, yet from somewhere inside me I had found a renewed determination to try. I supposed I could thank the horse surgeon for that, for I felt much stronger despite the frequent beatings.

"Hussa, we need to escape," I repeated.

There was a rustling, clanking sound as Hussa came closer. I could not see him, but I could feel his breath on my cheek as he whispered to me, "Aethelfrith worries me, Cerdic."

"What? I thought you his loyal captain."

"Well, I was. But I am worried how far he will go in his ambition."

"What you mean?"

"You were there that day at the stone circle. He started that fight over a minor disagreement. He did not seem bothered that he had just started a war with the Scots. He just wants to keep fighting and expanding and does not care what or whom he sacrifices to do it."

"Why are you telling me this now?"

Hussa did not answer and for a moment he seemed to be considering what to say. "Because of what he asked me to say to mac Gabráin," he said eventually.

"Well, we carried that message didn't we? We passed on Aethelfrith's offer of peace."

My brother gave a rasping laugh. "There was another message, Cerdic."

"Eh? What message?"

"One I had to wait to say. I had to let mac Gabráin believe he had tortured it out of me. I had waited long enough and today when the two thugs started on me I submitted and asked to see mac Gabráin. I was taken to his hall."

"*What!* Why? I don't understand."

"If I had just broken down and told mac Gabráin at the start he would have guessed it was a trick. This way he now thinks he knows where Aethelfrith is heading in the spring. He will go there with his army."

"What are you talking about? What message?" I said, still trying to get my head around what my brother was saying.

"I told him that Aethelfrith is taking the army into Rheged. We've defeated Strathclyde and the Gododdin and so now only Rheged remains of the British. I told mac Gabráin that Aethelfrith means to attack the frontier fortress of Degsastan, capture it and march on to Lugvalium."

I would have stared at Hussa if the room had not been black as pitch. Instead I shook my head and recoiled from him. Was my brother destined always to be a betrayer? "You told them *that*?" I hissed. "You do realise that now you've given Dál-Riata our plans, instead of the Angles just facing Rheged, one thousand of mac Gabráin's Scots will be on their way to Degsastan as soon as the winter storms are over?"

"Yes," he said patiently as though talking to a child. "That is exactly why Aethelfrith told me to give that information to mac Gabráin."

I gaped, "What are you saying? He *wants* the Scots there?"

"Exactly! Aethelfrith is gambling on smashing all opposition in the North in one huge battle."

"So *that* is why he persuaded Edwin to keep the army in the North," I said as Aethelfrith's plan slowly dawned on me.

"Indeed, but as I said earlier, I am worried because I think Aethelfrith is overreaching himself; he has gambled too much …" Hussa stopped speaking and spat then swore. "Another tooth gone, damn those bastards, I'll be forced to eat slops if I lose any more!"

I sympathised, I too had lost a couple of teeth and of those remaining two more felt loose. I pondered what Hussa had said about the Bernician king. "Why do you think that about him?" I asked.

"Because it won't just be Dál-Riata and Rheged at Degsastan. While I was in the king's hall I saw other men there: Nechtan, King of the Picts and Rhydderch, King of Strathclyde were present. Mac Gabráin has not been idle this winter. He has gathered his allies. We have made many enemies, brother, we Angles, and mac Gabráin has persuaded all of them to join him. If we attack Degsastan we will be fighting them all at once."

"Then we really have to get away and warn Aethelfrith!" I exclaimed. "If we don't, our armies will be annihilated! But it is hopeless. We haven't got a way out of here." I subsided against the wall in despair.

"No?" Hussa said. "Earlier you asked me if I believed the gods had plans for us. Well perhaps now is the time to see."

Before I could ponder his words, outside in the corridor I heard footsteps approaching and my heart sank. Was this our executioner coming for us? Now they had the information they wanted they had no more use for us. Mac Gabráin may well have ordered our deaths and I knew that Herring and Felnius would be delighted to carry out that order, bored with tormenting us at last.

"Now is the time, brother," Hussa said.

"What?" I said absently as I listened to the footsteps approaching the door and prepared to die. *Goodbye Aidith, my love. I will wait for you in Valhalla. Raise our son to be ...*

"Put your trust in Loki and all will be well," Hussa said urgently.

I shrugged and in the darkness my hand moved to Loki's symbol around my neck. In silence I sent a prayer to the god asking for his protection. The footsteps stopped at the door and there was the clatter of keys, the scrape as one slid into the lock.

Then a creak as the door opened.

Chapter Seventeen
Escape

When I saw who was standing in the doorway, a torch flaring in his hand, I was convinced I must be asleep and dreaming. Or alternatively, the torture, fatigue, starvation and sheer desperation must have finally taken its toll and I had indeed gone mad. For there, standing tall, was an impossible figure.

Lilla the bard!

Lilla my old friend; swathed in a great, floor-length, hooded cloak and exuding all his usual charm, his lips lifted in a warm smile, his fingers squeezing the end of his nose.

"Evening boys, I have to say what a very unpleasant place you had found to lodge in since I last saw you. These Irish Scots are reputed to be hospitable fellows, but this accommodation does seem a little basic. I would ask for my money back if I were you!"

"Lilla! What in the name of Woden's buttocks are you doing here?" I stuttered.

"Well, I have to say that is a quite fascinating story, Cerdic. Would you like to hear it?"

Hussa was on his feet straining at his chain, "Another day, Lilla," he muttered. "This is not the place for tales. All the same, I was glad to see you had turned up on time when I went to see mac Gabráin. Let's get out of here!"

My jaw dropped. What else had Hussa not told me? He did not seem anywhere near as surprised as I to see Lilla. Indeed, it was clear my brother was expecting him. I wanted to ask if he had known the bard was coming to rescue us and if so, how. And how

193

had Lilla known of our capture and where we were being held? More to the point, how in Loki's name had he persuaded our gaolers to part with the keys? None of it made any sense. My tired brain was teeming with questions, but Hussa was right - tales could wait for later.

"What about these," I asked, lifting up my foot to reveal the manacle tight around my ankle.

"Ah yes," said the bard, holding out a set of keys. "One of these should fit."

One of them did, but not our manacles, only the large padlock by which our chains were fixed to a ring in the wall. "No matter," Lilla said, unlocking it. "I have a solution. Come this way."

He led us, chains clanking, away from the guardroom and along the corridor to the chamber in which we had endured such pain. Gazing down at the bloodstained floor, the whip and instruments of torture hanging on the wall, I hesitated at the doorway, reluctant to enter it again.

"Come on, quickly Cerdic, over here, we don't have all night." Placing the torch in a bracket on the wall, Lilla moved to a small anvil in the corner. I saw that he held a hammer in one hand and an iron spike in the other. I joined him and winced as he positioned my foot on the anvil, smashed the lock on my manacle then used the spike to prise it apart. Once freed, I stepped aside to allow Hussa access to Lilla and bent to rub the welts at my ankle. The relief was exquisite.

"Thank you, Lilla. Now what?" Hussa asked, peering at the doorway.

"Indeed, boys, now what? Well, firstly, I found something of yours in the guard room. I wonder if perhaps you may need these," he said, lifting his hands. The objects he now showed us he must have had secreted somewhere on his person, mayhap

194

inside that great cloak of his, but I would be lying if I said I saw from where he produced them, for as if by magic, in a flash his hands were grasping three weapons. In one, which he now stretched out towards me, were Catraeth and my longsword and in the other was Hussa's fine blade. As my fingers wrapped themselves around Catraeth's hilt, I felt suddenly a whole lot better. I smiled at Lilla then a thought came to me, "But how are we going to get past the guards?"

He shrugged. "When Lilla the bard travels to a king's court it is not a minor occasion, Cerdic. The king, his warriors and chieftains, indeed most of the inhabitants of Dunadd came to the great hall to hear me tell a tale. I told them stories from the ancient folklore of Hibernia and tales of their ancestors' greatest battles. It was perhaps the best performance I have ever given, save those at the courts of Aethelfrith, Aelle and in the Villa, of course," he smiled. "It was full of humour, drama, titillation and bravado. In truth, I outdid myself! The ale cups were filled repeatedly. If that were not enough I soon had them drinking even more, for I suggested that we toast the hero of every tale. And then I led the toasts to mac Gabráin and his guests such that the ales and wines were flowing like never before. I doubt there is a sober man within a mile of where we stand tonight, save we three."

"And our guards?"

Lilla grinned at me, "Were extremely grateful that I had thought to bring them some mead to make up for missing out on my tales in the hall. So grateful they seemed not to have noticed it was laced with henbane. Removing the key to your cell was remarkably easy after that. However, we dare not dawdle here too long, lest someone sober up and find us. Come on," he said, heading for the door. I shoved my longsword into my belt and held on to Catraeth.

Still smiling at the silver-tongued bard's trickery, Hussa and I followed. At the end of the corridor were steps cut out of the rock upon which Dunadd was built. These led upwards into the king's hall. At the top of the stairs Lilla held out his hand to indicate that we should halt then placed one elegant finger on his lips. I bit my tongue as we peered around the doorway to look across the hall, expecting to hear a cry of alarm at any moment. However, I could hear snoring, but little else.

We crept forward, swords in hand, step by step, edging around the door and into the hall. Now I could see the tables and benches. At one a pair of mac Gabráin's warriors lay slumped forward fast asleep. An upturned tankard lay close by the head of one of them, ale dripping from it, running across the table and down onto the floor. The rest of the chamber seemed otherwise empty, the king's company having retired to bed, or so I assumed. That was until we reached the outer door. There near the embers of the firepit, which was now burning low, lay two more guards both wrapped in their cloaks and effectively blocking our route to the exit. Tentatively, Lilla lifted one foot and stepped over the nearest guard. I followed. Hussa went to do the same, but slipped on a damp patch - probably yet more spilt ale - and stumbled towards the man. Desperately I thrust out my arms and caught him, his knee just inches above the man's face. We stood like that for a moment, frozen, silently staring at each other, praying that the man stayed asleep. He gave a loud bubbling snore and rolled over towards Hussa's leg. I wrapped my arms around my brother's waist, not easy with Catraeth clenched tight in my fist, and heaved him off the ground then swung him over the man's head and deposited him on the floor in front of the door.

Desperation lent me strength, but had Hussa not lost so much weight in these last weeks I doubt I could have managed it.

Lilla tried the door. It opened, but creaked as it did so. Close at hand the other guard stirred, his sleeping expression becoming puzzled as if hearing the sound but uncertain what it was. We held our breath. Lilla gently pulled and gradually the door opened, the gap getting wider: one inch, three, six then twelve. A little more, creaking with each move and suddenly Lilla had slipped through the gap, followed by Hussa and lastly me.

What concerned me now was how we were going to get past the guards on the four sets of gates between here and freedom. When I asked Lilla this, however, he had the answer. Why should that surprise me!

"What gates? Since you lads smell like shit you might as well get tossed out with all the other rubbish."

"Eh?" I mumbled.

Lilla pointed across the starlit courtyard. We were surrounded by tall, palisaded walls but where he pointed I saw a small hatch swinging gently forward and back. I realised it must let into the chute through which the cooks and servants tossed their debris to get it out through the walls. We walked across to it, tilted the door open and peered through. Beyond it the side of the hill dropped precariously away into the darkness that shrouded the bottom of the fortress.

"You must be having a joke, Lilla," Hussa commented. "Very funny, but what really is your plan?"

Lilla stared at us both in silence.

"I don't think he's joking," I said.

"But it's a hundred feet at least straight down!" Hussa observed.

"Not straight down - it slopes a little. In addition it's a soft landing at the bottom - what with all that rotting waste. You'll be fine," said Lilla.

"You'll be fine? What do you mean, *you'll*? Aren't you coming too?" I asked.

Lilla chuckled. "Hardly. In the first place I would not want to ruin my clothes, whilst yours are ... er," he sniffed, "shall we just say the worse for wear. Secondly, it is you two who are the escaping prisoners. I am an honoured guest of the king. Your escape has absolutely nothing whatever to do with me – I shall be as amazed as everyone else when I wake come morning and learn you are gone. Now get on with it before we are discovered. I don't want to have to explain to mac Gabráin what I am doing out of bed with you two spies."

I glared at him and then down at the uninviting slope. "This winter just keeps getting better and better. What do we do when we get out?"

In answer he held out a sack. I glanced inside. There was bread, smoked meat, cheese and a bulging wineskin. The scent of wholesome food made my mouth water.

"If you attempt to go home by land you will be caught. Once they know you have gone, they will let the hounds out to track you down. The Scots are far better horseman than most of us Angles. Besides all this, you are exhausted, weak and feeble. You need a couple of days of decent food and rest before attempting any journey. Five miles south of here is a hill with a bent oak tree on its summit. Behind the tree is a ruined stone hovel. I have sheltered from the rain there before now when travelling these lands. Few people use it or know of it. Go and hide there and rest up for a couple of days. When you are stronger either get yourselves a boat or horses."

198

I nodded. He was right that we were exhausted and needed to recover. "But what will you do? And what of the hounds? Won't they track us down?"

Lilla smiled and produced yet more objects from beneath his cloak. These were clean tunics and britches. "Take off those filthy garments, lads, and put these on."

I did as instructed, happy for a change of clothes. I was about to throw the old tunic down the chute, but Lilla tugged it off me.

"Give that to me, Cerdic, you too Hussa."

"Why?" I asked.

"As soon as it is light I will take my leave - before most of the court is awake. I will drag those tunics behind my horse and lead the hounds north towards Pictland - away from you. When you get down this slope keep to the boggy ground as much as possible and off the paths. Wet ground will reduce the scent and hopefully the dogs will pick up my trail and follow me."

"Aren't you worried they will catch you? You said the Scots are better riders than we are," Hussa retorted.

Again Lilla smiled, "Than you, certainly. As for me? Well, I imagine I am going to find out how good *I* am."

"Well let's hope good enough," Hussa said, "for you must take news to Aethelfrith in case we don't get through."

"If I can I will, but I suspect I'll be stopped if I try to head that way. Mac Gabráin will be watching his borders until he is ready to move."

Hussa nodded. "Come on, Cerdic, we must go!" He tugged at my sleeve.

"Hang on a moment ... Lilla, tell me how you managed to plan all this."

The bard nodded his head towards Hussa, "That is a tale for your brother. Now go."

"Oh, very well!" I sighed. Stepping forward I squeezed myself through the chute hatch. My heels landed on the loose soil of the hill slope and I began sliding - faster and faster - desperately trying to keep my balance. Finally, with a cry of alarm, I stumbled, lost my already precarious footing, fell back on my rear end and carried on sliding and then tumbling, taking assorted rubbish down with me as I went, my hands taken up with holding onto my swords and Lilla's sack of food. Eventually I crashed into a massive heap of vegetable peelings and the rotten carcass of a pig and came to a squelching halt. The stench was unbelievable. A moment later, Hussa galloped past me and ended up face down in a pool of mud and filth at the bottom of the slope.

"Bastard!" he said, craning his neck to look back up at the top of the slope. But the swinging door was shut and Lilla had vanished back to his bed to play out his role of innocence.

I clambered to my feet, stumbled over to my brother and dragged him upright. "Well at least he got us out of there," I reasoned.

"He didn't have to enjoy it quite so much though, did he!"

We stood for a moment looking around us at the terrain. The countryside all about us was marshy. The river wound its way around three sides of Dunadd. This meant we could not just head out in any direction for soon enough we would become trapped in the quagmire or come up against the river. There was a path running around the base of the fortress, but we needed to avoid that. So it seemed we would have to find a route through the bog without getting stuck.

"Keep to the marshes and bogs, Lilla said," Hussa grumbled. "Huh, I don't think that will be the issue. More of a problem getting *out* of the bog!"

"Come on," I urged him. "We will manage somehow."

We made our way around the imposing wall of rock that now loomed over us and in the dark seemed like some huge creature from one of Lilla's tales - a dragon maybe or some other demon. If we were spotted out here where there was no cover, the likelihood was that the gates would open and the pursuit would begin. I peered upwards at the fortifications that rose layer upon layer above us. Here and there torches burnt and one of them silhouetted a man leaning against his spear. He seemed to be staring right at me. Yet he did not appear to move. After a moment, I realised that most likely he was dozing through his watch during these lonely hours of the deep night – and we were, of course, in shadow.

Eventually we reached a point close to where the pathway coming down from the front entrance to the fortress met a larger track. Following it eastwards would take us by land out of Dál-Riata and ultimately to Alt Clut. But we had no horses and in any event capture that way seemed likely, as Lilla had suggested. Westwards lay the sea. Directly in front was the route south through KinTīwe and past Lilla's ruined hovel. It was about five miles he had said. Yet we were weak and tired and even one mile seemed forever as we staggered on through the night, stumbling along over uneven ground, tripping over heather and clumps of long grass and reeds, our feet squelching in bog. All the while I looked out for the hill with the bent oak tree, but saw nothing. In the east the sky was beginning to lighten, lending us urgency. We needed to be under cover before daylight and the start of any hue and cry. In the end the faint pre-dawn glow helped us for it gave us just enough light to spot, not two hundred paces away, a small hill surmounted by a crooked tree. Sure enough, just as Lilla had described, behind it lay a tumbledown stone croft, a farmer's house once on a time.

We found that although much of the structure had fallen down, one room was intact, dry and sheltered from the wind. I opened Lilla's sack and we shared some bread, cheese, wine and a little meat and then lay down to sleep.

A few hours after we had arrived we heard the distant howling of hounds away to the north. We sat in the cold room and listened for any noise suggesting that men and dogs were closing in on us. After a while when we heard no more barking we assumed that Lilla's plan had worked. The dogs were tracking him and our filthy tunics. I sent a silent prayer to the gods to let him escape and drifted off to sleep again. When I came to later in the day I found that Hussa was awake and nibbling on some cheese. He threw me a lump.

"So then," I asked, "are you going to tell me how Lilla knew we were there in Dunadd? How did he know to turn up at exactly the right time with a plan to help us escape? And if you knew about it, which you seem to have done, why in Loki's name did you not tell me?"

"Because you might have given it away under torture – and I do not mean to insult your courage, so don't give me that look, brother. In extremity of pain any man can be driven beyond reason and not know what he says."

I nodded, remembering that I had indeed revealed a few things, albeit most of them lies.

"Aethelfrith told him. I agreed with the king before we left that Lilla would be told of what we were secretly planning." Hussa looked at me a little shamefaced, "You played into my hands when you suggested we go back to scout the harbour. I had wondered how I was going to get myself captured without mac

202

Gabráin seeing through the ruse. I had agreed with Aethelfrith that I would hold off revealing the route the Angle army would follow, at least until winter was drawing to a close. He did not want mac Gabráin charging rashly across the land until spring. Not before he had a chance to gather his own strength. Likewise, we knew Lilla would willingly come to our aid - you know how much he likes these foolhardy escapades. They appeal to his sense of daring and adventure."

"You took an awful risk. They might have killed us both long before Lilla appeared."

"I tried to make sure they didn't by giving them enough titbits of knowledge each time they questioned me. More to the point, I kept hinting that I knew where Bran was being held. Mac Gabráin got angry and treated me pretty roughly, but I think it was the chance of him finding Bran that kept us alive – if only just!"

"I am amazed you were willing to endure what they did to you for Aethelfrith's sake. I'm damned if I would have done, given the choice," I added sourly.

Hussa snorted. "What I do, brother, I do for myself. I learnt long ago that no one cared for me. Aethelfrith was my best chance for power and wealth. At least I thought so ... I told you I was having doubts about him. It seemed to me that in planning to overturn Dál-Riata and Rheged in one huge battle, he was overestimating his strength, but you don't tell kings where they are going wrong and anyway, once the die was cast what could I do but play the part? It was not easy and truth be told I could not have held out much longer, but I thought I heard Herring mention the bard to Felnius yesterday, so guessed – or at least hoped – that Lilla had arrived. Had I been wrong I doubt we would have survived the day, for I finally told them everything last night. As soon as he knew where Bran was mac Gabráin would have had us killed. But after I had spoken to him I spotted Lilla in the hall and knew that our chance had come, just so long as the king held off killing us until after the storytelling! So you see, I was not so much putting our fate in Loki's hands as in Lilla's," he grinned.

"Pass the wine, will you. I need some," I said weakly.

We stayed in the cottage for three days while life crept back into our bodies and by which time we had used up all our supplies. Although we were both still weak, on the third night we agreed to get on our way.

"What do you suggest we do now?" Hussa asked me when we had decided to leave.

"We steal a boat. It will be the quickest and safest way. Less chance of capture, I would say."

"More chance of drowning, though," Hussa muttered. "Done much sailing have you?"

He had a point. We had both grown up in inland settlements and had had little contact with or experience of boats. I shrugged. "We'll figure it out."

Thus it was some time later that we once more stood at the spot where we had been captured at the end of the summer and looking down into the harbour by the light of a gibbous moon. If anything, there were more boats present than before. Many had been dragged up onto the shore to protect them from the winter storms. Yet others remained at anchor. Still more were obviously being constructed from the evidence of a wooden skeleton nearby, which looked curiously like an overturned spider with its legs sticking up into the air like a claw. Next to it another framework was halfway through the process of being covered with cured animal skins, which were stretched over the wooden struts. I could smell the tar that was being used to seal them and

204

make them waterproof. Mac Gabráin was building a fleet of Irish curraghs to go with the longships he already had.

We had travelled slowly and carefully, all the time keeping to the shadows and watching our backs. By now the night was moving on and the dawn fast approaching. As we edged down to the shore Hussa let out a stifled cry and pulled me down beside him.

"What is it?" I hissed.

He pointed along the rocky beach towards the cluster of hovels where the ship builders and fishermen dwelt. One of the huts had a light showing in the doorway through which a man emerged. He turned, muttered some words and pulled the door to behind him. He then came walking towards us.

Sword in hand, Hussa shuffled across to crouch behind an upturned boat. Keeping low, I joined him. As we peered out, the man came closer, stopping at a curragh pulled up on the shore near to us, his feet crunching on the shingle. He threw some belongings into the boat and then pushed it towards the water. Hussa slowly drew his sword and advanced on the man. He lifted his blade and I thought he was about to strike the fellow down. Instead he reached out and gently tapped him on the shoulder. The man jumped about a foot into the air and spun round, an expression of outrage on his face. He looked about ready to let fly with a torrent of abuse, but when he felt the point of Hussa's sword pricking at his throat, he froze and swallowed hard. With a quick scan of the village to ensure we were alone, I drew Catraeth and moved out to join them.

The man was about forty-five years old, his back slightly bent and hands roughened by years of working at sea. He stared at us with dark eyes that matched his dark hair.

"You speak Welsh?" I whispered to him in that language.

He nodded.

"English?" Hussa asked him.

The man shrugged. "A little," he replied his voice quavering.

"Get into the boat. Hussa, you as well; I will push us off," I said.

"You're not going to kill me?" The man asked as he stood unmoving beside his boat.

"Not if you take us where we want to go," Hussa replied, "but get in the boat now or we might change our minds!"

The man cast an anxious glance at the sword then his gaze shifted past my shoulder into the gloom around the bay. I followed his gaze, but could see nothing in the darkness despite the hint of light stealing into the eastern sky.

"Get a move on!" Hussa urged him. Reluctantly, the Irishman clambered over the side of the boat and climbed in. Hussa followed and then sat down opposite him. I glanced once more around the shore, but could see no other sign of life, so I pushed the boat into the sea gasping when the cold water splashed and soaked my legs.

As the boat got underway I jumped in. "Row!" I ordered the boatman. With a clattering as he retrieved the oars and then a splash as the blades dug into the water, the boat jumped forward heading for the open sea.

"Follow the coast line south," I instructed him. With a surly nod he obeyed. After rowing for a while he stowed the oars, unfurled a sail on the single mast and then moved to the stern of the little boat and steered it from the tiller there. As we headed out to sea the boat started to rise and fall with the waves. It was the first time I had ever been on the sea and I began to feel rather queasy.

"How far are we going?" the Scot asked.

I looked across at Hussa and could see that he was as uncertain as I. We had been dreaming about escaping from that terrible place all through the weeks of our captivity, but now that we were away we really weren't sure what to do next. I had no knowledge of these lands and even less of the seas around them. But I did have an idea.

" Hussa - you said that Aethelfrith was taking the army through the fortress at Degsastan and on to Lugvalium?"

My brother nodded.

"That would be at the start of the spring?"

Again he nodded, but said nothing and I wondered if he too was feeling queasy. "You," I said to the boatman, "how long to spring?"

Our captive's jaw dropped and he stared at me as though I were a madman. "Where have you been that you don't know the month or the season?" he asked.

"Let us just say that we have been occupied," I replied.

His brow furrowed he looked from one to the other of us then shrugged, "The worst of the winter is behind us, the boats are putting to sea once more, the farmers are sowing their fields and I believe the first lambs are being born in the hills."

I looked with disbelief at Hussa - could it be spring already? Had we been captives in that dark hole through two seasons? Was it possible? Yet as I looked along the coastline in the early morning light I could see leaves growing on the trees and at their feet shoots of fresh, green vegetation pushing their way out of the soil. When we rode into Dunadd all those weeks ago the leaves in the woodlands had just begun to turn, but somehow, whilst we had suffered in the pit beneath mac Gabráin's fortress, autumn and winter had come and gone.

But that meant that if spring was truly on the way then Aethelfrith and Edwin would be marching on Degsastan very soon - perhaps even now as we bobbed along in the curragh. Likewise, if the Angles were on the march and if mac Gabráin had planned to intercept them, then his fleet would also be underway very soon, and unless Lilla got through to warn him, Aethelfrith would have no idea what awaited him. Hussa was right: the king had gambled too much.

I turned to look back along the coast. The Scot was steering the boat close to the shore. We came around a headland and another bay opened up beyond it. I suddenly realised why the boatman was holding so tightly to the shore. The next bay was also full of curraghs. Many of these were already occupied and out on the water. Close to the shore was a small village and I noticed two or three dozen tents and many more improvised shelters crammed into the space between the huts and the shoreline. The risen sun illuminated the camp and I now guessed what our captive had been looking at back in his village when he glanced over my shoulder. Presumably there had been a camp there too. We had blundered past it unknowingly in the dark. This camp, however, was awake and bustling with activity. At least four hundred warriors were up and about sharpening weapons and loading boats with equipment.

"That's close enough! Steer away back out to sea," I ordered. The Scot glared at me, but when Hussa tapped him on the shin with his sword the man complied, yanked on the tiller and the boat turned back out to sea. I saw some men in the nearest curragh studying us with suspicion.

"Wave and smile," I said and Hussa and I waved as we turned away. It was an anxious moment, but we must have been convincing for they did not follow us.

"You do realise of course what this means?" Hussa asked.

"It means that Aethelfrith in his arrogance and recklessness is going to get more than he bargained for when he sent you here. He was hoping to entice mac Gabráin to a battle at Degsastan. What neither he nor Edwin nor any of our army know, is that mac Gabráin has brought in the Picts and what is left of the British. Aethelfrith was probably gambling on facing, what ... one thousand men at the most?"

Hussa shrugged. "At the very most, less than that he would have hoped."

"But what's going to happen is that he is going to find the armies of the Picts and Strathclyde at Degsastan or at the very least on the way there."

"What do you mean Strathclyde? We defeated them in the autumn didn't we?"

I shook my head. "I am not so sure now. Do you remember those tracks we passed on the way to Alt Clut? Do you remember how determined Rhydderch Hen seemed to be to tell us he had no warriors left?"

"What you are saying is that it was all a trick? Do you think that even as far back as then, mac Gabráin and Strathclyde were plotting this together?"

I shrugged. "It would not surprise me to learn that Aethelfrith is leading our armies into a trap. Now do you see what happens when you get involved in the conspiracies of kings?"

Hussa did not reply but turned to look again at the camp behind us. "So what do you think we should do now?" he asked after a moment.

"We go and find Edwin and Aethelfrith and try to stop them attacking Degsastan." I turned to face the boatman. "Where is the fleet headed?"

209

He shook his head. "Why should I tell you, Angle?"

I leant towards him drew Catraeth and pointed it at his chest. "My brother and I have been prisoners of your king for months. The winter did not pass very pleasantly for us. So you can imagine that we are not in the best of moods. You are in a boat with two warriors who are enemies of your king. We both have swords and we have both killed men with them before now. So it is really up to you to decide what happens in the next few minutes. You can call for help, of course, but by the time it comes you will be feeding the fishes."

"I am impressed, brother, I didn't think you had it in you," Hussa grinned.

Looking at the two of us and then down at my blade the Scot seemed to make an extremely quick decision, "Lugvalium."

"When?" Hussa asked.

"Within a couple of days at most, we were told. We were to prepare the boats for immediate sailing and to expect to take as many men as we could fit."

"Then we don't have long." Hussa turned to me, "Cerdic, if we go on ahead of the fleet and get to Lugvalium first, then travel overland to Degsastan, we should be able to intercept Aethelfrith before he reaches the fortress."

I nodded. "Take us to Lugvalium," I ordered the boatman. He looked about to argue until I lifted Catraeth and waggled the point at him. His eyes widened, he swallowed and nodded.

"How long will it take?" Hussa asked.

The Scot looked up at the skies and then closed his eyes in concentration. Then he shrugged, "It depends on the wind, but if it continues to blow in the right direction then the rest of today and into tomorrow."

I groaned, feeling my stomach turn within me as the boat once more rode high over one wave and dipped on the far side.

"We will need food and drink, Cerdic. We're both weak and I for one could use a meal around now," Hussa pointed out. I groaned again and retched at the mere thought.

"Looks like someone is not a good sailor," the Scot laughed, a touch of hope in his voice, perhaps considering there might yet be an opportunity for him to overpower us.

Hussa heard it as well. "Just you concentrate on the boat. He might be seasick but I am not. And I am particularly good with this sword, *aren't I*, Cerdic?" My brother's Welsh was not that good, but the boatman clearly understood.

On another level, so did I. I didn't respond and eyeing me, Hussa chortled. I knew he was remembering the sword fighting contest he and I had once competed in when he had beaten me and won his sword. It had rankled at the time. Oddly it still did. I wondered if I could best him even now and somehow doubted it. Just then he leaned forward to look intently at the bottom of the boat. I followed his gaze and saw the boatman's satchel peeping out from beneath a coil of rope where he had attempted to kick it out of sight. With a grin, Hussa seized it and began ripping open the straps.

"Hey! That's mine," the sailor objected, glowering.

"It was yours, but not any longer … ah, praise the gods I am saved!" Hussa laughed as he opened the satchel and retrieved a hunk of bread, a flask of wine, some cheese and salted pork. I swallowed phlegm and looked away as my brother smacked his lips and tucked in.

The journey seemed to go on forever. My world shrank to some fifteen feet by four feet, made of wood and animal skin. A world that tossed up and down and quite often from side to side at the same time, becoming a world which to me seemed rather green ... very green in fact. To Hussa's jeers, I vomited over the side until there was nothing left but bile. As a result of my malady, I somewhat lost track of the passage of time until I became aware that the sun was setting. We were crossing a wider gap of water and travelling south by east. Ahead of us more land loomed.

"How much further?" I mumbled.

The boatman pointed to the headland we were approaching. "We have to go right round that first and into Solway Firth. It will take most of the night if you're determined to carry on that is. It would be better if we made landfall and anchored up ..."

"No! We carry on. If we stop and make landfall who knows who of your friends - our enemies - we would meet. We go on."

"At night it can be hard to find our way. The wind might drop."

"Then get out the oars!" Hussa pointed at the sky. "It's a clear night. The stars will be out soon. You can use them. Just don't stop," he ordered.

The boatman glared at him while I slumped back and returned to my misery.

"Take me back to mac Gabráin's fortress ..." I muttered to myself. "At least that cell did not move."

"What?" Hussa asked.

"Nothing," I said, turning away from him to stare ahead longingly at the solid land we were passing. I let my gaze slide along the shore to the point we would go around to find Solway Firth and our route to Lugvalium. The sea ahead of us seemed empty. Then I spotted a dot in the distance, then a second. No, five ... ten? Were they ... gods!

"Boats ahead of us!" I cried.

212

Hussa turned to stare. There were more now, maybe as many as thirty. They were anchored along the coast in a little bay that on this heading we would soon pass.

"More there!" Hussa shouted. "Behind us!"

He was right. We were bobbing along between two fleets of over thirty boats in each. Mac Gabráin's invasion fleet was already at sea and we were trapped right in the middle of it!

Chapter Eighteen
At Sea

"What're we going to do now?" Hussa asked. "There could be a thousand men in those ships."

I stared again at the boats ahead of us and those that were still a good way behind. They seemed to be gaining, but I could not see them clearly. Then it occurred to me that the light was fading; the sun sinking fast now.

"Bring down the sail," I instructed the boatman in Welsh. "We will wait." He gave me a look, but with a glance at Catraeth did as I told him. To Hussa I said, "The sun is setting and there is no moon. If we can sneak past those ones ahead of us during the hours of darkness we should be able to arrive at Lugvalium ahead of the Scots' fleet."

"Worth a try," Hussa remarked.

We waited, bobbing on the water and all the while watching the approaching fleet. I hoped that with so many boats ahead of us, they had no reason to be suspicious even if they spotted us, but the tension in our little boat was not improving my twisted guts.

As soon as the sun sank below the horizon, I ordered the boatman to hoist the sail and get underway. Sure enough, just as we caught up with the forward boats, which by now were anchored in the little bay, it was full dark. There was a makeshift camp set up and already I could see half a dozen fires burning. The bay had a little fishing village along the shoreline and I imagined the local British residents would have come out warily to trade. Soon fish and meat would be roasting over fires whilst pots of ale and mead were passed around. Did I not feel so ill it would have been a tempting sight, but as it was, outside the glow of those fires, unfed and cold I shivered as we sailed on by.

Eventually we reached the headland and started around it. The inviting scene on the shore slipped out of view and soon all was in darkness, punctuated only by the stars up above us and the occasional light ashore, most likely from a lonely house or farmstead. Lonely. That rather accurately described me that night. What is it about night time that makes you want to be home? I felt very far from home in that boat and fell again to thinking of Cuthwine and Aidith. I could see it in my mind's eye: the kitchen in the Villa, warm and snug, heated by the ever burning hearth and the blistering heat from the bread oven. On a winter's night we would often sit around it. Aedann's mother would serve us hot flatbreads and we would sip our ale and just enjoy being together. Cuthwine, sitting on my knee, would be dropping off to sleep, but I would be reluctant to give him to Aidith to put to bed for I could feel the warmth of his little body. Aidith, smiling at my gentleness would humour me. "Just a little longer, Cerdic, then he must go to bed. Then you and I ...." she would leave the suggestion open with just the faintest inclination of her head.

I jolted awake and felt the cold rush back into my bones. Above me the stars had moved - with the prominent shape of the Wagon having shifted a quarter way across the sky. I had clearly been asleep for almost half the night. I jerked my head around, drawing Catraeth from its sheath and staring at Hussa. He just chuckled at me.

"It's all right, Cerdic. I stayed awake. That food gave me energy and you looked terrible so I let you sleep."

216

I glanced across at the sullen Scot. He seemed weary, shoulders hunched, his hands occupied with sheet and tiller. "You should not have let me sleep through, brother."

"Well I did. Tomorrow we have a lot of land to cover and you are of no use if you can't keep up with me."

I saw his point.

"What were you dreaming of just then, anyway?"

"Huh?"

"Just then you muttered something about 'just a little longer'."

The words brought with them a flash of memory. For an instant I saw the kitchen. It was all fantasy, of course. In fact not even a real memory - more a collection of images and feelings. Cuthwine was now not as small as in my dream - in fact he would be even older now than I remembered, for this winter I had missed his fourth birthday. Likewise it had been a while since Aidith had looked quite so beautiful, the fever having taken much of her roundness. Not that I cared: I would take them both just as they were if I could be at home tonight. More than anything I yearned for that. Looking up into the skies again I could make out the single bright star on the horizon that was called 'Loki's Torch' and it reminded me of my pact with Loki that if he saved Aidith I would go where fate took me. Gods remember a vow like that and now here I was playing his game. But even a god must know a man can only take so much and that I was near to collapse, mentally if not physically. Had he sensed that and sent a reminder of home to my dreams, a vision of what awaited me if I ever made it back? Was he teasing me? Under my breath I cursed him, but then I realised that I did feel a little better. More than that, I no longer felt sick - in fact I felt very hungry.

"Never mind that," I dismissed Hussa's question. "Is there any food left or have you eaten the lot?"

217

In reply he tossed over the satchel and I found some of the bread and salted pork along with a little wine. After I had eaten I passed the rest to the sailor. "Come, let me take the rudder a while and you rest."

The man gave me a suspicious look, but I just shrugged. "It's like my brother here says ... we all need to keep our strength up. You get us to land just where we want to go and we will release you." He looked rather doubtful at the promise.

"You swear by the Son of God that you will not harm me?" he asked earnestly.

"The son of which god?" I asked.

"Oh, so you are heathen?" he frowned.

"If that means I worship the gods of my ancestors and not your Christian God, then that is so. But in any case, I will swear by my gods and by this," I added, patting Catraeth. "A warrior's sword is as good as an oath."

He nodded at me and shifted away from the tiller where I replaced him.

After a few moments I asked another question. "Er ... how do I steer this thing?"

When the sun was rising ahead of us, the land still dark and vast off to our left, I realised my plans were flawed and we were not going to arrive in Lugvalium ahead of mac Gabráin's fleet. There might be fifty boats behind us around the headland, but ahead of us, like black dots against the brightness of the sunrise, there were yet more sails - more boats.

"Damn!" Hussa swore. "Just tell me how many of the buggers are there?"

"We are still in the middle," I said with rising panic. "There must have been more boats further ahead. What do we do?"

218

"We could turn the boat around ..." Hussa began, but trailed off as he realised the futility of that. "No, we would just sail right into the bastards coming from the west."

"We can't go sailing around forever. It might have been the quickest way to get here, but unless we reach the army and warn them it will all be for nothing." I studied the fleet ahead for a while and then made a decision.

"We look identical to anyone else. We join the invasion. We follow the fleet, make landfall and then try and evade the army as it forms up on the far side."

"What? We try to evade a thousand Scots and the gods know how many Rheged and Strathclyde warriors on top?"

I nodded then turned to the boatman. "I gave you my oath that you would not be harmed, but if you so much as *look* at those boat crews, I will cut out your tongue," I threatened. Now come and take back the tiller. The Scot must have believed me for he instantly complied, deliberately lowering his head to stare at his feet.

"I can't believe we had the same father sometimes," Hussa mumbled. "All right, let's do it!"

The boats now coming out from the shore ahead of us were tacking against the strong, northerly breeze as they tried to reach the open sea before turning east towards Lugvalium. We, on the other hand, were already some way out from land and already heading in the direction of that distant city. Thus fairly soon we began to catch up with the fleet and indeed to overtake part of it so that by mid-morning we were pretty much in the middle. I was anxious that a boat with only three men in it would draw attention to us, so I had the Scot steer further out to sea so that we were a little apart from the rest.

219

By mid-afternoon we had entered Solway Firth and now the coastline of Strathclyde to the north and Rheged to the south grew closer and closer, until we came to the mouth of the River Esk - so the boatman told me. After a few miles the river split. One channel turned away towards the smoky haze that hung over a large city in the distance, away to the southeast. Meanwhile, the boats we were accompanying chose the left hand passage, which headed east and north.

"What city is that?" I asked, studying the stone walls of a Roman fortress.

"That is Lugvalium," the boatman replied.

" Lugvalium? Why is the fleet not going that way then?" Hussa asked.

"Who do you think I am, the king? I haven't got a clue. I was told we were going to Lugvalium, that is all I know."

"This river must get us closer to Degsastan," I guessed, "how far up is it navigable?"

"I don't know. I have been to Lugvalium before, but not up this river."

I was not sure if our boatman was being deliberately obstructive, but if so, he was as good an actor as Lilla.

Hussa and I watched the other boats, anxious that this was a trap, but the fleet continued to move upriver, necessitating the use of oars. No-one took any notice of us - maybe they thought we were just hangers on; fishermen come along to watch the fun. Hussa and I took it in turns to row, one of us always watching our increasingly sullen companion in case he tried to attract attention to our boat. We carried on for at least another five miles until once again the river divided. In the angle between the waters at this point was a small town. The enemy fleet was now landing on either bank or tying up to quays that projected out of the settlement.

"Looks to me that this is it," Hussa commented. "Both rivers are getting pretty shallow now. I think this is as far as mac Gabráin's army will go by boat."

I nodded in agreement. "But which way is Degsastan, do you think?" I studied the land all around, wishing I had Wallace's map with me, not that I would have been allowed to keep it had mac Gabráin got his hands on it.

Hussa pointed up one river. "I'm fairly sure it's that way. Aethelfrith told me that Degsastan lies near the start of a river called the Liddel Water where it comes close to the headwaters of the Tyne. It stands on a route through the hills between Lugvalium and Aethelfrith's lands north of the Wall, so that is in the right direction. It is border country and the British fortified it years ago when the Bernicians started to expand their territory. The king told me he would bring the army up to Degsastan then wait for Theobald to ferry more troops up the Tyne. Once reunited, they would attack the fortress."

"How far is it?"

"Maybe six or seven miles, but I don't know how far beyond Degsastan Aethelfrith means to set up his camp."

I squinted up at the sun. "We ought to be able to manage it by sunset, providing we can avoid the Scots and their allies," I said, pulling at the oars, my arms weary beyond words.

Hussa nodded, "Very well, we'll go across to that right bank and tie up. We need to make sure we are a little way apart from the other boats. Go upriver a little. Yes, that's it over to those trees. Hang on; I'll take back the oars."

I nodded and moved back, drawing Catraeth and waving it at the Scot, who looked longingly at his friends, so near and yet so far.

Hussa pulled more strongly than I and within minutes the boat thumped into the bank in the shade of a willow tree, which was bent and overhanging the river like an old women with long hair so that we were completely hidden from the other boats. The Scot jumped out with the coil of rope, tied one end around the prow and the other around the trunk of the willow. Then he turned to us expectantly.

"Well, I did what you said. I brought you here. Will you keep your promise and let me go."

I scrambled out onto the bank nodding. "I vowed that I would, but if I do, what guarantee do I have that you won't just run to your countrymen and tell them about us?"

"I could give you my word as you did me. On my honour I will stay here until sunset."

"I am sorry, but I just can't trust your word ... too much depends on it. You had no choice in the boat, but if our parts were reversed would you trust me now?"

He hesitated and then his shoulders slumped and he looked suddenly fearful. "No, I don't suppose I would. So what will you do?"

I considered him for a moment and came to a decision. "We will knock you out and tie you up. You will be found soon enough, but we will be long gone. At worst you'll have a headache."

The fellow took a step backwards. "Just wait a moment!" he pleaded, his hands held out in front of him to keep me away. His terrified gaze was fixed on me so that he did not see Hussa step up behind him. My brother placed one hand over the man's mouth and with a suddenness that shocked me, drew his seax and slashed it across the boatman's throat then held onto him while the blood gushed out and poured down the man's tunic. He thrashed around for a moment before his legs finally gave way then Hussa let him go and he fell to the ground, quite dead.

"What the hell did you do that for?" I glared at my brother, "I gave him my word I would not hurt him."

He knelt down and cleaned his blade on the man's tunic then stood, re-sheathing the seax before answering. "You might have given *your* word, brother, but I did not give mine. If we had done as you suggested, tied him up and knocked him out, he would have come round soon enough and hollered. We would have had half of mac Gabráin's army on our heels before we'd gone a mile, not to mention cavalry and probably hounds as well. And you, by the look of you, are not going to be able to run very fast. I did what was necessary. Now help me hide his body and we will be on our way."

I stared at him for a moment then I shook my head. "As you said on the boat, Hussa, sometimes it is hard to believe we had the same father." I sighed and bent to grab the man under his arms. Hussa took hold of the ankles and we heaved the corpse into the undergrowth.

I returned to the boat, salvaged the satchel and filled the empty wine skin from the cool fresh waters of the river and then turning back to my brother I led the way through the trees.

"Come on then, let's make the best of this."

We followed the stream upriver. As we left the village behind I noticed that most of the boats were moored on the left bank and that the majority of mac Gabráin's army was disembarking on that side. I also noticed they appeared to be making no immediate preparations for departure and indeed, most seemed to be setting up camp for the night. I pointed this out to my brother.

"Maybe they plan to march to Degsastan in the morning," he suggested.

"If that's the case then Aethelfrith must be making no move to attack the fortress yet. Else they would surely be hurrying to get there today."

Hussa shrugged, "Maybe, and if so there is a possibility we can prevent Aethelfrith and Edwin from marching into a trap. Come on we must hurry."

The Liddel Water wound its way northeast away from the River Esk. The road from the village behind us followed the west bank of the Esk and forded it a mile or so from the junction, then ran along the north bank of the Liddel Water - that is, on the opposite side to us. We decided to stay on the south bank of the river where we felt we would be less likely to be discovered. The terrain, initially low-lying fields and scattered woodlands, began to rise into hills, which themselves then blended into peaks several hundred feet high. The trees became sparser and there was gorse and heather underfoot. The terrain slowed us down considerably, but we pressed on as best as we could. After a couple of miles all I wanted was to lie down, my chest ached and my legs wobbled like a newborn lamb's, but the thought of losing face with my brother was too much to bear and somehow I kept going, though to this day I'm not sure how.

Just before it began to get dark we came around a bend in the river and could see a fort up ahead. The land all around us now comprised steep-sided hills dropping to the banks of the river, which divided again splitting the land into a 'Y' shaped valley with a stream flowing along each limb. The road continued on the far side of the right or southerly valley, but another track split off

224

from it and followed the left-hand stream through the northern hills.

Hussa gave a sudden, excited laugh. "This is it! This is Degsastan!"

I studied the land again and believed I understood it. I pointed to the southern road, "This road goes down the Tyne Valley?"

He nodded.

"The other, then, goes northeast towards Aethelfrith's camp?"

Again he nodded.

It was clear to me now why this place was important. It occupied the routes through the Pennines that armies to the north and the south of the Wall might follow to reach Lugvalium. Just as Catraeth had stood at the head of another mountain pass into Rheged, this remote place was also important. The kings of Rheged had realised it and had built a fortress up here in the northern part of their territory. The high land between the two arms of the 'Y' was raised up into a steep-sided plateau. What Rheged had done was to construct a pair of forts, one here in the southern valley and another twin fort in the northern valley. They were connected by a fortified embankment thrown up from a ditch that had been dug right across the plateau. From our vantage point we could not see the northern valley that well, but smoke rising from beyond the plateau matched that emerging from hearths in the southern fort, thus confirming the presence of the other.

I could see that however Aethelfrith attacked this place he would be coming up against a ditch, earth embankments and then wooden palisaded fortifications, just to get at the enemy army. The layout also provided Hussa and me with a problem: it was going to be just as hard to get from here to the other side of those fortifications. We could try to bluff our way through the village

225

next to the fort or maybe attempt to sneak up to the embankment on the plateau, find a quiet spot and tumble over it. But the land west of the embankment was quite open, so a stealthy approach would be impossible. The only other choice was to avoid the valley entirely by climbing the hills to the south. I looked up at the nearby hill on our right, which rose steeply a good thousand feet or so, and stared at it. Hussa followed my gaze, grimaced and then shrugged. There was really no other choice. So we turned towards it and began our ascent.

It was a tough climb and we were both gasping for breath after only a couple of hundred feet. We came across a stream descending the hillside, cascading as a waterfall down through a narrow crevasse. We soon found the going was easier up the rocky walls of this canyon than up the steep, grassy slope on which we had been labouring. It also had the advantage of being quite cool, which gave us some relief as we were both by then sweating heavily. Eventually we reached the top of the hill and looked down at the whole valley laid out beneath us. It was not yet quite dark and from our vantage point we could now see that between the arms of the 'Y' the ground was cut by a deep brook. It ran more or less parallel with the earthworks but further to the east. This brook flowed into Liddel Water. Beyond it the ground rose again into a heavily forested hillside.

The western road, along which the Irish Scots would march, passed through the village and fort in the south valley. It then crossed this same brook by way of a ford and accompanied by Liddel Water, turned southwards around the hill on which we stood.

Once past our hill that road continued southeast through more hills, which became mountains further back. I surmised that I was looking towards the Pennines and the Tyne valley in that direction. From our elevated position we could see many miles down the road and now, squinting through the early evening gloom, I was sure I could discern the movement of a large body of men in the valley.

I nudged my brother and pointed, "Look, over there. Do you think that is Theobald?"

Hussa squinted in the direction I was indicating and after a moment nodded his head. "I reckon so. I think he's about half a day's march away. What would you say?"

"Yes, I'd agree. But where is Aethelfrith?" I asked, turning to look northeast. Beyond the brook where the heavily forested hill loomed, and far back through the trees, I could now see smoke rising and by the look of it coming from many fires. I pointed this out to Hussa. "Aethelfrith?" I suggested.

He nodded again.

"My bet is if he is here already he will be in there spying out the lie of the land," I said. "The best thing we can do then is to go down the eastern side of this hill, cross Liddel Water and head into those trees."

We proceeded with our plan. I was anxious because although crossing the hill had brought us right around the fortifications that blocked the valley below us, there was the possibility of enemy scouts in the hills and woods beyond. It was almost full dark now, but a clear, starlit night and we might easily be seen. Once we came down the hill and reached the river we hid in some bushes whilst we studied the area. Seeing no sign of moment we forded the shallow waters as they tumbled over a rocky stream bed. On the other side we crossed the road and plunged at once into the woods. Fairly soon we came across a track leading uphill and decided to follow that.

After about another half mile of climbing, when I was on the point of collapse and knew I could go no further without a rest, Hussa suddenly pulled me down behind a tree trunk. "Hush," he murmured, "movement up ahead. Keep under the trees." He peered down at me, for I had subsided to the ground and was rubbing my legs. "Can you manage just a bit further or shall I leave you here?"

"If you can then so can I," I hissed. He grinned and nodded, holding out his hand. I grasped it and he pulled me back onto my feet.

We stayed inside the tree line and slowly picked our way along the path until it emerged into a small clearing. Again, Hussa held me back and we ducked into the shadow of the trees. A well stood in the middle of the clearing and nearby I could make out the ruins of an abandoned farmstead, which the surrounding woodlands had been quick to reclaim. The movement Hussa had seen earlier was a patrol of about twenty warriors. They were gathered around the well and seemed to be inspecting it as a potential source of fresh water.

"Water, yuk!" A familiar voice rang out.

"If you hadn't drunk all that ale last night, Eduard, we would have some left for tonight, you greedy horse's arse!"

It was Cuthbert and Eduard and others of the Wicstun Company. Breathing a sigh of relief I moved unsteadily towards them, walking up quietly behind my big friend before shouting at the top of my voice, "Call this a scouting party?"

Eduard spun round, his hand going to the axe he wore at his belt, before recognition lit up his face. He roared with laughter pulling me into a bear hug that squeezed the air out of my lungs.

There were cheers all round as he shouted, "Cerdic, you bastard! Where the hell did you come from? You're still alive.

Gods, but you're a lot thinner! Where have you been? Never mind - you can tell us later. Praise the gods though! Cuth, why did you let me drink all that ale last night? We have reason to get drunk tonight."

Cuthbert glared at him then turned to beam at me, his mouth working but no sound coming out.

I chuckled but then shook my head. "Maybe later, but probably not tonight I'm sorry to say. We bring dire news we must pass on immediately. Quickly now, tell me where are Aethelfrith and Edwin, Sabert and Harald? We must see them at once!"

"Harald returned to Deira to inform King Aethelric the army was staying up here over winter. We hoped he would order us home, but here we still are. The others are together nearby. Come on, I'll take you," Eduard said, his smile disappearing as he took in the state of me and that of Hussa standing awkwardly at my side.

Leaving most of the others in and around the well, Eduard led us further into the woods and along a path. At length - probably less than another half a mile, though to my weary legs it felt like a lot more - he brought us to a small valley where a camp had been set up. There were only about a hundred warriors in and around the immediate area, so I surmised the rest of Aethelfrith's army had not yet arrived. We located the tent in the centre of the camp, where Aethelfrith and Edwin, Sabert and others were sitting around enjoying an evening meal.

Sabert jumped to his feet as soon as he saw me. "Woden be praised! I was certain you had been killed."

The welcome from the prince was much less warm. "Cerdic, where have you been? It's been months since we sent you to Dál-Riata." Edwin demanded, without a hint of pleasure and certainly no expression of relief. If anything there was irritation in his voice.

Without waiting for me to answer, Aethelfrith's voice cut across us. "Did you succeed? Have you done what we set out to do?"

"I have, Sire," Hussa replied, "but we have news. Not only are Rheged's warriors up ahead at Degsastan, but mac Gabráin is coming with all his strength. We were in the fleet that set sail only two days ago and is even now unloading an army ten miles west of here. He is coming very quickly. By tomorrow or the day after at the latest, he will be on the march."

"Mac Gabráin! Here? We must withdraw," Sabert said, but Hussa interrupted him.

"Wait, there is yet more news. We had thought Strathclyde defeated, but in fact they have sent an army, at least another two hundred spears that may already be at Degsastan. That is not all, for the Picts have also made an alliance with mac Gabráin. They've put aside their differences and are coming too. My lord King, within a day, maybe two, I fear you may face between two and three thousand men."

Edwin looked pale and stared at Aethelfrith as if uncertain what to say. Aethelfrith, on the other hand, showed no signs of surprise. Indeed, he looked calm as he sat back and nodded his head at the news. Then a smile of a smug satisfaction flitted across his face.

What was he thinking and why did he look so pleased? There surely was only one course of action left to us. I forced my tired brain to think, but it was beyond me.

"There is time enough to withdraw," said Edwin. "We can back off towards Theobald and then retreat to Bernicia and make them bring the fight to us on home ground."

230

Aethelfrith shook his head. "No! We will not withdraw. I will send word to Theobald to increase his pace. I will send the same command to my own companies who are approaching from the north. I want them all here. Forget this talk of retreat and defence. Tomorrow at dawn we will be launching an attack!"

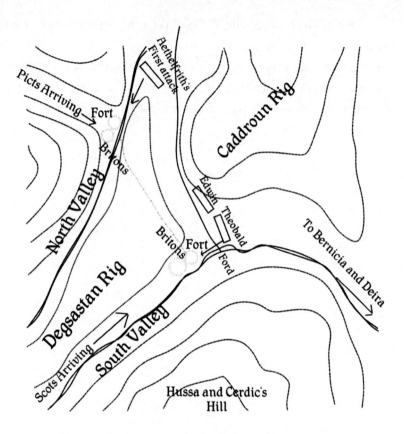

Map of the Battlefield of Degsastsan

Chapter Nineteen
Battle of Degsastan

There was complete silence in response to Aethelfrith's startling announcement. Edwin looked unsure how to respond to the king's decision to attack. I could see him struggling with conflicting emotions. On the one hand he would not want to appear afraid or indecisive in what would be his first full-scale battle. Conversely, he must know that such an attack would be extremely hazardous for everyone involved in it. I noticed that Hussa did not look quite as surprised as everyone else. He had, of course, been expressing his doubts about his new master and the wisdom of the King of Bernicia's foreign policy. But this must have seemed a step too reckless even for him. Sabert was shaking his head. He exchanged a worried look with me, which suggested he was unsure whether he should intervene or not. Somebody had to say something, but given Edwin's attitude to both Sabert and me, if we were the ones to point out the problems with Aethelfrith's plan, how would the prince react?

I sighed, realising that since Hussa and I had carried the information about the Scots and the Picts, it was we two and no one else who had maybe a brief moment of authority in which to speak.

"Your Majesty," I ventured, "I don't think I made myself very clear and if so I apologise. We are *severely* outnumbered. I am not sure how far away the Picts are, but Rheged and Strathclyde are already here. By afternoon tomorrow a thousand Scots may have joined them. I must emphasise again that it is quite possible their strength could rise to as many as three thousand men by the end of tomorrow. We have, even with Theobald's men, perhaps eighteen hundred? To attack with those odds is surely folly?"

Aethelfrith slammed his fist down onto a barrel of ale cracking the wood so that the dark-coloured liquid within gushed out to drench the floor.

"That is exactly why we must attack at once - or as soon as we are able to in the morning. The Scots and the Picts *will* join the battle tomorrow. I too have some news of which you are unaware. I have heard from my scouts that the Picts are less than a day away to the northwest, force marching in this direction. Everything is focused here at this battlefield. I do not intend to run away from this confrontation. On the contrary, I intend this battle to determine the future of this whole region for a generation. One big battle: one day of blood and then whoever wins will dominate all." He moved his goblet to catch some of the ale still streaming from the barrel, raised it frothing to his lips and downed it in one, slopping ale onto his chin. Giving a satisfied belch, he wiped it away with the back of his hand and slapping the empty goblet down onto the top of the barrel, looked around at his speechless audience and grinned. "And that, my lords, will be me!"

Again silence reigned across the tent. Sabert coughed and spoke at last. "It is too dangerous, Sire. Even if you win your battle tomorrow, the cost must be too heavy. Just consider how many men must die for this plan - even if we are victorious. My Prince," he turned to Edwin, "I counsel strongly against this. We should pull back into the hills and let them come to us, ambush them and let them bleed themselves to death trying to catch us. There is no need for this folly."

Probably his choice of the word 'folly' was unwise, for Aethelfrith's eyes widened in anger, but it was Edwin who now spoke. "You dare to question the king, Earl Sabert?"

"Highness, I meant no disrespect I ..." Sabert stumbled over his words, but he was not allowed to continue.

"I've had enough of the whining of old men," Edwin spat, "and I see at last that my father's faith in you, Cerdic, was also mistaken. I was always told you were a man of courage, but what courage is it you show us today?"

It was on the tip of my tongue to mention what Hussa and I had suffered at the hands of the Scots, but Edwin would not be able to imagine it. He was just a boy; his concept of courage limited to stories in the mead hall. "Highness," I said as patiently as I was able, "it is not a question of courage but of common sense. If we fight the battle at these odds and somehow we win, the cost could be too great to contemplate. The king mentions a generation, but we could lose a whole generation of men in a conflict such as he proposes. Is this necessary? That is what I ask: is it really necessary to do this right now?"

I thought of what Hussa had told me in the cell under mac Gabráin's fortress: that he had been ordered to let himself be captured then hold back his information so the enemy would believe he had been tortured into revealing Aethelfrith's plans. The Bernician king had known it was certain to draw mac Gabráin here. Had he also got wind of the Scot's alliances with Strathclyde and the Picts? It was obvious to me now that Aethelfrith had intended this big battle to happen. This was all just part of his plan to dominate the North at whatever the cost. Hussa had been alarmed to learn that the Picts would be at Degsastan, but I was not so sure that Aethelfrith was. His scouts had told him they were coming and yet he had told no one about

235

that until now. Was he really as ruthless as I feared? If a thousand or more Angles died tomorrow, but the North was crushed and he was all powerful between the walls of stone and earth, would he consider that a fair exchange and be satisfied with the outcome? I feared this was so.

"Prince Edwin, can we talk in private, please?" I asked.

Edwin glared at me. "We are in an alliance on the eve of war. I have no secrets from our brothers."

A faint smile flickered across Aethelfrith's lips. Hussa's expression was unreadable and I really couldn't tell how he felt about the way things were going.

"Please, Highness …" I tried again.

"Enough!" Aethelfrith roared as anger flared on his face and then just as swiftly faded as he turned to Edwin and asked politely, "Prince Edwin, may I request the Lord Cerdic be sent to carry a message to my brother to make haste and with all speed to join us on this battlefield?"

Edwin nodded, "Of course, Sire." He turned to me, "Go, Cerdic. Perhaps you can manage to do this right. Don't be gone for five months this time, eh?" he sneered. "Take a patrol and horses and bring Prince Theobald here."

Hussa finally spoke. "Sire, may I suggest that Theobald's best plan is to march along the road he's already on. That'll bring him up against the fort that Cerdic and I saw in that southern valley. It will be the fastest way to get him into battle." My brother glanced fleetingly at me before he added, "Of course, it will be a dangerous part of the fight, perhaps *the* most dangerous."

I was not sure this was right, but before Aethelfrith could say anything, Edwin interjected, "I would not have my allies assaulting the fort on their own. If that is a dangerous part of the battlefield then I would have Deira there as well!"

236

Aethelfrith smiled at the suggestion. "Agreed - it is fitting that my allies should face the danger side by side as heroes must."

Edwin's eyes lit up. He clearly liked the description 'hero' and I could imagine he was expecting this battlefield to be where he would make a name for himself. He looked across at me and frowned, "Then it is agreed, Cerdic, so you have your orders, now go. Bring Theobald to the southern fort. Get him there before dawn tomorrow and my Deirans will be ready to join him. We can attack the fortress at first light." He turned back to Aethelfrith, "Your Majesty, where will your companies attack?"

"I will assault the northern fortress, but I will hold back a strong reserve ready to attack the centre - the earthworks on the high plateau. If we attack as you say at dawn we must break through before the Picts and the Scots arrive. We then defeat them in turn."

As I moved towards the tent flap I glanced across at Sabert. His expression was glum, but we had our orders and there was nothing to do now but carry them out and put our trust in the gods and what the wyrd had in store for us.

I was dropping with exhaustion, but I gathered up Cuthbert and Edward, located some horses and set out.

"What's up mate?" Eduard asked, noticing my dark expression.

"I'll tell you on the way."

Theobald was not difficult to find. We had already seen his army in the distance from the top of that hill. So we headed across country, avoiding the fort and keeping out of sight of the enemy as best we could, until we had travelled a couple of miles to the south. We then emerged on the road and continued south along it. We found Theobald another ten miles further on. He had evidently set up camp almost at the time that Hussa and I had observed him. As it was already getting on towards night, he had clearly decided to break the journey and complete it in the morning. We rode into the camp and then, having identified ourselves, Eduard and Cuthbert looked after the horses whilst I was escorted into Theobald's company. I looked around at the army as we walked through it. There were perhaps five hundred men here. Some I recognised as veterans from Catraeth, but many were fresh-faced young boys. Aethelfrith had clearly scraped together as large an army as he could for this gamble he was playing. As I studied the faces of lads as young as twelve and old men who had seen fifty winters, I shook my head at the enormity of the gamble. If everything went wrong on the morrow many mothers and wives would mourn. Bernicia could lose its menfolk and its future. If things went right there would still be a price to be paid and it would be these men who would be paying it.

"My brother wants me to arrive when?" Prince Theobald asked when we had passed on the orders.

"Dawn, Highness."

"How far is it to these forts we are to attack?"

"Maybe twelve miles, Highness."

"Very well, get some food and then sleep, Cerdic. You look to me as though you could use both! We will wake you in a few hours and you can lead us to our battlefield."

I nodded and we were led away to a fire where some *briw* was bubbling. Each of us had some of the leek and barley broth along with bread and ale and then we settled down and prepared to sleep. Just as I was about to drift off, a familiar figure stepped into the firelight. Aedann stood there looking down at me, concern etched on his face.

"I am happy to see you are still alive. I ... spoke in haste when I left you and I regret that. Will you forgive me?"

I dragged myself to my feet, stumbled over to Aedann and embraced him. "Old friends do not need forgiveness, for they are always friends whatever their differences," I said.

I sat back on a log that had been dragged near the fire, feeling we should talk, but I felt shattered and Aedann spotted it.

"You look exhausted, Cerdic. From what Eduard tells me you have been tortured for months and barely a week ago escaped, battered, bruised and half starved. You are in no position to fight a battle tomorrow."

I gave a grim smile, "I don't think Edwin and Aethelfrith will wait for me to recover, do you? If there is a battle tomorrow the Wicstun Company needs its commander and I will be there. We can only win if we attack at first light. If we do not defeat Strathclyde and Rheged before the Scots and Picts arrive we will be outnumbered and we will be slaughtered. We cannot wait until I am rested. Do you see?"

Aedann nodded, "Then get some rest." He turned around, but instead of walking away he seemed to be checking who was close by, "But Cerdic," he lowered his voice, "there is something else I must tell you. You need to warn Edwin ..." he had no chance to finish as at that moment Theobald called out to him from the other side of the fire.

"Aedann!" he called again as he approached, carrying a chain shirt hung over his arm.

"Yes, my lord?"

"Go to my tent. I need to talk to you."

Aedann hesitated, glanced at me and then vanished into the dark. Theobald came towards me. "Cerdic, here is a chain shirt for you. A gift for the services of your former huscarl, now mine."

"Thank you, Highness," I replied, taking the fine shirt. "It is a worthy gift."

239

"Good luck tomorrow," he said and returned to his tent leaving me wondering what Aedann was trying to say and why Theobald had felt the need to suddenly present me with a gift.

I lay down again, pulling my cloak around me, aware that Eduard and Cuthbert were eyeing me, questioningly. I shrugged, "Come on, let's get some sleep." I said.

Within minutes Eduard was snoring happily by my side and after a few moments of fidgeting Cuthbert joined him in slumber. But for me sleep was something, despite my exhaustion, that took a long time to arrive. Tomorrow I would fight yet another battle. I had resolved to never leave home again - had promised myself I would not fight again - and yet here I was. My pact with Loki had brought me here and tomorrow's fight would be even bigger than Catraeth. Perhaps five thousand and more men would be trying to kill each other. Yet again I thought of home and that memory of the kitchen, the feel of Cuthwine in my arms and the soft words spoken by Aidith. I thought when I had escaped from mac Gabráin's fortress carrying a warning to Aethelfrith that he would heed it and retreat back through the hills. That maybe mac Gabráin would not follow or if he did we could fight at a place of our choice - one of our own fortresses perhaps - or we could ambush him and harass him along the way. I thought of Hussa and how he had expressed his doubts about Aethelfrith. That being the case I had expected that he would also try to persuade the king to retreat, and yet he had hardly made much in the way of an effort. Indeed, it was at Hussa's suggestion that this attack on the southern fort would be led by Theobald. Had it been my imagination or had my brother's emphasis of the danger caused Edwin to volunteer Deira for the attack there? It was a predictable response from the glory-seeking prince and Hussa must have known that. Then again, I was probably letting my imagination run away with me, yet I could not dispel the feeling that my brother had deliberately manipulated Prince Edwin, who had taken to him more than he ever had to me. But why would Hussa want to put Edwin in danger? It was beyond my tired brain to answer that question.

I groaned as I rolled over and muscles and bones that had suffered a pounding and no proper sustenance for months complained as they stretched. Aedann was right, of course. I was in no fit state to fight a battle and I was rather worried about that. Ah well, if I could just get some sleep then I might feel better in the morning. I finally did drift off into a restless slumber, but when I was woken by a rough shake to the shoulder, my muscles if anything felt even stiffer than they had the night before. I dragged myself to my feet, pulled the new chain shirt over my head, slapped a helmet on and buckled Catraeth and my longsword to my side. Cuthbert was testing his bow and sorting through his arrows. Eduard was sharpening his axe and strapping his shield to his back. I searched the camp looking out for Aedann, but when I asked for him I was told he had been sent out to scout the hills to the west and would rejoin us later.

We were underway three hours before dawn, marching briskly down the road. The foot soldiers' feet crunched the pebbles beneath their boots as we moved grimly forwards towards our doom. Eventually we passed the point where the road curved around the hill where Hussa and I had looked down upon the fort the previous afternoon. We marched around it until we reached a spot where in front of us lay the ford. We halted some five hundred paces from where the fortress waited for our attack. Just minutes later, Edwin and Aethelfrith came out from the trees. Behind Edwin the companies from Deira swung out and formed up to the right of those led by Theobald. The Wicstun Company

241

was near the centre of our army and I was heartened to see the wolf's head banner flying proudly above it.

Leaving the men behind, Aethelfrith, Edwin, Theobald, Sabert and I, along with the captains of the other companies, gathered and as the sun rose at our backs and lit up the fort and the palisaded fortifications, we stood and considered the enemy's position.

Our army was deployed on the lower slopes of the wooded Cauddroun Rig. Immediately to our front the cool waters of Cauddroun Burn ran from our right to join the Liddel Water on our left. Beyond the stream the ground rose steeply to the high plateau that was Degsastan Rig - a flat, open land covered with rough clumps of grass and scrub. Five hundred yards from where we stood it was cut by a deep ditch running parallel with the stream. Beyond the ditch was an embankment and on top of that the palisaded, fortified wall.

South of the plateau lay the valley of the Liddel Water through which passed the road Theobald had marched up from Bernicia. In the valley just beyond the ford was the settlement of Degsastan. This was itself encircled by a wooden palisade, but was out of sight beyond the fort, which was connected to the southern end of the earthwork that extended down from the plateau. Aethelfrith had told us that there was a similar arrangement on the far side of the plateau in the northern valley. All around us lay steep hills. It was a land that could have been marked out for a battlefield by Woden and Tiw at the beginning of time and one which favoured defence.

The British were already lining both the fort and the earthwork. On our side of the battlefield five hundred and more spears pointed to the heavens from over the top of the palisades and we believed these were matched by as many in the northern

242

valley. More than a score of banners in a multitude of colours hung limp in the still air above them. Mixed in with the spearmen we could see many archers fitting arrows to bowstrings. A good number of the spearmen were resting their weapons against the fortifications and were preparing slings.

It was not an encouraging sight, yet if we must attack then the earlier the better, for fifteen hundred more enemy warriors were on the way. If we were to breach these defenses and be ready for mac Gabráin and his allies the Picts, we needed to attack as soon as possible. This at least was obvious to everyone.

"Gather the skirmishers from all your companies and deploy them to your front. Try to take out some of the bastards before they can target our shield wall then form up as tightly as you can and smash into the fort. Throw everything you have at it. Any questions?" Aethelfrith barked.

There was nothing really more to be said or done. This was not a battlefield that allowed for manoeuvre. There would be limits to the use of clever tactics or strategies here. The only advantage we possessed was that we could choose the point of contact with the enemy and we could focus all our strength at that point.

Aethelfrith turned away, mounted his horse and rode towards the northern valley where even now his forces would be massing for the attack he would lead on the fortress there. The rest of us dispersed and returned to our companies. I looked across the army to where Aedann stood amongst Theobald's huscarls. He must have felt me watching him for he turned and waved. I nodded at him and offered up a prayer that the Valkyries would not come for him this day. He had made his choice and although he possibly regretted his decision, I could not begrudge the man his chance for land and a title. Returning to the Wicstun Company familiar faces looked expectantly at me.

"Cuthbert, get your men together out front. You know what to do. Just be careful."

My friend nodded and stepped out of the shield wall pulling his bow from his back, stringing it and sorting out his arrows as he advanced onto the open ground. He looked as anxious as he had done before Catraeth, but here, as there, once he had an arrow notched on his bowstring the trembles and shakes stopped and he became still and calm.

"Right then - everybody else get ready. See that fort down there? I am hungry and they've got my breakfast. I expect it to be inside me within an hour. The man who brings me some bacon will have earned himself a new seax."

That brought a few laughs and the odd cheer.

A hundred skirmishers splashed across the stream and then worked their way forward towards the fort. When they were a hundred paces short they halted and without any ceremony the battle of Degsastan began. The archers let fly and the air was dotted with arrows speeding away to fall like hawks upon their prey. A storm of stones and pebbles, as intense as a sudden downpour of hail but far more deadly, pelted the palisades and our men exposed in the open. The missiles were finding their mark in both armies, but whilst the British hunkered down behind their defences our boys had no such protection. Soon a dozen were lying motionless face down on the ground, skulls smashed, bloody and broken. The storm continued and more of our skirmishers crumpled and fell. Yet our own bowmen and slingers were having an effect, for I could see the enemy spearmen were avoiding the missiles and dropping out of sight. Only their archers stayed up on the battlements and when one of them revealed himself, ten arrows sped in his direction, two

244

finding their mark. Yes, Aethelfrith's plan was working, but to take advantage of the situation we had to act quickly.

Theobald could see this too and with a blast of Bernician horns and a wave of his hand his companies started forward. Edwin, just as eager to get to grips with the enemy as he had been at Aethelfrith's camp, waved at the Deiran companies and headed off at a run. With a bellow of orders each of the companies set off after him.

"This is it lads, Woden watch over you all. Forward!" I shouted.

Theobald had reached the ford and crossing it, his companies spread out on the far bank. Then, without halting, they continued towards the fort. Edwin and his huscarls followed them across and swung round to the right of the Bernicians.

"He's not learnt anything, has he?" Eduard grunted with a tilt of the head towards the prince.

He was right. Edwin was determined to reach the fort alongside Theobald and as a result was becoming separated from the rest of his army.

The ford was narrow and only one company could cross at a time. As it happened, the Wicstun Company reached the ford first. After we had crossed it I realised we needed to act fast if we were not to lose a prince. I sighed; we had been here before! Gods preserve me from glory-seeking youths.

"Double pace, come on stretch your legs, lads - let's catch up with those lazy palace guards."

With our shields and spears clattering and banging as we ran we overtook Edwin about thirty paces from the fort. I led the Wicstun Company into the gap to Edwin's right whilst Sabert slotted in beyond me. Directly ahead was the section of the earthworks that came down from the plateau and connected to

245

the fort. Like the fort itself this was lined by Rheged warriors. The skirmishers had advanced ahead of us and continued their assault, but their numbers were dwindling and as we came closer the British resumed their positions on the battlements and shifted their focus to us.

"Shield wall, tighten up lads!" I ordered.

The shields banged together as the men tucked themselves in tightly between their neighbours to the left and right and endeavoured to take what protection they could from these boards of wood. The problem with a shield wall is that whilst it can protect you, you cannot move very quickly, which meant we had to endure the spite of our enemies as they sent stones and arrows hurling into our ranks. I was reminded of Catraeth where it had been we who had been behind fortifications, desperately flinging anything we could at Owain's army as it advanced upon us.

The noise of the slingshots clattering on our shields reminded me of hailstones on the tiles of the Villa. Except that these were not lumps of ice but hunks of rock, as was brought home to me a moment later when a boy from Wicstun screamed. A stone had struck him on the shoulder cracking his collar bone. He dropped his shield and an arrow instantly found his chest and pierced his heart. He fell dead at my feet. I had no time to do more than glance briefly at him as I stepped over his body and moved on towards the fort. Meanwhile, Cuthbert led the survivors of the skirmishers around the flank of the company where they could shelter behind the shields and still direct intermittent flurries of stones and arrows at the enemy.

We were now closing on the ditch that had been dug in front of the earthwork and from which the earth would have been thrown up to create the embankment beyond. Again I had a sudden recollection of those Welsh warriors at Catraeth clambering or merely falling down into the ditch to reach us. This ditch was not quite as deep as the one at Catraeth had been. Yet as we reached its lip we still had to descend five feet. As men in the front rank turned to lower themselves into the ditch the enemy pelted at them even more furiously. Bloodcurdling screams of agony rent the air and still echo in my mind all these decades later.

"Press on, press on - it is the only way!" I encouraged the company, knowing I was guaranteeing that many would die. But what else could I do? We had to get across the ditch, break in and kill this enemy and get out onto the road and the plateau beyond. Then I realised what I was thinking: I was desperate to get through *this* enemy so we could be ready for the next - ready for the Scots and Picts. Bloody insanity all of it! But then again, that is war for you: the game of kings.

Far to my left, Theobald had reached the fort gates and his men were pushing and heaving at them. They had brought a tree trunk with them which they were attempting to use as a battering ram. The first charge with the ram got nowhere. The Rheged archers on the battlements focused their fire upon the men carrying it and who could not therefore protect themselves. Half of them were hit by a volley of arrows and the reminder could not bear the heavy trunk's weight so dropped it.

Meanwhile, ahead of me the company was floundering across the ditch and had now reached the far side. The wall ahead of us was guarded by spearmen, but not now by many skirmishers. I figured I could spare Cuthbert.

"Cuth!" I bellowed. "Where are you?"

"Here, Cerdic," he answered jogging across to me, loaded bow held arrow point downwards. Then as he arrived he looked up at the wall with alarm, elbowed me to one side and quickly brought

247

up his bow. His arrow sped to the battlements and an enemy archer tumbled backwards out of sight. Had he been aiming at me? I reckoned so.

"Thanks Cuth, but go quickly with as many men as you can. See that ram. Sweep the battlements. Let Theobald get it to the gates."

He nodded and without another word ran off, waving at the other nearby skirmishers as he did so. In life he may be something of a lamb, but in battle Cuthbert was a lion.

I did not have time to watch him, however, because the company had reached the embankment beyond the ditch. Eduard was giving one man a leg up and then jumping up to seize the top of the fence. He ducked back down as a spear thrust almost skewered his head and then reaching up again, grabbed his opponent by the tunic and jerked him forward over the palisade so he fell screaming into the middle of the company. Axes, spears and swords swung up and down and the screaming stopped abruptly. Eduard was over the fence and swinging his axe left and right. Time to join them, I felt.

Dropping down into the ditch, I pushed my way through the company past the bloody remains of the Rheged archer. Above me Eduard, who with a dozen men was fighting to widen our foothold on the battlements, turned to face me and was shouting something which I could not hear above the din. I flinched to the left as a sling shot ricocheted off my helmet, leaving my ears ringing. Blinking to clear my vision I again saw Eduard shouting at me and gesturing violently back over his shoulder to the west.

Reaching the far embankment I clawed my way up the ditch and then stretched my hand towards Eduard, who bent forward and grasped it heaving me up to join him. More of the company followed me up so we now occupied the earthwork for thirty yards above the fort, where the ground sloped upwards towards the flat hill to our north. There was a crash from the fort and from my position I could see that the ram was in action. Cuthbert's archers were sending a steady hail of arrows on the area around the gate and under their protection, Theobald's companies were pounding on the gate itself. I caught a glimpse of Aedann at the ram, his mouth open as he gasped in air and then strained again to swing the log forward. Between us and the fort the embankment was full of warriors from Rheged forming a tight shield wall across the fortification and blocking our progress.

Eduard tapped me impatiently on the shoulder. "You deaf or something?" he bellowed.

"Not that deaf," I replied. "What were you saying?"

In reply he pointed westwards. I followed the direction of his finger, over the rear wall of the embankment, past the huddle of villagers' huts inside the second ring of fortifications and down the road as it followed the north bank of the Liddel Water. There - a couple of miles away but marching fast - was a dense shadow. A body of maybe a thousand men and more were coming towards us.

We were too late.

Mac Gabráin was here!

Chapter Twenty
An Immense and Mighty Army

"Woden save us!" I cried. I searched the area for Edwin and Sabert. Then I spotted the prince with his Huscarls on the battlement close to the fort and just beyond the tight knot of Rheged warriors on the other side of us. Sabert's company was to our right, having breached the battlements about eighty paces above our position. In both cases we had not yet linked up with them. Edwin looked outnumbered and hard-pressed so I needed to reach him quickly. Taking Eduard with me I led the way.

"We need to join up with his company and warn him!" I yelled above the noise of battle – it is one of the things about battle that remains uppermost in my mind along with the stench of blood, faeces and viscera: the sheer bloody awful din.

Eduard nodded and with a roar charged the enemy. He is the strongest man I know and the power with which he could wield an axe was awesome. With two huge swings he had carved a hole in the enemy shield wall and now, oblivious to his own safety, he leapt into the gap. I followed him up and the Wicstun Company came after me.

One of the British hacked at me with a sword and the weapon scraped down my shield grazing my lower arm beneath the short sleeves of my mailshirt and making me cry out in pain. I smashed my shield into his face and struck back with Catraeth, the Roman blade cutting deep into his neck. As he fell to the ground I stepped over him. The man following me up from behind

251

finished him off with a slash of his seax to the throat. Suddenly we were through and I was standing next to Edwin panting hard and gasping for breath.

"Highness, look!" I shouted and gestured down the road. The Scots were closer now although still some six hundred paces distant. Edwin's face grew pale as he watched them approach. For once his certainty had gone and sounding like the youth he was, he turned to me, "W-what do we do? Do we w-withdraw?"

I grimaced at the thought. "That will be messy and nigh on impossible to do without great risk. They would fall on us like a pack of wolves."

I turned around and looked east into the hills beyond the brook, scouring Cauddroun Rig for signs of friends. Aethelfrith was attacking the fort north of the plateau at the same time as we were attacking here, but he was also meant to be crossing that brook to hit the fortification on Degsastan Rig itself. Where was he?

"No, we can't pull back now. We press on, take the fort and village, hold it and pray to the gods that Aethelfrith arrives."

"We need to send a messenger, Cerdic. Tell him to find Aethelfrith and get him to attack at once."

I turned to look about the company, wondering who to send. Down on the bloody grass outside the fort I spotted Cuthbert. He was fast, nimble and ideal for the job.

"Highness, your company and mine should try to enter the fort. If we can take the pressure off Theobald, maybe he can gain entry at the gates. I will get word to Sabert to start pushing up toward the plateau. Eduard, stay with the prince and get on with that attack. I'll be back."

Without any more discussion I lowered myself back down the battlements and picked my way across the ditch, stepping in

252

between the broken bodies of men with whom I had trained and who only months before might have drunk ale in my hall. Cuthbert saw me moving towards him and joined me. We stood together examining the struggle at the gate. Cuthbert's skirmishers were providing cover, aiming steadily at the battlements as our battering ram was crashing against the gate.

At that moment, Aedann and his companions gave another mighty swing and the ram smashed through the woodwork with an ear-splitting noise. They pulled the ram back out of the breach and then they were at the gate, pulling apart the wreckage and trying to fight their way in. A spear thrust out of the doorway and caught Aedann in the shoulder. I saw him go down in the midst of the melee and lost sight of him.

"Cerdic, did you see? That was Aedann!" Cuthbert gasped, moving towards the gateway and pulling another arrow from the quiver at his back.

"Cuthbert, come back! Theobald and his brutes are with him. I need you to do something."

He turned to stare at me, "But damn it, Cerdic, it's Aedann!"

"Yes, yes I know, I want to go and help as much as you do, but we have a battle to win and I need you to do something for me."

"What?"

"Find Aethelfrith. Tell him that mac Gabráin has arrived."

"*What!*" Cuthbert said, his eyes widening.

I held my hands up to silence him. "Please, Cuth, speed is essential now. Find Aethelfrith and tell him that mac Gabráin is here already. I don't know about the Picts, but the Scots will be on us very soon. Aethelfrith must attack across the brook and draw them away from us or we will *all* be massacred. Got that?"

Cuthbert nodded. "Yes, Cerdic, of c-c-course. I'll g-go at once," he replied, his stammer returning with his anxiety.

253

"Good luck," I said. "Keep your head down!"

"And let the g-gods keep you and Eduard safe," he shouted, then he was off scampering across the open ground to the ford, splashing across the stream and disappearing into the trees that covered the hills to the east. I prayed that he would find Aethelfrith quickly and persuade him to bring his men to the battle as speedily as possible otherwise … well, otherwise I might not live to find out what happened next so there was not a lot of point in thinking about it.

I had a second message to deliver and I'd better do it quickly before I could return to my men. I jogged along the ditch until I came level with where Sabert stood, up on the battlements in the midst of his company. Clambering up the palisade and heaving myself over, I pushed through the mass of men to find myself just behind him. Back on the battlements I could see that the Scots were even closer now and they did indeed appear to be marching directly towards the fort.

"What is it, Cerdic? Sabert enquired. I quickly told him what we had done and what the plan was now. He nodded, "Agreed, but let's link up our companies here first though, and then I will push mine up over the battlements to the hill and you take yours down into the fort."

I drew Catraeth, lifted up my shield and pushed through the throng towards the knot of Rheged warriors who were still holding out on the battlements between Sabert's company and my own.

"Eduard!" I yelled, and again, "Eduard!"

This time my friend heard me from thirty paces away, saw me pushing towards him and rallied the company. "To our captain! To Cerdic," he bellowed and then hacked into the enemy mass with his vicious axe.

254

"This way," I ordered the men around me.

With me stabbing and thrusting with Catraeth in the one direction and Eduard swinging violently with his axe from the other, we drove a bloody path through the Rheged warriors, young men and old. Gradually, slipping and sliding on blood and guts, smashing our shields into the faces of someone's husband and someone's son, stumbling over the bodies of men who only moments before had been full of life, we eventually met up with the remnants of the Rheged garrison fleeing back to the village beyond the earthwork. The men around us gave a huge cheer as they realised that we had won this particular part of the battle. I let them cheer and enjoy their moment of triumph then pointed down the road.

"Look men: that is the Scots coming. We don't have long. We need to take the fort and the village. So keep fighting!"

I sent Eduard and as many men as he could muster over the battlements towards the village to try to secure it and prepare it for defence. Sabert, meanwhile, was fighting his way further up the battlements, trying to clear the enemy from the fortifications so that we could be ready when mac Gabráin arrived. Prince Edwin and his huscarls were slowly edging towards the fort so I took half the company with me to join him.

Theobald had not been idle whilst we had been fighting on the wall. As we approached the fort I could see that his companies were pushing through the gate. I barged my way through the throng of men until I found Edwin near the front, his sword drawn locked in combat with a giant of a man. The prince was being battered backwards by the might of his opponent. Edwin's huscarls were doing their duty and trying to protect him, but the enemy chieftain appeared to have singled him out and just as I arrived he smashed his shield into one of the prince's bodyguards and then advanced yet again on the boy.

With a cry of alarm, Edwin slipped backwards letting go of his sword and shield and tumbling helpless to the ground. Bellowing his triumph, his opponent jumped towards him and swung back with his sword ready to land the killing blow. It never reached him, for just in time I had stepped over the prince's body and blocked the blow with my shield, then stabbed with Catraeth into the man's neck, sending him crashing backwards into the mass of men behind, blood spurting down his tunic. After twitching for a moment, he lay still.

I reaching down to pull the ashen prince to his feet and then shouted back over my shoulder, "Come on men, the gates are open!"

I led the way forward. With their chieftain dead, the warriors guarding the way into the fort hesitated, dropped their weapons and turned to run. We pursued them, cutting and slashing, then suddenly we were inside the fort and I looked at a scene of utter devastation.

Having fought their way into the fort Theobald's company was now locked in a deadly struggle with Rheged's army. The crush of bodies was so intense it was hardly possible for a man to lift a weapon, much less to strike with it. Instead they heaved and pushed against each other, yelling and spitting in each other's faces. Theobald was trying to force his way further into the fort, Rheged's warriors just as desperately trying to evict the Bernician army and its prince. How long this struggle would have lasted is anyone's guess: until one side or the other in a state of exhaustion finally gave way and fled I suppose. But our arrival at the flank of the British defenders caused fear to flicker on their faces.

As we surged into the battle screaming and shouting, men defending the fort began to edge backwards to the rear entrance that connected to the village beyond. Fear became terror and that terror turned to panic. In ones and twos, then half a dozen; a score then fifty, until almost as one the enemy turned and fled.

Theobald's companies pursued them, hacking at them to prevent as many escaping as possible. A man who escaped now might returned to fight again later. Better to kill him than allow that to happen. We pursued them out of the gate and into the village, were between the hovels Eduard and his men were already fighting survivors from the battlements. At the sight of more of their compatriots fleeing, the fight went out of the village's defenders and as many as could joined the defeated warriors in running down the road towards mac Gabráin.

We had secured the fort and the battlements and the fortified village beyond, but as we took up positions on the walls and looked west towards the approaching Scots we saw they would be in a position to attack very soon. We had barely time to draw breath and regroup. I wondered how many of the victors of the morning's fight would live beyond midday - and if I would be one of them.

In the trees and hills to the east of the fort I could still see no sign of Aethelfrith or Cuthbert. How long had he been gone? It seemed an age: surely Aethelfrith's companies had arrived by now? Had he committed them all to the assault on the northern forts, out of sight beyond the hill that loomed on our right? If so we might not be able to hold out against mac Gabráin for long. I found Edwin, Sabert and Theobald, together with the captains of the other companies discussing how the defence of the village would be fought. Seeing Theobald made me think again about Aedann and I looked around the fort, but could see no sight of

257

him. I asked Theobald, but he said he had not seen him since they smashed the gate in. I wanted to search, but there was no time: we had a battle to fight first.

Around eight hundred Angles had attacked the fort and settlement at Degsastan. A third of these had been killed or wounded in the initial assault - many of the latter were being treated for their wounds in the interior of the fort even as we spoke. We could put perhaps five hundred men to the defence of the southern valley. We placed two hundred under Theobald in the village. This would be a breakwater upon which mac Gabráin's army would first descend. If we could not stop them in the village, Theobald would retreat to the fort where another hundred men from the Wicstun Company were deployed. Sabert took a further two hundred men and lined the earthwork above the fort and village. As skirmishers scavenged as many arrows and stones as they could, we armed ourselves and prepared for the assault.

The Scots were near enough for us to see their faces now. Their king had at least one thousand spears marching with him. The remnants of Rheged's shattered garrison, which we had earlier defeated, had rallied and added perhaps another two hundred to that strength. So we were outnumbered by more than two to one and in addition to that, mac Gabráin's forces had not been fighting this morning and so despite some fatigue from the march would be much less exhausted than we were.

Mac Gabráin himself rode forward out of his army when he had closed to just one hundred paces. The enemy spread out into a dense shield wall that filled the gap between the stream and the steep hillside to our right. The King of the Scots approached us and reined in just thirty yards away. He looked up at the battlements upon which we stood and studied us in silence for a long moment. I was reminded again about the wolf metaphor he had himself employed. How like a wolf he was that day, studying his prey and deciding when to strike.

"I am Áedánn mac Gabráin, King of Dál-Riata. I come for justice. Justice for our allies whose land you have taken and whose people you have slaughtered. Justice too for myself. I demand retribution for the murder of my son, Domanghast and the unlawful imprisonment of my other son, Bran. Where is Aethelfrith? I would have him answer for these crimes."

I had wondered about Bran. What had happened to him? I assumed Aethelfrith had held him captive since that skirmish in the stone circle when Domanghast was slain, but I knew not where. In fact I'd heard no more about him aside from when mac Gabráin had questioned me and my brother beneath the fortress of Dunadd. I knew now that when Aethelfrith had sent us north he had told Hussa to use the promise of Bran's release to tempt mac Gabráin to come here. If Bran still lived perhaps mac Gabráin would not attack. It was a slim hope, but could at least delay things; give Aethelfrith a chance to arrive or better still, maybe even avoid the battle completely. The very possibility that the prince might be released to him might make mac Gabráin hesitant about attacking us. If Theobald was wise he would be careful about how he answered that question.

I realised my folly just as soon as I had this thought because if there is one word you would not use to describe Theobald it is 'wise'. Before I had a chance to counsel him, he stepped up to the battlements and shouted his response.

"I am Theobald, Prince of Bernicia and brother to Aethelfrith. We are just in all that we do. We only fight to protect ourselves and our people. Your sons insulted our honour. They paid the price for that. My brother would have me tell you that he gave

259

orders that Bran should be put to death. I have just come from Bernicia where I saw to the matter myself," Theobald said, a deliberate touch of taunting in his voice.

"Great," Eduard muttered to me. "An enemy outnumbers you almost three to one and you tell him you've killed his son. Not much chance of negotiation now is there?"

He was right of course, which made me think about what he had just said. Aethelfrith had gone out of his way to provoke all these enemies. It really seemed as if the man would do anything to play his gamble to dominate the North. 'Negotiation' was not in his vocabulary.

Mac Gabráin said nothing in response to these words, but his face looked terrible. In silence he stared at Theobald and then very slowly turned his horse and rode it back into the front rank of his army. Once there he shouted an order in Gaelic and then repeated in the British speech.

"Attack! Attack at once! We take no prisoners. We offer no quarter. Kill them all. A thousand weight of gold to the man who brings me Theobald's head!"

Woden save us, I thought. For a price such as that, half of our own army might just betray the prince. On the enemy this challenge had an immediate effect. A loud roar began somewhere in the middle of their shield wall and then rolled along it in both directions. Soon all of the enemy were roaring, shouting, stamping their feet and smashing their swords and spears against their shields. Above the enemy army I could see dozens of the huge, two-handed Irish swords swinging back and forth. Their owners were telling us that these weapons were destined for us. Upon them we would perish.

Mac Gabráin nudged his horse a few steps forward and then thrusting out his sword so it pointed directly at us he roared one word.

"Attack!"

As one the enemy surged in our direction. They abandoned the tight formation of a shield wall in exchange for speed. Twelve hundred men were charging right at us.

"Return to your companies, lords." Theobald shouted as we dispersed, I to the fort with Edwin, Sabert to the earthwork. I glanced once more at the hills to the east but could still see no movement. Where in the name of all the gods was Aethelfrith?

From the battlements of the fort we could look down on the village. Theobald's men let fly with arrows, slingshots and javelins. In the brief moments between the charge beginning and the enemy reaching the village several hundred missiles were flung high into the air to descend upon the Scots and the British. Most fell harmlessly to earth, but four score of the enemy fell - many struck dead and the rest writhing around in agony. Then mac Gabráin's men smashed into the village wall. It was like standing on a beach watching the tide coming in. Where the water reaches a rock the wave splits and separates and surges on around the edge of it. On that day the tidal wave of mac Gabráin's army hit the wall and his men spread out in both directions and gradually encircled the village. Soon all around it men were fighting. Part of the right wing of the enemy reached the fort just below us and tried to enter, but Eduard gathered as many men as he could and repelled the first attack and for the moment we were safe. Meanwhile, the other wing of the Scots swept past the village and up to the embankment. Here they assaulted Sabert's companies. He too was able to keep them at bay for the present.

261

But the full might and fury of the enemy led by mac Gabráin in person, charging forward like some vengeful war god, fell upon the village. Nothing it seemed could stop his assault. Reaching the outer wall he used the height of his horse to seize hold of the battlements and soon he was over. For a moment he was isolated and I thought he would surely be struck down, surrounded as he was by so many enemies. But these were mere fyrd; no match for a man who had been a warrior for thirty years. With a ferocity born of fury, mad with grief and a thirst for revenge, the King of the Scots laid about him with his blade. Where ten men had stood moments before, now only mac Gabráin remained surrounded by the carnage of his victims.

It was an awesome sight. There he stood upon the battlements, shield in one hand and a fearsome looking sword that was almost two-handed in the other. He roared out a challenge to Theobald. The Bernician prince responded. At the front of his huscarls Theobald led them hurtling around the perimeter of the fenced village. He reached mac Gabráin first and from a hundred paces away, above the noise of battle, I could hear the clash as their swords met. As the king and the prince fought, the Scots had finally reached the battlements and were clambering over the top. Soon the air was filled with screaming, shouting and cursing. Not yet engaged, I and the Wicstun Company watched as just a short distance away men were dying. Suddenly I spotted Felnius and Herring. They had come over the wall close to mac Gabráin. A Bernician archer took aim at Herring and let fly. The arrow leapt towards the bastard who had tortured me in Dunadd. Along with Felnius, he had caused me great pain, but at that precise moment I prayed to Woden that the arrow did not hit him. I wanted him dead, true enough - but I wanted to do it myself. With relief I saw

262

my enemy pull his shield in the way of the arrow, which embedded itself harmlessly in the board.

Herring and Felnius then led a charge around the east side of the village battlements. Meanwhile, mac Gabráin and Theobald were still locked in combat. Huscarls and warriors on both sides moved to help one man or the other, but both of the combatants shouted that they wanted to be left alone. Whilst Felnius and Herring were advancing through the Bernician spearman on the eastern side of the village, here the battle on the western half of the village seemed to have halted. Every man was watching the duel between king and prince. Theobald was young, agile and confident. Mac Gabráin was older and wiser and full of the experience the years give. But in the end it was not knowledge and wisdom or experience that made a difference here. If a man has killed your son there is strength to be found in the fury that only vengeance can assuage. Theobald dodged and weaved, rushing forward to stab and scampering away to avoid the counter blow. Mac Gabráin absorbed every blow with his shield and sword and even on his body. He was bleeding from a dozen cuts. Then suddenly, when Theobald must have believed that victory was moments away, the king threw his shield at the prince. Theobald jumped to his left to avoid the heavy board and found that mac Gabráin was charging at him. Unbalanced by his evasive manoeuvre Theobald tried desperately to bring his sword up. He wasn't quick enough and mac Gabráin's own blade plunged into his throat, the point emerging with a sickening 'crack' from the back of his spine. Theobald slid off the Irishman's sword and fell into a heap on the ground. His body twitched then lay still.

For a moment there was silence. Even the fighting on the eastern part of the village seemed to halt. Then I heard Herring shout one word: "Victory!"

With a roar of triumph the Scots and British surged forward again. Theobald's men took one look at their dead prince and turned and fled in panic back towards the fort.

"Oh, bollocks!" Eduard cursed.

The Bernicians were now flooding through the open gates between the fort and the village with the Scots and British pursuing them. I had to get the gates closed.

" Eduard!" I bellowed. "Get those gates closed now!"

We both ran down from the battlements and headed towards the open gates. As I galloped down the steps two at a time I could see that Edwin was standing just inside the gates clutching his sword in one hand as if he was prepared to hold the gates single-handed. I arrived at his side.

"Highness, what are you *doing*? We have to close the gates!"

"Let the bastards come. We will stop them here."

"Not if we can't shut those gates we won't."

"You held the gates at Catraeth, why should I not do it here?"

I ignored him, seized hold of one gate and nodded at Eduard who took the other and we started pushing the gates together. Theobald's panicked Bernicians continued to flood through the opening. If I shut the gates with them outside, they would be slaughtered. Yet if I left them open, mac Gabráin would be through them in moments and the battle would be over.

"Keep pushing, keep pushing!" I urged Eduard. More men came to join us and we heaved at the gates and gradually they closed even as more men were running towards them.

"For the gods' sake let us in!" Voices pleaded. Hands were scraping at the other side, fists pounding on the gates as

264

panicstricken men begged to be admitted. Then there was a cry of pain, a shout of terror, the clash of sword against sword, more cries of agony - and then silence. Eduard and I slid the bar across the gates and moved aside to let men pass, their arms full of items to blockade the gateway: barrels, sacks of grain and even a pair of benches. I left them to it and sick at heart for those Bernicians whose death I had indirectly caused, returned to the battlements. Prance Edwin, sour-faced, followed me.

In the village, mac Gabráin's men were shouting and cheering in triumph. The last Angle survivors were being hunted down between the huts and slaughtered. Then the Scots king started pulling his men into order. I watched him in grim realisation that although it would take him some minutes to gather his forces for another assault, an attack on the fort would surely not be long in coming.

Next to me, Edwin studied the enemy then scowled at me. "You did not answer my question, Cerdic!"

"What question?" I mumbled.

"I asked why, if you had held the gates at Catraeth, I could not do it here today." I turned to stare at the prince. This was all about a chance to win a reputation to him. Did he not realise how dire our situation was? I tried to explain. "Back at Catraeth I had no choice. The gates were opened and Owain was coming through. We had no chance to close them. It was a case of either stopping him or all would be lost. It wasn't about glory!"

"That is easy for you to say, Cerdic, you have your reputation and your glory. I am just a younger prince. The crown will most likely not come to me, but to Hereric, after Aethelric. Any man needs glory and reputation, but a prince more than most. I don't suppose you would understand that."

265

At that moment I thought just how much he sounded like me in the weeks before the Villa was attacked and my brother, Cuthwine, was slain. I realised that I understood Edwin more than he knew. He may be young and foolish, but as my father had once said, there was a fire in this prince's soul; an echo of his sire, King Aelle. He had the makings alright; he just needed guidance. In that realisation my feelings towards him softened a degree.

"Prince Edwin, you have the ability to make a name for yourself, I am certain of it. Yet no one will ever find out if you go and get yourself killed here today will they? Let's just get out of this alive, eh?"

Edwin glanced up at me sharply. His usual arrogant sneer, a habitual feature when talking to me, had gone. He seemed unsure how to respond, but at that moment an outburst of chanting began in the village, reminding us – as if we needed reminding - that we were in the middle of a battle. We turned to study the enemy: mac Gabráin's army had reformed and seemed almost as strong as it had been before they attacked the village. Still more than eleven hundred men, they were getting ready to attack again. We, on the other hand, had lost most of Theobald's command. We were now outnumbered more than three to one and our morale was low whilst that of the enemy was soaring. The odds were stacked against us: how Loki must be laughing.

I put Eduard back in charge of the men on the outside wall of the fort whilst I took control of the main body holding the gates and battlements. Sabert and his two hundred men spread out to hold the earthworks. They looked perilously thin. For the umpteenth time I glanced eastwards to search the hills, looking for signs of Aethelfrith and still I could discern no movement. For a moment I thought I could hear the sound of fighting to the north beyond the hill. Had Aethelfrith taken his whole force there? Were we being abandoned to our inevitable fate?

Mac Gabráin's horns sounded and the cry was taken up across the battlefield. Then he advanced towards us in three divisions: one wing swinging east towards Sabert; another circling around the village to come at Eduard from the south. The main body accompanied by mac Gabráin, Felnius and Herring - as many as seven hundred men - stomped through the muddy ground of the village and came right at me. This time, I knew there would be no stopping them.

The enemy reached the fort and started to claw and clamber their way up the outer fence, as well as batter at the gate between fort and village. The crude makeshift barrier we had created behind the gate was insufficient to hold them and after only moments of hammering and pounding, the gate gave and collapsed back over the barricade.

Herring was first through it, followed by Felnius and then, in a surge, the Scots were inside the fort. I led a counter charge and in a moment I was face to face with the two men who had tortured me through this last winter. Exhausted and weak I may be, but inside me a great surge of anger and the desire for revenge gave me strength.

They recognised me almost at the same moment and steered a course towards me. I wondered briefly if they had worked out how Hussa and I had escaped, but there was no preamble, no clever comments or threats. Herring simply swung his sword at me. I parried with mine and then slammed my shield towards his face. He stepped back and deflected the blow with his own shield and swung back at me. Felnius joined him, but the sheer crush of men on both sides carried the two Scots away from me and I was fighting another. For a while we held them in the fort. Then I

267

heard a roar from the southern battlements. Feinting a thrust at my opponent so that he stepped away I chanced a glance in that direction. Eduard and his men had not been able to stop the charge against them and were swept off the battlements and down into the body of the fort. Outflanked by the new arrivals my company was starting to panic and give way. Step by step we were pushed backwards towards the eastern gates that Theobald and his rammers had sacrificed so much to open. If we were forced outside the fort all would be lost. Yet moment by moment this was looking more likely. Another roar off to the north suggested that mac Gabráin's men had reached the top of the battlements there as well. Everything looked very grim. In front of me, just out of reach, following me up as I retreated, Herring was grinning in expectation of victory. It dawned on me that if they won here and Aethelfrith was killed then Herring would be king in Bernicia. A puppet king of mac Gabráin's maybe but it would still be bad for Deira . Gods help us if we lost today!

The eastern gates were being pushed apart and my company started to crumble at the edges as men turned and fled through them.

"Stand! Stand!" I ordered.

"No retreat men of Deira, no retreat," bellowed Eduard.

"Don't run!" Edwin added at my elbow.

It did no good. The men were not stupid. They knew the odds against us. They were thinking of themselves now, of their families and homes and whether they would see them again. The incessant pressure from ahead and the weakening of resolve from behind meant that we were being pushed past the gate. I was standing in the gateway now, Eduard on my left and Edwin on my right. Only fifty men were gathered around us willing to resist or just ashamed to lose. Perhaps Lilla would write a song about

268

us, I thought. Edwin was now being pulled to the rear by his huscarls and Eduard was roaring at the enemy, challenging them to take him on, probably thinking that at least in death we might sell ourselves dear. Maybe if we took enough of them with us some of the army could escape - maybe Edwin could get back home and the army might defend the country after all.

I stepped forward to stand beside Eduard with the enemy closing in on us and suddenly I remembered Lilla's story of my uncle standing in that sunken road near Eorforwic. Was this how he had felt? Was this the moment when my own story would join his, to be repeated through the long years. Would folk look at *my* sword with reverence? Then again, on that day Grettir had brought my uncle's body and sword home. Would anyone take my body home, I wondered.

Herring came on again slashing his sword at my throat. Flinching away, I slipped and fell over backwards losing my grip on my shield, which went flying off into the ditch outside the fort. Desperately I tried to parry the incoming blow with my sword, but the sheer force of it made my arm numb. I had blocked that attack, but knew that I would not be able to protect myself again. Eduard was being attacked by no fewer than ten enemies and could not help me either.

Suddenly, a shadow fell over me and there standing astride me, shield in one hand and sword in the other, was Hussa. He parried Herring's incoming strike, sending the Scot stumbling backwards into his men. My brother pulled me to my feet. I shook my hand to clear the numbness from it and picked up another shield and now the three of us, Hussa, Eduard and I, were standing side by side. I glanced briefly at Hussa and nodded at him. He grinned back at me. Never had he felt more like my brother than at that moment. On my other side Eduard roared at

269

the enemy, challenging them to come and die on his axe? And there, in the midst of utter horror I smiled, for my big friend showed no fear even now.

For a brief moment there was a pause; it happens sometimes in battle, as though men must rest their sword arms for a breath before coming at each other again. I looked around and felt as if my heart leapt into my throat, for there, amongst a pile of bodies close by the gate, I saw Aedann. Was he dead or just wounded? There was no time to check. I wondered then about Cuthbert. At least he was better off out of it. Maybe afterwards he would take our bodies home and hand over my swords to Aidith. Thinking of Cuthbert I wondered again where he had got to. And where was Aethelfrith?

"Here they come again," Eduard said, lifting the great axe. I readied myself, felt Hussa stiffen at my side; became aware that Edwin had escaped his huscarls and come up beside us.

"Woden's balls!" shouted one of my men, "look over there!" He was pointing to the north, where the brook ran between Degsastan Rig and the wooded hills to the east. There at last was the answer to my questions and prayers, for there was Aethelfrith. His men were emerging from between the trees. As we watched, one thousand and more carrying spears crossed the brook, clambered up the steep western slope and formed up on the highest plateau. Mac Gabráin's men must have seen his arrival for there was a sudden murmur and a word could be heard from five hundred lips and more: "Aethelfrith" - that was the word and it was as if lightning had passed through the enemy forces. Now the Scots were staring around nervously, no longer pushing us back, for they realised the terrible danger they were in. And I smiled and at the same time shook my head in wonder, for I could now see Aethelfrith's plan in all its cunning beauty. He had fought his battle here in the south valley and also in the one to the north. He had drawn the enemy into a fight, knowing they would come with their fresh troops and try to take back the forts from us. Because we had not attacked the plateau they had hardly placed any men there themselves. And now Aethelfrith was advancing westwards across that plateau with no opposition in his way. He could turn at will northwards or southwards and cut off their retreat.

If we could hold them here in the fort we could annihilate this army right here, right now, crushed between hammer and anvil, just as the king had foreseen, just as he had planned. I had misjudged the man's cleverness - if not his ruthless ambition that did not count the cost.

At that moment Cuthbert came running up behind me. "Cuth, thank the gods, you're safe!"

"Aethelfrith says to attack with all your might," he panted. "Attack the fort and keep them here. He will come round behind them and destroy them."

I nodded and started rallying as many men as I could. Not many moments before they had been backing away and some were already running for home. Yet many had seen Aethelfrith's arrival. Their captains were shouting at them to rally, pushing and cajoling them back towards the fight. A good many men came back of their own free will. Within moments we had formed up two hundred men and yet more were running to join us.

"Attack!" I shouted.

"Attack!" Eduard and Edwin echoed.

And forward we went.

It wasn't going to be as easy as we perhaps had hoped. Felnius and Herring and mac Gabráin himself were rallying their own warriors and they still outnumbered us. But they now had

271

Aethelfrith to worry about. At the rear of the fort the King of the Scots was pulling off whole companies and sending them back out to the village and up onto the hill. The Scots charged in front of Aethelfrith, trying to get in his way and halt his advance. But now I could not think of the larger battle, I could not do more than concentrate on staying alive here at the eastern gate. Herring came back at me and we were slashing and cutting at each other once more. He was clearly enjoying the fight, was doubtless savouring the expectation of finishing what he had started in that stinking hole in the ground. That was his weakness: he believed he was superior to me because of what he had done when I was helpless and in chains. Well if he wanted to believe that, I would use it against him. I feinted another slip down onto my knees and seemed to let go of my shield so that it started to slide off my arm. Herring, triumph shining in his eyes, took a step forward ready to strike the killing blow, but now I leapt back up, thrusting the sword up under his shield and into his throat. Triumph died to be replaced by disbelief as he stared at me for a moment and then slid off my sword onto the ground. Very briefly I glanced exultantly at his body, but didn't have time to gloat for other Scots were upon me and the fight continued.

So the great battle raged on. But step by step we pushed back and regained the lost ground. More and more Scots were pulled away from fighting us to try to halt Aethelfrith on the high plateau. Finally, we broke through their ranks and advanced upwards towards the plateau ourselves, coming into the flank of the very companies that mac Gabráin had already sent up there in a futile attempt to hold Aethelfrith and prevent a massacre. I do not like to think back on that day as I do not like to recall the terrible murder we did. For murder it was there on the high Rig as we surrounded the enemy and destroyed them.

272

Aethelfrith would have wanted to capture or kill mac Gabráin. In fact this was the only one of his objectives he did not achieve that day. As we stood around with the bodies heaped about us, spears thrust into the ground and pointing to the bleak sky, shields and swords abandoned in a scene of carnage so terrible that one can see it only on a battlefield, I chanced to glance off westwards towards the setting sun. Aethelfrith had continued his march across the hilltop, but we did not have horses in our army and the King of the Scots did, if only a few. He had somehow managed to reach his mount and alongside him I saw Felnius pull himself up onto another. Only a very few Scots nobles reached the safety and escape that the horses offered that day and mac Gabráin was one of them.

They looked back towards us and mac Gabráin seemed to hesitate as if considering one last charge at the man who had killed his sons. Mayhap he was of a mind to join them in the Christian's heaven, but I saw Felnius put one hand on his shoulder and steer him away. Perhaps he was telling his king that another day might come for revenge. I stared after Felnius and I had the same thoughts: he and I had unfinished business and he was escaping. However, I was beyond the point of exhaustion and I and the men who had attacked the fort that morning collapsed where we stood and amidst the groans and gore of dying foe, we tried to get some rest before we must turn to the gruesome task that awaited us. Overhead the carrion crows were already gathering to feast and in the distant peaks I heard the echoing howl of wolves.

I learned later that the Picts had attacked the north fort just as the Scots had attacked the south and had been swept up in the same trap Aethelfrith had set. He pursued the fleeing Scots, Picts and the British almost as far as the same river to the west where

273

two days before Hussa and I had landed. Then he had turned back. He had not abandoned us to our fate as I had feared, merely gambled that enough of us would still be alive to contain the enemy until he eventually returned to the battlefield.

Once rested, our thirst quenched by scurrying water boys, we piled up the bodies and placed cairns over them. Very few men had any more memorial than that. One who did was Prince Theobald. When Aethelfrith returned to the battlefield the following day, having chased in vain after mac Gabráin, he went to look upon the body of his brother and ordered that Theobald be buried close by the spot where he had died and a stone be raised to mark the location.

So the battle was won, there were no enemies left here north of the Wall and Aethelfrith's gamble had paid off. He was all powerful between the walls, but as I had feared, the cost had been horrendous. In the army of Aethelfrith's Bernicia the losses had not been that bad, except in Theobald's companies. Edwin's army, however, had not only attacked the fort but defended it from counter attack. Of the five hundred men we had taken north the year before, only two hundred were alive and uninjured. If we had to fight to defend Deira, I did not see how it would now be possible. But the gods willing, for the moment we had no enemies strong enough to try.

We found Aedann after the battle. He was alive, for which I thanked the gods, yet fearfully wounded, with a huge, deep gash down one side from which he had lost an awful amount of blood. We took him to a nearby hut in the village and cleaned his wounds. Mercifully he passed out, so we were able to stitch him up without holding him down, but I could not ask him what he had wanted me to tell Edwin before the battle. Whatever it was, I guessed it was no longer important. I prayed for his recovery, even sending a prayer to the Christian God to watch over His follower. It was with great relief that the day after the battle I saw that Lilla had turned up, having ridden from Dunadd across country.

He embraced me, "I see you live still, Cerdic. I told you Loki had plans for you."

"I live, but Aedann is badly injured. He needs your help."

"Then take me to him," the bard said, his jovial face suddenly serious.

Hussa came and found me after we had buried Theobald and I thanked him for saving my life.

He shrugged, "I told you in Dunadd that I was afraid of Aethelfrith. Now you have seen the extent that he will go in order to have his glory."

"Yes," I nodded, "the risks he took were extraordinary and the costs have been enormous, but I suppose from his point of view they have paid off. At least it is over now."

Hussa did not reply, but something in his expression made my heart sink. "What is it? What is wrong?"

"It is not over."

"But we have destroyed everyone - Aethelfrith is unassailable here north of the Wall."

Again Hussa shrugged. "North of the Wall, yes ..."

"What do you mean?"

"I mean that he was not as reckless with this battle as I thought. This was not just a matter of destroying his enemies here, Cerdic. He also planned to weaken his friends."

"You mean ..."

"Yes, I mean Deira."

"But ..."

My brother nodded. "Yes go on ..." he encouraged.

I stared at him appalled, "But he would only do that if ..."

"Yes?" Hussa regarded me, one eyebrow raised. I had a horrible feeling he knew what I was thinking and that what I was thinking might be right.

"Well, if he was going to ..." I faltered as the awful suspicion came home to me, "... attack *us* ... to attack Deira!"

"Exactly," Hussa said.

Chapter Twenty-One
Betrayal

W hat?" I gasped, staring at the man as if he was insane, which at that moment he seemed to be, at least to me. "That is sheer madness. I cannot believe I'm right." I shook my head, "What does he expect us to do: just stand around whilst he marches south towards Deira?"

Hussa shrugged and then with a tilt of the head indicated that I should look to the east. The army had camped out on the battlefield of Degsastan. Edwin's army had been allowed to use the huts within the village whilst Aethelfrith had his men sleep out in the fields to the west of the fort and further east near the ford. Now that I considered that decision, which had previously seemed to be generous, it was suspicious. Indeed, I now realised that half of Aethelfrith's army, perhaps a thousand men, lay between ours and our road south and home.

"He's not letting us go is he? He kept us here last winter when you and I were away in Dunadd with the excuse that this campaign required the presence of our army. But now no one opposes him north of the Wall. Nor for that matter in Rheged. Elmet was crushed by us only a few years ago. There are no enemies surrounding him now, are there?"

"No; only friends or vassal states. Remember what mac Gabráin said about Aethelfrith being like a wolf? In a wolf pack there is only one leader. He will not permit anyone else to be that leader. Aethelric may be weak, but he is still a king. Aethelfrith wants him out of the way. What is there to stop the Bernician wolf from turning south now?"

I didn't answer because Hussa was right. I was convinced of it now. There was no one to stop Aethelfrith. Deira lay open to conquest and the only men who knew the danger were trapped inside the enemy army.

"Are you sure of this?" Sabert asked Hussa a short while later when my brother and I had gone to see him and Edwin. We all went inside the hut where Aedann lay in fitful sleep watched over by Lilla. I shut the door after posting Eduard and Cuthbert as guards.

Hussa nodded, "He told us last night. He gave orders that the army of Deira should not be permitted to leave."

"Why are you telling us this?" Sabert asked. "You don't exactly owe Deira much loyalty do you - on past experience anyway."

"Why would I lie? Ask yourself what I would hope to gain."

"But why tell us at all?" I asked.

"I could lie and say that I have been thinking about Deira during these years up here, wondering about home. Maybe it's true and perhaps I find that I would like the ability to return. But to do so - to be accepted - would require an impressive act. Maybe I hoped this might qualify."

"I find that hard to believe, Hussa, after all you have said about Deira in the past."

"I dare say," Hussa smiled at me. "Very well, I'll tell you. It's Theobald - it is all to do with Theobald."

I had no idea what he meant and looking at the blank expressions on the other faces, neither did they. "What about him?" I asked.

"I wanted him out of the way."

"What?"

"He never trusted me, right from the start. He was always in my way; even more when I got up here."

I nodded, recalling the tension in the air on our first visit. "What do you mean, always in your way?"

"I figured I could become Aethelfrith's lieutenant, but Theobald kept casting doubts about my loyalty. I reasoned that if I got him out the way I could gain a high position in his brother's court. Theobald was stupid; brave enough, but impulsive and it was not hard to provoke him."

I had a sudden flash of memory. That stone circle: Hussa talking to Theobald. I had assumed he had been trying to calm him down. But no, quite the opposite, he had been goading Theobald into anger by hinting that the Scots princes were insulting him, but of course, they hadn't been. Hussa had caused the fight hoping that Theobald would die. Now I thought back on it Aethelfrith had seemed surprised by the fracas at the time. He had not planned it, merely taken advantage of it, realised he could use it for his own ends and seized the opportunity to kill Domanghast and capture Bran.

"The stone circle," I burst out. "You started the fight. You hoped Theobald would die, but it went wrong; he lived and Domanghast died in his stead."

Hussa nodded.

"Here too - at Degsastan," I went on, as everything slotted into place. "It was you who suggested that Theobald launch the attack. That he be the one to march into the worst part of the battle. You were again hoping he would die." I recalled now that Hussa had spoken to Theobald before the battle. "What did you tell him that morning?"

279

Hussa laughed. "Aethelfrith had told me that Theobald had killed Bran. I suggested to Theobald that it would be foolish of him to brag about that to mac Gabráin."

"Damn it, Hussa, you knew that would incite him to do just that and you knew, given how mac Gabráin felt about his sons, that this would inflame the Scots king to a killing pitch."

My brother raised an eyebrow, but did not deny it.

"Very well," Sabert said, "you wanted Theobald dead so you could take his place. Now you have achieved exactly that, why on earth betray Aethelfrith now, just when you are his trusted lieutenant? I don't understand."

"The king is a lot cleverer than his brother was, Earl Sabert. I am not sure he ever really trusted me; he just made use of me knowing I wanted advancement. Maybe someone told him I goaded the prince at the stone circle. As it turned out I did him a favour there, but he also knows I talked Theobald into bragging about Bran's death to mac Gabráin and he's put two and two together. Aethelfrith might be ruthless, but Theobald was still his kin." Hussa shrugged, a half smile lifting the corner of his mouth, "He is holding me responsible for what happened and he does not take kindly to my manipulating his brother's death. He has ordered my arrest to answer to the charge of treason. That is why I was sneaking around here avoiding his camp. I figured ..."

"Huh, you figured if we can get away, we will take you along and you will save your neck. Is that it?"

Hussa nodded.

"Well I for one don't believe you," Sabert said. "What trickery are you and Aethelfrith planning?"

"He ... he speaks the truth," came the weak voice of Aedann from the cot on which he lay. The Welshman was awake, though

280

still dreadfully grey in the face, his eyes looked bruised, sunk in dark hollows.

"Aedann, thank the gods!" I rushed over to the cot, knelt down and felt his head. He was still warm but the fever seemed a little diminished. I glanced up at Lilla and nodded my thanks. His magic or healing potion, whatever it was, had worked again.

"He is ... not lying," Aedann said again, lifting his head to peer at Hussa.

"What do you mean?" I asked.

"I was trying to tell you at the camp the night before the battle, but I could not get you alone. Two weeks ago some of Theobald's huscarls got drunk back in Bebbanburgh when we were waiting for the new companies to gather. One of them said he had overheard Theobald and Aethelfrith talking through their plans one day."

"Their plans to attack Deira?" I asked.

"Yes. They expected this battle with mac Gabráin; Aethelfrith had it all planned down to the finest detail."

"I can vouch for that at least," said Lilla.

"But not just that," Aedann gasped, "they kept saying that after they'd beaten the Picts and the Scots, nothing would stop them marching on Deira."

Sabert looked down his nose at Aedann, "I thought you were sworn to Theobald's service, Welshman. Why do you tell us this?"

"I am loyal to Cerdic and his house. I swore to that and though we have had harsh words I still count that promise above all others."

I got to my feet, "I am grateful, Aedann. If you would return to my service I would gladly have you back, but I still have no land to give you."

"Forgive me, Cerdic. I was chasing false gold. Hope of some obscure fields up here is not the same as belonging in the land where I was born."

"Yes, yes. All very touching I am sure," Hussa commented sourly. "Yet we still must decide what to do. Do I take it you now accept I am telling the truth?"

Sabert shrugged. "It seems so ... yet I still wonder ..."

Edwin, who had been listening closely to what was said, now spoke up. "Maybe we should not worry so much about why he is telling us this and more about what to do now." He had a point.

"Yes, that is a good question," Sabert conceded. "What do we do now? We can't march out east or west. The road is blocked. We can't fight our way out in either direction. What do we do?"

I looked at Hussa and suddenly I smiled and he must have known what I was thinking because he laughed and said, "Alas, it's an idea but we would be spotted."

"Not at night. Not if we created a diversion. It's a new moon and cloudy too. Nice and dark," I grinned, "lots of shadows ..."

"Ah yes," Hussa chortled, "real ghostly."

Edwin looked from one to the other of us and scowled. "Well, are you going to tell us your plan, gentlemen?" he asked irritably.

So we did, elaborating as we went along.

Midnight. I was standing at the gate between the fort and the battlements peering along the earthwork as it climbed the hillside and vanished into the gloom. Sabert stood beside me.

"How long have they been?" he asked, breaking the silence.

"Long enough I would say. They won't be much longer ... in fact here they come."

Eduard, accompanied by half a dozen Wicstun men, hurried along the battlements towards us, moving as quietly as they were able. The men passed us whilst my friend halted at the gate.

"Well?" I asked.

It is ready. Won't be long now."

"Right then, get down to the village and get the men ready. Make sure weapons are sheathed. No shields and no spears; nothing that will clatter. We will be along with Cuthbert and Hussa shortly."

They nodded and scuttled off.

"I hope to Woden that this works, Cerdic," Sabert said. "If it does not we will never get away."

"It will work," I said and added a prayer to the gods myself. But not to Woden or any of the others save one: I prayed to Loki, the master of tricks and misdirection. I needed his blessing tonight - because this was his type of game.

After a few minutes I saw what I was waiting for.

"There!" Sabert hissed, pointing west along the hilltop. A few hundred yards away, to the west of us a light flared up and then another and another, as small bonfires were lit.

"Now there!" I added as to the east more fires ignited. These were closer to us and we could make out shapes in front of the flames. It seemed as if an army was standing on the hilltop. I could see figures in front of the fire; see their spears, shields, armour and helms silhouetted by the firelight.

"Someone is coming!" Sabert hissed as Cuthbert came into view. A minute later Hussa too appeared.

"It's done," he muttered, turning to the west to admire his handiwork. Now over there too we could see shadowy figures around the fires. There was a shout from the west as the watch spotted the fires and ran to the edge of the camp to investigate.

"Right, let's go," I ordered and we all vacated the earthwork passing through the fort to emerge in the village. The remnants of our five hundred Deirans were standing ready beside the southern gate of the village. Two hundred men were unharmed or bore only minor cuts and bruises. Another fifty were injured. Some of these, like Aedann, were able to walk albeit slowly and certainly would not be able to fight for many days. Aedann insisted on carrying his sword nonetheless. Others - maybe a score - could not walk along with us. Sabert, Edwin and I had talked about these. Should we leave them to Aethelfrith's mercy? Should we put them out of their misery ourselves? We did not wish to take the chance of the former and baulked at the mere thought of the latter. In the end it was Eduard who suggested we build carrying frames with spears and cloaks roped together and carry the wounded as best as we could, four men to a frame, two at each end. It was all we could do for them. It was likely that most would die as we travelled, but at least they would have a chance.

Without a word of command I ran over, located Edwin near the gate and nodded at him as I led the men through. This then was the plan. The ways west and east were blocked, but south was a huge shadow - the hill that Hussa and I had climbed up just a few days before to circle the valley. The hill we had gone over to reach Aethelfrith and now the one we planned to use to evade him.

But first we needed to cross the road. It passed south of the village and on to the ford. The valley floor was flat and open. Silently, with backs bent to try to keep as low as possible, we scuttled across the road and down into a ditch that ran along the other side. I crouched in the bottom and turned to watch the hillside to the north. Whilst I waved the men on by, Cuthbert and

I searched for signs that we were being observed. High up on the hills the warriors of our phantom army were lit by the now blazing bonfires. They looked like the spectres of men rising from their graves; spirits come to wreak vengeance on those who had slain them. That at least was what we were intending the Bernicians to believe. As we watched it seemed that we had been successful, for in both camps men were emerging from their tents and standing huddled around as if unsure what they were watching.

In the meantime their former allies were crossing a stream and in ones and twos starting to climb the hill - men moving in ones and twos. Those who were carrying frames had lowered their burdens to the ground and each was now dragged up the steep hillside using ropes looped around the spears. The wounded must have been in dreadful pain, but not one cried out. If anyone did look in our direction I hoped the darkness of the hill's shadow was shrouding us. And for a long time it worked. All the men were across the stream and Cuthbert and I were fording the shallow brook when I heard a cry from the fort. One of the Bernicians had obviously gone to find out why we had not come out to look at the flaming soldiers and found the fort empty. Cuthbert and I had now reached the southern bank and were starting up the steep slope when a figure appeared on the battlements and pointed towards us.

Even then it took some time for him to get anyone else to take any notice. Our fire and light show had drawn their attention. Eventually, a courageous huscarl must have ventured to the top of the hill for we heard a shout and then a lot more shouting. We had used spears to prop up the empty armour, chain shirts, cloaks and shields and we guessed he had pulled one of them out of the ground and shown it to the men below. They knew then that all they were seeing was a trick. Just then the observant fellow in the fort managed to get a couple of his companions to look where he was pointing. After that it was only a matter of moments before the entire Bernician army had scrambled to the battlements to gaze in our direction.

Suddenly, Aethelfrith was on the road below us, sword in one hand gesturing violently with the other. He pointed south towards us and then east along the road. With another shout his army was sent into a flurry of activity - seizing swords, spears, shields and helmets and then setting off in pursuit. Some men came up the slope towards us, whilst others marched east along the road trying to cut us off before we were able to reach the route south to freedom.

Now the race was on.

"Keep moving, keep moving," I urged the men.

Panting heavily we kept clambering up the steep hill in the dark. Ahead of me a man gave a yelp of pain as his foot slipped into some unseen hole and there was a snap. It was obvious as soon as I reached him that the man's ankle had broken. He would not be able to climb anymore and would need to be helped off this hill. Eduard came running back down. Dragging the man up onto his one good foot and supporting his weight, my friend helped him limp up the hill.

"You need to leave me," the man said as bravely as he could, though I saw his gaze was fixed upon the pursuing warriors only a few hundred feet below us.

"We have lost enough good men here," Eduard said. "I am not leaving any more."

"But I can't walk!" the man said desperately.

Eduard did not answer, but simply reached down and pulled the man off his feet and up onto his back. I had lifted Cuthwine

286

like that and carried him around the Villa. Cuthwine was only two at the time, whilst this man was twenty years his senior and yet Eduard lifted him as if he were merely a bag of flour. Eduard was the strongest man I knew, nevertheless, he had not gone twenty steps before I could see sweat breaking out on his forehead and his breathing becoming laboured for the hill we were ascending was all but sheer.

We climbed and Aethelfrith's men pursued us, but we did have one advantage. Saving the burden that Eduard carried, no others had any weight on them apart from swords, seax, axes, bows and arrows. The men carrying the wounded made light work of it thanks to Eduard's frames, and knowing that our mail shirts would impede our progress we'd even left those behind, using them to clothe our phantom warriors. Our pursuers, however, were fully armed and equipped and soon found that climbing up that hill with all that weight was slowing them down.

Finally, we reached the top where a spring emerged from the hillside and here I let the men rest briefly and drink their fill from the clear cool waters. The spring became a stream which carried on down into the valley below us before joining the Liddel Water. From the hilltop I spotted movement along the road north and east of where we stood and although it was hard to see any detail I knew that Aethelfrith's men would be marching at full pace along it, trying to reach the eastern foot of the hill before we could.

"We will be cut off," Edwin remarked.

"Not if I can help it. Keep moving - everyone, keep moving. If you want to see your families and your homes again, don't stop."

We hurtled down the other side of the hill and now had to be careful not to run too fast for we could not risk any more broken ankles. Behind us Eduard was coming slowly down the slope, struggling with his burden, when suddenly above him and fifty or so paces behind, a pursuing Bernician archer arrived on the hilltop. Seeing Eduard and the injured man well within range he quickly notched an arrow on his string and took aim.

"Eduard, get down!" I shouted.

Eduard looked puzzled; he clearly had not heard what I said. I opened my mouth to yell at him again, but just then an arrow buzzed past my ear from behind me, perilously close. Instinctively I ducked and heard the scream as the arrow thudded into the chest of the enemy archer. He tumbled down the hillside ten yards from where the spring emerged, landing in a heap, quite dead. Glancing round I saw Cuthbert lowering his bow, an expression of grim satisfaction on his narrow features.

"Good man, Cuth."

"Well that bastard wasn't going to get Eduard - not with me here anyhow!"

Eduard stumbled on past us, oblivious to the whole episode.

"Bloody typical!" Cuthbert muttered as he watched the big man struggle by.

I grinned at him, "Never mind, Cuth, you can tell him later."

If there is a later, I said to myself, with an eye on the men marching along the road towards us.

As we pushed on down the eastern slope of the hill, Sabert and Edwin had also spotted the pursuit, whilst above us the Bernicians following us up the other side of the hill were now emerging in numbers there too. Sabert lingered until I caught up with him.

"We are never going to reach the road before those bastards cut us off, are we? Especially not with the wounded slowing us down," he said.

I shook my head. "I doubt it, unless ..."

"Unless one of us takes a company directly towards them and intercepts them, blocks their path and lets the others get away."

"No! That would be suicide for the men that did it."

"I will do it," he said.

"No," I repeated. "There must be another way."

"Well, tell me what it is."

I said nothing. Sabert nodded at me. You know there is not, Cerdic. We must get the prince out and as many men as we can. We sacrifice a few to save the rest."

"Maybe it is the only way. But I will do it, not you."

"No, Cerdic. You have a family ... a young son. Besides which, Deira will need you more than it needs an old man like me. If I must die, let me do it this way. I will take some of them with me and they will serve me in the next life."

I looked back up the slope and then at the approaching column on the road.

"Cerdic, we don't have time to debate it. I am still senior to you. I can make it an order, but let me do it for the sake of honour."

I put one hand on his shoulder and looked into his eyes, trying one last time to persuade him to let me go. "Sabert ... please ..." I could see it was no use. I withdrew my hand in surrender. He was right, there was no other way and he was determined to be the one to do it. "Very well. But who will you take?"

"My huscarls will not desert me. I will take volunteers from my company. Men who served me in life can fight with me. I will send away the married and the young. Pray to Tīw and Woden for me, Cerdic; pray that they will fight with me."

289

Nodding my agreement, I clasped his hand. "I will. Good luck. If I get out of this alive, I'll tell Lilla to sing of your courage. If not, we will feast together soon in Woden's hall."

He smiled and turned away, calling his men to him and then leading them in a charge down the slope towards the road. As he left I did what he asked. I sent a prayer to Asgard, to the warrior gods, Tīw and Woden, but I added one to Loki: '*Let Sabert be your man this day.*'

"Cerdic, what is Sabert doing?" Edwin asked me as I caught up with the rest of the army.

"Paying for our freedom with his life. Let us move so it is not in vain ... what are you doing?"

Edwin had moved to run after Sabert, but I strode after him and seized his tunic.

"Let me go! I am going to join him."

"No you are bloody not, mate. Deira needs you. He is doing this so we all - but you in particular - can get away. Now move ... Highness. Hussa, Cuthbert take him. Now move all of you. Get down to the road. FAST!!"

On the road the company had noticed Sabert's approach and had halted, spread out and formed a shield wall. Sabert ran on towards them, his men surging after him. With the momentum of the sprint downhill rushing them on, they crashed into the shield wall and laid about them like rabid dogs.

"Cerdic - behind us!" Cuthbert gasped.

The pursuers were now after us, galloping down the hillside with abandon. Though some fell, too many were quickly closing the gap.

"Archers, drop them!" I shouted.

Cuthbert and a dozen of his skirmishers quickly notched arrows, their flights streaming like a cloud of starlings over our heads. When three of the pursuers died the rest slowed and looked about, waiting for others to take the risk. Thanking the gods for the accuracy of Cuth and his archers I charged on down the hill.

We reached the road three hundred paces south of where Sabert and his men were fighting. With a final look in his direction I turned the Deiran companies south and picked up the pace. We now had a road beneath our feet. I asked Cuthbert and his men to linger in the trees and slow the pursuit by letting arrows fly at intervals, but to run as soon as the enemy got close. I did not want Cuth's life sacrificed too. Sabert's sacrifice would allow us to put maybe two miles between us and the Bernicians. The valley was narrow and the hills and forest around blocked easy alternative routes.

All of Bernicia's army was behind us. Not far to the south there lay a Roman road that connected to the Great North Road, which would lead us to Deira ... to home.

What then?

Aethelfrith was not far behind with all of fifteen hundred spears at his command. With the fyrd we might muster five hundred at best. Sabert was almost certainly dead. A weak king, a courageous but impulsive prince, five hundred men and my friends were all that lay between the wolf and his prey: the fields and villages of my childhood.

My land - Deira.

Chapter Twenty-Two
Gathering Storm

It took us two weeks to reach the bridge at Catraeth. As I had predicted we lost almost half of the wounded, but were still burdened with those who clung onto life. The men were exhausted and hungry, for pickings were hard to come by and we dare not stop to hunt. As a result we found it hard going to make more than a dozen miles a day. All the way home we watched the road behind us, expecting at any moment to catch sight of pursuing Bernicians. I found it hard to believe that Aethelfrith had simply given up the chase and yet we saw no sign of them.

The people in the villages and farmsteads we passed watched us carefully, but though hostile, did nothing to impede our journey. Whether this was caution at the sight of a warband they did not recognise or they were deliberately observing us in order to send back reports of our progress, I was unsure, but it was with great relief that we came in sight of the bridge and crossed into Deira. At that moment I began to believe that we had left Aethelfrith far behind and perhaps he was not coming after all. Maybe Aedann was mistaken and Hussa lying. Just as I was beginning to relax and the war weary veterans of the northern campaign marched over the river and fell out of line to make camp, Cuthbert, who was lingering at the rear, gave a cry of alarm and gesturing wildly back up the road called Edwin and me to him.

"What is it, I see nothing," Edwin said, peering up the Roman road through the gloom.

"What is it Cuth?" It was true the road seemed empty, but I trusted my friend's sharp eyes.

"There!" He pointed and now I did see movement. Emerging from beneath the shadow of the beech trees lining the road, I could see half a dozen riders galloping hard towards us.

"Stand to!" I bellowed and behind me the companies stirred, groaning and complaining and expecting that my alarm would come to nothing as it had done a dozen times a day for the last fortnight.

Cuthbert notched an arrow on his bow string and a couple of his archers did likewise. I formed the Wicstun Company up across the south end of the bridge whilst Edwin and I waited on it with drawn swords as the horsemen approached.

"Get ready, Cuth. If it's Bernicians drop them on my order. But don't let fly your arrows till I say."

The half dozen riders galloped on towards us.

"There are more behind them. It's Aethelfrith ... it must be," Edwin said, pointing at a body of horsemen that had just come into sight. Maybe fifty more men.

"Cuth, get ready. When they are in range ... let go!" I shouted, expecting to hear the twang of bowstrings.

But Cuthbert did not obey me - he was studying the approaching riders.

"Drop them, damn it!" Edwin shouted, but still Cuthbert did not obey. His companions bent their bows to comply, but he shook his head.

"Don't aim at the leaders, but over their heads," he yelled. "The ones behind! Hit the ones behind!" With that he let fly at last with his arrow. It flew over the heads of the leading riders to plunge into the chest of the nearest of the larger body of men,

294

who was knocked off his horse and lost in the dust thrown up by the hooves of his companions.

"Why ...?" I asked, but the words died in my throat as I could now see the answer. There, leading the six horsemen was ...

"Sabert! Damn me if it ain't," Eduard roared.

He was right. Sabert and five of his huscarls clattered over the bridge and reined in on our side, their mounts flecked with foam and steaming.

"Picts! Kill the bastards," was all he could say between gasping for air.

"Picts? What the hell are they doing here?" asked Aedann, who in the last two weeks had made a better recovery than I had dared to hope.

"Aethelfrith's allies," Sabert panted, by way of explanation.

"I thought he was fighting them just a few weeks ago?" I said, watching what I recognised as Pictish light cavalry, unarmoured but armed with lances and fast across flat ground.

"Times change," Hussa muttered from behind me. "He beat them at Degsastan and now I expect that he has demanded their allegiance as his price for peace between them."

"Great. That is all we need. Bloody Picts attacking us too!" Eduard muttered.

But they did not attack. The sight of almost two hundred warriors in a tight shield wall blocking the narrow bridge was clearly enough to put them off. Instead they pulled back out of bow range and waited, quietly observing us.

"What are they waiting for?" Edwin asked.

I turned to Sabert with a questioning look, still not quite able to grasp that he was not only here and alive, but mounted.

"Infantry I would guess," was the answer he gave. "What we see here are Pictish cavalry acting as scouts for Aethelfrith's army.

295

The spearmen may be a day behind. We have time to pull back - warily. Let us not waste it. King Aethelric needs to know about the Bernician duplicity."

"Agreed," I nodded, "but first tell us what happened after we left you. I was sure you would die."

"Damn well should have done. But we gave that first company a fair hiding and they upped and routed on us. You will remember it was full dark and all was confusion. We took advantage of that and ran as fast as we could, but Aethelfrith released the Picts. We fought a running battle for two days, losing a half dozen men with each charge. But we managed to unhorse a few of them and ..." Sabert's voice faltered and he looked down at his boots. When he looked up, his face was wet with tears. "My men forced me to leave with just the huscarls that you see here. The rest sacrificed their lives to let us get away."

I glanced again at the Picts waiting on the other side of the bridge for their spearmen. "We must delay them a little while. But how?"

"Cerdic – look!" Aedann yelled, pointing. In the field close by was a hay wain loaded with timber, spare planks and offcuts from those that had been used to make running repairs to the bridge. I knew exactly what Aedann was thinking. It wouldn't give us much time, but enough, maybe.

"Get them!" I instructed. "Apologies, my Prince, but I am about to commit arson on your property!"

"Eh?" Edwin looked puzzled.

Eduard, Aedann and a dozen other lads pulled and pushed the wain into the middle of the bridge and piled some of the driest offcuts beneath it. Meanwhile, I foraged around for a bundle of twigs and dried grass then I stepped forward and thrust it in amongst the timber, using my strike-a-light to ignite it. It took a while to catch being damp and I was all fingers and thumbs. I could see some of the Picts moving forward to see what we were doing and swore under my breath wondering if they'd try to rush us. "Burn, damn it," I muttered. And it did. First the offcuts caught and soon the wain was ablaze, the bottom falling out and tipping the rest of the burning timber onto the bridge. In no time we had a fire going fit for funeral pyre and soon enough the planks of the bridge beneath it were ablaze.

The Picts moved closer, perhaps considering a dash to the river in an attempt to douse the fire and save the bridge. No sooner had their leader ridden in range, however, than Cuthbert released an arrow, which caught the Pict in the chest. He toppled off his horse and lay unmoving in the dust to cheers from our entire company.

"Bloody good shot," Eduard roared.

"Yes, excellent shot, good man," Prince Edwin said. "Look there – see?" He pointed, "It has scared them off."

He was right. The cavalry had abandoned attempts to rescue the bridge and pulled back out of range. We watched until the burning planks blackened, buckled and finally gave way, sending what was left of the wain plunging into the deep waters beneath and throwing up a cloud of steam. The old stone piles remained, of course, but the bridge now had a gaping hole in the middle, which would take some time to repair even if they could find more planks.

"Right, get moving!" I ordered. The companies fell in and started marching in quick time along the road to Eorforwic, all hoping the destruction of the bridge would delay pursuit sufficiently to give us time to escape and find somewhere safe for the night. Then in the morning we would carry on to Eorforwic and finally Godnundingham.

We arrived at the king's hall at midday two days later and marched into the fortress. In the daylight I could see that in the months we had been away, Aethelric had been adding to his father's construction. The ditch had been deepened and the palisade strengthened. In addition there were two long, single storey buildings to the west of the main hall and on our left as we marched through the gate.

We later discovered that these were quarters for troops. Aethelric had decided to organise his warriors and part of this approach was to provide accommodation for his garrison. We were shown to one of them and then the men were ordered to rest and prepare a meal. I went to give my report and Sabert and Edwin went with me.

We found the king holding court in the great hall, sitting in Aelle's old throne. To his right was Prince Hereric, who was now fourteen, but he was a serious lad and seemed older. Osric, now eleven, was also present but looking bored with the proceedings. Earl Harald stood up as we walked in and turned to address us.

"I saw your arrival. What has happened? We heard rumours of a great battle in the North and first that you had been destroyed and then that you were victorious. We did not expect you back so soon."

So I told them of all that had happened since Harald himself left the North to return home: of my capture and torture and of Aethelfrith's grand plan for a great battle. I sent a huscarl to fetch Aedann and Hussa to corroborate my story and we told of Aethelfrith's betrayal, his turning on us and our eventual escape.

"He will come south soon and attack," Hussa was saying. "He knows that Deira is weak and he is strong. Doubly strong now that he has Pictish allies."

"Accepting for the moment your presence here, traitor," Harald growled, unhappy that Hussa was allowed to live, albeit under guard at Sabert's insistence, "can you tell us where he will attack?"

"He did not tell me his full plan," my brother replied. "The idea was to weaken Deira's armies and then attack where he felt he had the most chance of success. I suppose the Picts ..."

"Yes, the Picts," interrupted Edwin. "They were on the Eoforwic road. That is the way they will come: down the Great North Road and into Deira that way."

I agreed that it did seem the most logical and easiest way.

"We must send out scouts, Sire," Harald suggested. "We have no way of knowing how far behind Sabert Aethelfrith is. He might be here within days."

The king nodded in that vague way he had, as if his mind was on another matter entirely. "Yes ... yes, see to it my lord."

"Sire, we must summon the fyrd," Sabert added. "All of it this time. Along with your own company we have here only those that are left after the Degsastan campaign. It is not enough. We need more men and we need them quickly."

"Very well," Aethelric agreed. "Harald, Sabert and Cerdic, return at once to your earldoms. Summon the fyrd. They must be here quickly."

Quickly: that was the word. I feared that we could not possibly be quick enough. We would go home and send out riders who would gallop from village to village and farm to farm. They would instruct the men to arm themselves and muster at given points and then march to the king's hall. It sounded simple enough, but it was not. Many would not come, those that did would take longer than they should. Many would be poorly equipped. But we had to try and so I went home. I was happy to,

299

of course. My family must think me dead and I was desperate to see them.

Throughout that last terrible winter and the horrors of Degsastan that followed, it was the image of the kitchen at the Villa that sustained me. It was there that I went when I arrived back. Of course, you can never go back to a moment, never recreate its perfection. Thus, as I walked through the door, I had low expectations of what I would find. I also did not care. I did not care if the kitchen was full of dirty washing. I just wanted to see Aidith and Cuthwine. As it happened, Cuthwine saw me first. He was sitting at the table eating bread hot and fresh from the oven just as I had done many a time. When he spotted me he looked uncertain who I was. He had been three when I left and I had been gone for almost a year - an eternity for a child of that age. Then something stirred in his memory and he turned his head to ask a question of someone out of sight behind the door into the atrium.

"Mama, it's a man. Is it Pa?"

A figure came into view. When I had left her she was still thin and wan from the plague. That evening, in the glow of embers from the fire dying down in the bread oven, Aidith looked stunning. She stared at me for a moment and then just nodded in response to our son's question.

Cuthwine let out a scream of joy and the next thing I knew, a flying ball of four-year-old boy head-butted me in the belly and knocked me onto my back.

"Pa, it is you! It is you. You are back! Did you win?" he asked with enthusiasm and all the warmth that only a child can have when they have decided that everything is all right.

"We beat the Scots, yes, but I will tell you about it later. Let me kiss your mother."

I managed to drag myself to my feet, heaving him with me over to Aidith. She was weeping. "You are back then ... I thought ..."

I knew what she thought. That I was dead: she had heard nothing from me in almost a year, what had she done to survive, how had she coped?

There was a strange hesitation between us. I wanted to enfold her in my arms, but something stopped me. It was as if we were strangers. "Yes, I am back, but ... I am sorry ... not for long. Aethelfrith betrayed us all. He is coming to attack us."

"To Deira? What will you do?"

"The king is calling out the fyrd. I have to return in a few days."

"But you have only just come back. Why do you always have to be the one to fight? Why not others?"

Her tone was accusing – as if I *chose* to go to war! "It is not only me, Aidith. Others too."

"So for now you are back, but you might die in a few days and I would have to lose you all over again."

"Would you prefer it if I had not come back?"

She walked towards me shaking her head, "No ... but if I hold you tonight I will know you are real and here. Then if fate decides that you don't come home ... well then ... again it will be real and I don't know that I can cope with that. How could I go on if that happened?"

I frowned, struggling to follow her logic. "So what are you going to do?"

"Oh, Cerdic! Come here you great ox!" She reached forward and pulled me by the tunic toward her, "I will take what I can today and fate be damned!" She kissed me.

And then we weren't like strangers any more.

301

"Are you serious about this?" Millie asked me the following day.

We were sitting in the ale hall. Cuthbert was standing on the far side of the table staring open-mouthed at me and then with a sort of disbelief at Mildrith.

"I had intended agreeing to your betrothal with Cuthbert, but something Aidith said changed my mind. Cuth, in two days we go back to Godnundingham. We don't know how soon afterwards Aethelfrith will attack, but he will come soon. You, me, any of us could be dead in a week. I should have resolved this a year past, but there you go. But yes. If you wish to, you may marry tonight. I can send for the priest. What do you say?"

"By way of answer Mildrith jumped over the table and into Cuthbert's arms. Cuth threw me one brief, embarrassed grin as he collapsed under her.

Time travels quickly, more so when those times are sweet and joyful. Three days later, my new brother-in-law and I, along with Eduard and Aedann and those of the Village that we could muster to the fyrd, had returned to the king's hall. With us were a handful of others that my riders had managed to call to Wicstun and whom we had collected on the way. I had not even tried to summon Guthred from Bursea as after his response the last time it seemed rather futile. I again left Grettir at home. He protested, of course, but I told him that if the worst happened I wanted him there to protect my family. "I would die before harm comes to them, my lord," Grettir had promised.

I found Sabert and Harald in council with Aethelric and Edwin. Advisors were reporting on the preparation of the fyrd, and scouts on the enemy's movements. It appeared that Aethelfrith's army was now below the River Tees. If he marched his men straight south, they might be in Deira within a few days. Envoys had been sent with renewed offers of friendship and to ask for a negotiation, for Aethelric wished to avoid war at all costs, but none had returned as yet.

I noticed that Hussa was present at the council and stood close to the Edwin, which was a surprise. Even more of a surprise, now I studied him, was that he wore the rich cloth and chain armour of a huscarl.

"Your eyes do not deceive you, Cerdic," Sabert said sourly as he wandered over to greet me. "Edwin made your brother one of his huscarls in reward for saving his life. A man can betray his country, but save a prince's life and it is considered all in balance."

Hussa felt me watching him, turned and smiled at me. It was a smug rather than a kindly smile. I raised my eyebrows then looked away and focused my attention on the council.

"What of Elmet?" Aethelric was asking. If possible he looked quite a lot older than he had when I had last seen him. News of Bernicia's betrayal and the likely invasion had clearly aged him. His eyes had a haunted look as if he had not slept in days and his ruddy complexion suggested he was enjoying even more wine than usual - enjoying it, or perhaps taking solace in it. He looked like a man hoping that the inevitable was not about to happen.

"There has been no dispute or fighting with that country in the last five years. They have traded with us and received our envoys and paid their tribute. We have heard nothing to suggest a threat from that direction," Harald replied.

"There was nothing to suggest a threat when they attacked us before, Harald, how can you be so sure now?" Edwin asked.

"I believe they were persuaded to raid us then and to back their fellow British at Catraeth for the promise of lands or

303

wealth," the Earl replied. "Since then they have not received much of either, were weakened by our raid there some years ago and I believe they will now try to stay out of this war. Relations between us have improved of late. I am certain they will see to their own defences."

The king seemed to ponder on this point for a while. Then he said, "We will have to hope that they do not attack us. We cannot fight both Bernicia and Elmet. Truth be known we cannot even spare men to *watch* Elmet. Aethelfrith outnumbers us at least three to one. Alone he is a great threat. However, now he has these Pictish allies we need every man here and even that will not be enough."

The council went on for some time. I listened as they spoke of the intentions of Mercia and East Anglia, both Saxon kingdoms who seemed disinterested in affairs north of the Humber. Finally, Aethelric welcomed me.

"Greetings, Lord Cerdic. I thank you for bringing the Wicstun Company. It will form part of the reserve of my army. Sabert will command the moorland companies and Harald those of Eoforwic. You will command the reserve comprising your company along with my household troops."

"Sire," I bowed.

Hereric looked at me, "Are you sure, Father? There are five score other men you might choose right here within the walls of the palace or its garrison." He cast a sly look at Edwin, "Do we really need to give command to a farmer?"

He was clearly expecting to be applauded by his uncle, but Edwin frowned at him and shook his head. "I have seen Cerdic fight and he is brave and resourceful. He also has a good head for strategy. You could do no better, Sire."

I exchanged a glance with Sabert and saw his eyebrows go up in surprise. I had expected Edwin to make some rude comment as so often in the past. It was true that his attitude to me had softened after I got everyone away from Degsastan, but this was the first time he had complimented me. I saw Hereric's face flush and had a strong desire to laugh, but I kept a straight face and said quietly, "Thank you, Highness."

Oblivious to the undercurrents, the king nodded and went on, "I want you two, Hereric and Edwin, to join Cerdic's company for training. Make the most of the next few days."

Thus I became the princes' tutor and they liked it no more than I did. Each morning we drilled in the courtyard. We practiced as a company and fought mock battles against the Wolds' companies and those from the palace. I had already seen Edwin fight. He was impetuous but skilled and even Hereric, un-blooded as he was, appeared to be well tutored in arms. I found myself wondering why the king had asked me to teach them.

Over the next few days we learnt that the enemy was moving south and gathering at Catraeth. Then, finally, Sabert arrived in a hurry and reported that his scouts patrolling out beyond Eorforwic had spotted a large number of troops moving south towards the city. This information now spurred Aethelric into action. He ordered that Sabert take his own companies and link with Harald's in Eorforwic. Together they would have five hundred spears. I watched them depart and then turned to more practice in the yard. We all expected to follow within two days with the reserve and no one complained.

Later the same day I was walking the ramparts as the early evening sun cast long shadows across the ground. Hussa stood alone looking at the sunset. He turned as I approached.

"I see that you have risen in the world," I commented. "From traitor to prince's huscarl is quite a step."

He shrugged. "You have done well too, brother. I am sure our father would be proud of you."

There was a shout from a sentinel twenty yards away near the east fence. Hussa and I ran round to where the man stood. It turned out to be my sharp-eyed brother-in-law.

"What is it, Cuth," I asked.

"There, Cerdic." I followed his pointing finger. At first I could see only the scattered copses of trees to the east. Then I realised there was movement between them. A deer, I thought, or maybe a boar. Then I spotted men emerging: men in huge numbers.

One of them lifted his pennant, which flapped in the breeze and at that moment a chill raced up my spine and lifted the hairs on the back of my neck, for I had seen that emblem before. At Degsastan

It was a Bernician flag!

Chapter Twenty-Three
King's Hall

Aethelfrith had tricked us!

Aethelric had sent three hundred men and his most senior captains towards Eorforwic because of the news that the enemy were marching from Catraeth south to that city. Both Sabert and Harald had gone. The king had planned to follow a day or so later after gathering as many of his other companies as possible.

It was clear that the reported march on Eorforwic was a feint. How had Aethelfrith managed to evade our scouts with the main body of his men? Had he landed on the coast? Or had he sneaked across the moors? We did not know. But somehow he had escaped our notice and here he now was - on our doorstep!

At the palace we had just two companies - seventy men of the king's own house guards and my sixty Wicstun men. If Godnundingham fell and Aethelric was slain it was certain the army would melt away like snow on a warm day. The men would run home to protect their families - and who could blame them? If I'm honest I was sorely tempted to be off to the Villa myself and I could see similar thoughts in the eyes of all the men in my company, not least Cuthbert, doubtless thinking of Mildrith with whom he had shared so brief a time.

Looking at the emerging men I could now see more banners confirming my fears. It was Bernicia all right and moreover, here came Aethelfrith leading them. I would have recognised his sturdy, energetic figure even had he not been wearing a golden torque. I could see it glinting at his neck in the last rays of the setting sun. Some banners were strange to me as were the men under them, but many more I had seen at Degsastan. Cuthbert ran to sound the alarm and soon Aethelric and the princes had joined me. All of our men had now mustered on the ramparts. We watched the enemy form up to the east and then march round the fortress to the south. There must have been fifteen hundred of them: ten times our number. They paraded just out of bowshot, blowing their horns and banging their drums. They were announcing their presence; intimidating us. Even mocking us – some of them bending over and flipping up their tunics to show us their bare buttocks. *'Look at us,'* they were saying, *'and be afraid, for we have defeated countless foes across all the lands. You will be just the latest. In a year we will have forgotten you as will all men.'*

I watched Aethelfrith. He rode forward to just within bow shot. He was showing us he was not afraid of us and our fortress. More than that: he was showing his own men. Victors they may be and more numerous, but he was still asking them to assault us behind our tall walls. Many would die. One arrow here and now would finish the arrogant, scheming bastard. I beckoned Cuthbert forward, but Aethelric held up his hand and shook his head at me and one does not disobey a king and live.

Aethelfrith stopped opposite the main gate and Aethelric moved round to look down at him. The two men locked gazes. "We meet again little king," the Bernician shouted, "just a prince at Catraeth as I recall. Remember what happened to your army? You were lucky to escape. It was I who rescued you then. Despair now, for you have no hope today; there's no-one to rescue you this time. Look around you. I have at least a hundred men for each ten of yours - perhaps more. There can be just one outcome to this battle. You, your princes," Aethelfrith pointed at Hereric,

Edwin and even little Osric, who was staring in stunned silence at the horde, "your captains, your army. At dawn tomorrow all will be destroyed!"

He let that thought play on our fears for a moment before continuing. "Yet it need not be like that. Bow down and acknowledge me as king and I will let you keep your throne as vassal. Serve me and your men shall live," he promised. "We are kin, you and I, joined by marriage. Your sister, my queen, would have us be at peace. Submit to me and it can be so. Hand over your princes as surety of your good behaviour and I will leave you to live out your life in peace. They will not be harmed."

"Like Bran wasn't harmed?" I hissed, turning to look at the boys. Osric was staring at his uncle and clearly pissing himself, but both Edwin and Hereric gazed back fearlessly, Edwin fingering his sword. Aethelric said nothing for a long while. Turning his back on Aethelfrith, he looked round at his men. Some had fear in their eyes. Some seemed stunned by the spectacle. I am sure that many felt, as did Cuthbert and I, that they would rather be elsewhere. But in the end a man is worth as much as the promises he makes, the oaths he swears.

A little to my right, Eduard voiced my thoughts, muttering as if to himself but clearly enough for even the enemy king to hear, "I would give up my place in Valhalla before I would serve this traitorous son of a pig!" A faint ripple of agreement passed among our men. One or two chuckled. There was no great fuss. Everyone knew we would fight and fate would decide the outcome.

Aethelfrith showed no sign of irritation. "So be it," he said and galloped back to his men. His army dispersed and began making camp fires, though a score or so sentinels moved up to extreme bow range and spread out to observe us.

For a moment Aethelric seemed uncertain what to do now. He had never really wanted to be king and knew his own limitations, but he was no coward and if he had to fight and die here, he would not shirk from his fate. He drew himself up and turned to us and for that moment the overweight, ageing nobleman was gone and a king stood before us. It was the first time I had ever seen in him an echo of his father, Aelle.

"Get yourself a mount," he said to a huscarl. "Fast as you can, ride after Sabert and Harald. I need them back here by morning. Tell them to march through the night. I need their spears tomorrow."

The man tapped his spear against his shield. "Yes, My King, at once," he said and rushed off. A few minutes later the gates were opened and he galloped out. Cuthbert and a few other archers covered him from the ramparts, their arrows finding an enemy spearman who had moved into range to hurl his weapon at the horse. And then Aethelric's huscarl was away into the gloom and the great gates closed.

Aethelric meanwhile had organised the watches and ordered men not on watch to bed. I followed him into his hall but he sent me away. "You too, Cerdic. I want my captains rested come dawn." I turned away, but he called me back. "One more thing, Cerdic."

"Sire?"

"I must hope for victory if Sabert and Harald can reach us in time, but I have to face the fact that against such impossible odds we might be defeated. If we lose tomorrow and the palace is overrun, if you can see there is no hope, then you have one duty left to me. The only hope for Deira is that Osric, Hereric or Edwin survive. If I am lost, get the boys out and keep them safe. Do that for me; for Deira."

310

"Let it be someone else, my King," I protested. "I will not leave you. I will die in battle rather than run away." It was true. After Catraeth I had never wanted to be a warrior, would prefer to be at the Villa than here, but I am not a man to run from danger for my own sake and, as my father would say, without honour and duty a man is nothing.

Aethelric slammed his hand down on the high table. We were alone in the great hall and the noise echoed up to the rafters. "No Cerdic! You saved Deira before at Catraeth and I must ask you to do it again. I am nothing but a weak king, but Deira must have another king and you must keep them safe ... if the worst happens. You alone I trust to do this. Give me your oath."

What could I do? I nodded and promised to obey him, although I hardly felt that it would be necessary. After all we had tall ramparts and a sturdy gate. If we could hold until the companies from Eorforwic returned we might be saved. Or so I told myself, for a warrior who thinks of defeat has lost the battle even before it begins.

Around midnight the gates opened again. The rider had returned. He reported that he had caught up with Sabert's camp just this side of Eoforwic and given him the king's orders. According to the exhausted messenger, Sabert had sent a fresh horseman to carry the order on to Harald whose company was some way ahead of him, and had promised to turn back at once. It might be late morning before he arrived, but he would come as fast as he was able.

Well, I thought, we might be outnumbered, but by midday tomorrow the odds would have improved. Feeling a little more hopeful, I checked on the guards at the gates and set more on the walls then I obeyed my king and went to the barracks to get some sleep.

I could hear the clanging of swords and the screams of battle. At first, still more asleep than awake, I thought I was back at Catraeth, it sounded so real. Then, as I came up through the layers of slumber I realised this was no dream. It was not the nightmarish echo of a battle fought six years ago. No, it was happening now! The noise was coming from just outside the barracks and could mean only one thing. The enemy were here within the walls! But how could that be?

Fully awake now, I sat up and looked around me at the other warriors who were coming out of sleep, bleary-eyed and confused. Like me, many could not believe what they were hearing. The ditch and tall bank surmounted with the wooden palisade would prove a daunting barrier in the day time. But an assault in dead of night must surely fail. And yet my ears told me that somehow Aethelfrith was inside. A moment later a horn was sounded: one of the sentinels raising the alarm, no doubt. I leapt up, quickly pulled on britches, tunic and boots and ran for my weapons, helm and shield. There was no time to don a mail shirt. Sheathing my longsword at my side, I grabbed up Catraeth.

All around me the other warriors were staggering to their feet and fumbling for their weapons. Cuthbert was trying to string his bow whilst rubbing his eyes. Eduard looked confused. I told myself that if I lived through this night I would remember that a night attack certainly brought surprise – perhaps enough to turn the outcome. We had surprised the Bernicians by our escape in the dead of night and here they had returned the favour. We had been merely trying to get away, but this night the Bernicians had our deaths on their minds.

We rushed out through the door of the barrack block. The night was lit by fires burning in the roofing of the stables over towards the gate. Our hut was to the west of the gate on the left

312

hand side of the compound. The gate itself was wide open and Bernician warriors were streaming through it. In the space between the gate and the great hall a swirling melee was raging between the attackers and the outnumbered Deiran defenders. My countrymen were trying to form up into a shield wall, but the steady arrival of new troops through the gate heading for the flanks threatened its security. The wings were curling back and soon were abutting the front of the great hall.

Some of the warriors in the hut started toward the fight whilst others held back looking uncertainly at me for instructions. "Form up," I ordered. "Shield wall in three ranks!"

The men rushed to their positions as we had practiced so many times over the years. Eduard and I stood in the centre of the company in the third rank. Cuthbert and five of his best skirmishers ran up in front of us and began releasing their arrows into the left wing of the enemy as it curled round the palace guard.

"Lock shields, fast advance!" I shouted. There was a clattering of boards as the shields were firmly overlapped. Then we began moving quickly toward the battle.

"Spears overhead," I gave the order. Now we were ready for attack.

The enemy had seen us as we closed and new troops coming in to the fortress formed up in a line that angled away from the main fight and faced toward us.

Thirty yards to go.

Cuthbert risked another arrow, which caught a young Bernician in the throat. "Good man," I breathed as Cuth ran back round our flanks to join the shield wall.

Twenty yards to go.

I heard a shout behind me. Glancing round I saw the princes, Hereric and Edwin, running toward us with shield and sword. I had forgotten they were nominally in this company since I had agreed to train them. Too late to think of them now.

Ten yards to go.

There was the ear-splitting sound of shields crashing together. Then the killing began. From the third rank, too hemmed in to draw my longsword and armed only with Catraeth, I could not reach the enemy but had to watch as men on both sides died. As they did I pushed forward men from the third rank to fill the gaps, but felt a jolt of anxiety as Eduard stepped over the body of one of the villagers to take his place at the front.

Now the princes joined me. Hereric looked excited and frightened at the same time. Of course, I thought, this was his first battle. I prayed to Woden that it would not be the last. From where I stood I could see more of the melee in front of the great hall. Aethelric was there now, fighting in the centre of his personal guard. He and they fought like devils. Yet the numbers against us were too great. As we fell there were few to replace us. As the enemy fell, men stepped forward from the pressing mass at the gates. I looked around for Hussa, but could not see him and felt a pang of anxiety. Had he fallen as the Bernicians attacked? Had they taken revenge on the man who was wanted for treason; the man who had served their king then returned to his own people and helped them escape?

I looked beyond the enemy to our fore. Then, in the red glow of the burning buildings, I saw my brother standing in the midst of the enemy. I rubbed a hand across my eyes in a moment of confusion. Hussa it was – but alive - and talking to one of the enemy lords. The Bernician turned. It was Aethelfrith!

314

What a fool I was! What fools we all were. I recalled what he had said in that dark dungeon: *'What I do, brother, I do for myself.'* Hussa had only ever acted in his own best interests. Always it had been the same. Why had I imagined he had changed? How could I have been so gullible? I felt sick to my stomach as I pondered what he had done. Had he, seeing the impossible odds, once more turned traitor to put himself on the winning side or had this always been the plan? It did not matter now - he had let them in. That was how the enemy had got within the gates: Hussa had opened them and betrayed us yet again.

Just as I realised this, Aethelfrith slapped my brother on the shoulder as if giving thanks and Hussa, glancing towards us, caught my eye and knew that I had seen. Our gazes locked and in that instant an understanding passed between us. If we both lived this night there was unfinished business between brothers. A reckoning to be had.

Turning my attention back to my men, I could see that the arc of defenders in front of the doors was being pushed back whilst we were being driven away from the hall. I moved to the left of the company dragging Eduard and ten others with me. There was a small gap between the left of our line and the side of the hall. I led a charge against that point trying to break through to Aethelric. The two princes came with me despite my shout to them to stay back. I could not blame them: after all, this was Edwin's brother and Hereric's father in danger of his life.

At first we made progress. The enemy held this point fairly thinly. It was the angle between their main body pressing against the front of the great hall and their left flank, which was thrown back to face my company. I cut down a Bernician warrior and leapt over him to take on another. Edwin and Hereric were to my left and Eduard to my right. I thought we might break through.

315

Then I saw a counter charge led by the man we all feared. Aethelfrith had arrived. He chopped down two men from my company and turned on me. He gave a curt nod of recognition before swinging his sword in an arc, aiming for my throat. I ducked.

Then suddenly, launching a ferocious attack that drove through the Bernicians, we were joined from our left by Aethelric with his huscarls. He burst out from the front of the hall and cut his way through to us. For a moment the two rival kings stared at each other and then began to fight.

"Cerdic, follow my last order!" Aethelric shouted above the din.

I felt a terrible, hollow feeling of despair that swamped my brief feeling of triumph when, for a fleeting moment, I had thought Aethelric's counter attack had overcome his enemy. But this was not to be. Aethelric fought like a lion, but he was no match for Aethelfrith. My king had seen that all was lost. His command was falling. He had tried a final attack hoping perhaps to kill his enemy, but what he really intended was to distract the Bernicians to enable his son and brother to escape. His words of the previous day came back to me: *'If you can see there is no hope then you have one duty left to me. The only hope for Deira is that Osric, Hereric or Edwin survive. If I am lost, get the boys out and keep them safe.'*

I could see that he was losing, and yet I hesitated. Hereric and Edwin were still fighting at my side. I could leave now with what men I could gather and get the two princes out. But what if by staying I could change things? The thought tormented me. It was hard to think. Catraeth was rising and falling, slashing at throats and limbs as I laid into the enemy about me. The press of men around Aethelric increased. I could now no longer see him. There

316

was a cheer to the left and a crash as the doors of the great hall were breached. Inside I heard a woman scream. The enemy that had surrounded me moments before were backing off, turning to run gleefully towards the sounds that told them pillaging and worse had begun. Somewhere inside was Prince Osric, but I could not save him now. I knew I was condemning Aethelric to capture or death, but I had to leave, for that is what he had asked of me and I was oathsworn. Damn it! Damn you, Loki! Damn it all!

Fire now leapt from the side of the great hall. Dozens of Aethelfrith's men were streaming out into the open space beside it. They were looking for plunder or women. Yet soon they could outflank us. That decided it. I had a moment's grace. I grabbed both princes and yelled in their faces, "We are leaving now!" They stared at me blankly. What did I mean? We could not run away and leave the king, their faces said.

"The battle is lost," I said desperately. "We cannot save the king. We must get out now!"

"I am not leaving my father. And what about Prince Osric?" Hereric shouted.

Edwin nodded in agreement, "My duty is to die here if I must, to defend my brother the king." He started to pull away from me.

I had known this was going to be difficult. "Your duty is to the kingdom. I am sorry, but the king is lost. He may already be dead. You must live. We cannot get to the hall. If we try we will die too. It's hopeless. Live today and fight tomorrow. We must go now. It is what the king asked of me. He has given his life for you. Do not let his sacrifice be wasted."

I saw doubt enter Edwin's eyes, but Hereric stared at me, his face screwed up with grief and anger. "I am not going anywhere. You cowardly bastard *farmer*," he screamed at me.

317

Suddenly a fist flew past me and landed with a cracking sound on Hereric's face. The prince dropped senseless to the ground. I looked to my left. Eduard was shaking his hand. "Sorry," he said, "but I could not really see any other way out of the problem." He bent over, lifted the unconscious youth and heaved him up onto his great shoulder. Then he turned and glared at Edwin. "Are you coming now?"

Edwin shrugged and then nodded. I smiled briefly - Eduard was a lot bigger than Edwin and as intimidating as a bear, but I think the older prince, who at least had some experience of battle, knew we were right.

I ran back behind the company. Eduard and Edwin followed as did half a dozen others. The battle was lost and a great weight of enemy was pushing my company back. I had to get as many men out as I could. The palace would be swarming with Bernician warriors. Their blood was up; they would kill any of us they found and rip our corpses to pieces.

Suddenly, there was a roar of triumph from near the great hall. Swords were being lifted high and then a bloody cloak - Aethelric's cloak. It was over, the king was dead.

"Step backwards!" I shouted. There was no response. The noise of shouting and screaming men was too great. I ran up to the rear ranks and grabbed two men by the shoulders and dragged them back.

"Back, back!" I bellowed. A few more men turned and started edging back, shields up, spears at the ready position. Slowly I managed to get the rear rank to begin stepping back. What I was trying to do was one of the hardest tasks in battle. Once a body of men begin retreating with the enemy still pressing hard from the front, the urge to turn, drop weapons and run is almost irresistible. It is at these times that the majority of men who die in

318

battle are slain. Most mortal wounds are not in the front but in the back as the victorious enemy leaps forward to cut the vanquished down.

A score or so Bernicians had broken through where I had last seen Aethelric. I tried not to think what desecration they would do to his body. They were running round our left flank. In a moment they would be behind us. This was it. No option now. Time to run. Fate would decide who would live.

"Men of Deira, RUN!" I yelled. "Follow me." I knew few would get away, but the princes were my concern now. I turned and pushed Edwin towards the western palisade. We would have to escape over the wall. I prayed that most of the enemy were now inside the palace. Eduard was already hurrying towards the fence with Hereric still out cold on his shoulder.

The rear ranks of our company were running on either side of me. I glanced behind and felt a moment of guilt. The enemy were breaking through our front rank. Few of those young warriors would escape. A man from the Village turned away from the enemy and started to run. A moment later he stumbled and fell as an enemy warrior leapt at him and hewed him down sending a fountain of blood spraying up into the air.

I kept running. We now reached the palisade. It had been built to stop assault from without. From the inside the wooden posts only came up to chest height. Men threw themselves over. I got to the wall and helped Edwin over and then, needing both hands, I sheathed Catraeth. Just as I started to pull myself up I felt a hand on my leg. Looking down I saw a Bernician warrior pulling me back, his seax swinging up for the killing blow. I kicked him in the abdomen, but he held on. I panicked now. I was going to die here spreadeagled on this blasted fence.

Then I saw him stiffen and collapse. Behind him was Cuthbert, his dagger covered in blood and a surprised grin on his face. I reached out and pulled him up beside me, gasping my thanks as we tumbled over the wall together just before three arrows slammed into it behind us. On the far side the wall was eight feet tall and the bank beneath it sloped steeply into a dry ditch. We landed there with a sickening thud, which stunned me for a moment. I shook my head to clear it. When I could see again I found that apart from the princes and my friends there were perhaps two dozen from our company in the ditch. Looking up I saw the enemy swarming at the palisades. Some started throwing spears and axes down at us. A man next to me was pinned to the ground with a spear through his chest.

"Up the ditch, quickly!" Eduard shouted. It amazed me to see he was still carrying Hereric. We started climbing the outer ditch slope. All around us we heard the hiss of arrows, the thud as they hit the earth. The screams as they found their targets. We reached the top, Cuthbert helping Eduard with Hereric, I pushing Edwin up ahead of me.

"Now run!" I shouted. They needed no orders. The score of us sprinted west, away from the palace, across the wide expanse of grass and into woods still shrouded in the dark cloak of night.

On we ran until our lungs burnt. Then exhausted we rested a few moments before running again. We went on like this until we reached the Roman road north of Wicstun, some five miles away. By then Hereric had come round and was on his feet, but all the fight had gone out of him. Dazed and speechless, he nursed his bruised jaw, his glazed eyes staring in shock from Edwin to me and back again. I could hear no sounds of pursuit. It might be a while before Aethelfrith realised the princes, Aethelric's heirs, had escaped him, but when he did he would come after us for sure.

320

He would not rest while a potential threat to his plans for Deira still lived.

I looked around at the exhausted men and knew they could go no further. "Get back off the road into the trees," I said.

Only then did I permit them to rest.

Only then, when there was time to think, did despair begin to drown us.

Chapter Twenty-Four
Where Now?

The light of the quarter moon illuminated the sorry remnants of the Wicstun Company. I looked around at our ragged band. We were fewer than twenty men. Deira had been betrayed and had fallen. Aethelric was dead and Aethelfrith had won again and was now in effect King of Northumbria – all of it.

The speed at which it had all happened was startling and now that I had a chance to catch my breath and think about it, I was bewildered. Hussa and Aethelfrith had tricked us. For how long had they planned this night? How many twists and turns on the road had they foreseen - or maybe more than foreseen? I began to see that Hussa's opening the gates was not, as I had thought at first, an impulse born of his fear of being on the losing side. It had been planned after Degsastan. As soon as Aethelfrith had learned that my Welsh friend Aedann was still alive – Aedann, who knew of his plans for Deira and could not be trusted not to warn us – he had planted Hussa in our camp to gain our trust and be ready to aid him in just such a situation as had occurred this night. Hussa had been working for the Bernician all along. How much of all that had transpired since Aelle's death had they brought about? Sabert had been right not to trust my brother. How could I have been so blind? I had no answers, just questions. I slumped back against a tree trunk utterly exhausted and mentally shattered.

I was not the only one. My friends all looked totally lost. The world they knew was suddenly turned upside down - all its certainties swept away. But I knew we had to do something. We

323

could hardly sit on this road for ever. But what could we do - a mere handful of weary men against fifteen hundred enemy warriors and the might of Aethelfrith?

I became aware that the men were studying me, looking to me for guidance. What was I to say? Not for the first time I made a silent wish that I could have been left to live out this life in obscurity farming my little valley. But I knew that was not possible and it never really had been. I may have made my pact with Loki, but even before then I felt in my heart that the gods wanted more from me than just being a farmer. Clearly fate had decreed that I had more to do and for good or ill I had no choice now. I sighed and began considering our options. The princes seemed to have their own ideas.

"I intend returning to the palace and killing Aethelfrith," said Edwin.

"My lord, I do not think that is a good idea," I argued.

"We were not asking your opinion, Cerdic. It's not your brother back there. Or your father, come to that. Nor for that matter is your cousin there. Do you have any idea what will happen to Osric? A prince of the line of Soemil," snarled Edwin.

I very much doubted he was still alive, but forbore to point it out. "But Prince Edwin,' I protested, 'you cannot go back. It would be futile."

"We are princes of Deira. We do not take orders from *farmers!*" snapped Edwin. Clearly the shock of defeat that had stunned him for the last hour had faded. It was replaced by anger and with it had resurfaced his irritation that he had lately been under the command of a mere farmer, which is what he still thought of me despite his recent mellowing.

"Edwin, calm down a moment, Cerdic is only trying to help," Hereric interceded.

324

I stared at the younger prince in surprise. Given his behaviour earlier this was unexpected.

"Him, help? For all we know he might be the traitor!" Edwin spat.

"Don't be a fool, Uncle! That's a stupid thing to say."

Edwin flushed, clearly stung. "Think about it, *Nephew*. Who let Aethelfrith in? For all we know Cerdic has been working for Bernicia since Catraeth."

"Wait a moment, Edwin, you're not thinking clearly," Hereric argued. "If Cerdic was going to betray us, why would he have done so much to save us this night? He could simply have handed us over and got his reward."

Edwin seemed a little taken aback by that and fell silent.

"Besides," I said into the silence, "it's not me who is the traitor. It's my brother. I saw him with Aethelfrith back at the palace. It was Hussa who betrayed us."

It was all so obvious to me now. I should have suspected him from the start, but he had been too clever for me. I had never fully trusted him, of course, but I had been lulled into hoping that somehow he might come round. There were signs of that – or so I thought. He had saved Edwin's life when he could easily have let him die. Then he started talking of his doubts about Aethelfrith and warned us of the Bernician's plan to capture us after Degsastan. We had escaped that night and it seemed as if his warning had allowed it, but as I had now realised, Aedann would have warned us anyway and Hussa knew that. As a reward for saving Edwin's life, he had infiltrated the prince's personal retinue and by demonstrating his 'loyalty' he had succeeded in sweeping away the stain of betrayal at Catraeth. But it had all been a sham.

325

I said all this to the princes, finishing with, "He and Aethelfrith planned it all down to the finest detail, manipulating events so that Hussa was at the heart of our camp ready to betray us at an opportune moment should the need arise. That moment came tonight when he opened the gates and let the enemy through."

There was silence when I had finished. I waited to see what the princes would say, wondering if they would blame me anyway simply for being Hussa's brother. Then a thought occurred to me, wiping everything else from my mind.

"Sabert and Harald do not know!" I blurted out.

"Of course, Cerdic," Hereric said excitedly. "Sabert and Harald are the answer. If we can find them and their three hundred men there is still a chance. Don't you see, Edwin. Cerdic is right. To go alone to the palace would be foolish. We need men. We must go to Eorforwic."

Edwin stared at both of us for a moment and then, seeming to calm down, said, "You are right. I agree. Let us go to Eorforwic."

I had no better plan. It seemed fruitless: three hundred men against how many? And yet we might have surprise on our side. And we had to do *something*. Better to die trying than to be hunted like deer before a wolf pack until Aethelfrith finally caught up with us.

The princes both wanted to depart at once. I pointed out that it was the middle of the night and the men were exhausted, as was I. We needed at least some rest. We agreed that we would get moving at dawn. I did not think Aethelfrith would send his scouts out before first light in any event. The princes looked strained. Hereric particularly, was still shocked at the loss of his father and clearly had a thumping headache, for which Eduard repeatedly apologised. Edwin seemed more angry than upset, but I knew that for some men it was easier to hate and desire revenge

326

than to fully confront their grief. To an extent that was how I had coped with the loss of my brother, by swearing revenge on Samlen.

I set the watch and then slept until the last watch before dawn, which I took myself. From my vantage point in the hedgerow along that road, I observed the sun rise in the direction of the palace a few miles away. There was no sign of pursuit yet, but it would surely only be a matter of time. I roused the party early and sending Cuthbert up ahead to scout out the road, had us marching before it was fully light.

Hereric walked alongside me. "I notice you have rather taken command, Cerdic," he observed.

"I suppose I have, my lord. Do you object?"

"I do," said Edwin coming up behind, "Hereric and I should give the orders, not you."

"Oh shut up, Edwin," snapped Hereric. "As a matter of fact I feel Cerdic should command the men."

"You do?" I asked, again surprised by the younger prince's changed attitude.

"You do?" chimed Edwin, looking irritated by his nephew's comments.

"Yes I do," Hereric replied, and then seemed to be putting together his thoughts. Not a gifted young man it took a while, but what eventually emerged made a lot of sense and I confess I was taken aback by his maturity.

"I had my doubts about Cerdic," Hereric cast an apologetic glance at me, "and it was you, Edwin, who spoke up for him and showed me that his experience was important. Why have you changed your mind?"

"I could ask you the same question," Edwin retorted.

327

Hereric shrugged, "The dozen or so men here are all from Cerdic's company. Some of them served with him at Catraeth and Degsastan and come from his village. He has fought in several battles and as you said the experience must count for something. But it is more than that," and now he lowered his voice so that only we three could hear. "Right now these men are confused and bewildered. Half of them will want to go home. They will be thinking that maybe Aethelfrith will leave them alone and perhaps he would not be so bad a king. They are wondering why they are still here instead of home in a warm bed. We have to give them a reason to stay. Cerdic can hold their loyalty at least for a while. Finally, it was my father who gave him command and who put our fate in his hands. A few days ago he said to me that he trusted Cerdic."

He turned to me now saying, "He told me to trust you as he felt whatever happened you would be loyal. He knew you would rather be at home and that perhaps you'd had enough of war after Catraeth, but it never stopped you."

I stared at him, speechless.

"Oh, I know my father is ...," he gulped, "was not a scholar, just as I am not, but he understood men all right. He could see you had no desire for glory. Perhaps that is why he trusted you. You don't want to be part of all this, yet you will not walk away. You will see it through. Whatever is meant to be, you will have a role in it. I am content for you to be in command and I'm sorry about what I said before."

Edwin stared at him as if his nephew were not totally sound of mind. Maybe wondering if it had something to do with that blow to the head, but reluctantly he nodded his assent. "Perhaps I spoke harshly, but remember this, Cerdic, *we* are the princes. Command the men and lead us, but we decide where we will go."

"I understand, My Prince." I picked up my pace to catch up with the head of the column. I'd had enough of proud princelings to last me a lifetime!"

Then I looked north along the road to Eorforwic and I blinked. Was that movement further down the road? Rubbing my eyes I looked again. Yes it was. There were men moving towards us. I raised my right arm to halt the company and then indicated that we should move to the hedgerows. We scattered and each found a hiding place in the ditches or hedgerows. I readied my sword and saw that the other men were also preparing themselves.

The men moving down the road could now be seen more clearly. There were about ten of them. Several were wounded and most were bloody, as if they had been in battle. They were hurrying towards us but it was clear they had not seen us. Every so often one of the men would glance behind as if fearing pursuit. When they reached twenty yards away I recognised Sabert. The man had an uncanny knack of coming back from the dead! He was wounded and dishevelled, but it was he, the commander of the army that had departed to Eorforwic only a few days before. Alongside him, for once looking tired and not at all elegant was Lilla.

"Stay out of sight!" I ordered my company then I stepped out onto the road. The band of men halted and brought spears and swords up to defend themselves.

"It is I, Cerdic," I called out. "Fear not, Sabert, you are among friends," I indicated the others stirring in the hedgerow.

Looking doubtful, Sabert squinted at me in the early morning light then he turned to scan the road behind him. In the distance I could now see pursuers moving through the morning mist. Sabert looked towards us again, hesitant, uncertain.

"Come quickly, "I said, my voice echoing down the lane.

"Cerdic? It really is you! I don't understand ..." Then he looked behind him again. The approaching enemy spurred him into action and he and his men limped towards us at a shambling run.

"Quick, Sabert, move past us. Don't stop. We will ambush the pursuit," I instructed.

He nodded and led his men past me and on toward Wicstun. Now I could see the enemy warriors more clearly: they were about a dozen or so in strength, strange-looking men with coarse clothing, dark hair and blue-painted faces. It was those blasted Picts again! These were some of Aethelfrith's Pictish allies come to help him gain Deira.

I waved down my men and ducked back out of sight, praying we had not been seen.

The Picts came on, running after their quarry. We kept still and quiet in our hiding places and let them pass. Then I waved the men out onto the road and raising my uncle's sword high shouted "For Aethelric and our fallen friends!"

We all gave a huge bellow and then fell upon the rear of the Picts. We gained total surprise and six of them were dead before they could turn and face us. A few seconds after they did, Sabert turned and led his men back to help us. Within the time it takes to string a bow, all the Picts were slain.

We dragged their bodies off the road and laid them in a nearby field. We then retired to a copse and saw to Sabert's wounds and those of his men. Then we all started talking.

It seemed that Sabert had never reached Eorforwic. The messenger Aethelric had sent overtook him to the east of the city. He had send a rider on to summon Harald from the city and then turned back at once. Harald, marching at speed had caught up with Sabert during the night. Shortly afterwards, their two companies, numbering three hundred men, had been ambushed

330

by a much larger force of Picts that had hidden off the road and must have watched them go by, much as we had done only moments ago. In the surprise that followed almost all Sabert's and Harald's warriors were killed, taken prisoner or scattered. Sabert and his personal guard had managed to cut their way out of the disaster and were trying to get back to warn the king, but had fought a running battle with the pursuing Picts every step of the way and only half had survived to reach this far.

When Sabert had finished this sorry tale, I saw his gaze resting on the princes and knew from his expression that he feared the worst. "Sabert, I need to tell you something," I said quickly, stemming the flow of questions that I could see springing to his lips. Then I told him all that had happened the night before.

Sabert was aghast to hear the news of the loss of the palace and even more so the death of the king. It now seemed clear that Aethelfrith had sent only a feint directly to Eorforwic, enough to trick us into believing it was the main aim of the attack. He had expected an attempt to reinforce the city and had sent several hundred Picts to lay an ambush for just such a move. Then he had taken his main force and must have come across the moors or along the edges so as to come at the palace from the east where we least expected him. Finally, the traitor Hussa had enabled the plan to succeed by opening the gates.

"And what of Harald?" I asked Sabert.

He shook his head, "I am sorry Cerdic; we got separated in the ambush. I have no idea if he lived or died," Sabert answered simply.

Edwin and Hereric greeted the news with profound gloom. Any chance of meeting Aethelfrith in battle in the near future was gone. We were now just thirty men. Hardly a warband let alone an army. The princes looked lost now and obviously had no clue

331

as to what to do next. Once again, there was some mad talk from Edwin of challenging Aethelfrith personally.

"He will kill you," I said shortly then at sight of his indignant face, added hastily, "that is, he will refuse single combat and set a dozen of his warriors against you."

Appeased, Edwin nodded, descending once more into gloom.

Sabert then proposed trying to come to an accommodation with the enemy. "Perhaps he might permit you to hold some lands, my lords."

But we all knew that would not happen. Deira was destroyed and there was no reason for Aethelfrith to offer anything to us.

Eventually, well aware that we must do something but unable to suggest what, my big friend, Eduard, who in the rare times spoke his feelings out loud and was usually plain speaking, said what we had to do and we all knew he was right.

"You have to leave, don't you? You cannot stay in Deira. Aethelfrith will find you and kill you. One day perhaps you can return. Perhaps. But it is senseless to lead us into battle. Our thirty against seventy times that number or more. Both you and we would die. I'd rather live and fight when we can be sure of winning. The two of you are all that's left of Deira now. You must stay alive and somehow we must build another army."

We all stared at him and then finally Edwin spoke.

"Well, Cerdic, your man here sees sense where we see confusion. I don't like it. Particularly as we have left Prince Osric behind. But we cannot go back now. Woden forgive us, but Hereric and I must leave. Perhaps we can rally support in Mercia. The other English kingdoms can hardly look forward to a strong Aethelfrith. We two must go. But we cannot call on any of you to follow us. It was the king's responsibility to protect you. In return you owed service. But the kingdom has fallen. We cannot help

332

you. You should look to your own families and homes now that we can no longer protect them."

We were all thinking that of course. Perhaps we should just wander off into the night. It was just a few miles to home. Mother, Aidith, Cuthwine and Mildrith were there as well as all the villagers. I glanced at Cuthbert and Eduard. They were gazing to the south too. Yet I knew it was not as simple as that. This night had not just destroyed Deira; it had reawakened an old rivalry. Hussa would seek me out. He had told me at Catraeth that his vengeance was directed at me. He had kept it buried these years but was it really over? No. I had known that the moment we locked gazes outside the burning palace. When he did not find my body he would know I was alive and would come to find me. And I knew where he would look first.

I had to go home, but there was no way that I could just retire there and hope, as I had so often in the past, that the world would ignore me. I had to get my family away from the Villa. If I was not there and Hussa got there before me, who knew what he would do? The thought curled me up inside: I clearly had to go and quickly.

That, of course, was my chief concern, but I had not forgotten Aethelric. I had given him my word that I would look after Edwin and Hereric. And one of them - I was not sure at present which - was now my king. The loyalty of a warrior to his king was the measure of a man's honour. How could I abandon them to their fate? But how could I abandon my family and leave them to Hussa's mercy? I could in truth do neither.

I took a deep breath. "I at least will come with you, Highnesses. I made a promise to the king and I will keep it ... but I am going to Cerdham to get my family first."

Edwin nodded and gave me a peculiar, appraising look, seemingly changing his view of the man he had dismissed so often as a farmer. I saw Cuthbert raise his eyebrows at Eduard who nodded back.

"Where you go, Cerdic, we go too, for our folk are there also. We get them all out."

I turned to Aedann, who had been silent throughout. "You have no need to come with us, Aedann. I can offer you nothing now. No lands, no title ... nothing."

"Cerdic, I go with my friends. I had land in Bernicia and put it aside to follow you home. There is always a chance for land and glory, but if I abandon you now where would I find friends like you again?"

"So be it," Edwin addressed the men. "We march to Cerdham and the Villa. Then we are leaving Deira. Prince Hereric and I go into exile. Those that wish to can come with us. Those with families elsewhere may depart with no ill feeling." He spoke like a king and I acknowledged it.

"Thank you, Your Majesty," I said and saw his eyes widen at the title. Hereric noticed it too and nodded at me, a smile lighting his face. Although he was Aethelric's son, it seemed he was content to relinquish kingship to his uncle.

In the end half a dozen of the youngest lads asked to be allowed home. Most were from the moors. The rest agreed to come with us. As we wished to reach the Village we took the Wicstun road, avoided the town for fear of meeting Aethelfrith's scouts and circled to the west, although two more men who had wives there left us. We headed on toward the Villa, now down to twenty-two.

We hurried south past farms and hamlets whose occupants were still sleeping or were just now stirring to look out at what the new day would bring, unaware of the horrors of the previous night. A few, seeing a band of armed men rushing along, scuttled away to hide, clearly hoping that we did not come with sword and spear to attack them.

Hungry and thirsty, we marched on tired and blistered feet. One man was limping and could not keep up, so Eduard and Cuthbert propped him up between them and laboured grunting to keep up with us. As the sun rose towards midday we reached a high point on the road and came in sight of the Villa.

Ahead of me the company suddenly halted and as I caught them up I too stopped and stared. For down in the valley smoke was rising. Like a memory of a nightmare of years before, I could now see that the Villa roof, the great barn and store rooms and most of the village was burning. The wind changed direction and blew toward us and upon it I heard the crying of women, the screams of children, the smell of the smoke and worse - the hint of burnt and charred flesh, which lingered on the cool air.

Chapter Twenty-Five
Ashes

With a cry of alarm, which took me back six years to the last time we had seen smoke rising from the village, Eduard and Cuthbert dropped their burden on the road and ran towards the Villa. Aedann and I were right behind them. I heard Sabert yell, "Wait, Cerdic, it could be a trap!" but I paid no heed to the warning. Reaching the path that led to the Villa we sprinted towards our homes.

When the Elmetae had raided in that long ago summer – the summer when we changed from boys to men - they had started some fires, but the damage done then was as naught compared to the wanton destruction we could now see as we pressed on along the path. As we ran, details became clearer. The new mead hall was smouldering, but not yet aflame; beyond it half the huts in the village were also burning, but it seemed that the full spite of the attackers had been vented against the old Roman house that would never more be my home. The roof of the Villa had partially caved in and flames were erupting through every opening and doorway. Thick, acrid smoke billowed out and rose in a plume high into the spring skies. No one could be alive in there. Aedann and I frantically circled the Villa. When we came round to the east side where the great barn had collapsed in on itself and now resembled a funeral pyre, we spotted a sign of life.

Two figures were outside the Villa rear entrance where the kitchens were. They were taking water from the well and trying to douse the flames. As the smoke cleared a little and I saw it was

Aidith and Grettir I almost wept with relief. Grettir's tunic was stained with blood and he was limping badly, but he was still trying to put out the fire. My wife looked terrified, but she was helping him lift the buckets and heaving them at the flames in futile desperation. I called out, but neither of them heard me over the crackle of the flames and the groans of falling timber as the rest of the roof collapsed.

As I approached, still yelling, the old warrior spun around, drew his seax and took a step in front of Aidith, staring through the smoke towards us. For a moment his face was fierce and then he recognised me. At the same moment Aidith saw me too and ran over to me, tears streaming down her face as she flung herself weeping into my arms.

Grettir stumbled over to join us. "Oh, Master Cerdic, forgive me ... we cannot put it out."

I set Aidith back on her feet, "Where is Cuthwine? Are Mother and Mildrith safe? What happened?"

Before she could reply, Aedann pushed past us, "Where is my mother?" he asked, rushing to the kitchen door but then recoiling from the intense heat. Grettir limped after him and threw another pail of water at the house.

Beside myself with anxiety I yelled, "Grettir stop that! The Villa is lost!" The old man startled by my tone stared at me before his shoulders slumped and he sat on the edge of the well, a picture of abject surrender. I turned back to my wife and seized her by the shoulders, "Gods, Aidith, where is Cuthwine? Tell me!"

She stared at me for a moment, tears tracking her soot-streaked face. "Safe, Cerdic. He is safe. Mildrith is with him, she glanced over at Aedann, "Gwen too. They went and hid when we saw the bastards coming ...." Overcome by racking sobs, she stopped speaking.

"Then what is it? What is wrong?"

"It's your mother, Cerdic, th-they ... killed her ... in there!" Aidith pointed into the inferno that once was the kitchen.

"What?" I asked, aware of a pounding in my ears, my mouth suddenly bone dry. I started towards the Villa, but could not get within ten paces, the heat being so intense.

"Mother!" I shouted.

"I'm sorry, Master Cerdic," Grettir said, looking bleakly towards the fire. "She is gone. I failed you."

"What happened? What ... *happened*?" I stared at them both. Aidith started sobbing again and I took her into my arms. I just held her for a moment and eventually she calmed down while Grettir told me everything.

Aethelfrith's men had come on swift horses at dawn. They searched the Villa and all around and grew increasingly angry when they could not find what they were looking for, namely me and the princes. One of the men turned on Aidith and made to ravish her, at which point Grettir knocked him down. The Bernicians retaliated and that made the youths of the village and their grandfathers – boys too young and men too old for the fyrd - rally to Grettir's aid.

"Damn them for joining in. It just got three of them killed," the old warrior growled. "It was pretty one-sided, although one of the scum won't be going home," he added, patting his seax. "At least it gave the rest of the villagers a chance to get away. But the Bernicians were not bothered about them. They were asking about you and Prince Edwin, and they wanted Aidith ..." he faltered, "but more than that, they wanted your mother too." He shook his head, tears spilling from his rheumy eyes.

339

I stared at Grettir in horror as the story unfolded. He told me that my family had been hiding with the wives and children in the woods to the west, where once we had led the villagers after the Elmetae raid years before. Meanwhile, the leader of the Bernicians had set fire to everything that would burn, including the Villa. My mother had run back to the house when she saw what they were doing thinking to stop them and that was when they grabbed her.

"Forgive me, Master Cerdic, they were too many and too strong. They caught her and dragged her to their leader. I recognised him straight away, that lad from Wicstun – your father's bastard. I knew they should have executed the traitor," he whispered, then slumped to the ground, his breathing laboured. I crouched down next to him and pulled his tunic up. An ugly gash ran down the side of his chest, blood dripping from it, beginning to congeal. I sent Aedann to the well for water to clean it. "Lilla is with us, I'll get him to look at it," I said. "What happened, Grettir? When they caught my mother?"

He wheezed and tried to sit up. "Bastard seemed to go crazy. Blamed her for ruining his life. Said it was time to pay. Then he had her wrists bound and threw her in the kitchen, barricaded the door and let her burn to death. I tried to save her, but that was when they skewered me."

"She won't have felt any pain, Cerdic," Aidith whispered. "The smoke would have killed her before she ..."

At that moment, Sabert and Lilla arrived with the company and the princes. Lilla at once joined me and started working on Grettir, stitching and binding his wound. Sabert meanwhile took charge of organising the men into teams to fight the fire. They wanted to start with the Villa, but it was a lost cause. I pointed to the Village and the hall, "Save what can be saved, the Villa is gone." The words felt like ashes in my mouth.

"So Hussa got here before us?" Sabert asked.

I did not answer, but just stared as the fire engulfed my home and became a funeral pyre for my mother. I thought I had already paid Loki's fee for Aidith's life. It seemed I was mistaken. Was there to be no end to the mischief-making of this jealous god?

"Cerdic?" Sabert said, jolting me out of my thoughts.

"Yes, he did. He was looking for the princes and me and ... for revenge. He got it and I will kill him for it. But he is gone and we cannot linger. We must press on south."

Just then a small figure came hurtling towards me and wrapped his arms around my leg. "Pa, Pa, you have come. I said you would."

Speechless, I lifted my son into my arms and held him a moment, then put him down and ruffled his hair, by which time Mildrith had emerged from the woods leading a small band of frightened women and children. She held me a long time when we greeted each other.

"Oh, Cerdic, it was horrible," she whimpered and started to cry again.

"Millie, I am sorry I was not here. I ..." My voice trailed off, for what can you say at a time like this? I was spared having to find words because Cuthbert rushed over and grabbing her by the hand took her to sit on a nearby wall. She stared at him a moment, her hands going to his face as though she feared she was dreaming, and then she let herself be held.

Eduard stomped over to me fury in his face. "So the bastard Hussa did this?" I nodded.

"Well he is going to have to suffer now," he said and kicked a blackened brick in anger. "He's killed my brother, Cerdic. I'm

341

going to cut out the bastard's liver and feed it to the pigs while he watches!"

"Not if I get to him first you're not! I'm sorry about your brother, Ed."

Despite the need for speed our party was exhausted in mind and body and so no one argued when I said we would bury the Village dead before moving on.

I was not alone in grief. Husbands, sons and fathers had been lost in Aethelric's last battle and women and children mourned. Cuthbert's cousin had been one of the boys killed when Grettir was attacked, along with Eduard's brother and several others. We buried those we could find, including the charred remains of my mother. She we placed near my father on the family burial hill and the slain villagers joined them, slightly lower down on the same slope. My fondest memory of Mother was how jealously she used to guard the keys to the store houses and pantry, shooing us children away, but always relenting and giving us something nice to eat, usually an apple or a few hazelnuts. I retrieved the keys from Aidith, who had taken them over when she became my wife and mistress of the Villa, and we buried them with my mother. Prince Edwin – I had not yet got used to thinking of him as our potential king – said a few words in the absence of the priest, who had fled when the raid started. Prince Hereric also expressed his sorrow and Lilla sang a song of my mother's many kindnesses. I knew that both my father and my mother, together now in Valhalla with my brother, would be proud.

Afterwards, we all gathered together in the part of the hall that remained intact and discussed the future. The village was destroyed and many of its people dispersed. There seemed nothing left to stay here for. Indeed, to do so was very dangerous, for Hussa might return to finish what he'd started. I explained that I had promised to aid the princes in exile and any who wished to come with us were welcome. We would not abandon the womenfolk or children so they would come too, but we needed to go quickly.

So it was agreed. We would try to escape south across the Humber to Mercia or Lyndsey. Those nations had been friends in the past and would accept us for a while. We would spend a short time there and gather support and plan our next action. We might even be back in Deira within a year.

"It'll be a slow journey with the children. It's ten miles or more to the Humber and the bastards took our oxen and all but one of our horses," Eduard pointed out.

I nodded gloomily, remembering Autumn. I hoped whoever had my mare would look after her. The little colt they'd left behind was not much use to us, he was barely broken and had probably kicked them when they tried to rope him. I hoped so.

"There is a quicker way," Lilla suggested. "We can go by boat. There is a quay on the Fulganaess at Bursea, it's not so far."

The small River Fulganaess ran along the bottom of our valley beyond the orchard and flowed into the Humber. There was an insurmountable snag, however. "We have no boats, Lilla."

"No, but Lord Guthred has several. He uses them to ship goods across the Humber to Lyndsey. "

I grimaced. I had not seen Guthred since the dispute about Mildrith's betrothal. How would he react now? Would he help us?

"I hardly see Guthred agreeing to help me, do you?"

"Perhaps not, but he will help me, Lilla said."

I thought for a moment; if anyone could talk Guthred into giving us a boat, it was silver-tongued Lilla and the bard's idea seemed the best way so I nodded my agreement.

We then set about organising the departure. We had to be ready to leave at first light. We would take what provisions and clothing we could from the stores at the Villa – those that had been locked in the small stone room below ground level and had survived the fire. It was where I had kept our few valuables, my father's rings, one or two old Roman coins, items of my mother's jewellery – trinkets only; nothing as precious as the Amber Treasure, but I took them anyway – and more importantly, Earl Wallace's map, which would doubtless come in useful now. I stuffed them all into a small satchel. The last item I removed was Cynric's sword. Cuthwine was still far too young to wield it but I would not leave it behind. I strapped it to the satchel and gave it all into Aidith's care. Finally, we released from their pens such livestock as we had – a few pigs, a couple of cows and half a dozen goats - to forage for themselves, since there was no time to kill them for the meat and we would have to travel too fast to think of herding them.

As we prepared to depart I noticed Eduard gesturing to me frantically from high up on the roof of what was left of the mead hall. We had posted a watch up there since our arrival. He was pointing towards the road, but I couldn't quite hear what he was saying. Cuthbert's face, however, was pale when he turned to me.

"He says there are men coming from the road."

"How many?" I shouted up towards my big friend.

Edward held up both hands, closed his fists and then opened them again - twenty then. He shouted something more. I strained to hear the words. Finally one phrase reached me.

"Hussa is coming back, Cerdic!" he shouted.

Chapter Twenty-Six
My Brother

"It's Hussa. He's back!" Eduard shouted again from the hall roof. He gestured up the lane towards the road and then slid down the thatch and landed near me, bringing a bundle of soggy reeds with him. "Let's kill the bastard!" he added, dusting off his backside.

"Agreed, but we get the princes, women and children away first. Lilla! Grettir!" I shouted.

The old retainer hobbled over to me, still looking very pale but at least he was on his feet. The bard walked beside him, a caring hand resting on his shoulder.

"We will just have to hope Guthred is in a good mood. Get everyone to Bursea. Try to find a boat then get them down to the Humber and across if you can."

"But Master Cerdic," Grettir protested, "what about you?"

"We will be along shortly."

The gruff old man looked doubtful. "Please Grettir, I need to know everyone is safe." As I spoke, I eyed Lilla, who nodded. I thanked the gods that he was with us – his reassuring presence was a comfort to me.

At last Grettir agreed and moving away as quickly as possible, proceeded to gather up the survivors of the Village, my family, Sabert and his huscarls and the two princes. Edwin and Hereric were all for staying behind to confront Hussa, but I dissuaded them, pointing out that the whole reason for fleeing was to keep them safe. Eventually they too agreed and allowed Grettir and Lilla to lead them away southwards.

Besides myself and my three closest friends, the dozen survivors from the Wicstun Company remained behind. Common sense suggested that we should flee with everyone else. Yet there were three reasons which held me back. Firstly, we needed to give Sabert and Grettir time to get the princes and vllagers away. Just as Sabert had done at Degsastan – the sacrifice might allow them to escape. That was only if it came to sacrifice – I had no intention of dying here and now, not if I could avoid it. That was where the other two reasons came in.

The first reason of the two was that I wanted to know what part Hussa had played in all that had happened these last few years and why he had done all that he had done. When he'd had the chance to do right by Deira why had he betrayed it again? The third reason was revenge – and if I'm honest, it was the most pressing of the three.

"Here they come," Eduard reported, peering around the corner of the hall.

"Get ready everyone," I ordered, drawing Catraeth, my long sword sheathed at my hip. Aedann and Eduard came to stand on either side of me and the rest of the company gathered about us. Cuthbert, meanwhile, found a vantage point and loaded his bow.

A few moments later Hussa appeared leading a patrol of Bernicians. He did not look surprised to see me. "There you are, my brother. I am so glad to have found you."

"I bet you are, Hussa. Have you come here to tie off your loose ends?"

Hussa nodded. "You could say that. I had hoped you would come here and here you are, the last part of my old life left to sweep away. But before I come to that, tell me where I might find

346

Edwin and Hereric. King Aethelfrith is anxious to know their whereabouts."

"You mean they are still alive? I was sure you and he would have slaughtered them along with King Aethelric."

"Come on brother, I saw you climb over the palisades at Godnundingham together with the princes not two days ago. I could see you were shepherding them. So tell me where they are."

I laughed at him. "If I knew where they were do you think I would tell you? In any event, what makes you think I do? They are nothing to me," I lied.

Hussa stepped a little closer to me and as he did so I heard the creak of Cuthbert's bow string as he tensed. I held up my hand to signal that I did not want him to release his arrow – not yet. I wanted to drag out this moment for as long as possible. Aside from which, I wanted the pleasure of killing Hussa myself. My brother knew this, of course. He looked not at all concerned as he glanced at Cuthbert and then back at me.

"You are lying. Now tell me where they are."

"You tell me two things first. How long have you been planning all of this? Was it all thought up even before Degsastan?"

Hussa sneered at me. "Long before, brother. Aethelfrith is the power in the North. He is the wolf come to destroy you. I saw that as I stood in front of him not long after Catraeth. He saw in me someone who would do anything for vengeance. The longer I had to wait for it, the more elaborate the deception, so the greater the taste of revenge would be." He smiled and looked round at the still smoking Villa.

"I was right, it is indeed sweet. But anyway, to answer your question, Aethelfrith and I began planning all this soon after Catraeth. Every action we took, everything we did was designed to create that one big battle at Degsastan. We knew that if things went well Aethelfrith would be unassailable north of the Wall. But we had to be certain the next part of the plan - the invasion of Deira - would go well. Two things were needed to ensure success."

"Which were?"

My brother held up two fingers, "One, we had to destroy as much of the army sent from Deira as possible. Manipulating foolish little Prince Edwin into volunteering to attack the fort along with Theobald was very gratifying. Two, we needed to infiltrate Aethelric's palace. That was my job - the humble penitent son of Deira returning to his beloved homeland. Saving Edwin's life, well ... that was unplanned, but it certainly helped to persuade Edwin and later Aethelric that I was indeed a reformed character. When I warned you all about Aethelfrith so that you could attempt that daring escape, I was well placed to betray Deira for a second time by opening the gates and letting Bernicia in. It might not have been entirely necessary, of course, but we were concerned about what Aedann might reveal of our plans. In any event Aethelfrith had learnt that Aethelric had strengthened the defences at Goddnundingham and we thought it worth the deception and letting a few of you escape to get me inside in order to open the gates. Even so the brilliance of your escape plan succeeded better than we expected."

"The idea was at least half yours," I pointed out.

"Again, I felt that it would make my defection sound more convincing to contribute to the plan . In the end infiltrating your camp was worth letting a couple of hundred Deirans get away."

It was all as I had surmised, but to hear it spilling from my brother's sneering lips made my blood run cold. "So what you said about Aethelfrith wanting you arrested after finding out you had plotted against Theobald? That was a lie just to give you an excuse to run away with us?"

"Well, Aethelfrith was not after me - that at least was a lie, yes. We planned for my escape with you, but he left it me to come up with a plausible explanation. As for Theobald - let's just said that I felt you might believe me. A good lie works better if there is some truth in it."

"So you *were* trying to get him killed? Do your men know that, I wonder?" I scanned the faces of his warriors. They did not seem surprised by the revelation.

"Theobald and I never did get on, everyone knew that and yes, I wanted him out of the way. As for these men," he gestured behind him, "I chose them because they had no love for the prince either and my gold buys their silence and loyalty."

He smiled a mocking smile and it came to me that he was actually proud of himself. There was not even the tiniest shred of remorse. It was staggering to think the same blood ran in our veins. I often felt as if the gods were manipulating me; as if we all were mere game pieces on Loki's board. But I could now see that it was my brother who most resembled the trickster god. Like a child of Loki he had manipulated all these events. Yet the game was not yet over, the winning move not yet made. Indeed, even now the game was being played, for the longer we delayed these Bernicians, the further away Edwin and Hereric were getting from Aethelfrith's clutches. So I let Hussa boast on, asking questions and widening my eyes in pretended admiration at his prowess. Perhaps I overdid it a touch for suddenly Hussa's eyes narrowed in suspicion.

"You delay me brother, do you not?" Then he turned to his men, "The princes must be nearby. Attack these fools at once!"

349

"Get ready men!" I shouted, and finding that I no longer cared who killed my brother so long as he ended up dead, I yelled, "Let go, Cuth!"

Cuthbert's bow string thrummed, but Hussa was ready for it, he brought up his shield and the arrow embedded itself harmlessly in the wooden board. Those of my men who had shields drew close together creating a small shield wall that protected the rest of us. I was conscious of Eduard growling at my side like a hound straining at the leash.

Hussa's men also lifted their shields and brought their spears level so that their tips were pointing straight at us. Then as one they advanced upon us. There was no preamble, no challenges or exchange of javelins and throwing axes. They simply charged us. Cuthbert let fly with another arrow, which pierced one man in the shoulder knocking him back out of the fight. Then the two bodies of men met with a crash of shields. Spears thrust forwards and then returned, some dripping with the blood of the men who now lay screaming on the ground. The work was too close for me to draw my longsword. I slashed with Catraeth at the man facing me, but he blocked with his shield and then swung back with his axe. I dodged back to avoid it and at that moment noticed that the Bernicians were not pushing as hard as they had been. Indeed, they were falling back, letting us advance; leading us away from the orchard through which our folk had fled on their way to the river. Why?

I craned my neck and searched for my brother. With alarm I realised that Hussa must have spotted their tracks, for he had left the shield wall and was leading half a dozen men around the flank nearest to the still smouldering Villa, heading towards the orchard. He must have told his Bernicians to keep us busy and taking six men had set off in pursuit. My blood ran cold as I saw they all had bows: if they caught up they might inflict many casualties from a distance, including striking down the princes from afar.

"Eduard, it's a trick! Get the men down to the river. Cuthbert and Aedann come with me!"

Eduard turned briefly and must have seen Hussa's bowmen vanish between the apple trees for he nodded at me and started pulling men back. I could not wait for the company to retreat, however. Without stopping to see if they were following, I ran after my brother. These were the trees my friends and I had played amongst as children; the ones beneath which Aedann had become our friend. How long ago it all seemed at that moment. Under Grettir's critical eye the entire company, including Hussa, had trained in this orchard at times. And now I intended to kill him there.

I almost lost sight of him as I entered the trees, which were in full leaf now. I paused to listen; a brief flash of sunlight reflecting off his sword showed him to me a moment later. He was almost out the far side of the orchard. Beyond it lay the long meadow that sloped gently downwards to the distant river. Once he was there the villagers and the princes would be in plain sight - a sitting target for his archers. I had to stop him.

"Hussa!" I shouted. I thought he had not heard, but a moment later I saw him turn to face me. Behind him, his men ran on.

"Get those bloody bowmen!" I shouted to my friends, who were now running at my heels. They charged on past me, but hesitated as they closed on Hussa.

"Leave him to me!" I ordered and they resumed their pursuit of the archers.

Re-sheathing Catraeth and drawing my longsword as I walked the last fifty yards to stand in front of my brother, it occurred to

351

me that I had not yet named it. The name came to me as I looked into Hussa's face and tutted, "Tch! That was very rude of you, brother."

"What *do* you mean?" he asked, his tone puzzled.

"Running off like that before you'd answered my questions. I did say I had *two* questions for you and you only answered one."

He grinned at me, "All right then, brother, I'll humour you. What was the other question?"

"Why?"

"Why? You mean why did I do all this?"

I nodded. "You had a second chance. You could have remained a loyal huscarl to Edwin and gained lands and a name for yourself here. You could have told us earlier of Aethelfrith's plan or fought with us at Godnundingham. Whatever you believe, Hussa, you are still Deiran."

The grin left his face and for the first time I was struck by the cruelty in his narrow features; the ruthlessness in his dark eyes. There was nothing of our father in him and for that I was suddenly glad.

"This is nothing to do with Deira," he snarled. "I have no love for it, that is true, but for me this was always more than Deira. This was about our ... father."

"But Father bought your freedom, gave you your sword back and let you go when he could have seen you hang. He forgave you."

Hussa spat. "Did he tell you that?"

I shook my head. "Well, no. He never told me what happened at the bridge when he left you. He would never talk about it."

"Then you know nothing. Oh, he told me that he forgave me, told me he was sorry that he had never been there for me; never raised me as his son. He gave me money and my sword back."

352

"Well there you go then."

"HIS forgiveness, Cerdic! I never wanted *his* forgiveness: the sanctimonious bastard. He should have been begging me for *mine*! All those years he ignored me and let me suffer. Made me feel like my mother was a whore and I a smear of shit on the bottom of his boot. Then suddenly he feels guilty and I am supposed to bow my head and accept his forgiveness. Yes, Cerdic, he let me go and did all that he did, but out of guilt not love."

"How can you be sure of that? Surely it is what you wanted ...?"

"It was years too late, brother. Did he think that buying my freedom would make me love him when he had always rejected my love? A man does not turn his back on you for seventeen years and suddenly get to be accepted as the loving father. I told him that. I told him what he could do with his forgiveness. I told him that one day I wanted to stand over him as he lay dying and look into his eyes and smile. Yet even then he had the last laugh, dying of plague before I could see him suffer."

"But my mother. You killed her. Why?"

"You know why! It was her fault. It was always her fault. Had it not been for your mother, Father might have stayed with me. Might have been the father I wanted. It was because of her he denied my mother. I swore that one day she would pay and pay she did."

"Bastard!" I spat at him.

Hussa moved towards me, his sword held out to his side. "Yes, I am that, it's true: a bastard. But what would you know about that? You, the pampered favourite who inherited everything and left me with nothing. Well I've had my revenge. Most of it. There is just one part left. You!"

I brought my own sword up to face him and looked down its length. "I have not named this sword yet, you know. But I realised, just now, that it has a name and you helped me to choose it. For this is the sword I will use to kill you. Therefore I will call it 'Wrecen' - for with it I will wreak vengeance upon you."

Hussa spat at me and attacked, but I was already on the move myself, off to the side, circling past him as he charged me, then spinning back to slash at his side with Wrecen. The point scraped along his chain shirt and bounced off, but he roared in pain and aimed a cut at my neck. I recoiled away from the swing and with a shout of alarm toppled backwards into a bramble-covered ditch. Above me a shadow blotted out the sun. Hussa was standing over me.

"I was always better than you, *brother*." His sword came swinging down towards me!

Chapter Twenty-Seven
Exile

Suddenly all was confusion. The orchard seemed full of running men. There was the clash of swords, the crash of spear against shields and the screams of wounded men. Someone clasped my hand and pulled me to my feet.

"Cerdic, come on!"

It was Eduard. I glanced around. The wood was now a battlefield: a swirling maelstrom of steel and flesh. Our company had retreated through it, pursued by the Bernicians. I looked around for Hussa. He was on the other side of the clearing, holding his arm which was drenched in blood, I could see it dripping from his fingers. I made to move towards him, but Eduard tugged me the other way.

"No time for that. We must get away!"

Then we were running through the trees, the undergrowth catching and tugging at our clothes and suddenly we burst out from the orchard to stand blinking in the sunlight. Ahead of us Cuthbert and Aedann were firing bow and sling at the Bernician archers, who had set themselves up and were sending arrow after arrow into our fleeing folk, among them my wife and son. They had reached the far side of the meadow, not far from the river, but I could see one man was lying dead with an arrow sticking out of his back. As I watched, scarcely able to breath for fear, another of Sabert's men was wounded. Then Cuthbert's arrow took one archer in the back and he fell screaming to the ground. His companions turned to face us, reloading their bows, taking aim ...

355

"Charge!" Eduard yelled and he and I and as many of the company as were alive ran them down, mercilessly cutting them to pieces. I then turned to go back for Hussa, but the edge of the orchard was now lined by Bernician spearmen who were emerging from between the trees. It was no good. We had to flee.

"To the river!" I shouted and we ran for our lives. The Bernicians ran after us and the race was on. My lungs were burning and breathing was agony but we reached the water's edge and - the gods be praised – the boats were there. Lilla had got everyone loaded into one and was already halfway across the river. Grettir was standing next to a second boat waiting for us, but he was not alone.

For standing around him, spears and swords drawn, was a very angry group of warriors lead by Frithwulf and Guthred and accompanied by half a dozen frightened women and children - his family. We moved closer and were spotted. Guthred turned and smiled at me. It was not a nice smile.

"So, not only do you default on a betrothal, but now you want to take our boats too!" he sneered.

"Guthred, wake up! Can't you see who is in that other boat?" I pointed at the two princes. "Don't you know what has happened?"

He glanced at the boat and then back at me. "Oh I know well enough. Lilla told me. Why else do you think I'm here? But as it happens your own brother explained it to me only a few hours ago. Made me an offer too, didn't he, son," he said, glancing across at Frithwulf, who nodded back at him.

"*Cerdic we don't have long!*" Eduard hissed at me, looking back to where Hussa's men were closing in on us.

"What offer?" I asked.

356

"I hand you over, should you come this way and then I become Earl of the Southern Marches in your place."

I moved closer to him, Wrecan held out to my side.

"Well?" I asked him. "Now is your time to decide what you will do. Will you betray the king you swore to obey, betray his heirs, or will you let us pass?"

Guthred looked toward Hussa and the Bernicians, who were now barely a hundred paces away. Then, remarkably, he stepped aside.

"Whatever I think of you, Earl Cerdic, I am no traitor! I am loyal to Aelle's line. I will let you pass. But, like it or not, we are coming too! Into the boat everyone!" Without more ado his men grabbed up the women and children and waded out to where Grettir was holding the boat.

"Run you bastards!" Grettir bellowed at us, pointing at the Bernicians and gesturing that we should make haste. And suddenly I was eight again and old Grettir was in his prime and roaring at us to get a move on as he had so often in the past. It was a voice we had always obeyed instantly – even now.

Splashing into the water we heaved ourselves over the side of the boat. The Bernician spearmen had almost reached the river, one of them thrust forward with his spear, but Cuthbert let fly with an arrow to his throat and the man went down choking. Guthred's women and children screamed. Eduard gave the boat a huge push as he and Grettir dragged themselves aboard and we were away, oars cutting the water as we followed the other boat and turned to row southeast towards the Humber.

We were thirty paces downstream when I spotted Hussa on the water's edge looking after me, still holding his wounded arm.

I pointed, said over my shoulder, "Cuthbert, quick, kill him!"

357

"I have no arrows left, sorry, Cerdic, that Bernician spearman had the last one."

"Damn!" I swore and could do nothing but watch my bastard half-brother, the child of Loki, who in turn watched me back. Even at that distance I could see his dark eyes brooding. Our business was still unfinished and we both knew it. He gave a short, sharp nod and turning vanished into the bushes and in my mind I seemed to hear a great belly laugh and knew that it was Loki.

The small river took us the short distance to the Humber and once out on the larger waterway we rowed across to make landfall on the far side. As soon as I could get out of the boat I dashed to Aidith and Cuthwine waiting on the shore and enfolded them in my arms. Twice that day I had nearly lost them and I had no words to express my gratitude to the gods who had seen fit to spare them.

We abandoned the boats and set off again on foot. Close by the south bank of the River Humber, like a black shadow against the coming night, was a dense forest. I led the way with Lilla at my side, and stumbling after me in the semi-darkness, the confused, terrified company of refugees and their wailing children followed, with Sabert, the princes and my friends bringing up the rear. I had no idea what I was doing or where I was going. The woods were filled with wolves, wild boar, brigands and so the tales went, ghosts, dragons and goblins too – as the bard gleefully reminded me. To take refuge at night in such a place was foolish beyond words, but I knew it was death or slavery if Aethelfrith sent men across the river after us. They might think twice about following us through here, at least until first light. This part of the south bank was still Deiran territory - a small enclave beyond the Humber. As soon as we were able to we needed to reach Mercia. There we might be safe.

We floundered on for maybe four miles, but it was slow going and we were all thoroughly exhausted. I knew the children especially could go no further without rest. I called a halt in a small dell with a stream running through it. We collapsed, and having slaked our thirst, everyone huddled on the soft, damp leaf mould of the forest floor and fell at once into deep sleep. Aidith, Cuthwine and I curled up together, entwined beneath Aidith's cloak. None had the energy to stand watch - not even I could keep my eyes open, so shattered was I. If we were caught so be it. But I prayed to Loki that whatever his game was now, he would at least let us sleep this one night.

I was woken by the early dawn light filtering between the overhead branches. Disentangling myself from Aidith, I struggled to my feet and looked around our makeshift camp. I could hear infants whimpering for food and the muted groans and curses of a few waking folk suggesting they felt as cold and stiff as I, but most still slept. On the other side of the dell, however, one man was wide awake. In fact he looked as if he had not slept at all - or at least not much. Sitting on a log, staring into the shallow stream, was Edwin. I stepped over my still sleeping wife and son and went to him.

"My Prince, I ..." I stammered not really sure what to say.

"Ah, farmer, have you slept well?" he said, without turning his head. His voice was soft and despite the habitual insult carried none of his usual spite. I blinked, almost it sounded as if he were teasing me.

"Sorry, my lord, I was tired," I explained.

"Relax, Cerdic." He looked up at me and I could see that his face was ghastly pale. "No man could have done more then you have done to help us. I can see that now. I am sorry for what I have said about you in the past." He rubbed his face with his hands and I stared at him, unsure if I had heard right. He had never apologised to me before.

"Yet," he went on, "it is all in vain. We cannot hope to challenge Aethelfrith. He is mighty and all powerful. And we ..." he indicated the two dozen warriors, "are few."

He was silent for a moment and again I did not know what to say. Behind me, Sabert had woken and come over to stand close to us.

"If that was not enough there is also my sister, Acha," Edwin went on. "She and Aethelfrith already have a son and will have more children: sons and heirs to unite Deira and Bernicia into one bloodline. Where does that leave Hereric and me? What of our cause then?" He stared at me for a moment, then shook his head, "I will not lead you all to death." Turning, he regarded the village women and the children lying in their arms, all but the youngest still sleeping in sheer exhaustion. "You, Cerdic, will lead the men on to Mercia and offer your service to their king. Hereric and I will go back to Deira and submit to Aethelfrith. Enough of running!"

Looking down at Edwin, Sabert shook his head firmly. "No, Highness, that is not what we will do," he said defiantly.

"Sabert, Cerdic, are we not princes, Hereic and I? Indeed, one of us is now your king. You will obey my orders!" Edwin insisted.

"My lord, we will follow you into battle. We will risk our lives to defend yours. We will do all in our power to regain the throne of Aelle your father and Aethelric, your brother. But we will not just surrender or go about the land hiring our services like masterless mercenaries. It is our duty and our honour to serve

360

you. To do otherwise even if we would live longer has no honour and we will not do it," Sabert said.

"Damn right!" said Eduard emphatically from where he was nursing a nearby fire into life. Most of the men were now awake and listening intently. Some of the women were stirring too. Several nodded their heads at Eduard's remark. Good old Eduard. Life was black and white and required no soul searching for him. He followed his code of loyalty to me and to his king and left the thinking to others.

"But why bother just for honour?" Edwin asked. Hereric had come over to join us now and was also listening intently.

"Because," I said, Eduard's words finally stirring me to speech, "a man without honour is nothing. My father taught me that. There is more."

I paused trying to collect my thoughts. "You refer to me as the hero of Catraeth," I half-smiled, "well, that is when you are not calling me a farmer! But I am no great warrior lord. Since even before Catraeth, aside from the usual yearnings for glory of an unblooded youth, all I really wanted was a quiet life. Yet fate seems to have had other ideas. Every time I felt I had finally managed to hide away in my little valley something came along to drag me back out of it and into the world. It might be fate, it might be the tricks of Loki and the will of the gods or maybe I am just bloody unlucky, but I now accept that a man cannot hide away and avoid his destiny. You and I have not always seen eye to eye, Prince Edwin, but I meant what I said at Degsastan - I believe you have it in you to be a great king, one who will make a difference and leave a mark, but that will only happen if you accept your destiny."

I stopped a moment surprised at myself, for I was not normally given to eloquence – I was just a farmer after all - but

361

then I realised I was expressing ideas that had rolled through my mind for some time. I saw Lilla, who had come to stand beside Edwin, smile at me. Edwin, meantime, had flushed and dropped his gaze to examine his boots.

"Even if we do go on, what real chance is there of ever challenging Aethelfrith?" Hereric asked.

"We are not saying it will be easy," Sabert answered. "It will take a great deal of luck, a lot of effort and not a small amount of danger, and it might take a long time. To be frank, I cannot see any hope of getting support and help to launch an attempt any time soon. You may be a much older man when you return. But that does not mean it is not worth the effort."

Edwin looked up again. He gazed from one to the other of us and then at the faces of the men. Eduard was forcefully nodding. One, more outspoken than the rest, said, "He's got that right." Others murmured their agreement.

Looking surprised and quite taken aback by their obvious support, for a long moment Edwin said nothing. Then he tilted his head.

"Very well. I am not yet totally convinced by all that you say, Cerdic, or you, Earl Sabert, but much of what you say I will think on and I will lead you and accept your service. One day I hope I can grant each of you a reward befitting your loyalty. I ... that is, *we*," he glanced up at Hereric, "will be your princes if you will follow us."

"Not us, Uncle; you. You are older, than I," Hereric said. "I may be Aethelric's heir, but you are Aelle's remaining son and let's be honest, much more like him that I will ever be. We must have just one leader. It is you ... Sire," he added with a bow. "I shall be your heir until such time as you have sons of your own, but I do not, nor have I ever, wanted to be king."

I bowed too and the others joined me. It seemed we had decided on who was king and who heir - if indeed we ever had a kingdom!

"I give you the king!" announced Lilla, on cue as usual; one hand rested lightly on Edwin's head.

It was not much as coronations go, but for the first time since the disaster in Deira we had pledged our loyalty to a lord and he had accepted it. We had a king and he had an army. Well ... of sorts! Eduard cheered and was joined by the men. Even the children, who had lived through a nightmare these last few days, smiled and laughed as the atmosphere lightened. Sabert tried to quiet them down reminding them we were still in Deiran territory, but Edwin let them cheer for a few moments – we all needed it. Him more than the rest of us, perhaps.

After a brief meal of stale bread and very old cheese, we marched on through the forest. All day we trod anxiously, always looking behind for pursuit and sending sharp-eyed Cuthbert ahead with a few scouts to seek out any ambush and steer us around all signs of habitation. I expected the arrival of Aethelfrith's warriors at any moment. Yet as the sun began to sink towards the west and the shadows to gather, we had still seen no one, travelling as we had planned through a fairly uninhabited part of the forest that at times was almost impenetrable.

At last the trees began to thin and the going became easier. The light was beginning to fail when Cuthbert came running back to us, waving his arms and shouting. My heart plummeted: what now?

But then I saw the wide grin on his face. He waved us on and up a small rise. As we crossed the crest line we could see a river running to the south. I laughed out loud. It was what we had

363

been aiming for: the River Shaef and the border with Mercia. We had made it.

Sabert suggested we rest a brief moment and no one argued – it had been a tiring day and we had not paused much. As folk foraged in their bundles for a bite to eat, I retrieved my pack from Aidith and pulled out Wallace's map, studying it in the fading light. "Well, My King," I said to Edwin, "here is Mercia," I pointed at the map, "and here the river that we can see. There is a ford marked a little further west. Shall we cross over and try to find some friends?"

Edwin nodded his agreement. Then he stood and stepped away from me to look back over the forest towards Deira and raising his voice, said, "I swear an oath this day by Woden that I will not rest until I regain my kingdom."

For only the second time since I had known him, Edwin no longer sounded like a spoilt prince, but a king. I glanced at Sabert and for a moment our eyes met. He gave a slight smile and nod of his head and I knew he was thinking, as was I, that perhaps this boy would be a great king one day. And yet I felt a faint chill in my bones. An echo of what the future might bring. A fear that the bright flame of revenge might one day consume Edwin. I shook off my fears. That feeling was as true for me and Hussa as it was for Edwin and Aethelfrith. Our fates were truly linked now.

Edwin turned to look at me. "I have reason to regret some of the things I said and how I acted towards you in the past, Cerdic, and indeed before then. I guess the pride of one who was born of a king found it hard to take advice from a ... er," he struggled for words.

"A mere farmer's son?" I suggested.

"Yes," he agreed with a fleeting smile. "Well, farmer's son, of all the great lords who served my father and my brother, only

364

Sabert and Guthred here survive. I have no one else save my young nephew, two lords and a farmer!'

"And these loyal warriors," I added, indicating those of my company who were with us still."

"Indeed," said Edwin, regarding them. "I owe you all a lot. I am too weary and too mournful of my brother's loss to say more for now, but make no mistake, you men have my heartfelt gratitude."

There was a muted cheer from the men, who nodded and smiled.

"Come let us press on," Edwin said. "We still have enemies close by."

Yes there were enemies, traitors and a nation that wanted us dead close behind us. And one man who hated me, Hussa, my brother, child of Loki: the man I would one day kill or die trying.

So we marched west. We marched away from our homes and all that had been our lives.

I was first across the river into Mercia. Behind me came my friends and family, what was left of a proud army and the remnants of the blood line of Aelle.

I, Cerdic son of Cenred, led the princes into exile.

Historical Note

The time period in which *Child of Loki* is set is one of the most obscure and confusing of this Island's long history. These are the birth pangs of the British nations we know today when the English, Irish, Welsh and Scots emerge, clash, amalgamate and go their separate ways on and off for centuries. These climactic times shatter forever the remnants of the Roman Province of Britannia and forge a new land. Britain in 598 A.D. when the book starts is indeed a divided land.

Reliable documentation for this time period is sparse at best and most of what we think we know is pieced together from fragments in manuscripts usually written in the 8th century or later, very brief mentions in the Welsh or Irish Annals of the day, bits and pieces of Welsh poetry and the evidence of archaeology.

We begin to emerge from this dark cloud into a period we are more certain about as we move on towards the mid-7th century. But this book refers to events that occurred between 598 and about 604 A.D - right in the middle of the darkest part of the Dark Ages.

So what do we really know?

The nations of Deira, Elmet, Bernicia, Rheged, Strathclyde, Manau Goddodin, Dál-Riata, Mercia and the Picts did exist and came into conflicts and alliances with each other. The Battle of Catraeth - fought around 597 A.D. weakened the northern British to the extent that Aethelfrith's Bernicians were able to move on into the lands "between the walls" – that is, to threaten that area between Hadrian's Wall and the Antonine Wall, including Manau Goddodin and Strathclyde and probably the Picts and the Scots of

367

Dál-Riata too. This seems to have provoked the Scots under Áedán mac Gabráin to become interested in Bernicia. A diplomatic mission from Dunadd (of which the ruins still exist in Argyll and Butte) to the Angles appears to have occurred about 601 A.D. and we know that Bran and Domanghast died at that meeting or shortly afterwards and that Aethelfrith was held to blame. There are references to a plague in the Annals Cambriae about the same time which MIGHT have explained why the Scots took two years to respond to the loss of two princes. Eventually they gather an alliance and march to Degsastan.

In Deira, Aelle probably died - an old man- about A.D. 599 and it seems that his son or possibly brother, Aethelric succeeded him. He is recorded in history as being a weak, ineffectual leader. Around this time Acha, daughter to Aelle married Aethelfrith. Aethelfrith had another wife - Bebba after which Bebbanburgh was named. It is unclear in which order they were married - indeed it is possible that Aethelfrith was polygamous. However, it seems probable that Bebba only had one son -Eanfrith (Aethelfrith's oldest son), whilst Acha had many children and so probably Bebba died earlier in his reign.

From this union would come a dynasty of kings of a unified Northumbria - but that is a story for another day, a later book maybe.

Aethelfrith may have used the marriage to draw Deira under his influence. It seems probable that Deira as well as Bernicia fought at Degsastan. What we do know is that the great chronicler, Bede, writing in the 8th century says:

Ethelfrid, king of the Northumbrians, having vanquished the nations of the Scots, expels them from the territories of the English, [a.d. 603.] At this time, Ethelfrid, a most worthy king, with ambitions of glory, governed the kingdom of the Northumbrians, and ravaged the Britons more than all the great men of the English .... where upon, Aedan, king of the Scots that inhabit Britain, being concerned at his success, came against him with an immense and mighty army, but was beaten by an inferior force, and put to flight ; for almost all his army was slain at a famous place, called Degsastan. In which battle also Theodbald, brother to Ethelfrid, was killed, with almost all the forces he commanded. ... From that time, no king of the Scots durst come into Britain to make war on the English to this day.

The actual location of the battle is not known with certainty. Historians have suggested that it occurred at Dawstone in Liddesdale. I have visited this place with my family when writing this novel. It is a remote location and at first glance seems an unlikely place for a great battle. It does, however, have some supporting evidence. Geographically it occupies the watershed where rivers and streams flow away west and east and gives access to routes through the hills of the Scottish borders and Northern Pennines. Thus an army heading for Carlisle might just go that way.

Furthermore, archeological digs on the site in the early 20th century found evidence of iron weaponry and arrowheads in the area. There is even today in the southern valley the outlines of a circular fort, a settlement as well as a shallow ditch cutting across Dawstone Rig (the plateau). The top of the rig is littered with the vague remnants of stone cairns - possibly raised over the bodies of the fallen.

In the very old papers of a local archaeological society there is a record of a rather interesting monument which is now lost. There is a photo - of poor quality - of a black tombstone. It was supposed to be found in the south valley near the remains of old

369

fortifications and a settlement. Could this indeed be the place where Theobald died as recorded by Bede?

Soon after the great battle of Degsastan Aethelfrith takes over Deira. Now it is possible that he just absorbed it but it seems more likely that he invaded. Aethelric is supposed to have died around 603 or 604 A.D. Was this during a battle? We are not sure. What we do know is that, accompanied by a small party of followers, Edwin went into Exile along with Hereric about this time. Their kinsman, Osric, probably remained in Deira.

The story of their exile and what happens next will be taken up in the third book of the Northern Crown Series, **Princes in Exile**.

It seems that Cerdic still has a part to play ...

... and Hussa too.

Lightning Source UK Ltd.
Milton Keynes UK
UKOW030154230312

189434UK00001B/14/P